A TRAP

for the

POTENTATE

a novel
by Michael Atamanov

Wishing you safe travels on your fantasy journey,

Michael Atamanov

Dark herbalist
Book Three

Magic Dome Books

A Trap for the Potentate
Dark Herbalist, Book 3
Copyright © Michael Atamanov 2018
Cover Art © Vladimir Manyukhin 2018
English Translation Copyright ©
Andrew Schmitt 2018
Published by Magic Dome Books, 2018
All Rights Reserved
ISBN: 978-80-88231-56-1

All books by Michael Atamanov:

The Dark Herbalist LitRPG series
Video Game Plotline Tester
Stay on the Wing
A Trap for the Potentate
Finding a Body

Reality Benders LitRPG series
Countdown
External Threat
Game Changer
Web of Worlds
A Jump into the Unknown
Aces High

Perimeter Defense LitRPG series
Sector Eight
Beyond Death
New Contract
A Game with No Rules

League of Losers LitRPG Series
A Cat and His Human

You're in Game!
(LitRPG Stories from Bestselling Authors)

You're in Game-2!
(More LitRPG stories set in your favorite worlds)

Table of Contents:

New Director

"**D**ID YOU CALL?" I asked, knocking politely and walking through the wide-open doors of my new boss's office. Before entering, I pumped the breaks for a second, reading a copper plaque that a workman was screwing into the door:

> *Max Tohner*
> *Director of Special Projects*

He was the fourth person to occupy this office in a month. Truly, it was a cursed position. The new head of the special projects division didn't look all that glum about it though, reflecting confidence, gravitas and power with his whole appearance. When I entered, he gave a scant nod and motioned to the guest chair.

It should be said that my recent late-night conversation with the Keeper had given me an utterly mistaken picture of my new boss. Based on the voice and behavior of his glowing winged character, I supposed that the person playing the Keeper was fairly young, maybe even my peer. But the man sitting in the immense director's seat left by the rotund Mark Tobius, was short, around fifty and had a noticeable gray streak in his otherwise dark chestnut hair. He had a huge bald patch that practically reached the back of his head. And I was also struck by his eyes. They were chalky, cold and had a very light-colored iris. They looked somehow inhuman, like those of a snake or fish.

"You already know my name," Max Tohner said with a nod to the plaque, "and I know yours. So then, let's get straight to business. Timothy, what kind of character do you play?"

"A Goblin Herbalist," I answered, surprised at his ignorance.

How could he not have known that?! After all, he had met me in *Boundless Realm*, seen my big-eared Amra with his own eyes and probably read the race, profession and level as well! Had he seriously forgotten? But, as it turned out, it wasn't forgetfulness or ignorance that served as the reason for his question.

"So then, you're an Herbalist, not a Pirate, or a Wolf Rider or a Beast Master! But meanwhile,

~ A Trap for the Potentate ~

Herbalism is your most waning and neglected skill! You still haven't even leveled it to first specialization, even though your character is at level forty! That's a downright mess! The corporation hired you to do a specific job: show our users all the advantages of playing as a Goblin Herbalist. But somehow, you just keep doing all manner of things other than your explicit profession!!!"

With every new phrase, my boss raised his voice more and more. By the end of his incriminating speech, he had built up to a scream. I tried to vindicate myself, reminding the director with a smile about the great hunt for my Amra and how I had to constantly flee, so I didn't have much time to gather plants.

But I should have just kept my mouth shut...

My boss found my response inappropriately jocular, which struck him as very disagreeable. He also clearly disliked having a subordinate try to contradict him. A stream of reproaches and cursing poured out onto me. I was accused of not respecting my superiors, having a defiant attitude, exhibiting boorish behavior, holding a negligent outlook on work and damn near treason against the *Boundless Realm* Corporation. Only at the very end of his hateful monolog did Max Tohner begin to calm down, noting justly in a more or less normal tone:

"Timothy, the great hunt for you ended several days ago. But you have missed a number of work shifts since then, and your goblin didn't gain a single level in Herbalism over the whole ten hours of your last gaming session. Your character didn't grow in any other way, either. You just flew to your heart's content over the desert at night and lollygagged instead of working."

I really had no way of denying his last accusation. After leveling up the Royal Forest Wyvern to the point it could support my small weight, I really had forgotten about everything on earth and just enjoyed the sensation of flight, while my orcish army made its way across the Great Desert. But there were plenty of other complaints without the senselessly wasted gaming session. I was in shock and didn't even know how to behave.

No one had called me out like this in a fairly long time. I suppose the last time I'd gotten such a chewing out was ten years ago from my school principal for missing my final algebra exam without a good reason. At that time, I was poorly prepared for an important test, so I thought I'd be clever and skip it, claiming I had sharp chest pains.

I was only ten at the time, and I naively supposed I would simply be allowed to go home, then take the test a day or two later, getting the questions from my classmates and finding the answers to them in the comfort of my own house. However, it all turned out wrong. My awkward attempt at faking illness was quickly uncovered by the ambulance workers and, instead of maximum points on the test, I got a call to an enraged school principal...

But then, ten years ago, I could have guessed that the school director wouldn't have anything good to say, and was morally prepared for his stream of sharp enraged proclamations. Now though, the new special projects director for the *Boundless Realm* Corporation had caught me off guard with his fervent criticism. I didn't know how to act. I could either demonstrate submission and agree with him or, on the other hand, tell the boorish man what I thought about treating subordinates that way and sign my resignation right then and there.

In the end, life did exist beyond the *Boundless Realm* Corporation. I'd find myself another job with leadership that treated me right. Also, the half million credits I'd earned in the great hunt allowed me to have an optimistic outlook on the future and not worry too much about losing this job. But I still didn't rush such an irreversible decision. My boss had already said his fill, blown off steam, and was returning to normal. Some of the things he said were completely correct.

What was more, I noticed that he looked tired, as if he hadn't gotten enough sleep. His excessive irritation was probably rooted in that. What was more, Max Tohner had most likely gotten an emotional send up from his bosses intended to push him into adapting quicker to his new position, and he was just transmitting this rage to his underlings.

Nevertheless, I was expecting a totally different evaluation of my gameplay. No matter how you sliced it, Amra had kept the wonderful flying mount, acquired a unique mythical hound for the Gray Pack, made it away from the big chase and kept up an exciting pace the whole time. The fact that my video clips enjoyed such success in the rankings was evidence of that. Taking advantage of the pause in the stream of the director's rage, I reminded him of my accomplishments.

And yet, on that account, my boss had a totally different perspective:

"Timothy, I don't see anything to your credit in this sudden spike in popularity. You got the unique forest wyvern from nothing more than one stroke of luck. I don't know all the details of what happened, but I've heard rumors that your much-vaunted quest was not entirely free of foul play, and that other directors of special projects were fired over some of the murky details. From there, you just rode the current. The reason your clips were so popular wasn't because you're such a brilliant player, but simply because the players were interested in the valuable trophy of the great hunt. Soon, your fleeting glory will pass, and all that will remain is a barren remnant — an abominable Goblin Herbalist who hasn't even developed his main skills."

I wanted to disagree and even opened my mouth slightly, preparing to speak, but just kept silent and lowered my head. Actually, I had to agree with him there. Max Tohner then continued:

"If you were just a normal player, no one would have said a word to you about your poor skill leveling. But you're employed by the *Boundless Realm* Corporation, and everyone knows it! You must serve as an example for the others, show the advantages of playing as an Herbalist, reveal the potential of that path and then, at the very least, don't lag behind in your profession. But what we have on our hands now is a rotten mess. The average level-forty Herbalist has their Herbalism skill at around level forty-two, or three. But yours is just fifteen... I'm not afraid to say that that someone who works for a game developer should be ashamed of that. How much time do you need to correct the error? Will one week be enough?"

"More than," I answered with an even and absolutely confident voice, trying not to show my feelings.

Inside, I was cringing in horror. Was it really possible to raise my Herbalism skill by thirty levels in one week?! Even if I crawled around the forest and swamp day and night collecting herbs and flowers, it wasn't certain I'd make it! But I didn't want to show my lack of confidence in front of my boss. I was still a senior tester, a quite famous player, and wanted my boss to see me as an experienced employee who knew his value.

"That's great then!" Max Tohner lit up. "Then let's come back to this issue in a week. And for now, Timothy, I say we should look over how to use your unique flying snake for the shared interest and benefit of the whole *Boundless Realm* Corporation. There are very few flying mounts, and your advantage over other players needs to be constantly emphasized. How about exploring some undiscovered lands?"

It cost me great effort to hold back an acrid comment. It was hardly possible to both actively gather herbs for the whole next week and take VIXEN on prolonged flights. But I didn't provoke my boss, instead answering that I was already working on something like that.

"A wyvern is, of course, good. But it alone isn't enough for long scouting missions. The flying snake is still small and weak. She gets tired quickly and has to land often. In any place inhabited by dangerous monsters, we'd be devoured the second VIXEN lands. And also, don't forget about flying beasts. *Boundless Realm* is full of them. In far-off unknown places, such monsters will be beyond high-level. VIXEN and I won't even be a mouthful to them. But as it turns out, I currently have about three hundred brutish orcs under my command. Of course, I could just let the NPC pirates go free, but I don't think that's the right decision. No matter what, they are a valuable resource, which just needs to find the proper application. Maybe I could use them for a big expedition to hard-to-reach undiscovered lands."

"Continue," the director replied, his interest piqued. He folded his hands together and leaned over the table toward me.

"My troop is moving through the narrowest part of the Great Desert and, today or tomorrow, we will have reached the other side. I told my warriors the way, then spent all night flying back and forth on the wyvern, bringing them strength-restoring water from an enchanted spring near a copper mine. The water is a special elixir that restores endurance, but it spoils quite fast. So, I had to carry it on the Royal Forest Wyvern to get it there in time. At any rate, my cutthroats are moving fast, and will soon cross the desert and reach a deep, wide black river, on the very edge of the known world. I could make a map of these new territories and even, if I'm dreaming big, construct a defensive outpost on the river, where players can wait out the dangerous nights in safety."

The director turned on his computer screen and spent a few minutes checking something, scrolling through text on his monitor. Then he sat back in his leather armchair and looked at me with a smirk:

"Timothy, you have no idea what you're talking about. That black river you're leading your orcs to is called the Styx. It's also known as the river of death, because it contains water that is dead and completely unfit to drink. What's more, the river has overgrown swampy banks, with infectious bloodsucking animals, and that's an easy way to catch an untreatable disease. The biggest draw of those areas is the abundance of high-level dangerous creatures. What's more, further upstream, the monsters get deadlier, and have bigger, sharper fangs."

"There is a constant law in game worlds: the further you get from easily reachable places, the harder the conditions, the more dangerous the beasts, but also the more valuable the loot," I noted in an even tone, although this new information put me on high alert.

"That is true," the director agreed. "And the upper reaches of the Styx hide a great many interesting locations with unique trophies. But taking them is extremely difficult. I found some curious information, saying that twenty-six big expeditions have already been organized, and by quite serious clans at that. And as for how many lone travelers or small groups have tried to find the upper reaches of the Styx, I can't even count. None of them have made it. They all turned back sooner or later. Now you want to tell me that you hope to make it where much higher-level and better-prepared players got clobbered?!"

I didn't give an unambiguous answer to the director. I just promised to think as seriously as possible before this evening, then tell him my decision in this very office at eight PM. On the one hand I was, of course, not glad to hear that the river I had seen from VIXEN's back, was the legendary and ghastly Styx. On the other, I had a flying wyvern at my disposal, which made it significantly easier to reach remote locations.

My boss, then, was left none-too-satisfied with my cautiousness, and began to openly goad me into agreeing:

"Timothy, if you can complete this mission, I'll take back all my insults about your worthless Goblin Herbalist! What's more, in that this mission is directed at exploring *Boundless Realm* and will be useful to all players, I will try to get the leadership to give you a valuable reward, appropriate to the difficulty level."

But I just repeated my promise to seriously think about it, said goodbye and left the office. Despite the obvious difficulty of the mission, I was in no rush to refuse. The perspective of Amra's video clips falling in popularity after the end of the great hunt gave me an unexpected shock. You get used to popularity and glory quite fast. They're like a drug. And after having millions of people waiting with bated breath for your video clips each day, suddenly becoming an unknown loser... would be unbearably painful.

I was prepared to participate in this resounding and dangerous adventure, if it could help restore viewer interest in the adventures of my big-eared goblin. But such important decisions needed to be discussed in advance with my little sister. No matter how I looked at it, we played as a team, and I would never drag Val to such gloomy and unwelcoming places without her agreement.

* * *

Just after waking up, I rushed to my computer to see how many viewers had watched my new clip about the orcs' journey through the Great Desert and my riding the wyvern. Two thousand one hundred four people. Not so very long ago, that number would have made me jump up to the ceiling in joy but, after getting millions of views, it looked pitiful and didn't make me happy at all...

No matter what you say, my boss was right today. My Goblin Herbalist's glory was fleeting. With that sad thought in mind, I went out into the hall... and stopped short.

Kira was sleeping on the sofa, covered with a light blanket. Her glamorous red hair was spread out on the pillows and she was squeezing a huge plush rabbit. Precisely when my girlfriend had come into the apartment I did not know, because I had been sleeping like a rock for half a day, making up for my active night. But now, I didn't even know how to behave. Probably, for a start, I should at least get dressed so I wouldn't be wandering around the apartment in nothing but my underwear. Trying not to be too loud, I tip-toed back into the bedroom. But my girlfriend woke up nevertheless:

"What time is it?" Kira mumbled drowsily, not peeling back an eyelid.

"Seven PM."

She responded with a dismayed bleating:

"Damn, seven already. Time to get up. But my head is just humming... Timothy, do I have to go to work today?"

I smiled at the strange question and answered with a happy chuckle that I personally had nothing against giving my girl a day off but, as it happened, Kira was my boss somewhere high up in the corporate hierarchy, and maybe even the president of the *Boundless Realm* Corporation so, technically, it would be subversive for me to tell her what to do.

Kira opened her eyes and threw the comforter aside, revealing that she was wearing nothing but a semi-transparent nighty. She sat up on the edge of the sofa and said:

"You're funny, Timothy... How long have you

been working as a tester for the company? A month? Are you seriously saying that, in all that time, you never bothered to find out who is in charge of the *Boundless Realm* Corporation?"

I grew embarrassed, lowered my gaze and shrugged my shoulders. Yes, I was just a senior tester, and my job was to play a flap-eared Goblin Herbalist in *Boundless Realm*. All these appointments and changes of directors, stock payouts to beneficiaries and other lofty topics were not quite in my sphere. Kira shook her head in reproach and, looking me shamelessly right in the eyes, brought me up to speed:

"The President of our corporation is named Thomas Heywood. He's a tall, stately dark-haired man with singular charisma, excellent education and a surprisingly broad perspective. I feel like he knows everything on earth! And on every floor of the company skyscraper, there are portraits and quotes from his speeches! How could you not have noticed?! Anyway, as it turns out, I personally know Thomas very well. Once upon a time, my grandmother Inessa did her best to marry me off to him. Thomas and I even dated for a while, but we had a mutual break up after not too long. I was of no interest to him as a woman, he needed a tool to influence the Board of Directors, and a convenient stepping stool to reach the heights of power. All that said, we remain good friends and periodically cross paths at private company parties and various get-togethers for city elites."

I don't think Kira was purposely trying to make me feel low but, in the end, that is exactly what she did. The beautiful redhead had never before allowed herself to point out the bottomless pit that separated our social standing. All around, it was a very painful slap to the face, although it was honest. Yes, my girlfriend was an elite and, although she didn't advertise it on every corner, a financial bigwig of the metropolis. The chic lady only allowed me to be near her out of a fleeting whim, tired of rich admirers from her circle and people searching for unusual distractions.

No, I didn't say anything to Kira and didn't show that her words had hurt me in any way. But it was precisely at that moment that I decided once and for all: I needed to find the upper reaches of the Styx! Even if my sister refused to accompany me. I headed to the kitchen and put some coffee on for me and Kira, reached for the mugs, but my phone rang, stopping me. The ringtone was unusual, and also the number was unknown... strange. Nevertheless, I accepted.

"Hello?"

"Hi, Amra! When will you be back in *Boundless Realm*? I've started to miss you and am horribly tired after this never-ending day. This red-hot desert has simply finished us all off. Even the orcs with the highest endurance are staggering. No matter where I look, there are nothing but scorching hot dunes..."

Taisha?! What the hell?! I shook my head and even gave myself a hard pinch to make sure I wasn't dreaming or losing my mind. I had just gotten a call in the real world from an NPC from a game! This was just not possible! Probably, it was just a friend playing a trick on me!

I asked the suspicious voice a few questions to check, knowing that only my NPC bride could have the answers. And she did! All my doubts passed. This was definitely Taisha, a computer character from a virtual game!

"How did you find out my number, and how did you manage to call the world of the undying?"

The green-skinned beauty cracked up laughing, clearly satisfied at the effect she'd produced:

"Amra, you're the one who showed me how to do it! You even said your number in front of me, when you called the ambulance. Did you forget?"

No, such things could not be forgotten... I remembered the ghastliest moment in my life perfectly. My frightened big-eared goblin was holding his unconscious forest nymph sister in despair, as Valeria died in the real world... I had called right from the game and told my address to the emergency phone operator, also giving my telephone number. But the last thing on my mind at that moment was that my NPC bride might memorize that information and use it to call me in the real world.

But I had to answer Taisha somehow. I tried to reassure and perk up the NPC thief by promising to come into the game as soon as the sun set, when my Goblin Vampire would no longer be threatened by its glaring rays. I also asked Taisha to pass along an order to First Mate Ziabash Hardy to keep up the march. They needed to make it through the Great Desert no matter how hard it was to travel over the red-hot sands. Taisha promised to transmit the order and hung up. I lowered my hand with the phone.

"Timothy, who was the girl that just called you, and what language were you speaking?" Kira asked in agitation, standing in the kitchen door, having found the energy to get off the couch and come figure out who I was speaking to.

"What do you mean 'what language?'" I answered with a smile... And sharply froze. She was right! I was not speaking my usual native language but... what even was that? Goblin tongue? I couldn't find any other explanation, and answered just that to the owner of the apartment. I also told her the call was from an NPC thief by the name of Taisha, a computer character from the game *Boundless Realm*.

"Are you mocking me?! Do you think I'm the kind of naive fool who would buy such a tall tale?! Tell me the truth right now, or I'll be very angry at you!" Kira shouted, boiling over.

But I stayed firm, repeating again and again that I had said the whole truth. I had really just been called by a computer character asking when I would come into the game. My redheaded girlfriend started hissing like an enraged cat, and said through tightly clenched teeth:

"I, of course, will give you a chance and check your story with corporate specialists, even though it sounds like obvious crap. But if it all turns out to be a lie, and you make me look like a fool in front of serious people, I... I..."

Kira didn't finish her sentence, just turned sharply and went into the other room, slamming the door loudly as a grand finale. I still didn't know what exactly the redheaded fury was planning to do, if the NPC thief's call had not been detected by any corporate workers. Would she break up with me? Kick me out of the apartment? Complain about me to her influential grandmother? And if it wasn't any of those things, I could be sure that would lead to something nasty.

When I came back into the room a few minutes later with two mugs of aromatic freshly-brewed coffee in hand, Kira had already left the apartment...

* * *

When I got to the hospital, Val wasn't in her room. Her wheelchair wasn't there either. Had she just popped out for a minute and would be right back? But a nurse walking down the hallway told me she had seen my sister in on a lower floor talking with the other kids. My eyebrows shot up in surprise. My shy and unsociable Valeria had taken it on herself to go on a walk and talk with peers? Until I saw it with my own eyes, I'd never believe it!

But the nurse was not wrong. Even from the stairs, I could hear happy childish laughter and cries of joy, Val's voice included. I stopped sharply. For a girl who had tried to kill herself just a few days earlier because the "real world is unbearably gray and boring," positive emotions were as vital as oxygen. So, it certainly would not be a good idea to pull my sister out of the common room away from her active playtime and burden her with my problems.

So, I didn't interrupt the children's game and returned to my sister's hospital bed. Time was pressing, and I needed to go to work very soon, so I just left a bag of fruits and a gift for Val on the bed, leaving a short note on the table:

"I talked with the new director. I'm supposed to raise my Herbalism. When you have the time, look up how I could raise it by thirty levels in a week. I'll see you in the game at nine tonight."

This morning, I had promised the new director I'd give him my final decision about the expedition to the upper Styx at precisely eight tonight. It was already near eight, and I was really afraid of being late to a meeting I'd set myself. That would be extremely irresponsible and a sign of disrespect to my superior. So, in a lather, I flew up the building steps, ran to the elevator and, at seven fifty-five, was standing at the door with the plaque reading: *"Max Tohner. Director of Special Projects."*

But the door was locked... Had the director not waited for me?! Then my phone gave a beep. It was my friend Max Sochnier, the Naiad Trader.

"Hello, Timothy. Have you already talked with the new director?"

I could sense a certain subtext in that seemingly normal question so, before answering, I asked my friend why he wanted to know.

"Well, I just left his office ten minutes ago. And now I'm just awash with despair... If he hadn't been called to some kind of emergency meeting, I'm afraid he would have bit my head off. Leon is sitting next to me at the table. He's all pale, his arms are shaking and he's smoking inside."

I could hear the former builder's shaken-up voice:

"Yeah, they really got me worked up. If I get fired for smoking, then to hell with this job! It took me a lot not to break that old bastard's jaw with an uppercut!"

I admitted that, this morning, I had about the same feelings when talking with Max Tohner. I was not used to having someone shout at me so flagrantly. And I didn't know whether or not to be glad about the fact that I was standing in front of the locked door of his office and the second half of that difficult conversation would be put off.

"Yep, I get that!" Max Sochnier smiled. "Anyway, come down here to the tester floor. Leon and I are sitting in a nook by the vending machines waiting for you. There's a lot to discuss."

Precisely three minutes later, I left the elevator on the tester floor and headed over to my friends. Both Leon and Max Sochnier stood up when they saw me, and we greeted each other warmly.

"Guys, the new director is a wild animal," said the former music teacher, raising the relevant topic. "He shouted at me and threatened damn near prison time just because I withdrew money from my character's game account. I really did convert thirty thousand in-game coins into three thousand credits. I was planning to trade in my old electromobile for a more modern model."

"Was there something criminal in that?" I asked. "I mean, you're an employee and, if your contract allows it, you absolutely have the right to withdraw money."

"That's what I thought!" Max Sochnier flared up. "But apparently, it wasn't so simple! The finance department complained to the director about me. Apparently, since my character is holding lots of loans and client money, our boss had to figure out the situation and calm the financiers down. Instead of that, he started shouting at me, saying that a person in my position withdrawing money from *Boundless Realm* could be accused of embezzlement, which breaks corporate rules, and tax law in general. It's totally surreal. I cannot get my own salary without the agreement of an auditor appointed specially by the corporation, who will check the legality of every withdrawal! I'm a trader, and I will always have some money that technically is an advance from someone. Why should that mean I sit here without a salary?!"

"Yeah, that's total nonsense," I agreed. "And what if you change your contract to a fixed salary?"

Max Sochnier gave a glum chuckle and said that was exactly what the new director had tried to force him into today. But in that case, his salary would be four times lower...

After that, Leon told the story of his talk with the new boss. He tried to use only appropriate words, but my straightforward friend didn't always manage. The director was unhappy with absolutely everything: the Ogre Fortifier's low level, the lack of a sensible game-plan, the sharp drop-off in progress, and even his romantic relationship with a tester employee. It was all used to make the former construction worker feel guilty.

I also shared my experience with our new

boss, after which my friends got totally sad and hung their heads. Seeing their gloomy state, I steeled my nerves and told them my plan: we would go together to a place where nary a foot had fallen, and not just human, but of any player of any race. The upper reaches of the Styx!

"And how will that help us?" Leon asked sullenly.

"Popularity, unique trophies, and not only that," I chuckled. "The department head will be forced to treat us with respect, if we announce for all to hear that we are corporate employees carrying out a special, extremely risky mission for the good of all *Boundless Realm*. We could even name our boss and say he was officially instructed by the corporation to give us this mission!"

Max Sochnier and Leon exchanged glances and both snickered, imagining our boss's face after getting that kind of news.

"He'll definitely come at us for that..." the cautious Frenchman noted.

"He won't. First off, he was egging me on to take this adventurous journey, so it's the pure truth. Second, I'll try really hard to get a bunch of players watching our campaign, I've got a couple trump cards up my sleeve. We could even stop doing the short daily video clips, and switch to live streams without any cutting, showing all the problems, dangers and deaths. But the most important thing for us is to present the situation in such a way that all viewers will associate us not with the private initiative of a small group of players, but with a project organized by the *Boundless Realm* Corporation. We need to make it so that our success or failure will be seen as the company's success or failure."

My friends went silent in thought. Finally, Max Sochnier stopped drumming his fingers nervously on the table and spoke up:

"That's all well and good, Timothy, and I'm prepared to accompany you on this adventure. But I'm not really getting how you plan to drum up all that interest in your video clips. After all, there are thousands and thousands of streamers in *Boundless Realm*, and only some of them manage to become popular."

I gave a sad chuckle and, with a heavy sigh, admitted to my colleagues:

"Well, I have one very important difference from the other streamers. My character is infected with vampirism! He was made that way from the very beginning of the game and, all that time, my Goblin Vampire has been forced to play only at night and regularly drink blood. I think now is the very time to tell that secret to the whole world. We can even present that fact as yet another whim of the developers."

My friends stayed silent for a long time, shocked at my admission. Finally, Leon squeezed out:

~ A Trap for the Potentate ~

"A lot of your Goblin Herbalist's behavior is clear now. Both how you play at night, and how you take blood samples for 'antivenoms.'"

"I bet people really will watch your streams," Max Sochnier continued in deep thought. "Just think — one of the very last vampires in the game! What matters now is for our group not to be set upon by a huge group of paladins, fighters of the undead and various other vampire hunters..."

My friend's fears were very well founded. I had already thought them through, though.

"That is precisely why we'll announce the vampirism only once our crew is a bit further from inhabited areas. If someone wants to bag a vampire, let them follow us into the gloomy and dangerous lands around the river of death. I imagine there won't be many impatient enough for that, if any such busybodies are even to be found. Most players will watch our journey and wait for us to return, hoping to catch my Goblin Herbalist after the dangerous trip."

"But, sooner or later, our campaign will end," Leon noted justly. "And what will you do when your Vampire comes back, and hordes of players are waiting for you with wooden stakes, silver crosses and wreathes of dried garlic?"

I shrugged my shoulders indefinitely. Why worry now about what might happen in the very distant future, and may not even happen at all. What was more, there was an important nuance:

it wasn't enough for the players to merely know about the Goblin Herbalist's vampirism from my video clips. In the game, that knowledge wouldn't help their characters one bit. In order for the quest to trigger, they'd need to uncover the vampire in the game itself, and I was certainly not planning to help with that. Furthermore, my level-20 Veil skill allowed me to hide my name, and my sister could use her illusions to disguise my big-eared goblin in any number of ways. And then, try to find the Vampire in the crowd, if he looks totally different and has a different name! Also, no matter what, I always had the option of flying away on VIXEN and losing them again. In general, I didn't consider myself doomed, and was even sure I'd be able to squirm out of it.

My friends and I spent another hour sitting at that table, arguing and vividly discussing the concrete details of our forthcoming campaign. Above all else, in order to solve the problem of supplies and provisions and, at the same time, help Max Sochnier avoid chicanery from the financial control service, we agreed to buy supplies for three hundred orc pirates with all the money the Frenchman had borrowed from me. We agreed on the array of purchases and delivery location carefully and in great detail.

Beyond that, I asked my friends to look for any old maps left after the twenty-six unsuccessful expeditions to the upper Styx. I was certain these maps wouldn't be publicly available. I'd already checked, but maybe we could find a player willing to sell.

What was more, we also needed more companions, preferably NPC's, who could serve as guides and scouts in wild and dangerous locales. Neither we nor my goblins and pirates had the requisite experience and knowledge to survive in the harsh swampy climes. But such characters could probably be found in the game, so I asked Max Sochnier to find and hire them in the ports and cities his *Tipsy Gannet* passed through on its trade route.

We discussed further plans as well, but then my alarm rang out at nine, and I came to my senses. It was time for me to go into *Boundless Realm*.

Lost Oasis

SO THEN, loading. There weren't any new messages, which served as yet another confirmation of the fact that my Goblin Herbalist's popularity had fallen among both players and viewers. During the great hunt, I was reminded, I had grown tired of digging through the huge mountain of constant incoming messages. Well, I'd hope this was all just a temporary phenomenon.

A table displaying my character's stats jumped before my eyes.

Name	Amra
Race	Goblin Vampire

- A Trap for the Potentate -

Class		Herbalist
Experience		513172 of 540000
Character level		40
Hit points	6	336/336
Endurance points	3	293/293
Statistics		
	Strength (S)	42 (42)
	Agility (A)	49 (150)
(I)	Intelligence	5 (21)
(C)	Constitution	44 (55.5)
	Perception (P)	3 (45.3)
(Ch)	Charisma	78 (96)
Unused points		**0**
Primary skills (6 of 6 chosen)		
A)	Herbalism (P	15
	Trading (Ch I)	18
	Alchemy (I A)	23
	Dodging (A P)	22

Stealth (A C)	23
Exotic Weapons (A P)	13
Secondary skills (6 of 6 chosen)	
Veil	13
Acrobatics	18
Athletics	16
Foreman	26
Riding	18
Animal Control	14

No matter how you spun it, my Herbalism really was limping with both legs. My other skills needed attention, too. But this was business as usual with a character that earned experience primarily for completing quests, and not by slogging through hours' worth of farming. At any rate, I'd think up something to correct the situation.

So then, the world finally loaded. It was late evening. The sun was already beyond the horizon. Lots of stars were scattered in the sky. Orcish tents were densely packed all around me and, behind them, I could hear a dismayed crowing from many throats and bickering in elevated tones. I was standing next to a small fire pit, where a group of orcs was boiling a pot of something that didn't smell too appetizing. My arrival was met with a storm of adulation:

"Captain! Captain Amra is back! He can solve this for us!"

I could already tell by the increasing volume of the shouting behind the tents that my immediate intervention was needed. I pushed the pirates aside and hurried to the din of the fight. I had come just in time. There were already sabers and knives drawn. As far as I could tell, one of the groups of rioting pirates was led by the shaman. The other side was a horde twice as big as the first, commanded by my first mate.

"What is going on here?!" I shouted. My rage-filled cry stopped the knife fight, and both sides of the conflict hurriedly sheathed their weapons.

Fortunately, I made it in time. Only the troll had been hurt, but the huge green creature had perfect regeneration, and pulled a curved blade from his chest, which had gone in to the very hilt. In silence, he returned the weapon to its owner. First Mate Ziabash Hardy took a step forward and set out the essence of the conflict:

"Captain Amra, I got an order to continue our path through the desert. But my guys are dead tired, and have already been walking for days on red-hot sand without a break. More and more often, they ask me where they're even going. The sea, after all is in the complete opposite direction, and before us is only sand and death... Still, I drive them forward, as I was ordered. But the crew is reacting less and less to my angry shouting. It's practically reached the point of open rebellion!"

"We nearly died today under this unbearably scorching sun!" rang out the dismayed voice of an orc.

However, the speaker preferred not to say that to my face, and hid behind the others.

"Anyway..." sensing the attitude of the crew, the first mate continued his speech now much more confidently. "Our last day in the desert was a total shit-show. Our water reserves were gone by midday, and the sun just kept burning mercilessly. Any of us would have killed for a gulp of water. Only by evening did we find this tiny oasis, hidden amongst the dunes."

The troll, whose wounds had already fully healed, continued the orc's speech:

"Here, we have water and shelter from the sun but, as for food, it's totally barren. A couple palm nuts for three hundred hungry mouths is basically nothing. And meanwhile, none of us have had a bite to eat in two days. A dozen volunteers led by Shaman Ghuu headed out toward those cliffs to the south on a hunt, but they didn't even get a thousand steps from camp before an ifrit attacked..."

Now an ifrit... We already had enough

problems... I understood my crew's dismay perfectly, but I also didn't know what I should do in this situation to reassure the pirates and restore order.

"Ifrit?" Valerianna Quickfoot had now also loaded up *Boundless Realm* and reached the dustup, jumping right into the conversation. "Are you sure it was an ifrit?"

"Yes, madam enchantress," said the shaman Ghuu Gel All-Knowing, stepping out in front. "It was a Sandstorm Ifrit, level-77. A huge semi-transparent spirit, looking like it was made all of sand and flashing lightning. We didn't even manage to draw our weapons before the demon spun up a bunch of dust storms around our squad. Lashing, howling wind and sand blasted us right in the eyes. We couldn't see at all, or orient ourselves. And after that, as if in a ghoulish nightmare, the sand under our feet opened up, and three orcs fell in up to their belt. They were crying out in such pain it was as if they were being skinned alive. And with every moment, they were pulled deeper and deeper..."

"It was horrible, captain!" confirmed the very orc who had stabbed the Troll in the chest with his saber a minute earlier. "The shouts of those three unfortunate souls is still ringing in my ears. We turned to stone in fear and couldn't move. We just stood and watched as our comrades died. A few moments later, they were pulled completely under the sand and the screaming stopped. After that, it was as if our invisible fetters fell off, and we could move again. We ran away in panic."

"And I beat a retreat with the rest, captain. My magic was powerless against such a ghastly demon..." the shaman told me, lowering his head. "As soon as we got back to camp, I summoned some spirits for advice and they told me the further we went in the desert, the worse it would get. There would be more and more ifrits like that one, and the demons would get stronger. The spirits advised us to turn around quick, before it's too late! They told me the only thing we could expect from going forward is death!"

The pirates started talking in raised tones. There were some who thought we should return to the copper mine as the shaman suggested. Now here was some grief... I hadn't even considered the fact that my pirate crew might not want to make the dangerous journey to the upper reaches of the Styx. What should I do now?

Fortunately, my sister came in with a very timely comment about the ifrit, although it was from a slightly strange perspective:

"Well I can't believe what a stroke of luck this is! Ifrits are considered great sources of loot by the undying. They live for hundreds and thousands of years, and collect lots of treasure. Somewhere near where it attacked you, there should be a lair with all his riches. Normally, ifrits live in caves with very well-concealed entrances, using magic among other things. But Captain Amra is good at finding hidden places, and I can draw back the magical curtain. I think we should return to the site of the attack and look carefully for the entrance to the treasure cave!"

I immediately sensed the mood of the horde changing. Just a minute ago, the Sandstorm Ifrit had caused the Orc Pirates to feel nothing but tense horror and a desire to get as far away as possible. But now, my brutes were hesitating. Their fear of the ghastly demon was struggling with the temptation of its riches. And while the scales were tipping, I needed to support my sister's idea.

I took a step forward, calling for silence with a gesture and announcing loudly, so all the pirates would hear me:

"It really is rare luck on our part to find such a creature. Whichever of you was first to see the ifrit will get a reward of fifty coins from me personally! If he is alive, of course," I said with a happy chuckle, and many of the orc pirates laughed.

Foreman skill increased to level 27!

"Ifrits are dangerous only because they catch you by surprise, but a well-prepared team can take down such a creature without particular problems," the mavka assured everyone just in time, and the last doubts of the pirate crew passed without a trace. Now, everyone saw the ghastly monster as nothing but a valuable prize.

"We really were lucky to find the ifrit. We'll have to clear the desert spirit's cave, so our suffering through the Great Desert won't have been in vain. But only the strongest and bravest will come with me for the treasure. I can't have my warriors scampering away as soon as the wind picks up..."

"I'll go!" my NPC wife Taisha called out without even waiting for the end of my sentence. She was decked out in a full suit of green dragon-hide armor and looked very impressive and resolute.

I gave a nod of approval, and the goblin beauty burst forward with a joyful cry, hanging off my neck. Then, Shaman Ghuu walked forward, squeezing his gnarled staff and muttering something about wanting to dig through the demon's treasure. After that, gathering a team of volunteers was very simple. There were more than enough takers.

"I really hope you weren't wrong and we can take down the monster," I whispered into the mavka's ear when we'd gone away from the pirates and could talk one on one. "Otherwise, I'm afraid my authority as the successful captain of a pirate crew will nosedive and never recover."

"I hope so too," Valerianna Quickfoot

answered me just as quietly. "Anyway, dumbo, you should get over to those far-away palms. I see a respawn circle there..."

* * *

"The best part about ifrits is that the weakest defense they have is to physical damage," the forest nymph informed me, already having studied the article on them in the *Boundless Realm* Bestiary. "Ifrits are magical creatures. They are very hard to kill with magic. They actually have complete immunity to air magic. But at that, they are very vulnerable to normal arrows and simple physical weapons. Also, they are not exactly famed for their brainpower. It's generally recommended to send one or two tanks with good armor and high HP against an ifrit, then have others shoot it from a distance. A pretty dumb strategy, but it works."

"Are you saying a desert demon doesn't even have enough smarts to dodge an arrow?" I asked, somehow doubtful.

"Tim, can you really expect intelligence from simple desert winds? Beyond its huge size and ability to summon whirlwinds, an ifrit is just an idiotic stream of burning air and sand, brought to life by demonic magic. And it will stubbornly attack whatever enemies are found nearby. So, if we use our troll, pack him in some decent armor and let him take the hits..."

I imagined the plan and rejected it:

"No, Val. A level-77 monster will quickly shake our level fifty-four troll down, regardless of his armor and regeneration. And even healing magic from our shaman won't help. The level difference is too great. So, I say we use Taisha and I as lures, darting around before the ifrit's very nose. Meanwhile, twenty orc bowmen will shoot it full of arrows, as Taisha and I dodge the gusts of wind and shifting sands. The shaman will support us, increasing our Strength and Agility. And you can create copies of us with your illusion magic. That'll really throw the ifrit off his game. We can even take the Gray Pack and our Goblins Irek and Yunna with us. They cannot die, and extra experience won't do them any harm."

The plan was extremely simple, and I had no doubt it would work. Here, the main thing was provoking the ifrit, to force him to expose himself and crawl out of his hiding spot. Then, from there, we could handle him quickly. In theory, it was all simple, but reality had a surprise in store. No matter what we did, the ifrit just didn't want to show itself. We spent a whole hour in groups and alone wandering around the darkened desert, but the malicious sand demon was in no mood to come out. I walked the area up and down, activating my Search for Life and Night Vision skills, but didn't discover a thing.

"Maybe you were wrong after all, and this

isn't the right place?" the mavka asked the shaman for the umpteenth time. But Ghuu Gel All-Knowing continued assuring her that he was not mistaken, and this was the very place where the ifrit had attacked the orc hunters.

The shaman's words were also confirmed by a trail of huge orc tracks I found leading from the oasis and back, which cut off abruptly. The dust devils the Ifrit had conjured must have wiped away all traces, leaving nothing but unmarked desert sand.

"Maybe, the sand demon ate his fill with those three orcs and is resting now as he digests his prey. Or maybe he gathered strength and changed location." Valerianna Quickfoot suggested, but Taisha, standing not far away and looking at something, shook her head.

"No, the Ifrit definitely isn't full. He died..."

"What?!" my big-eared Goblin was instantly next to the NPC thief. Taisha pointed at a small colorful rock half covered with sand:

Sandstorm Ifrit Heart (alchemy ingredient)
Insufficient Intelligence to determine characteristics

Successful Perception check
Experience received: 160 Exp.

The stone seemed wet. Strange. Water in the

sands of the Great Desert? Perhaps it was just dew, of course. But how could there be dew at the very beginning of the night? And after such an unbearably hot day, at that? I picked up the strange stone. It was fairly heavy, quite wet, and somehow sticky. It didn't seem to be water. I looked a bit closer. It wasn't water at all!

Ifrit Blood (alchemy ingredient)

A very rare thing, given how extremely difficult it was to come across an ifrit. For my vampiric collection, it was invaluable! Only Taisha and Valerianna were nearby at that moment, so I had nothing to hide. Not wasting time, I stuck the stone in my mouth and sucked all the moisture off it.

Achievement unlocked: Taste Tester (42/1000)

The message was, though pleasant, entirely predictable, so I wasn't surprised. But the next events showed me how little I knew about *Boundless Realm.* The stone suddenly gave a pulse in my mouth, as if the Ifrit heart was still alive, and my goblin swallowed it in surprise... I choked and fell down on a knee, because the stone was fairly large. It took a good bit of effort to pass. Still, I managed to work the stone down my gullet. The next message I saw made my Goblin perk up his ears in surprise:

Fame increased
Present value: 5

You are the first player to use an Ifrit Heart in this way

You have activated a magical item
You may choose one effect:
- *One-time experience-gain of 500000 Exp.*
- *Permanent +5% defense against air magic*
- *One item in your inventory will be stripped of level and skill requirements*

Holy crap! Half a million experience points could instantly level up my Goblin Herbalist to 51! Eleven levels in one go! Although... I imagined my director saying, "your character is at level fifty-one, but Herbalism is still at 15," and my enthusiasm crashed. So, defense against air magic or... I also had Fenrir's Claw, which I could not use at all due to level requirements! That was right! I opened my inventory. There it was:

Fenrir's Claw amulet (unique item)
Gives +250 Constitution, +250 Strength,

~ Dark herbalist Book Three ~

+50% resistance to physical damage, +50 to reaction of the following creatures: Dogs, Wolves, Wargs, Volkodlaks

Attention! Your character's level is too low to use this object
Requisite level: 125

A great candidate for removing level requirement! I chose to use the Ifrit Heart for that. Nothing happened for five seconds, and the information on Fenrir's Claw didn't change. I even got worried it hadn't worked. Although... I could now place the amulet in the proper equipment slot, which I immediately did. And, just then, the game system started spewing a whole bedsheet of text:

You have equipped two items from Fenrir's Cursed Regalia

Hidden mission completed: True Alpha of the Gray Pack
Experience received: 40000 Exp.
Gray Pack member limit increased to ten

Set bonus unlocked: all Gray Pack members will receive a bonus of +50 Strength, +50 Agility, +50 Constitution, +25% movement speed, +25% experience gain

- A Trap for the Potentate -

Level forty-one!

Level forty-two!

Animal Control skill increased to level 15!

Mission received: Fenrir's Legacy (1/4)
Mission class: Unique, personal
Description: Collect and equip the four remaining items of Fenrir's Cursed Regalia
Reward for each item: 100000 Exp., +10 Animal Control, +50 Strength, +50 Agility, +50 Constitution, +2 to Gray Pack member limit
Optional condition: Equip all items of Fenrir's Cursed Regalia
Reward: 1000000 Exp., Fame +3, Gray Pack member limit removed, making number depend only on Charisma and skills
ATTENTION!!! If Optional Condition is completed, your character will receive the Criminal tag, visible to all players and active until your character unequips all items from Fenrir's Cursed Regalia
Your character's death will not remove the Criminal Tag

It took me some time to carefully read and

digest all that information. The game had offered me a unique quest, which was a very rare occurrence all on its own. What was more, I had just been revealed a path that would allow my goblin to achieve truly limitless power. No more Gray Pack member limit! That would mean... My breathing seized from the number of possibilities. Just raise Charisma, level Animal Control and, at the same time probably Foreman, and I could add many hundreds of fearsome predators to my pack!

And at that, I could give each of them the Pack Hunter specialization, making the strength, survivability and combat abilities of each fanged beast grow proportionally to the total number... Plus, the pets would also be strengthened by my skills... Then the bonuses from Fenrir's Cursed Regalia...

Yes, a permanent Criminal tag was extremely unpleasant, giving anyone the right to kill my big-eared Goblin Herbalist, but my vampiric character was already preparing to become a wanted criminal, so that didn't really change much.

All that remained was one tiny issue: I had to find the four items. And before I could do that, I needed to find out their names and what kind of items they were... After all, I didn't even have a near appreciation as to what I needed to look for. Boots, or maybe a helmet and cloak? My only clue was that the name of the object would most likely reference the huge mythical wolf Fenrir.

I took a heavy sigh, returning from the heavens to unhallowed ground. I didn't have enough information. Finding unique items based on what I knew, given there was only one copy of each in the huge *Boundless Realm,* would be very, very difficult. Although... I had a flash of inspiration... Perhaps they were still in the hands of players who had killed Fenrir a few months earlier! Determining the participants of that notorious event wouldn't be all that hard. After all, there were a ton of video clips, and associated topics on the game forum. There was probably a detailed chronicle of the final battle practically down to the second!

Although... the players that got those trophies may have sold them long ago, or given them to someone, not seeing any value in the cursed items. I suspected that these items hadn't been made a set until quite recently. After all, the Ring of Fenrir had been made by the game admins just three weeks ago. The players had seen just a heap of odd items in the loot left behind by Fenrir and his army of wolves, and a lot of it was fairly useless, and also cursed, making it nearly impossible to remove.

Just then, I was visited by another mystery. After all, even if I was able to find the third item from the cursed regalia, I wouldn't even be able to put it on! The amulet said I had to be at least level one hundred twenty-five! Probably, the other items also had very high requirements...

Overall, I needed to think about this. I called the forest nymph, and told her in detail about my unexpected discovery. My sister immediately dug out the most important bits:

"Tim, you should cruise the *Boundless Realm* forum tonight to find the other items from Fenrir's Cursed Regalia. That whole story with the fall of the Gray Pack didn't end all that long ago, and I'm sure there are some traces left. But it should all be done as delicately as possible, so none of the forum lurkers notice the suspicious interest in cursed items and strange search queries. Lots of players hang out on the forum, and some are very savvy, on the lookout for strange activity in the hopes of making off with items of underestimated value. I should probably do it, Tim. I'll be better."

I was in complete agreement with my sister there. Val was quite a bit better than me at such missions, as well as being faster and more delicate. But, just in case, I told Valeria another potential avenue to look down:

"All alone, these items have no practical value, but they are unique, so it is totally possible their owners simply put them up for auction. Then you could find the traces. Also, Val, you should check all currently active auctions in all provinces of *Boundless Realm*. Maybe someone just put an

~ A Trap for the Potentate ~

Ifrit Heart up for sale. It's just an alchemy ingredient, and no one else has any idea of its true value. If we get lucky, maybe we can buy one or even a few. If you find any, pay for fast delivery by magical messenger!"

"Alright, Tim, I'll do it. The doctor said I shouldn't spend more than four hours a day in the game anymore, so after midnight I'll have to log off. Then I can look through the forum and auctions. But for now, seeing as the ifrit died unexpectedly, go look for his lair."

* * *

The entrance to the cave was discovered soon after my sister cast Dispel Magic. Of course, we could have done that earlier, but we weren't exactly burning with desire to fight the high-level magic being in dark and confusing underground corridors. Now though, the threat of meeting the terrible ifrit gone, we equipped some torches and, one after the other, snaked into the narrow, short entrance.

"Careful! There's a trap here!" Taisha warned everyone, walking first in the file.

The pretty thief spent three minutes studying a gap in the wall and loose stones on the ground, after which she confidently pressed an unremarkable rough patch in the low ceiling. A mechanical click rang out, and Taisha lit up with colorful flames, having reached level thirty-three.

"Alright, trap disarmed. We can go," the green beauty assured us. "But the entrance to the ifrit's lair isn't where it seems. That path..." Taisha pointed into the darkness down the corridor, "leads to a cave-in. Most likely, death awaits careless treasure hunters down there. The real path is that way, right through the wall."

The mavka increased the power of her magic torch and carefully looked through the obstacle.

"Hey, Taisha's right. That wall is an illusion," my sister agreed and quickly removed the illusory barrier.

The ifrit's lair was a fairly small cave. Its floor was covered in a thick layer of old dry bones mixed with rotting fabric, tarnished silver and bronze tableware, and ancient weaponry. The amount of coins mixed into the trash heap was so great that my sensitive eyes began to hurt from the many flickers reflecting our torches. But the main thing was that my nostrils picked up on the scent of fresh blood. Orc blood, as I could immediately tell.

I got my bearings and carefully walked toward the source of the vampire-intoxicating aroma. I threw back a carpet and discovered three thoroughly battered fresh corpses... Although... my gaze unexpectedly met with a the utterly maddened eyes of an orc. With huge effort, I recognized him as being one of the oarsmen from the *White Shark*. He didn't have any intact parts left, just open wounds.

"Cap-ptai..." the bloodied sailor rasped out almost inarticulately, his gaze focused on me. "I... I sa... it all with my ow-wn ey... two whirl-rl-winds... Fighting... One... of... sand... and... and... the other... something different..."

With his last words, blood sputtered out of his mouth, and his eyes glazed over. The shaman standing behind me removed his hat without saying a word. I kept silent and read into an incoming system message:

Mission received: Something Different...
Mission class: Unique, group (no more than eight), time-limited
Description: Find the Sandstorm Ifrit's killer within 23 hours and 59 minutes
Reward: One Wish

"What does it mean by 'Wish?'" Valerianna Quickfoot had also received the quest and could not hide her amazement. "This is the first time I've heard of such a strange reward. Wish? But what if my wish cannot be described in stat and skill numbers?"

I had also never before seen or even heard of a quest like this. This mission was so unique, that it promised something one of a kind. But then everyone was struck by Taisha. The green-skinned

NPC thief spent a long time in silence, as if she was looking at something we couldn't see, then asked in surprise:

"Amra, what does 'Mission received' mean?"

Taisha's Wish

NPCs CANNOT RECEIVE and independently complete quests. That's a basic rule of any virtual game, an inviolable truth, a dogma! After all, what use are living players, if the mobs can deal with all their problems on their own?! Sure, NPC's generate missions for players, accept finished quests, and even sometimes get experience and objects after an assignment is completed. But they never get quests, period! That made it all the more surprising when Taisha got a unique mission at the same time as us two living players.

Valerianna, who also understood this was impossible, was looking at me with her eyes wide in surprise, not capable of giving my NPC bride any kind of explanation. I had to bluff my way out of it:

"Taisha, remember when you wished to become exactly the same as the undying? It seems the gods of *Boundless Realm* heard your prayers, and you are now becoming more and more similar to our kind. You are reborn after death, you can make independent decisions and, now, you're also seeing missions, and getting experience and rewards for them. Maybe, in a little bit, you will be able to enter the world of the undying!"

When I made these bombastic statements to my bride, I was just reassuring and encouraging her. While I spoke, though, I was thinking about something else entirely. Unique missions were so abnormal that most players got them quite rarely. Of course, I didn't have any concrete statistics before me but, somewhere on the forum, I had stumbled upon information that, even among experienced high-level players, over eighty percent had never received a unique mission. So, I simply didn't believe it was possible for my bat-eared Goblin Herbalist to get two of them in less than ten minutes by complete coincidence. It just couldn't happen!

What was it then? It looked like the admins were interfering in our gaming, watching carefully to see how the situation would develop. But at that, I had the firm suspicion that they wouldn't do such a thing just for the sake of my Goblin Herbalist. I wasn't such a high flyer that they would rewrite the rules and change the surrounding world for me. And the admins also wouldn't intervene on behalf of Valerianna Quickfoot, even though my sister was a remarkable player. But in my inner circle, there was a curvaceous green-skinned NPC-girl, who had aroused the interest of the *Boundless Realm* specialists for quite some time with her bizarre behavior and strange algorithms. I suspected that the NPC's call to the real world was the last straw and they had now decided to look into Taisha seriously.

"Well, what do you say, dumbo? Should we complete the unique quest right away, or invite others to help us?" My sister's question brought me back to reality.

What did she mean, right away? I stared in incomprehension at the forest nymph and asked her to explain. My sister then chuckled with a gloomy smile, as only she could do, indicating my mental capacity had yet again been cast into great doubt.

"Amra, are you seriously saying you don't know what killed the Sandstorm Ifrit?!"

Her question made me embarrassed. I blushed in shame. I confirmed that I didn't even have any near guesses about the killer's identity. Valerianna turned to Taisha and asked her the same exact question. If the NPC had answered positively, I would probably have died in embarrassment, but the green-skinned thief also admitted that she didn't know. The mavka gave a heavy sigh and started unhurriedly giving us one hint after the next:

"The dying orc pirate said that two whirlwinds were fighting... But, in the bestiary of a great many computer games, there are plenty of transparent creatures that resemble whirlwinds, and hate ifrits... They are mortal, inconsolable enemies who will always fight to the death, if ever they should meet... Amra, you cannot seriously not remember yet, right? They usually grant three wishes, if you free them from a bronze lamp!"

"A djinn???" the answer tore itself from Taisha and I at the exact same time.

"That's right!" the mavka gave a few claps, applauding our mental epiphanies. "This cave is full of old junk the Ifrit dragged from caravans he robbed. I suspect that, somewhere among all these bones and bronze plates, there must be a lamp. All it would have taken is a light touch to make the djinn trapped inside burst out and see his mortal enemy before him!"

In fact, my sister's guess looked very, very believable. The ifrit had dragged the three captives down under the earth and, in this small cave, one of the still living orcs might have touched an old magic lamp. It was already too late for that to save the orc but, at that, the djinn he released got revenge, killing the deadly Sandstorm Ifrit. By the way... I was reminded that not every djinn in fairy tales was blazing with gratitude for his liberators. In fact, it was more the opposite. In most cases, these magical creatures tried to kill whatever impudent fellow had dared to disturb their many-century slumber...

"There's an old oil lamp, but it's empty! And here's another! And another! And here's a bag full of them!" Taisha dug out from under a carpet a whole array of kitchen and domestic implements, including oil lamps.

But for some reason, I no longer wanted to experiment with releasing a djinn on my own. At one point, Kira had given me some great advice: "If you find a unique quest, but aren't sure you can handle it yourself, sell it!" This seemed like just such a case.

Boundless Realm had hundreds of millions of players. Some of them were quite wealthy in real life and put a significant amount of money into the game in premium credits. And at that, some inveterate gaming addicts would be willing to sell their last pair of pants just to stand out from the crowd and distinguish themselves in a rare mission or participate in an interesting mass event. And here, we had a unique quest ready to go, and eight players were promised a mysterious "wish," if they successfully completed the mission. And although three places were already taken by me, Valerianna and Taisha, I could sell the other five!!!

But they would need to get here, to a nameless oasis that was quite far from large cities, so a real problem arose of how to get the players here in less than a day. My orcs had taken a whole night and practically the entire next day to get here from Dotur-Khawe, the city of dwarves. And sure, mounted players could move faster, but they'd still need many hours to reach us. Although... there was also the *Legion of Steel*, the strongest clan in *Boundless Realm* and also one of the richest. They had five fleet-winged Silver Pegasuses, so they could get to this oasis from Dotur-Khawe quite quickly. And moreover, the *Legion of Steel* still had teleportation scrolls to the city of dwarves and the Prika Mine, where they had guarded the place I had reentered the game.

I had the contact information for a representative of the *Legion of Steel*, Alexander the Great3st, a level-230 Priest of the Sun, who had offered to help my Amra during the great hunt. I wrote a paid message to him with a description of the unique quest. I wasn't really expecting any answer before morning, so it caught me by surprise when a magical purple messenger devil appeared in the cave a few minutes later, handing me a scroll that read:

"It might be of interest, but I need to gather info about the quest and talk with the clan leader. Don't sell your five slots to any other players. My phone number is down there. Call me in twenty

- A Trap for the Potentate -

minutes, and I'll tell you my answer.

Alexander the Great3st. Human. Level-231 Priest of the Sun [LEGION]"

* * *

The telephone conversation was surprisingly short. He was of a quite advanced age, based on his creaky voice. Instead of greeting me, he got right to business and asked just one question: "What do you want in exchange for the quest?" Trying not to betray my excitement with my voice, I named a few wishes: food for three hundred hungry orcs delivered to the middle of the desert, as much of a map of the river Styx as the *Legion of Steel* had, and Ifrit Hearts, at least two, and maybe more.

The Ifrit Hearts were a last-minute addition, and I was expecting negotiation or some kind of limiting conditions, but he calmly heard out my demands and answered shortly that the *Legion of Steel* agreed. From what I understood, the powerful clan had all kinds of alchemical ingredients in its storage rooms, so he had no doubt there would be ifrit hearts.

In the end, the old man asked me for the coordinates and answered after a few minutes of silence that a Silver-Pegasus-rider would reach us in an hour and a half, and he would activate a portal scroll for the other players to come through.

When I came back into the game and told my sister the results of the conversation, Valerianna was very unhappy:

"Tim, it was very stupid of you to reveal our interest in Ifrit Hearts! I was gonna dig through the auction announcements from various regions tomorrow morning or even tonight to look for them! Now, it's no use. If there was anything there for an acceptable price before, it's probably already gone... The *Legion of Steel*, and all other TOP clans have very strong analysts. Naturally, your unexpected interest in such a resource won't have slipped past their attention, and the best alchemists and crafters of the *Legion of Steel* are probably already studying them for hidden properties. Our secret, if it hasn't been uncovered yet, will stop being a mystery to the *Legion of Steel* very soon, after which all Ifrit Hearts on all three continents of *Boundless Realm* will be bought up in a matter of minutes!"

My sister was probably right about the missed opportunity. Although, on the other hand, I had chosen to receive a couple of the alchemy ingredients for certain instead of a hypothetical chance to find more later at auction. First of all, there was no guarantee that there even were more than two Ifrit Hearts at auction, much less that we could win them. Second, once again, we were not insured against the possibility that our interest in the ingredient might give rise to stubborn research into them by big clans, and then we would be left looking all the more foolish. Overall, I preferred one in the hand to two in the bush.

While the orcs carefully sorted through the heaps of bones and garbage, removing everything valuable from the ifrit cave, Taisha my sister and I returned to the tent encampment. VIXEN came down from the sky, set a barely living level-21 Desert Monitor at my feet and stretched out her long neck in anticipation of her portion.

"Who's my pretty little girl? You never let your master starve or get thirsty!" I said, stroking the soft scaly skin under the wyvern's lower jaw. The flying snake lied down on her belly and even slightly closed her eyelids, entirely dissolving in bliss and delight.

There were no other people looking, so I killed her prey with a Vampire Bite.

Experience received: 105 Exp.

Achievement unlocked: Taste Tester (43/1000)
Racial ability improved: Taste for Blood (Gives +1% to all damage dealt for each unique creature killed with Vampire Bite. Current bonus: 25%)

After equipping the Claw of Fenrir, my Strength had grown to 294, meaning I could deal from 367 to 2202 units of damage with a single bite. Now, I could easily take down a player or monster of equal level, even if I could only get one move off. And my over fifteen hundred Endurance Points meant my Goblin Vampire could bite enemies nearly without end.

I tore the Desert Monitor's body in half with my bare hands. I fed one half to the hungry wolves of the Gray Pack, and brought the other to the unfortunate chefs, who were still boiling their unappetizing, disgusting smelling stew in the vain hope of turning it into something edible. The wild orcs didn't throw the bloody meat into their pot, or even roast it over the fire, tearing it to pieces and devouring it raw on the spot. I'll admit, that shook me:

"On *White Shark*, there was a decent chef, who knew how to cook. Where'd he go?" I asked my brutes.

"Well Captain, our cook died during the sea battle with the undying!" one of the orcs told me, wiping his bloodied toothy maw with the backside of his hand.

Alright... Well, the idea of structuring and organizing this collection of wild cutthroats had long been maturing in my mind. I suppose the time had come. I demanded that the orcs pour out the stinking mess they were boiling in their pot somewhere far away from camp, and invited First Mate Ziabash Hardy and Shaman Ghuu over to the fire.

* * *

"Captain, I don't understand. You want to turn our pirate crew into a regular army?" Ziabash Hardy asked, not too happy, and stroking the back of his head with a huge paw.

"You might say that," I answered, agreeing with his assessment of my plans. "Any orc is bigger, stronger and fiercer than a warrior from the human or elvish race. But when it comes to big groups or armies, humans defeat the orcs time and again, driving them from their lands and capturing their cities!"

Ziabash Hardy bared his teeth and snarled, but I was insistent:

"That is the truth, however bitter you may find it. Tell me of even one large battle orcs have won against humans. Not some raid on yawning farmhands or a sluggish wagon train, but a real battle between two armies. What, none come to mind? No surprise there, seeing how no such examples exist! People, weaker creatures by nature, have always won due to their strict discipline, good weapons and armor, better training and coordination."

"But orcs are naturally different, not like people," the shaman objected. "People are led by their aristocratic families and are trickier and less honorable. They're always first to enslave their brothers and sisters and eliminate pretenders including their own parents. Human commanders always stand behind their divisions and send others to die. Orcs are much more honest in that regard. Orcs have braver and stronger leaders, who have earned respect through their feats on the battlefield, and not by the ancient origins of their family. Our commanders always go in the first rows, setting an example to others with their bravery and..."

"Are the first to die in battle, leaving their army dejected and rudderless..." I said, finishing the shaman's ardent speech.

Shaman Ghuu choked mid-word and stopped, forced to admit I was right after a pause. I then continued:

"We won't have the kind of army that fights battles for far-off kings and spills its own blood for others and barely comprehensible interests. Orcish warriors, honest and direct, need a clear and easily comprehensible goal. All of our fighters need to know what they personally stand to gain when the whole group completes a mission. And everyone needs to understand exactly what they must do for victory. So, I will no longer stand to see my fierce and strong soldiers forced to make their own food, hunt their own meat, pitch their own tents and wash and mend their own garb. This must be done by skilled individuals with the proper training!"

Foreman skill increased to level 28!

For the first time, I saw a little fire of curiosity light in the eyes of my orcs. My words managed to break through the ice of doubt and conservatism. For the first time, the pirate cutthroats started imagining a different future than burials at sea. My first mate, shaman and the other orcs gathering in greater and greater number around our fire were carefully listening to their captain. I needed to take advantage of this moment and gradually lead the savages to the idea that we needed to make a dangerous voyage up the river of death.

"I want to build a strong and organized squadron, capable of surviving in this cruel world and holding its own under any circumstances. A trained, brave and audacious team that reacts in good time to changes around it. One where everyone is certain of their place in formation: scouts to find the way, soldiers to cut down hordes of enemies, healers to treat the wounded, mages to support with their magic, and decent cooks to make tasty food."

When they heard me talk about food, I heard the gnashing of teeth and moaning of hungry stomachs. Good, let the pirates think again that the present state of things was utterly unacceptable, and needed to be changed.

"In this world, which the undying call *Boundless Realm*, the very rarest and most valuable trophies are found far from the beaten path, and getting to them is very difficult indeed. But only there can one find a good haul of truly valuable loot, the kind that can provide for us all! I want us to have stories we can tell our children and grandchildren over a mug of foamy beer with pride. But now, we merely make do with pitiful scraps from poor fisherman and freight ships that can barely make ends meet themselves!"

"Captain, that's all well and good, of course. But I'd like to know: where can we find places with such rich bounty?" Ziabash Hardy asked.

"It isn't too hard to find out..." I said, beginning to answer and immediately noticing silence descend around me. The orcs, it seemed, even stopped breathing and tried not to say a single word. "The closest such magical location is past this desert up a black dead river, which is known by the name of Styx. Rumor has it that there is unheard of treasure hidden in those wild and terrifying places. But getting there will be hard, and you still aren't ready for such severe trials!"

I heard many orcs give a dismayed, insulted roar. The whole pirate crew thought their captain shouldn't be doubting their strength and capability.

~ A Trap for the Potentate ~

But I just chuckled, twisting up my lips:

"Today, just one lone ifrit was enough to put the fear of god in you. That creature sent a group of my best warriors running on their heels! That's where you're at now! But around the upper reaches of the Styx, the monsters are quite a bit scarier and more dangerous than some mere ifrit! So, before heading off somewhere, you must be trained and organized. And also, you all need good armor and weapons. I've already paid for them, and the galley *Tipsy Gannet*, loaded with supplies, will reach the Styx any day now. We will meet them there. But first of all, you need to be fed. My crew deserves not to walk in hunger! So, your Captain paid some undying to come here to the very center of the hot desert, and bring you tasty food and strong drink! Before the sun is up, I swear by my green ears that you will all be full and content with life!"

Trading skill increased to level 19!
Foreman skill increased to level 29!
Foreman skill increased to level 30!

Their elated screams made my sensitive goblin ears nearly fall off. My crew had never before experience such admiration and adoration of a captain! And the most pleasant part was that, when the din slightly abated, my sister jumped up and pointed her hand at a barely visible bright spot in the starry night sky:

"There's the undying rider now! Put more wood on the fire so he'll notice us!!!"

* * *

The arrival of the *Legion of Steel* was brilliant and impressive. A level-290 scout flew overhead on a huge Silver Pegasus and, without even landing, threw down a pulsating object that opened a large ovular portal right on the ground. From the bright, unbearably shining gates poured a huge river of terrifying soldiers encased in armor, mages in bright robes, severe necromancers and priests chanting mantras. And at that, they were all riding the most unimaginable mounts and surrounded by an innumerable variety of pets. I didn't see anyone at a level lower than two hundred. I even saw some characters over 300. The last to flitter out of the already flagging portal were four TOP players of the *Legion of Steel* astride Silver Pegasuses.

I didn't think the whole clan was represented here, probably just the rapid response force. But even so, the all-crushing concentrated might that poured into our small patch of the Great Desert in a matter of seconds could make even the demons and gods of *Boundless Realm* shiver. I don't know for whose benefit all this magnificent splendor had been organized, but even the wildest orcs were impressed. My brutes started crawling out of their tents, crowding up around the edge of the oasis, commenting vividly on the never-before-seen spectacle. But none of the pirates was afraid. The forces were so incredibly mismatched that the thought of conflict didn't even cross their minds.

The *Legion of Steel* got into formation three hundred meters from the oasis. The four Silver Pegasuses landed in front of the stock-still rows of high-level players, and the leaders of the clan hopped off of them. Overcoming a slight timidity, I ordered my orcs to stay in place, then moved out on the shaggy icy-white Fimbulthul, level-58 Mythical Hound. Behind me came the Gray Pack in full force: Akella, Lobo and White Fang, the level-38 Hardened Forest Wolves, Blanca the level-37 she-wolf, and Darius and Darina, two level-32 Wargs.

Successful Perception check
Experience received: 400 Exp.

The nighttime breeze carried the quiet conversation of the clan leaders to my keen ears. They were discussing my big-eared Goblin Herbalist:

"Seems to have quite a lot of pets for one player, and not the type you'd expect."

"Mhm. An Herbalist really shouldn't have

that many."

"And notice: the pets are of a higher level than they should be."

"Cheater?"

"He's either a cheater, or the *Boundless Realm* Corporation fudges the numbers for their testers."

They thought I was a cheater!

I didn't like that, but during the Great Hunt, I saw all kinds of accusations and insults thrown my way! And in large part, I didn't care what other players thought of me, even if they were world-famous stars from the very strongest clan in the game. Leaving the Gray Pack ten steps from the players, I jumped onto the sand from my huge white hound and read their information:

Kristina Mozzi [LEGION]
Human
Level-332 Valkyrie
Leon Shadow_Hunter [LEGION]
Drow Elf
Level-305 Assassin

Violetta Bestia [LEGION]
Light Elf
Level-323 Chaos Mage

Antonio de_Pirienne [LEGION]
Human

~ A Trap for the Potentate ~

Level-317 Inquisitor

Strange. I was sure I'd read on the forum that the leader of the *Legion of Steel* was a player named Till Quick_Fingers, a level 350+ Thief, the deadliest and highest-level player on the Southern Continent. And he was also supposedly in possession of one of the five Silver Pegasuses, which the *Legion of Steel* had won in a large PvP clan tournament. All five Pegasuses were accounted for, though. Four were on the ground, and the fifth was still being ridden by the scout, spinning circles in the night sky. But none of the five riders fit the description of the clan leader. Maybe he was using Veil to hide his real name?

After all, I had read about the big clan tournament and its victors... And here my memory obligingly provided me the names and classes of the lucky prizewinners. There was definitely no Inquisitor among them.

"Till Quick_Fingers, I presume," I said with a bow, turning to the Inquisitor standing to the far right.

Veil skill increased to level 14!

Based on the Inquisitor's reaction, I already knew I wasn't wrong. The player exchanged surprised glances with his companions, but they just shrugged their shoulders. A moment later, instead of the severe old Inquisitor, whose eyes burned with a fanatic fire, I saw a tall man in clothing the color of a moonless night, his face obscured by a hood.

Till Quick_Fingers [LEGION]
Human
Level-357 Thief

Together with their master, the pets also changed appearance. Instead of the trio of ghastly looking hellhounds, I now saw a dark shaggy spider the height of a person, a little gremlin with a miniature crossbow and a translucent boy ghost, barely visible in the dark.

"Have you found the lamp yet?" the Chaos Magess joined the conversation, immediately confirming my sister's guess.

"We found eighteen lamps. We don't know which it is yet. But we put them all in a row next to the cave exit. We haven't touched them with our bare hands."

"Rational caution," the Magess replied, praising our actions. "This is only the fourth time this quest has fired in the game. The last three times, the attempt to call the djinn ended fatally for the one who found the lamp and, even worse, the djinn himself ran away and moved to a different place. Do you know the level of the monster?"

~ A Trap for the Potentate ~

I shook my head "no." I could be sure the djinn was higher than level-77, as it had defeated the Sandstorm Ifrit in its very den, but the question was: how much higher?

"We'll treat this mission with all due seriousness. The most important thing is not to allow the djinn to flee." Till said, turning to his companions, then he turned to me. "You need to include five players in the group, I'll send the list in a private message!"

And just then a private-chat window flickered open, and I familiarized myself with the information. Now that was a surprise! Four of them were standing right in front of me, but the fifth was not the owner of the fifth Pegasus, or even a player from the *Legion of Steel* at all!

Larsen Lucky
Human
Level 237 Trader

Surprise must have shown on my face, because Till Quick_Fingers hurried to explain:

"He's an old friend of our clan, and we have certain understandings. What's more, he pays generously for the chance to take part in such activities."

And really, what difference did it make to me? I included the five names into the list of quest participants, after which the players standing before me grew noticeably happier and more relaxed. They couldn't seriously think I was tricking them, and didn't have a unique quest, right?!

"Yes, it's all on the up and up, like we agreed," the Valkyrie confirmed. "And now I ask you not to interfere, or even come close to us as we complete the quest! We'll call you when the mission is done, and the time to collect the reward has come! Our diplomat will give you the map and ingredients. The provisions are already unloaded. Your hungry mobs can wolf down everything there as soon as our soldiers walk away."

The starving orcs devoured their food. They didn't "dine" or "eat." What they did could only be called "devouring." Hurriedly shoving food into their tusked maws, they were all trying to tear off the biggest pieces, swallowing, gagging, belching and champing. The spectacle was fairly unsightly, but I understood that this was not the right moment to teach manners to my wildlings. The humans, though, who weren't accustomed to orcish ways, shot them dismayed frowns and turned away.

The only member of the *Legion of Steel* who stayed with us and didn't take part in the battle with the djinn was Alexander the Great3st, the level-231 Sun Priest, who was riding a huge level-150 Tyrannosaurus. He'd stayed behind as a rear guard instead of going to fight the djinn. At first, I was surprised at that fact, but remembered soon enough that the diplomat was of an advanced age and didn't ask a tactless question. All the same, the old man soon confirmed my guess:

"At eighty-two years, one starts to value peace and quiet, not brilliant sensations. There are plenty of people in the clan willing to spill their own blood fighting monsters without me. I am valued for other talents. I'm quite a good organizer, and my great life experience helps determine which type of rhetorical approach will work best on a person, which aids in negotiations."

The old man fell silent, staring at the twinkling glow coming from the battle. The mages of the *Legion of Steel* had covered the location with a translucent dome, allowing them to enter, but nothing to leave. Based on the ghastly whelping and flashes of lightning coming from that direction, my caution hadn't been misplaced, and the djinn had tested the magical boundary several times.

A trade window opened. Alexander the Great3st was offering me three Ifrit Hearts, and asking for zero coins in return. Naturally, I agreed immediately.

"Today, our mages discovered that these hearts have a property we hadn't detected before..." the man began with a crafty chuckle. "I'm sure, Amra, that you already know about it.

Half a million experience points is only interesting to a noob. Level 200+ characters get that much for killing just one monster. Removing level requirements from objects is also only useful to beginners. But improving resistance to air magic is a very interesting thing indeed. In fact, we can now even farm cloud palaces and the heavenly fortresses of air elementals. Before, those places were too harsh even for TOP alliances. So, the price of Ifrit Hearts is sure to take off into the heavens, and they'll soon be in very high demand. Now, as for the maps..."

Alexander the Great3st [LEGION] offers you a private contract

I opened the contract and read the conditions. I was being offered to buy a map for zero coins. He waited for my agreement, and asked only after that:

"May I inquire, Amra, why you needed a map of such a desolate area?"

It wasn't a secret, so I honestly told the old man that my boss at the *Boundless Realm* Corporation had given me a difficult mission as a tester and employee to journey to the upper reaches of the Styx. My boss told me that the owner of a flying mount was the very person for scouting new territories, and that such exploration would be to the benefit of all the millions of players

~ A Trap for the Potentate ~

of *Boundless Realm*. My boss also told me that many before me had tried to go up the black river, including large clans. So, I asked for a map of those places, supposing that the *Legion of Steel* may have already been there.

"You've been given a very difficult mission..." the old man said after a long silence. "The *Legion of Steel* was planning to make an expedition up the Styx a year and a half ago, just after it was added to the game. New locations, new quests, unique resources. All of that represents a fairly great value, which attracted us. But then a war came to a head between us and an alliance of three other clans, so we never even started our journey. After that, we simply watched other large clans break themselves one after the other trying to explore the river of death. I have no idea why the developers made these regions so impossibly hard to get through, or what reward is meant to compensate all these difficulties, or if such a prize even exists..."

The old man fell silent, but then gave a sharp shudder, as if he had seen or heard something I hadn't noticed. After turning his tyrannosaur toward the site of the battle, the diplomat commented:

"It's over Amra. The djinn has been pacified. Call your friends. The time has come to take your rewards."

~ Dark herbalist Book Three ~

Along with Valerianna Quickfoot, Taisha and I walked over to the shining dome, which many *Legion of Steel* mages were holding up with obvious strain. Guards stationed along the perimeter advised me to proceed on foot, because the spell wouldn't allow NPC's, including pets or mounts. I jumped off Fimbulthul and stopped, offering to let the girls go first through the magical barrier. I had serious doubts about Taisha, and I was already mentally preparing to ask the mages to remove the dome, but my NPC wife passed through without any resistance. Not wasting time, I followed after her.

Based on the dozens of bodies lying breathless and black patches of vitrified sand, it must have been very, very hot here, in the literal and figurative senses, and the djinn had made them pay handsomely for his freedom. Soon, I saw the thing that had caused all this mess, a nearly transparent, pale blue spirit restrained with a great many brightly glimmering power lines leading to a ball about one and a half meters in diameter hovering motionless in the air.

Al-Hassan Godsbain
Djinn Sultan (unique creature)

A unique creature! His marker on the mini-map was golden! The rarest type of being in *Boundless Realm*, of which only one could exist. I could not determine its level. To me, the Djinn Sultan was marked simply with a black skull, which meant there were more than fifty levels between us.

Kristina Mozzi, the level-333 Valkyrie came out to meet me and my companions. After calling for our attention with a raised pointer finger, she led us through a quick set of instructions:

"To be brief, the mission conditions are thus: this son of Shaytan won't create anything material but, other than that, the 'wishes' he can grant can be of nearly any nature. The only limit is that the wish must be clearly described with numbers and statistics. You can reinforce a stat, raise a skill level or resist, determine the coordinates of a rare object or quest... Basically, just try some stuff out. We've already made our wishes, now it's your turn!"

Hmm, it would be interesting to hear the wishes of TOP players from the strongest alliance in *Boundless Realm*! Probably, after all, they needed something extremely rare, very interesting or global! Most likely, we were invited late in order to leave us in the dark as to the demands of the leaders of the *Legion of Steel*.

For my own wish, I'll admit, I was lost. You might think I'd had plenty of time to think it over, but I just kept putting the decision off for later, thinking I'd figure it out when I got there. But now, nothing sensible was coming to mind. Valerianna Quickfoot, seeing my hesitation, was first to take a step forward to the restrained being:

"I wish to double the effect of my Insect Swarm specialization, under the Animal Control skill!"

The djinn didn't say anything aloud, but clearly my sister got some kind of answer, because she immediately adjusted her wish:

"Alright, if doubling it is impossible, then increase it by the forty percent the game rules allow!"

Based on what I saw, the djinn agreed, because the forest nymph spent a few seconds standing in silence, then jumped for joy:

"Amra, instead of twelve hornets, I now have seventeen! And they all have reinforcement bonuses from the total number of insects in the swarm! Dang, this is cool!"

After my sister, I stepped forward to the tethered djinn, already more or less having formed my thoughts:

"I'd like to know where the items from Fenrir's Cursed Regalia are!"

"Not possible," came a voice in my head. *"For one wish, you may receive information about only one unique item."*

"Alright, tell me the location of at least one item from Fenrir's Cursed Regalia," I said, agreeing to his limit. But before the djinn managed to answer, I hurriedly added: "except those I already have!"

"Ugh... You ruined such an amazing joke," the djinn answered, clearly upset. *"Alright. You can find the Boots of Fenrir in the Harpy village of Sini-Nalle in possession of a Minotaur rag-dealer named Rho."*

Mission   completed: Something Different...

Reward: One Wish

Fame increased
Present value: 6

Sini-Nalle? Where was that exactly? I didn't have any idea, but I was sure going to find out! I now had a new goal!

But meanwhile, Taisha was in no hurry to tell the djinn her wish. Instead, my NPC wife turned to the Valkyrie standing nearby:

"And what will happen when the last of the eight wishes is granted?"

Kristina Mozzi gave a predatory chuckle, displaying a set of pure white teeth:

"The djinn thinks we'll let him go... So naive! Who would refuse the chance to kill a unique creature?! That's both huge experience and unique loot, and also more fame for everyone who takes part in the battle! So, make your wish quick, we're already getting sick of waiting. Also, it's night time, and a lot of us have to work tomorrow."

"Alright, I won't keep you any longer..." Taisha turned around and walked over to the doomed creature in an unhurried gait.

I'll be honest, at the very last moment, I guessed what Taisha would wish for, and froze in horror, anticipating the now inevitable catastrophe. And my intuition didn't mislead me...

"I wish for the Djinn Sultan Al-Hassan Godsbain to be set free!"

Taisha said this in Goblin tongue, so very few understood her. But I did. And so did the Chaos Magess Violetta Bestia, because the she-elf gave a blood-curdling scream of horror and tried to protect herself, raising her magic staff for some kind of spell. But she wasn't fast enough. And no one else nearby was either...

You have died
55808 Exp. lost
You will respawn in 59 minutes, 58 seconds at the last respawn point you set

Adjustment in Plans

I CRAWLED OUT of the virtual reality capsule, soaked in sweat and feeling like a mouse that just escaped a cat. My arms were shaking in pain. I wasn't as overexerted as after that long-ago night of rowing with heavy oars, but I felt not only depleted, but depressed. Just to think, my NPC girlfriend Taisha, who I'd known for many weeks now, had not only killed my character with her actions, but had also humiliated me in the ugliest way possible before very, very influential players!

I reached for my phone and called my sister. Val answered instantly, as if she was already holding her phone.

"Bro, I can't say I have good news. I lost a level and a whole hour for respawn. And although my forest nymph has the Polyglot skill, I still am bad at understanding Goblin tongue. What just happened?!"

I explained exactly what Taisha had wished for. In reply, my little sister couldn't hold back her emotions and started cursing in the most natural fashion. This time, I didn't even tell my sister off. I had similar feelings myself.

"And what now?" Valeria wondered. "If the loss of experience from death is noticeable even to us, just imagine how mad the high-level *Legion of Steel* players are gonna be! It's much harder for them to gain a level. They take a few days to level up, maybe even a week!"

"You're right..." it was hard not to agree with my sister in this matter. "I feel like I can no longer count on their help..."

"Timothy, call their diplomat right now, apologize and explain what happened," Val suggested. "If you do, the *Legion of Steel* might not think we set it all up on purpose, and put us into their KOS list (kill on sight)."

It was the right idea, and I dialed the familiar number of Alexander the Great3st. All the same, the old man refused the call, not even wishing to speak with me. Bad sign, very bad sign! It meant an official representative of the strongest clan in the game was mad at me.

Such a large clan could express its anger at my big-eared Amra in many ways. And they wouldn't have to join forces with the *Goons* and loudly declare a hunt for me, include me in their KOS list, or set a bounty for my big-eared head. If they wanted to, they could simply ruin this game for me once and for all.

For example, they could buy an item from Fenrir's Cursed Regalia, thus stopping me from ever getting the full set. After all, I had technically just revealed my character-development strategy, and the representatives of the *Legion of Steel* had heard my wish. Or, for another option, they could simply kill all my orc pirates. For soldiers of such a high level, such a thing wouldn't even be hard. Without the help of the NPC orcs, it would be practically impossible for me to complete my new mission, and reach the upper parts of the river of death.

So, there were options and, to be honest, my shoulders were slumping due to all that happened. My mood was as low as could be.

As if sensing my gloomy state, I got a call from Val with words of encouragement. My sister understood that I was having a hard time, and assured me that the run of bad luck would end eventually. Beyond moral support, my wonderful little sister told me that she had found something interesting in an auction in the Lars province: a unique item called Wolf Claws, which seemed to be gloves.

"What, is that right?" I shuddered, gradually returning to life. "Tell me more!"

Valeria, with clear pride at the work she'd done, started telling me. There was no game-wide auction in *Boundless Realm*, each province had its own trade squares. So, she'd begun her search from the regions where Fenrir's Grey Pack had once raged. All in all, it was logical, seeing how the majority of battles had taken place in the Urtez and Lars regions, and the players who'd faced off against the wolves were primarily from there as well. She had done a context search for wolf, gray pack or Fenrir in active and old auctions and, fairly quickly, she turned up the Wolf Claws.

In the description, there wasn't a single word about the object being part of any set, and the gloves also had fairly weak characteristics:

+4% melee damage
+15 Agility +20 Strength
7% of damage dealt is transferred into healing
Immunity to fear

But the object was related to wolves, had first gone up for auction around the time of the Gray Pack's defeat, and was also unique and cursed! According to my sister, the owner of these gloves had placed them up for auction several times, trying in vain to palm off the unique item on any takers. The price had decreased in the previous months from thirty to eight thousand coins. But at that price, there still wasn't a single taker for the cursed yet mediocre gloves, which could never be removed. Now, the auction would be over in just five days, yet not one bid had been placed. They were still valued at eight thousand, though. For thirteen thousand, I could buy the item now, without waiting for the auction to end.

"It looks a lot like what I'm looking for, but I'm still not that sure. But thirteen thousand coins is a totally acceptable price for an attempt, I need to try! Val, look at the list of trader players from the Lars region. They usually relentlessly advertise their services on the *Boundless Realm* forum. Pick one that's active now, at night, but make sure he's reliable, with a good history. Pay all his costs and commissions, let him buy the lot and immediately send it on..." I thought for a few seconds... "to Dotur-Khawe, the subterranean city of the dwarves. As soon as I respawn, I'll fly there on VIXEN and pick them up."

"Timothy, I'd be glad to do all that, of course, but there is one little detail. My mavka simply doesn't have that much money!"

"Don't worry, I'll send two thousand credits to your card now. Just use it to buy in-game coins. Twenty thousand coins should be more than enough for all the commissions and delivery."

I said this sentence, myself not even fully believing that these words belonged to me. Just a month ago, two thousand credits had seemed an unrealistically huge amount of dough, so much I may have even been willing to commit a crime for it. But now, I was spending two thousand real credits without a second thought and not even to buy a virtual object I definitely needed, just hoping I had found the right one!

Valeria hung up, planning to do as I said. I then opened the player made *Boundless Realm* database and looked for the village of Sini-Nalle, where the djinn had pointed me to, and where one of the items from the set was definitely located. Unfortunately, there was no information about any location with such a name. A search on the forum with all kinds of variations also didn't bring me any useful information. Fail...

There was still some time before I could go into the game, so I got dressed and went out into the main hallway, preparing to drink coffee and have a bite to eat. The only cabin in use tonight belonged to Kira. The Queen of the Harpies was hard at work despite the fact she had said she was tired and wanted to play hooky this evening. By the way... the djinn had said the village of Sini-Nalle was inhabited by Harpies. So, who better than their ruler, Kirra'ellita Huntress of the Night, to ask about this question?

Sure, when we had parted ways this evening, it hadn't been on the most pleasant of terms, and Kira was angry at me. But now, she had most likely figured everything out about

~ A Trap for the Potentate ~

Taisha's call into the real world and understood I was right. If that was so, the redheaded beauty should have forgiven me and may have even been feeling stupid for starting a fight.

I grabbed my phone and scrolled down my contact list until I reached Kira. There was no reason to call her now. She was in a virtual reality capsule, so she wouldn't answer, but I sent her a message saying to call me. An automatic reply came in instantly:

"Invalid number. The destination number is not in use."

What the hell?! I had called this number several times before! Maybe Kira had set up a block on incoming messages because her high status drew lots of spam? To check, I tried to call Kira.

"Invalid number. The destination number is not in use."

Now that was really bad. Either my girlfriend had changed her phone number, or added me to her block list. Basically, nothing good...

As soon as the one-hour penalty for entering *Boundless Realm* was over, I hurried into my virtual reality capsule. My big-eared Goblin appeared next to the respawn stone on the edge of the desert oasis. Just like Valerianna Quickfoot, I had lost one level due to the stupid death, and my Goblin Herbalist was now back down to level-41.

It was a shame but, over the past hour, I had

already managed to digest all my negative emotions on the matter and was not going to waste any time on lamenting, indignation or pulling my hair out (especially because my bald Goblin had no hair to pull). I needed to leave it all in the past and act from there.

First of all, despite the high cost of communicating via magical messenger in the game, I sent a request to Kirra'ellita Huntress of the Night to find out about the village of Sini-Nalle from her Harpy subjects and buy the Boots of Fenrir for me from a Minotaur rag-dealer by the name Rho. I promised to compensate her immediately.

Having already sent the magical messenger, I belatedly decided to add to Kira that there was really no reason for her to be mad at me and block my phone number. My seemingly unbelievable words about a call from the Goblin Thief Taisha to the real world were probably already confirmed, after all. The *Legion of Steel* had also learned today that the NPC by the name of Taisha was very, very unusual. I paid for another message, but the little winged devil just spread his tiny hands helplessly:

"There is no a player in *Boundless Realm* by that name. I regret to inform you, but you spent the money on a postal messenger for nothing."

"Cut the crap! I sent her a message just a minute ago!"

But there was no one to listen to my

outraged cries anymore. The messenger had dissolved into thin air without a trace.

The forest nymph appeared one step from me, surrounded by a whole swarm of huge ghastly hornets. The Mavka was obviously yawning, covering her predatory-sharp teeth with a hand.

"I did everything just as you asked," my sister praised her efforts. "I found a trader and payed for his services. The Wolf Gloves have already been bought, and I paid for express delivery to the Trader's Guild warehouse in Dotur-Khawe. The gloves will arrive in around an hour. Listen, big-ears, you're gonna fly off for the goods soon anyway, so there's no reason for me to stick around here. What's more, I'm dying to sleep. I'm just about to pass out. So, I guess I'll be logging off until morning. But first share the map of the black river of death you got from the *Legion of Steel*. Tomorrow, I'll study it at my leisure. Maybe I'll find something interesting."

I created a personal contract for Valerianna Quickfoot, added my entire known map of *Boundless Realm* and set the desired price at zero coins. My sister received the contract and, after wishing me pleasant gaming, logged off.

* * *

Approaching the orc camp, I had no idea what to expect. Perhaps there would be ashes instead of tents, heaps of bodies, a *Legion of Steel* ambush, or even an enraged djinn, having decided to hang around a bit and send me to respawn one more time. But everything was surprisingly calm. All the tents were in place, the pirate crew was sleeping peacefully, and I even noticed a night patrol, walking around the camp and maintaining order.

My very highest captain's tent, or now more like chieftain's, was also where it belonged in the middle of the camp. Having eaten their fill, the wolves of the Gray Pack, with the mythical hound Fimbulthul, were dozing off peacefully near the entrance to the tent. Blanca lazily lifted her head a bit and moved her ears when she saw me approaching. It was all insanely calm and ordinary, as if there hadn't been death and destruction just one hour earlier. I opened the tent door and went inside.

Irek and Yunna were sleeping near the entrance on pelts. Darius and Darina were back in human form snoozing away, hugging in their sleep. I was walking carefully, trying not to wake my companions. Taisha was dozing in the middle of the tent, languidly collapsed on a pile of blankets and pelts. The goblin beauty was wearing nothing but a nighty. Something was different with my companion, but I couldn't tell what it was right away. Then it hit me. Taisha was at level-51! How? When? Just an hour ago, she was only level-33. Could it be...? I opened my bag to test my suspicion. There it was! I had only two Ifrit Hearts of the three I had gotten from the *Legion of Steel* diplomat. How?! I couldn't believe Taisha had been brazen enough to rob her companion and husband!

Before waking her up and starting a fight, demanding explanations for her most recent strange behavior, I opened her info and familiarized myself with the current state of my unpredictable companion:

Taisha Spark
Goblin
Level-51 Thief
Hitpoints: 580 of 580
Endurance points: 452 of 452
Primary skills:
Lockpicking (A I) level 27
Trap Disarming (A I) level 14
Dagger (S A) level 20
Stealth (A C) level 22
*Dodging (A P) level 24 * Perk taken: Arrow Dodging*
Crossbow (S A) level 3
Silent Step (A P) level 1
Secondary skills:
Pickpocket (A P) level 16
Athletics (C S) level 18
Culinarian (P A) level 13
Light leather armor (C P) level 12

Riding (A C) level 11
Lothario (Ch P) level 9
Shadow of the Leader (I Ch) level 1

Typically for a character who had leveled quickly through quests and other bonuses, her skills were quite low for her level. However, my Goblin Herbalist was in a similar position. So... that meant, at level fifty, Taisha Spark had taken Silent Step as a primary skill. What could I say? It was a totally natural choice for a thief trying not to give herself away with too much sound. But then as for the skill Shadow of the Leader, which she had taken as a secondary? I called up the in-game information and read the description.

Shadow of the Leader (former name Acolyte): A skill that allows the lower-level companion of a strong leader to project some of their master's glory onto themselves and act as their representative. As this skill grows, it will allow the companion to receive increased experience and boost their basic statistics. The effect is linear, based on the difference in levels between master and companion.
ATTENTION!!! This skill will not work or level if the companion and master are equal in level, or if the companion has surpassed the master.

I'll admit, this was a very strange choice for Taisha, considering that, after using the Ifrit

~ A Trap for the Potentate ~

Heart, the thief was higher than me by ten whole levels. It would be quite a long time before my companion could get even a slight return from this new addition. Alright, noted. I looked a bit further through the information.

> **Next missions to trigger: Taisha's Envy (normal, personal), Taisha's Disenchantment (unusual, personal), Taisha's Rebellion (unique, personal)**

I could receive a unique quest??? Would you look at that! My experience as a player in all kinds of computer games was simply screaming at full volume that I must not miss this chance under any circumstances. I would have to create the necessary conditions to receive the unique mission, even if the Taisha's Rebellion name implied something problematic. The names of the other quests were also not too positive either, in fact.

So then, finally, Taisha's opinion of me. Now that was unexpected... Just +50 (friendship)?! Considering the positive modifiers, the base value was just a pitiful +30. How?! Not very long ago, her opinion was the maximum possible +100. I also had a crazy high bonus guaranteeing that any check for Taisha's approval would succeed, excluding only the very most impudent and ill-advised. I had also fulfilled a bunch of quests, raising Taisha's opinion of me. Where had that all gone?

It seemed the time had come to wake the NPC thief and figure this all out! But how should I wake her up: with a tender kiss, a shake, or maybe a firm slap on the behind, in order to immediately show my upset mood? The beginning would determine the rest of the conversation, or so I thought.

Successful Perception check
Experience received: 40 Exp.

I noticed a flicker in Taisha's eyes through her squinting eyelids. The girl was not asleep and was watching me carefully. Alright then, one problem down...

"How am I to understand your behavior with the djinn and stealing the valuable alchemy ingredient from my inventory?" I decided to go right on the attack.

Taisha stopped pretending and opened her eyes. With a languorous stretch, she sat up on the bedroll and answered with two questions.

"What has you so surprised, Amra? The fact that I didn't allow it to end illegally?"

I choked on my next words, after the unexpected rebuff. Before I could come to my senses, Taisha threw herself at me with reproaches:

~ A Trap for the Potentate ~

"Amra, you have huge ears, so you probably also heard the Valkyrie from the *Legion of Steel*. The undying had promised to set the imprisoned djinn free, but instead, they were going to kill him! You must have heard all that perfectly, admit it! But you did nothing! How are you any better than the undying that tricked the djinn, or destroyed my home village of Tysh, considering them mere mobs to be killed unceremoniously?! After all, these cases have a lot in common!"

Well damn. My own virtual girlfriend had made me feel shame! And I didn't know how to answer my NPC companion to make her understand. I couldn't just explain to a computer program that it would cause me huge problems both in *Boundless Realm* and the real world if I had tried to stop the *Legion of Steel*. And if I had purposely set the Djinn Sultan against them, it would be even worse! But Taisha was not going to close her mouth, continuing to dress me down:

"Anyhow, if you had simply expressed disagreement, the most powerful Djinn Sultan Al-Hassan Godsbain would have spared your life! Al-Hassan is the only one there who acted nobly and honestly. He didn't kill all the undying, even though he had both the ability and right to do so. Al-Hassan Godsbain killed only those who had tricked him and prevented him from getting free. And right before he disappeared, scattering most of his enemies and driving the rest away, the sultan of the djinn returned to me and thanked me for his freedom! And, seeing how I wasted the valuable wish on his freedom, the djinn promised to come help me and bail me out of problems three times!"

Woah! She now had a very powerful ally, who had proved himself capable of dispersing a well-organized team of TOP players all by himself. And she could call him three times! Taisha's wasted wish had earned her a very cool companion! That didn't do much for me though. After waiting for the beautiful Goblin to say her fill, I asked her what had happened after the djinn got free.

"At first, all the surviving undying were very angry, confused and didn't understand what had happened. But after that, they very quickly realized I had set the djinn free."

"Did they curse at you? Threaten you?" I guessed, but was mistaken.

"It was actually the opposite. I was asked a few questions about my race, my life and my relatives. The undying wanted to know literally everything! I told them honestly about my childhood in the village of Tysh, my family, meeting you, and our marriage. There were so many unbelievably powerful and blindingly beautiful members of every race under the sun! I have never before felt such attention from the undying! I was praised for doing the right thing and not letting the glorious *Legion of Steel* break an oath. I was showered with gifts and asked to join their clan. I have never been heaped with compliments like that in my entire life!"

Taisha smiled from the pleasant memories. Clearly, my companion was very happy with the attention and streams of flattery poured on her by the *Legion of Steel*, competing in eloquence and applying their whole arsenal of charms, spells and skills.

"The head of the clan Till Quick_Fingers [LEGION], the best thief in all *Boundless Realm*, offered to let me be his companion! He promised to teach me all his thief wisdom in just a week, so that I could go with him on all kinds of interesting adventures! But still I refused, because I swore before the gods to be with you, Amra. That is precisely what I said to him. He didn't argue, and soon went back through the portal. But before they left, they asked me to think hard about whether to stay weak and pitiful with you, or rise up to the level of the gods of *Boundless Realm* with them."

Everything became extremely clear to me — the players of the *Legion of Steel* quickly realized how unusual an NPC Taisha was and were interested in her. And really, how could they not be? She was an NPC that got quests, calmly walked through their barrier, which only players could cross, had her own point of view, and basically just behaved totally independently!

Blowing up at her with rage for releasing the djinn was totally senseless, and the strongest clan in the game would never act so low. But they still did try to take the unique NPC thief girl away from me. They had praised her to the heavens, given her gifts — what girl, even if virtual, didn't love gifts and compliments? They'd probably told her a bunch of negative things about me. What was it that I'd heard slip through in Taisha's speech: "weak and pitiful?" That must have been where the fall in loyalty came from too. It was actually strange they didn't manage to convince her in the end. Clearly, my connection with Taisha was very strong to begin with, as even these players from a TOP clan were not able to tear her away. But they had significantly weakened that connection... And Taisha's next words confirmed that:

"I'll admit, Amra, I don't feel that you need me at all. All this time, you've never said a single word of kindness to me. You have no interest in me at all, you're always busy with your own stuff. Over the last five days, you've showed up a few times, and didn't even find any time to talk to me. Just tell me, what good is a husband like that?"

Mission received: Taisha's Disenchantment

Mission class: Unusual, racial, time-limited

- A Trap for the Potentate -

Description: Manage to convince your NPC wife in less than ten minutes that you really are good enough to be her husband

Reward: 16000 Exp., +5 to Taisha's opinion of you, +1 Charisma

Penalty for failure: -30 to Taisha's opinion of you, event Taisha's Departure will trigger

Taisha's departure?! Now I really was afraid. No matter how flighty the green-skinned beauty was, I really didn't want to lose her. Sure, I couldn't get used to the idea that I had an official wife in the game, and didn't experience the tender feelings that Taisha wanted. But I was accustomed to her, and found her fun and useful. Also, one of the reason my clips were so popular was my beautiful goblin companion. So, I would have to fight for Taisha.

Just ten minutes? So little time! But I understood that pouring out like a nightingale and starting to whisper sweet nothings to my wife now was senseless, as was telling her I'd had a sudden flare-up of passion. First of all, Taisha was smart and would easily detect that I was being false. Second, I was sure not to outdo the *Legion of Steel*'s professional charmers, who had brainwashed my NPC companion just an hour ago. I needed to act a bit differently. But how?

What separated me from the other players?

I was a goblin just like Taisha. I should take advantage of that, all the more so given that the quest description said "racial."

"Taisha, the last few days have been harder than I was expecting, and I haven't had the time to give you the attention you deserve. But I'll correct all that tonight!"

"And how are you gonna do that?" my green-skinned girlfriend asked.

"Tonight..." I said, fitfully trying to think something up, "is the Night of the Wolf Riders!"

"I've never heard of that..."

"What are you talking about?!" I asked, feigning amazement. "It's one of the most celebrated Goblin holidays! Maybe, in your village of Tysh there weren't any wolves to ride, so you didn't celebrate it? It was actually Goblins that invented riding in the first place! Our far-off ancestors were the first to saddle a wolf many centuries before humans even tamed the first horse! Ever since then, there has been an ancient connection between goblins and wolves, and Night of the Wolf Riders is one of our most beloved holidays, especially among young goblins!"

I was spinning pure nonsense, whatever came to mind, all the time keeping an eye on the countdown timer, which showed how long I had to finish the quest. Taisha then nodded unconfidently, digesting the information. Finally, the girl inquired:

~ A Trap for the Potentate ~

"And how is this night celebrated?"

"Young Goblin boys and girls ride their wolves as far into the night as they can. To places far from the prying eyes and ears of their meddlesome parents, where there are no nosy neighbors, and they won't be tripping over curious babies. When they get away, they act foolish, chase one another, compete in strength and agility. This is the celebration where young boys meet their future girlfriends, and couples can finally be alone together without the older generation bothering them."

Taisha thought intensively in silence. It seemed to me that I had made a wrong move and led the situation into a dead end, having gotten caught in too deep a lie.

Successful Charisma check
Experience received: 160 Exp.

Successful check for Taisha's opinion
Experience received: 400 Exp.

The redheaded beauty started smiling unexpectedly. Her eyes lit up with a happy flicker:

"What a wonderful holiday! Too bad it wasn't celebrated in Tysh. And this is a moon-lit night, just right for a romantic outing. But I don't have my own wolf, and all members of the Gray Pack belong to you and only listen to you. Also, after a whole day walking in the desert, I have no interest in seeing more of these dreary sand dunes all around. But I'd never refuse flying with you on the wyvern!"

"Ehh..." I tried to object. "But VIXEN is too little to fly with two on her back!"

"If that's what you call little!" Taisha snorted. "Your flying snake has already shot up to eight steps long! She could swallow a person whole! But if you're right, and she still doesn't have the strength... Do you want to know how to give your winged snake a few levels in one go? After all, you have two more Ifrit Hearts!"

Wait, stop! I asked Taisha how she even know about the contents of my Inventory, and how she wasn't ashamed to steal my things?! Her reaction was unexpected:

"That isn't true! I didn't steal anything! I just looked at your things when we were standing next to the djinn. And so what? Is that not allowed?! And I only took what belonged to me. After all, I found the Ifrit Heart! You just asked me to look at it but, instead of giving it back, you popped it in your mouth and wolfed it down!"

What a bizarre interpretation of events... For a second, I even wished I'd failed Taisha's Disenchantment. But I quickly got myself back together and didn't even express myself too rudely. Instead, I ordered my companion to remove every more or less heavy item from her inventory, and promised to do the same, so the Royal Forest Wyvern would be able to take off with both of us on her back.

Taisha didn't argue. Thirty seconds later, on a carpet in the center of the tent, there was a towering mountain of seven-sided silver coins, a heap of magic scrolls, a whole set of armor and weapons from the Kingslayer set, a porcelain statuette of a dancing girl (which I had been looking for, thinking I'd forgotten it on *White Shark*), a leather case with a bunch of magic elixirs, a heavy ring of lock picks, a dwarven monkey wrench, and a few pretty baubles and trinkets the thief had managed to pilfer during our journey.

Taisha had taken only a couple daggers, and was wearing only the practically weightless thief's outfit I'd given her so long ago. I also took almost all the coins and the majority of my things out of my inventory, leaving just the minimum necessary reserve of alchemical elixirs, my blowgun and some ammunition.

VIXEN came to my first call and, although she did give a few dismayed hisses and flashes of her poisonous fangs, even allowed both riders to get up on her back. I had to sit first, otherwise my winged mount refused to obey. It was too bad. I had been hoping to hold onto my companion's nice body during the flight. She looked so beautiful in the form-fitting dark clothes.

"We're flying toward Dotur-Khawe!" I told Taisha, and she didn't object in the slightest.

"Let's get on our way! I finally feel like your wife! Let's celebrate this wonderful night!" the girl shouted out provocatively, embracing me firmly by the shoulders.

I set my mount's trajectory for the subterranean city of the dwarves, and VIXEN tore off into the night sky, flapping her huge wings.

Mission completed: Taisha's Disenchantment
Reward: 16000 Exp.
Taisha's opinion of you has increased to +55
Charisma increased by +1

Riding skill increased to level 19!

Animal Control skill increased to level 16!

Level forty-two!

It seemed the situation was gradually starting to blow over. I'd already gotten back the level I'd lost by dying, and my relationship with Taisha was getting back to where it had been. I was hoping greatly that it was a good sign, meaning my unlucky streak of difficulties and failures was over, both in real life and the virtual world.

We flew in the night sky over the desert. From this perspective, it seemed to be made of pure silver. Taisha howled in elation and thanked me for the wonderful journey. But just taking my NPC girlfriend for a ride on my winged mount was not my aim. And also, my boss might not like to see me spending my time this way, which he would see as pointless, even if I was flying to Dotur-Khawe not just because, but to get a package I'd acquired at auction.

I still had the potential unique quest Taisha's Rebellion. So, for that reason, continuing to laugh and joke with my green-skinned girlfriend, I thought through the options of how to bring Taisha to that state. I could see that I needed to act extremely delicately here. On the one hand, I needed to make her upset, but I could not afford to allow an irreversible situation like Taisha's Departure.

We'd already been flying for around a half hour, and I still couldn't think up anything good enough for the quest. VIXEN then started to clearly sag. The flapping of her broad leathery wings was becoming more and more frequent and abrupt. I was looking for somewhere flat and secluded to take the wyvern in for a landing.

"Great," said Taisha, approving of my actions. She was no longer in a fun mood and had sharply grown serious. "This is just what we need: a solitary place for a most serious conversation."

Taisha's Rebellion

AS SOON AS VIXEN touched down on the sand, the Gray Pack appeared next to me in full formation. My girlfriend was very surprised by that. She thought the wolves, wargs and mythical hound would be left far behind.

"Well, they're my companions, so they will always appear next to me, if they die or get too far away," I explained.

"And me too?" the girl cringed in dissatisfaction. "After all, after I die and am reborn I always show up next to you again!"

I nodded in silence, trying to guess what exactly my NPC bride was implying. After all, Taisha clearly had something she wanted to talk about. The last thing she'd said during our flight seemed to imply she had some kind of plans.

"Amra, I'm not satisfied with this pitiful role! I don't want to be your shadow anymore, I want to be independent!!! And also, you're a goblin yourself and you know our laws. Only the strongest has the right to command! And I'm stronger than you now, so I want to be free of your meddlesome guardianship. I can take care of myself now and make my own independent decisions! Why aren't you saying anything?!"

I was just watching to see how my NPC girlfriend's flash of discontent would end. If Taisha thought I would get upset at the demonstration of disobedience or try to talk her out of it, she was deeply mistaken. Using my positive relationship and modifiers, I might be able to talk to the girl and get her over her present dismay. But I didn't want to. In fact, behind the careless look on my face, I was trying to hide an internal glee. Could it really be that this was leading to the unique quest Taisha's Rebellion?! Without waiting for me to answer, the girl continued her speech, gradually heating up more and more:

"Amra, we are bound by a holy oath, so I cannot simply up and leave. But I know a way out now. I will call the gods of *Boundless Realm* as witnesses and challenge you to a duel! One on one! Right here and now!"

Everything became clear to me at once. So, this was where all the disobedience had come from! The experienced players of the *Legion of Steel* had pinned down the reason for all their failed attempts to lure Taisha to their side. Taisha was bound to me by a divine oath, which they were powerless to break. All the same, the players knew the rules and had told Taisha a way to break this bond — rebel, challenge me to a duel and call the gods as witnesses. But I couldn't understand why the rebellion quest had yet to trigger. Clearly, I'd have to talk to my defiant NPC girlfriend and figure out all the conditions of the duel.

"Taisha, I can understand your motivation. But explain to me what I have to gain from that? I'm fine with our current situation, so why should I want to fight with you?"

Apparently, the goblin girl wasn't expecting me to refuse, and even got confused. But then, the lack of confidence on Taisha's face changed into determination:

"You have to fight! My stake in this battle is freedom and status as your wife! If the battle goes my way, you will completely lose power over me. I'll be able to go wherever I want and be whoever I want, and be reborn wherever I choose. But if you win, you can set a punishment for disobedience, and I'll agree in advance to any sentence. But I have one condition: the battle must be one on one. None of your beasts can interfere! And I will not use my right to summon the Djinn Sultan, even though I can!"

"Well, that's fair," I agreed and gave an order

to the Gray Pack, and also VIXEN to rest and not interfere no matter what happened.

Mission received: Taisha's Rebellion
Mission class: Unique, personal
Description: defeat Taisha in a ritual duel
Reward: 40000 Exp., Fame +1, one-week bonus of +50 to Taisha's opinion of you, +100 to any checks for Taisha's loyalty, absolute protection against any relationship decreases with Taisha
Penalty for failure: -50 to Taisha's opinion of you, -10 to Goblin race opinion of you, event Taisha's Departure will trigger

Finally! I read into the mission conditions. What could I say? It was harsh. Go big or go home. All or nothing. But what was so unique about this mission? After all, unique quests were usually accompanied by proportionally valuable rewards. Just then I saw only the ability to get, instead of a lively and interesting Taisha, a fully obedient NPC doll, in no way different from stupid bots, controlled by simple program scripts. Did I even need that?!

I valued Taisha for, among other things, how unusual and unpredictable she was, which meant she was sometimes even contrarian. I had no desire to break the NPC girl and make her an obedient slave. Although, I still did need to prove who was in charge of our group. Her current behavior just crossed every line.

"I summon the gods of *Boundless Realm* to witness our duel and swear to fight honorably!" Taisha declared smugly, and I repeated after her.

Next to us with a deafening crack, a blindingly bright bolt of lightning struck the sand. The gods had heard our oaths. Alright, time to get started! I'd already known my strategy for some time: hold the thief girl at a distance, threaten her with my throwing net and shoot her with my blowgun. Sure, Taisha did have the crossbow, and she could also shoot from a distance, but her skill level with that weapon was just three, giving me a clear advantage. Taisha could also go invisible, using her Stealth skill, but she could not shoot while invisible. What was more, the bright moon and open space of the desert didn't favor stealth, so I was hoping to see the girl by using my vampire abilities Night Vision and Search for Life. And if Taisha decided to come in for close combat and take out her daggers, I was hoping to immobilize her with the throwing net and hold her down with my greater Strength.

But the green-skinned thief girl caught me by surprise. One moment and, instead of the flexible female figure in thin dark clothing, I had a woman warrior before me, vested in an emerald suit of dragon-skin armor. The full Kingslayer set, probably with insane bonuses to Agility, damage, crits and all that! The situation sharply turned against me. My emotions must have been reflected on my face, because Taisha gave a happy chuckle:

"What, Amra, not expecting this? Did you think I'd be standing before you in that ultrathin form-fitting clothing all vulnerable and defenseless? No, I was never planning to return to that desert oasis, so I took all my items and coins with me. And I took yours too. I'm gonna need them in my journeys. By the way, you still could even out the chances by eating one or even two Ifrit Hearts. Don't be ashamed, I'll wait!"

For a moment, the thought of eating an Ifrit Heart and gaining ten levels really did flicker past in my mind. But I didn't do it. I just looked more carefully at Taisha's equipment, especially the two throwing daggers, which she was deftly twirling in her hands, and... laughed right in her face!

"No, Taisha, I have no need to waste an invaluable item. I'm already quite sure of my victory! In fact, you've already lost, even though you don't know it. However, if you put away your weapons right now and surrender, I will take mercy on you."

Instead of answering, Taisha went invisible.

Holy cow, that was unexpected. I couldn't see the thief girl, despite all my skills. Neither Search for Life, nor Night Vision were of any help. Unpleasant, of course. But all in all, that didn't change anything.

I waited, looking around carefully from side to side doing my best not to present my back for a strike. A Thief stabbing you in the back with a dagger was considered critical in all games, dealing damage that was increased by many times, and *Boundless Realm* was no exception.

Successful Perception check!
Experience received: 80 Exp.

Sand!

To be more accurate, footprints appearing in it.

Now, I knew for certain where the NPC thief was located and, pretending it was a coincidence, I tried to turn my face in that very direction.

Successful Perception check!
Experience received: 160 Exp.

Sound! My huge sensitive ears picked up the sifting of dry sand and little pebbles, as well as the rustling of my opponent's leather clothing.
Successful Perception check!
Experience received: 320 Exp.

Smell! Now this was an obvious error on Taisha's part. The girl had used cosmetics, and my nostrils could distinctly discern the scent of her powders, pomades and floral perfumes. The wolves of the Gray Pack could also detect the strong smell and were following Taisha's movements by turning their snouts.

My green-skinned girlfriend had never been distinguished by patience. After just four minutes, she got tired of spinning circles around me.

I first caught the sound of her clothes rustling as she wound up, then the whistle of a throwing dagger in flight.

In theory, I could calmly dodge the flying danger, but I didn't actually want to. I intentionally let the throwing knife hit me.

Damage taken: 285 (659 Dagger strike — 46 armor, 50% defense against physical damage)

Bleeding effect (30 damage per second, lasts 20 seconds)

Successful check for Poison Resistance

Successful Constitution check
The bleeding has stopped

Although my health bar went down to 1563 of 1848, It was still in the green. In theory, I could calmly survive a strike from the second throwing knife. Taisha became visible, now preparing to make another throw. But she couldn't get it off. I pulled the razor-sharp serrated dagger from my shoulder and simply placed it in my inventory.

At that very second, the throwing knife fell out of Taisha's hand, and almost all my attractive companion's clothing dropped off her at once, leaving her in nothing but tiny lacy undergarments. And though that was unexpected to the now practically naked girl, I had been anticipating this moment since the very beginning of the duel. I immediately threw my net at the confused thief girl, lost in her own fallen armor.

Exotic Weapons skill increased to level 14!

Taisha came back to her senses fairly quickly — just a second later, the girl had another set of daggers in her hands, and was trying to cut the net off her body. But she couldn't! I didn't catch her just so she could run away so easily! My Amra was next to her instantly, holding her down by both wrists.

Successful Strength check
Experience received: 200 Exp.

Successful Strength check
Experience received: 400 Exp.

Successful Strength check

Experience received: 800 Exp.

The thief girl was squirming vigorously, clearly not believing that my weak Goblin Herbalist, with lower level than her, could hold her down. This spasming could go on for a very long time yet, so I had to squeeze my fingers even harder.

> *Successful Strength check*
> *Experience received: 1600 Exp.*

Taisha yelped in pain and unclenched her hands, causing both of her daggers to fall to the sand. I could read incomprehension, confusion and fear in my companion's eyes. She still couldn't believe that she really had lost. I then picked up one of the fallen daggers and held it to the Goblin beauty's neck and Taisha stopped resisting.

"Do I need to make a clear demonstration of my victory and send you to rebirth with loss of experience and level? Or are you just gonna agree I won the duel?" I asked. And Taisha, after a second's pause, said distinctly:

"No, you won. I can see that already. I admit before all the gods of *Boundless Realm*, that I overestimated my abilities and lost the duel. Amra, you are my unquestioned sovereign, and I am prepared to take whatever punishment you give me."

~ A Trap for the Potentate ~

Mission completed: Taisha's Rebellion
Experience received: 40000 Exp.

Fame increased
Present value: 7

Level forty-three!

After quickly throwing the stat points into their habitual scheme (Strength and Constitution were raised by one point with every level automatically, and I added one to Agility and two to Charisma), I turned to my NPC companion. Taisha, still entangled in the throwing net, was just sitting motionless on the sand next to the pile of fallen equipment.

With a purposely rude and authoritarian voice, I ordered her:

"First, stand up spread out that cloak on the sand and set all your things on it. I want it all to be there. You cannot keep any secrets from your master."

Taisha stood up meekly, untangled herself and threw the net off, after which she began piling things from her bag, and pockets onto the cloak. The shimmering Kingslayer armor. A whole mountain of coins and scrolls. A lustrous black warg pelt. The very same porcelain statuette (what was that even worth to Taisha?). The dark thief's clothes, my elixirs and alchemy ingredients. The very last things to fly onto the pile were her lacy underwear, a ring with onyx inset and gold earrings with sapphires. The green-skinned girl, her cheeks crimson in embarrassment, was standing in front of me, covering her nakedness with her hands and expecting further commands.

Now, when I told her to set her items out, I had meant just the contents of her inventory, not her jewelry or underwear. But still, I didn't stop the girl. Knowing how easily embarrassed my companion was, this would be a lesson to her! I ordered her to spread her arms, then unhurriedly walked around Taisha, frozen in fear, looking shamelessly at the nice curves of the naked beauty at my own pace.

"You know, I should make you walk into the desert looking just like this, so you will never again feel a desire to raise a hand against your master!" I threatened the girl severely, and understood by the frightened expression on her face that the threat was taken extremely seriously. "And also, I forbid you from ever again using Stealth around me, or stealing from me, to once and for all break this habit of stealing your master's things!"

Picking up the onyx ring from the heap of items, I spun the unfamiliar object in my hands. I could not determine its properties, and asked if this was the object that could summon the djinn.

"Yes, that's the one," Taisha confirmed.

~ A Trap for the Potentate ~

I threw the valuable ring back with the other things and continued talking with the NPC thief:

"Now, I need honest answers to a whole lot of questions, because you have been acting very strangely for the last few days."

First of all, I asked a few questions about the reasons for my girlfriend's pent-up dismay. However, I didn't learn anything new. Taisha assured me, as before, that goblins generally obey the strongest, and I had allowed my wife to doubt my strength and thus right to be leader.

"And you didn't think with your bird brains that I might not want to attract excessive attention and demonstrate my true power? It didn't occur to you that my Goblin Herbalist might look weak and inoffensive on purpose, so no one would guess a powerful vampire is hidden in this fragile body? Just watch!"

I walked up to a massive boulder and, without apparent strain, lifted it with one hand, demonstrating Amra's Strength. After that, I took one of the thief girl's reserve daggers and easily snapped it with just three fingers. Her eyes went wide in astonishment. She wasn't expecting such a funny and frail-looking Goblin Herbalist to be able to do that.

"Forgive me, master, I was wrong. I only saw that you weren't even capable of holding me close or pulling off my clothes, when I was in a frisky mood and pretending to try and get out of your embrace. If I had gotten even the slightest hint that all this weakness was faked, I'd never have doubted your strength!"

I immediately reminded her of the story on the *White Shark* pirate bireme, when I had kissed Taisha in the captain's cabin, but she twisted out of my embrace and sent me a sharp lowering of her opinion. It turned out that was an element of play from my green bride. Woah!

Actually, my Strength and Constitution had only grown significantly long after that incident in the bunk, due to the bonus from two items from Fenrir's Cursed Regalia. All the same, I didn't clarify that, because Taisha didn't need to know.

I continued asking my questions. Now, I was interested in all the smallest details of what had happened after Taisha had made her wish to the Djinn. What questions had the undying from the *Legion of Steel* asked her? What had they done, used spells on her? What had the undying discussed amongst themselves? Above all else, I was worried that Taisha might have let slip that I was a vampire.

On that account, the thief girl reassured me. No one had asked her about vampirism, but if anyone had asked such a question, she wouldn't have been able to tell them the truth. Taisha reminded me that she had sworn an oath before the gods to keep my secret, and no one could make her violate it.

~ A Trap for the Potentate ~

It was as if a stone fell from my shoulders. But, as it turned out, not for long. I asked about Fenrir's Cursed Regalia, and Taisha said the very last thing I wanted to hear:

"Yes, the undying really did ask me about that."

"And what did you tell them?" I asked, my voice cracking in anxiety.

"I told them everything I knew: my husband had long held the Amulet of Fenrir, which gives some useful reinforcements to your wolves. But that you could only put it on after eating the Ifrit Heart. I don't know anything else about the Fenrir stuff."

I didn't curse Taisha out for her chattiness. First of all, it was too late to change anything no matter what, and my words of rage didn't overcome the regrettable fact that my secret, that I was trying to collect the entire set of Fenrir's Cursed Regalia, had become known to other players. Second, it would have been totally unfair to blame this on my companion. I had already figured out that the players of the *Legion of Steel* must have placed a huge number of spells and effects on her, starting with Charming a Humanoid and Intoxicating Flattery, and ending with Elixir of Truth. Taisha couldn't not answer the questions they asked, and she could only answer with the truth and nothing but.

But what Taisha said next forced me to first

shout out in fear and dismay, then start thinking in the most serious fashion:

"The most important undying around me was Till Quick_Fingers, and he demanded his servants find out everything they could about Fenrir's stuff. Soon after that, an old man by the name of Alexander the Great3st told him one such item was stored in the storeroom of the main *Legion of Steel* citadel. He said it was Fenrir's Pelt, a unique cursed suit of fur armor that cannot be removed after its put on. The old man rattled off some numbers to the thief, and Till Quick_Fingers scornfully replied with some strange phrase. I didn't understand a word of it: 'shit for a unique, total dregs.' After that, the undying lost interest in the Fenrir stuff, and changed the topic."

Taisha said everything she knew and fell silent, awaiting further instructions from her master. I finally allowed her to lower her hands and relax as I stood in agitation, thinking. So, one of the items I needed was in the *Legion of Steel* citadel. That was bad, very bad. I had no doubts that the *Legion of Steel* would refuse to sell the armor, if I asked. Most likely, they would even get on guard if I started a conversation about it. After all, they didn't fully understand Taisha's uniqueness and didn't know that the NPC could tell someone else about their negotiations.

Stealing an item from a TOP clan's store room was harder than getting gold from Fort Knox.

~ A Trap for the Potentate ~

Other than the usual watchmen, there were probably so many guard spells packed in there that any criminal who got inside would be turned to ash on the spot. And taking the citadel of the strongest clan in the game by force was such a hopeless mission, that I just needed to forget about it. So what now? Had my chance to gather the complete set simply been left by the wayside?

Perhaps... I looked at the goblin girl, who was patiently awaiting my orders.

"Taisha, how were you planning to get to Till Quick_Fingers after our duel?"

The thief girl, no longer embarrassed at her naked body and even strutting a bit, gracefully pulled out her lithe leg and pointed with her fingers at a parchment bound with a ribbon.

"There's the teleportation scroll. All I have to do is unfurl it, and I'll be brought wherever I need to go."

Hmmm... Interesting. What if I took advantage of this chance to send Taisha to the *Legion of Steel* and get the item? It sounded extremely risky and, if the plan was revealed, the consequences for me personally promised to be extremely disastrous. But I didn't see any other way.

"So then, Taisha. I heard your explanations carefully and am prepared to tell you my decision..."

The green-skinned beauty froze at complete

attention, I even noticed her ears perk up.

"As for you challenging me to a duel, I don't see anything reprehensible in your actions. You did exactly as a proud goblin girl should!"

Taisha's opinion of you has increased by +10

I skimmed the text that popped up before my eyes and surprisingly noticed that my girlfriend also seemed to be looking at something invisible. Could Taisha read game logs now?! Impossible! But, if that really was the case, influencing her using flattery and even finishing quests would become much more difficult, as the NPC girl would be able to guess exactly what happened.

All the same, my guesses weren't confirmed.

I continued my speech,

"But as for the theft of my things, you really did commit an offense and will be punished in the most serious fashion. But even more than the theft itself, I was hurt by your hypocrisy. I thought you were sincerely joyful to fly over the desert on my wyvern tonight and grateful to me for the chance. But the entire time you had in your head that you were tricking your naive companion, running away with stolen items and not planning to return. That is loathsome and, I cannot forgive you so easily for such villainy."

Taisha grew ashamed. At the very least, the thief lowered her eyes in guilt.

~ A Trap for the Potentate ~

I continued my speech:

"And now, I have a bunch of questions for the leaders of the *Legion of Steel*. After all, they openly took advantage of your lack of experience and trusting nature, putting spells on you to get secret information, tricking you and using you for their own purposes. They used forbidden magic to gain your confidence and besmirch me in your eyes. They soiled my beautiful bride with their nasty wizardry and thought you a naive and obedient fool! So, I'm horribly mad at them!!!"

Successful Charisma check
Experience received: 160 Exp.

Successful check for Taisha's opinion
Experience received: 400 Exp.

It seemed to me once again that the redheaded beauty was looking at a popup. Two times now! That could not be a mere coincidence. Finally, Taisha smiled and said:

"Amra, I'm insanely glad to hear that you care. And the thing I want most of all in this world is to atone for my sins against you. And so, if there's anything I can do for you, just tell me! I'll do anything! I swear!"

I had been expecting something like that from my companion, but this was more than I was even hoping for. Taisha wanted to get back to our former good relationship. What could I say? I had just the proposal for how to get us there.

"Till Quick_Fingers promised to quickly improve your skills and level. It would be stupid to refuse such a great chance for progress. So, you will take the teleportation scroll and go to the *Legion of Steel*!"

Taisha gasped in surprise. With a gesture, I told her to wait for me to finish.

"Before that, you will take all your things back, and everything you took from me in the desert oasis. You will tell them you defeated me tonight in the divine duel in the desert. You didn't kill me, no. That's too easy to check. Just say you forced me to retreat, recognizing your victory. And you won't simply say that, you will sincerely believe it, and any magic checks will prove that you are not lying."

"Why do I need that? Why do I need to fool them, and also believe it myself?" Taisha was, to put it lightly, shocked by my words.

"Don't interrupt! Keep listening. You will study all the wisdom of a master thief from the best one in *Boundless Realm*. You will take part in all *Legion of Steel* events together with its head Till Quick_Fingers, improving your level and skills. You will be sincerely glad at the ability to join the strongest undying clan and be a companion of its much-vaunted leader. You will demonstrate sincere joy at your new fate whenever they check and will obey every order except utterly brazen acts of harassment, if such things come to pass. The only thing you will keep silent on is your unique ability to respawn after death. And if you do happen to get asked about that, tell them that both of your rebirths came after I called the Keeper and reached some understandings you are not aware of."

Taisha clearly didn't yet understand why I was saying all that to her, but still was nodding obediently, taking all the limitations into account.

I continued my speech,

"In a few days, the undying from the *Legion of Steel* will get used to you and start to trust you completely. You will probably be able to understand when that happens on your own. They will stop shunning you and start discussing secret things in your presence. And after that, as if by coincidence, you will start a conversation about Fenrir's Pelt and ask them to show it to you using whatever excuse necessary. You're a smart girl and can probably think up a pretext on your own. I trust you on this. Your strange request will probably catch the attention of the leaders of the *Legion of Steel*, and any object you demand will be given at the very least out of curiosity, just to see what you'll do with it. And if the undying of the *Legion of Steel* have any doubts, you can even joke that they can put an anti-magic dome around you, so you won't slip away with the pelt. And now, the most important part! As soon as you make certain that they really did give you the very item you requested, the Pelt of Fenrir is in your hands or inventory, you kill yourself immediately!"

The goblin beauty shuddered in fear. But I hurried to reassure Taisha that she would remain immortal as long as she stuck with me. Such was the promise made by the Keeper himself, and I had bought her eternal life for a very high price.

"You will simply return to me, much stronger and with an item that is very valuable to me. As soon as you do, you will immediately be completely forgiven. You will be my wife once again, a loyal girlfriend and my very closest companion, who I trust fully. Yes, all this will threaten me with lots of problems in the future. The players of the *Legion of Steel* will realize that I tricked them, and they will huff and puff! But I cannot forgive them for using their dirty magic to try and steal my beautiful wife from me! This will be my revenge on the *Legion of Steel*!!!"

"Amra, I... I... I simply cannot find the words to express my admiration! You are willing to make such powerful enemies for my sake! I will do everything you ask, I promise! And then I will return to you and regain your trust! But before I use the portal scroll and leave you for some time... I want to give you a gift!"

The naked beauty Taisha blushed in embarrassment and started giggling uncontrollably, tousling her fiery red hair. She then picked up a fine black warg pelt from the pile of things and laid it out on the sand. After that, she laid her down on the thick fur, spread her legs wide and made a come-hither gesture:

"My master, today you showed fully that I chose the right husband! I doubted you for a long time and delayed this heart-pounding moment but, after this magical night, you deserve me like never before!"

Subterranean City

I HAD NEVER experienced such utter bliss from being with a woman. All of my previous experience with sex with all kinds of real world girlfriends, and even nights of love with Kira had been a faint shadow of the sincerely magical sensations I felt with the NPC girl Taisha. In the virtual *Boundless Realm,* everything was simply ideal, the way one can only dream of. Taisha was passionate, and insatiable, at times tender, at times wild, at times violent, and at times submissive but, at every second, sincere and loving. I could feel that. I wanted to extend these moments of sweetness indefinitely. The night was too short for us to get enough of one another.

But, unfortunately, morning came. Taisha and I were sitting in embrace on the soft black pelt, watching the pinkening sky in the east. As vexing as it may have been, the magical night of love had come to an end.

"I need to fly to the dwarven city of Dotur-Khawe, so I can get under the earth before the sun comes up," I said, straining massively to gather my will into a fist, break our sweet embrace and stand up.

"Yes, Amra, it's time for you to fly away," Taisha agreed with pity, also standing and gathering her strewn-about things. "I'll be so lonely without you these next few days..."

"You won't. Because you'll hide your memories of this night in the deepest recesses of your mind," I reminded my girlfriend. "And in a few days, we'll be together again, and you will remember everything!"

"Yes, Amra, that's exactly right," Taisha confirmed, smiling sadly. "But I really don't want to leave you... I'm now certain there's no one I can trust more or get on better with than you. I want to press myself up against you, pour out my soul and share all my secrets. I've never revealed this to anyone in my life, but I can simply open up to you..."

I was getting dressed just then, preparing to fly away on VIXEN, and figured Taisha's admission was nothing but fine words, coming out due to the emotional overload of our night of love. But what kind of secrets could the NPC girl have, even if she was so advanced and sweet? All the same, Taisha's next words caught my attention:

"Amra, do you want me to tell you the whole truth about what happened after the djinn was set free? After all, I could clearly see the undying from the *Legion of Steel* working me with their magic. I read exactly what spells they were using on me, and what effect they achieved. I understood it all perfectly, but did nothing to stop it. In fact, I wanted them to work."

"What?!" I froze, having forgotten about my plan to fly, and unable to hide my amazement. "But why, Taisha?"

"It's just that yesterday, the world changed for me. I didn't even understand myself exactly how it happened but, at a certain point, I started seeing everything through the eyes of the undying. Hints everywhere, little bits of text, everything in my usual world was reflected with dry numbers. It must be so boring for your kind! There's no real friendship, only increasing relationship numbers. No risk, just crude calculation before a duel. Anyone you come across is just a set of statistics. Much became clear to me. Experience, classes, missions, skills, reputation... I had heard these terms many times in your conversations with your sister and friends, but only yesterday realized exactly what they meant."

Now that was news! Taisha had really become more and more undying in the usual sense of the word. She had even practically realized that the world around her was just a game. She only had a few more steps to go before she reached that conclusions herself. The NPC thief girl then continued her story:

"At a certain point, I came to the sad conclusion that you were no better than the rest of the undying. That, to you, I was nothing more than some bot, whose opinion you'd increased by completing a few quests and artificially calling me to you. Realizing that was very hurtful! Then I decided that, if I was fated to be the companion of some undying, then let it truly be the strongest master! For example, someone like Till Quick_Fingers, leader of the strongest clan. That was precisely why I took the Leader's Shadow skill. Yes, I'll admit, I wanted to leave you. I was such a fool! How wonderful that you managed to keep me by your side! But now, after revealing my secret, I can go with a clean conscience to complete my mission. Personal quest: "Becoming his True Wife" with variable reward. See you in a few days. Expect to see me much stronger and with the Pelt of Fenrir!"

I now had a lot of questions for Taisha, but the goblin beauty had already managed to unfurl the teleportation scroll and disappear in a flash of light. I picked up my fallen jaw. Look at that! Apparently, the words I'd said to my girlfriend had transformed into a personal quest for Taisha!

* * *

I just barely made it, driving VIXEN on so hard my winged snake could barely stay in the air. There was just one minute and a half before the sun would rise when I jumped off the Royal Forest Wyvern and ran to the entrance to the subterranean city. The dwarven guards looked me over carefully, but didn't stop me, and I entered Dotur-Khawe. Just in the nick of time! It was six o'clock in the morning, and the edge of the deadly sun had already appeared over the horizon.

After quickly catching my breath, I started making a plan. At first, I had to pick up the package and get my new item fitted. Then, I'd find the Craftsman District and pick up some equipment appropriate to my level-43 Goblin Herbalist and replace the old stuff I'd bought back in the village of Tysh. Yes, I also should visit some subterranean Alchemists and Herbalists, given the chance, and exchange the huge amount of Bank of Thorin the Ninth notes for real silver and gold, which was no work at all in Dotur-Khawe.

For one seven-sided silver coin, the first dwarven boy I came across led me to the Trade Guild, a whole underground floor with lots of separate rooms and corridors leading into the unknown darkness. Fortunately, I didn't have to look for long, and a polite dwarven trader told me where I could pick up the package. All I had to do was introduce myself, and a package of thick folded paper became my property.

Wolf Claws

My purchase was a set of raggedy gloves with long, sharp steel claws like daggers. In the item's characteristics, my eyes were immediately met with a bright red warning flashing alarmingly, saying the item was cursed so, once donned, it could never be removed (to be more accurate, there were ways to rid ones' self of cursed items, but they were all very complicated and expensive).

There were no mentions of the item belonging to a set, though. And I really could get into a complicated situation by putting on the utterly unneeded, and also relatively weak cursed item. But, for some reason, I had no doubts that Valerianna's intuition had not misled me.

And I was not wrong!!! As soon as I put the gloves on, the item's characteristics changed:

Fenrir's Front Paws (unique item)
+50% melee damage, 17% of damage dealt goes toward healing self, Immunity to fear, Immunity to charms

You have equipped three items from Fenrir's Cursed Regalia

~ Dark Herbalist Book Three ~

Set bonus unlocked: all members of the Gray Pack will receive a bonus of +75 Strength, +75 Agility, +75 Constitution, +50% movement speed, +50% experience gain

Mission completed: Fenrir's Legacy (1/4)
Reward: 100000 Exp., +10 Animal Control, +50 Strength, +50 Agility, +50 Constitution, Gray Pack member limit raised to twelve

Level forty-four!

Level forty-five!

You may now choose your first specialization in the Animal Control skill

I'll admit, at first I was very glad... then I got afraid. Yes, yes, a true wave of panic swept over me. I was on the path to sharply increasing my character's strength and there was no way back now. My Goblin Herbalist was gradually changing from the peaceable goofy plant gatherer my audience had grown accustomed to, into a terrifying bloodthirsty alpha of a fierce pack of predators. Yes, my big-eared Goblin's appearance was purposely inoffensive, but I couldn't hide the true strength of my character forever, and the truth might not be to everyone's liking.

Amra already had plenty of ill-wishers in *Boundless Realm* due to the unique flying mount. But now, on the path to becoming the reincarnation of Fenrir, a true horror of *Boundless Realm*, I would certainly be gaining many more enemies. Beyond that fact, I would get many more enemies when my vampiric essence was revealed. And then in the future, if I did manage to gather the whole set of cursed wolf armor, my character would just be declared a criminal. No matter how I looked at it, that was a ghastly perspective.

But I was not planning to get off my chosen path. Only forward! Only hardcore! The mission now was extremely clear: get stronger in as compressed a timeframe as possible, while my character still had the chance!

New levels, new equipment, improved vampiric abilities. But the main thing was looking for the still unknown objects from Fenrir's Cursed Regalia! The claws, fortunately, didn't have any level requirements, and could be put on without even eating a single Ifrit Heart. I was very much counting on eventually getting the other two objects (Fenrir's Pelt and Fenrir's Paws), and the two Ifrit Hearts I had would allow me to don those items even if my level wasn't high enough. All that remained a secret was the location of the last, sixth item in the set, and I was planning to search for it in the next few days.

* * *

I distributed my new stat points and now was frozen staring at the first perk to Animal Control skill. I could choose to increase attack strength, endurance, defense against physical or magical attacks, or to add one more pet. I wanted all of that but, most of all, I wanted another pet. After carefully reading the skill description and perk hint, though, I realized with deep disappointment that the additional pet would not join the Gray Pack, so would be much, much weaker than the other animals and fairly useless to me. Increasing attack or defense of the Gray Pack would give a much greater beneficial effect. In the end, I decided to increase attack strength.

After closing the stat window for my Goblin Herbalist, I left the underground floor of the Trade Guild, planning to get new equipment. But before I managed to ask the way to the local armory masters, bootmakers and tailors, my attention was drawn by an emblem on the door of the neighboring shop: variously colored cones, a mortar and pestle for powdering ingredients, bundles of herbs. The local alchemist?

What could I say, I was planning to drop by an alchemist's, so I immediately headed for the door.

~ A Trap for the Potentate ~

Pirona Zealous
Level-65 Dwarf Alchemist

The owner of the shop was a redheaded bearded lady, quite tall for a dwarf and so wide at the belt that she was almost spherical. The expression of dismay and fastidiousness she reflected when seeing goblin on her doorstep gave way to a polite smile as soon as she took a closer look at me.

"Honored Guest of Dotur-Khawe. Alright then, what an important fellow visiting my shop! To what do I owe the honor, Mr. Amra?"

I had received the status of an honored guest a few days earlier after completing a chain of Socialization quests in the dwarven city. Cool, it really did impact my relationship! I asked if Pirona Zealous had the rare alchemy ingredient Ifrit Heart.

"No, sir. I've never had such a thing. But I do have lots of other items in stock. Elixirs and magic bombs, and a full array of body fragments of subterranean creatures from all of Dotur-Khawe! Tusks, hearts, brains, blood, poisonous glands... Everything an alchemist might need!"

Of course, my interest was piqued by one part in particular: "full array... subterranean creatures... blood," but I screwed up my green mug into a bored expression. With these traders, if you let them know an item has your interest, the price will instantly take off into the heavens! So, I approached from afar, first looking over some subterranean mushrooms in a glass case and even buying the cheapest ones for my Alchemy pursuits. After that, I filled out my empty bottle reserves, picked up a few crucibles and flask holders, magic ice for storing tissue samples and a porcelain mortar for powdering plants. And I actually bought two magical bombs: Frost Breath and Flame Rage. And only after that, as if by coincidence, did I agree to look over her collection.

In the end, my preparations came to naught. No matter how I tried to veil my interest in blood samples, even purposely adding things I didn't need to water down the purchase, like teeth, glands and claws, Pirona Zealous guessed nevertheless. We were negotiating for every new vial at screeching tones, raising my Trading skill to twenty, twenty-one and then twenty-two. I acquired forty-three new blood samples for my vampiric collection, and left only two unbought, the rarest ones:

Horror of the Depths Blood (alchemy ingredient)

Balrog Blood (alchemy ingredient)

The trader wanted fifteen thousand coins for each of the vials. I considered her price excessive, because that was about as much as all my previous purchases cost put together. The trader explained that, first off, the balrog was an extremely rare creature, which was to say nothing of the fact that killing such a powerful and dangerous fire beast was a serious undertaking. This particular monster had been found around three years earlier in the depths of the catacombs under the capital of the dwarves, and a large army of hundreds of undying had gathered to kill it. The trophy drop at that time was rich, and some of the loot was unloaded by the undying right here in Dotur-Khawe. Its fire-resistant pelt, tusks stronger than diamond, bones, blood and horns. But over the three years since then, all that had been bought and used by alchemists and craftsmen, and this vial of blood was all that remained. And now, the trader couldn't say when there might be more, or even if there ever would be.

I opened the *Boundless Realm* bestiary and searched for information about the balrog. Yes, everything was just as Pirona Zealous said. It was an extremely rare and dangerous monster that inhabited the very depths of the subterranean. My eye caught on the part saying the first balrog kill was by a Human Wizard named Gandalf the Gray, and that he had done it solo. But there were no links to his profile, which led me to think he must have been permanently banned from *Boundless Realm* for cheating.

The situation with the Horror of the Depths was approximately the same. The extremely rare and deadly dangerous monster was also invisible, so any trophies received from it were extremely rare. Everything added up. Trophies from such monsters should cost a lot. But at that, I understood perfectly that, in order to fully reveal the potential of my Goblin Vampire, these blood samples would be needed one day, and there was no guarantee I would ever find such a thing again, if I didn't get these two rare vials now. But still, I was not morally prepared to pay fifteen thousand coins for each one.

But Pirona Zealous balked, not wanting to lower the price no matter how I tried to convince her. Even the first specialization I took in the Trading skill, Honest Reputation, which was supposed to increase relationship with any NPC traders, didn't help one bit. To be more accurate, the prices for all the rest of the goods in the alchemy shop were lowered but, as for those two vials, she wouldn't budge. It seemed I was coming up against a programmed-in rule against lowering the price. Once upon a time, I had come up against the same in the village of Tysh, when Nyle Miser had not agreed to lower the price on the thief clothes for Taisha but, then, the trader's stubbornness was part of a quest.

What if this was a similar obstacle? Sensing, that I was on the right track, I began to carefully sound it out, touching on various topics and carefully observing the lady's reaction. Offer to trade the vials I needed for equally valuable elixirs? Clearly not it. The promise to buy goods for an insignificant value, like armor and weapons, from Pirona Zealous's relatives? Also didn't help. Although as for relatives, the lady still did express some interest. Something connected with relatives. So thus, by probing blindly, I eventually figured it out:

"Amra, my children are grown up, I have six wonderful sons. But if only you knew how hard it is for young dwarven men to find a bride. After all, in our submontane folk, only one girl is born for every five boys, and competition for the heart of every subterranean beauty is just bonkers! Nevertheless, I managed to set up my eldest three sons. Another two are now vying for the heart of their chosen woman, currying favor and earning respect with their mastery. And just my youngest, little Tondik, still cannot find success in love. He's modest and easily embarrassed, and every girl he ever liked was capricious and finicky. They only want the richest, bravest, strongest and most vaunted. But where is a peaceable Cook to earn his glory and fame?! So then I thought... Amra, take him with you on your adventure! As a reward, take any of the two monster-blood vials you were offered. You'll get the second after my little Tondik comes home from the adventure intact and unharmed!"

An unexpected turn of events! The shrewd trader had surprised me with an unusual suggestion. Before that, I had already told Pirona Zealous about my plan to travel up the river of death. But I was not expecting our conversation to take this turn. And also, I immediately noticed the flaws in Pirona's suggestion:

"And what if your little son doesn't want to come back home? For example, if he takes to life on the road or meets the love of his life and decides to stay with her?"

"Amra, knowing my homebody son, I'd never believe that my little Tondik would enjoy the restless life of a nomad. But if he does find love in far-off lands, what mother would talk her son out of marriage?! Right on the day my beloved son is married, I'll give you the second vial! But now, I'll fill your bag with healing elixirs and all kinds of plants to aid you on your journey. And I'll tell every alchemist I know about your kindness and concern for me. Well, goblin, what do you say? Shake on it?"

I thought over the suggestion of the corpulent trader. I saw very serious downsides to the suggestion to drag a momma's boy who was totally unprepared for such a journey along with me. And also, constantly protecting someone else's son from danger and bringing him home in one piece sounded difficult. On the other hand, the reward I was promised was more than generous. I agreed, squeezing the bearded lady's calloused hand.

Trading skill increased to level 23!

Foreman skill increased to level 31!

Mission completed: Recognition of the Alchemists' Guild (2/10)
Experience received: 160 Exp.

Alchemy skill increased to level 24

Mission received: Marrying Off a Son
Mission class: Rare, personal
Description: lead Tondik Exuberant to the upper reaches of the Styx and bring him back to Dotur-Khawe
Required: Tondik Exuberant must survive
Reward: 40000 Exp., vial of Horror of the Depths blood
Bonus condition: Make Tondik Exuberant a famous dwarven traveler and find him a wife
Reward: 80000 Exp., +10 to the opinion of all Dwarves in Boundless Realm

Pirona Zealous, clearly having planned this

out, squeezed my hand strongly in her iron grip. I don't know what the lady was expecting, perhaps she just wanted to laugh at a little bat-eared Goblin, or to demonstrate her power, but I had to put the trader in her place.

"Ow! That hurt! Let go, I was just joking!" the corpulent woman pulled her hand away and spent a long time blowing on her reddened palm.

I then took the Balrog Blood vial from the shelf and placed it in my bag. After that, I said severely:

"As for getting equipment for your son, that's up to you. Just consider this, woman. The lands around the river of death are dangerous and unwelcoming. If you want your beloved son to live, don't cheap out on good armor and weaponry. I'll come back to your shop at precisely eight PM. If Tondik isn't ready, I'll leave without him. And also... You probably have some good armorers around, right?"

The corpulent trader gave a very fast nod, that looked funny on her body, as if a ball filled with water slightly shuddered, or a wave ran over the surface of a pond.

"Well, I have no time to look for good craftsmen in your huge and confusing city. If you have any acquaintances that want to sell their goods, they can find me at eight PM in your shop. Tell them that I want a helmet, boots, leather armor, a cloak and a blowgun with a set of ammo.

~ A Trap for the Potentate ~

All of the best quality, with bonuses to Agility, Perception and Intelligence. As for skill improvements on the items, it'd be nice to have Stealth, Dodge, Acrobatics and Exotic Weapon. The success of the whole journey depends largely on whether the commander of the squadron can survive. So, I hope greatly that you understand that overcharging for my equipment would not be the wisest decision, if you want to see your youngest son return alive and well. I'll pay a fair price for expensive and quality items, but I will not allow anyone to shamelessly squeeze money out of me!"

Trading skill increased to level 24!

After making sure the trader understood the gravity of the moment, would find truly good craftsmen for me and not allow any of her acquaintances to fleece me, I bid farewell until evening and left the alchemy shop.

The clock before my eyes was showing almost nine o'clock in the morning. I hadn't noticed that so much time had passed in Pirona Zealous's shop. I wanted horribly to sleep. I couldn't keep my eyes open. But before leaving *Boundless Realm*, I looked for a quiet corner in the city of the dwarves, where none of the locals would notice me. And I started to uncork the vials of blood, tasting the vampire-tempting treats one after the other.

Achievement unlocked: Taste Tester (44/1000)

Achievement unlocked: Taste Tester (45/1000)
...
Achievement unlocked: Taste Tester (50/1000)
ATTENTION!!! Resistance to sunlight increased
Sunlight will now cause damage at a rate of 800 HP/second
...
Achievement unlocked: Taste Tester (60/1000)
Regeneration improved to 7 HP/Minute
...
Achievement unlocked: Taste Tester (70/1000)
Regeneration improved to 10 HP/Minute
...Achievement unlocked: Taste Tester (80/1000)
Regeneration improved to 15 HP/Minute
...
Achievement unlocked: Taste Tester (87/1000)

I'd never before drank blood in such

quantity, so the extreme intoxication that followed came as a surprise. My big-eared Goblin Herbalist was not able to stand firmly, which was to say nothing about performing complicated actions. It was absolutely impossible to play such an unresponsive character. Fortunately, I was already about to leave. After making sure Amra had no penalties against exiting *Boundless Realm*, and thirty seconds later the character would just disappear, I called up the game menu and chose "Exit Game."

New hardships

I**T WAS LOUD** and crowded on the tester floor today. A wave of newbies had arrived, completely green. Some of them hadn't even set up their virtual reality capsules or generated their characters yet. Taking advantage of the fact that no one knew their work neighbor, I also pretended to be new, thus avoiding unnecessary attention. First off, I was too tired to talk with the ones who were having a gab fest in the hallway instead of quickly entering the game. Second, I understood perfectly that the trial period for this whole huge crowd would be passed by very few, and I simply didn't want to waste my time. And third, I had absolutely no desire to tell them about myself or my character. I really had quite a bit to hide, and understood Kira with her paranoid reserve more and more.

After taking a shower and getting a quick snack and mineral water in the break area, I returned to my gaming room. My phone, which I'd left there to charge, had one missed call. The number was stored in my contacts under the name Voldemar KSM, but it took me some time to remember who that was. Ah, it was my former neighbor from the criminal neighborhood. A long time ago, a year and a half or maybe two, he and I had played *Kingdoms of Sword and Magic* together and talked fairly in depth. But then, Voldemar found stable work and left the game, then moved to a better neighborhood, and our friendship had come to an end. I'll be direct, it was an unexpected call from the past. We'd never been true friends, just acquaintances. What could he want from me.

Now, I was deciding whether to call him back or not. Another call came in from Voldemar. I accepted.

"Hello, Timothy! If you don't recognize the number, it's your old neighbor from the old 'hood. I'm calling to warn you. I had to drop by my old place this morning to ask a friend some questions. Anyway, I was stopped in the stairway by dangerous thugs from the Grave Worms gang. They interrogated me about you. Of course, I just said that I don't know shit and haven't seen you for three years. But, from the conversation, I realized that someone was willing to pay very handsomely to have you killed, and that they're looking for you actively. Timothy, the gangsters don't know where you live but, for some reason, they're sure you work as a tester for the *Boundless Realm* Corporation. They discussed ways of getting to you at work right in front of me. Like one of them was gonna call about the job advertisement and interview, then find you in the corporation building and take you out. And they even offered to let me join in. They promised me two thousand credits!"

I whistled in surprise. For the criminal outskirts of the metropolis, two thousand credits was an unimaginable amount of money! Of course, I was no expert in the matter, but it seemed to me a typical murder cost a lot less.

"That's what I'm saying," Voldemar agreed. "I mean, out there, every other person is ready to cut someone down for a hundred coins, and if we're talking about a few thousand, then the line of takers would stretch to the horizon! I can't say for sure what you did to make them so mad, but you should know they're after you! Alright then, I warned you. Be careful, Timothy!"

I thanked my old acquaintance for the warning, said goodbye and started thinking hard. I understood how the gangsters knew where I worked. It was probably from Jane, my old boss. But to be honest, I was expecting the unpleasant story with the racketeers from the Grave Worms to be left in the past after the gang got taken out by a special brigade of *Boundless Realm* Corporation soldiers. I didn't know how that special operation had ended, and didn't want to know for the sake of my own nerves, but I was counting on never again hearing about Jane, who turned out to be a surprisingly unprincipled slime-ball, nor her dangerous cohorts.

My phone rang again, and I looked at the name of the caller on screen, shuddered in fear and nearly threw the phone across the room. It was Jane herself. After a moment of hesitation, I accepted the call.

"Good morning, Timothy. Max Tohner is expecting you in his office on floor forty-four."

The voice of the girl on the line was young and pleasant, but totally unfamiliar. It took me a few seconds to realize I wasn't hearing Jane's voice, but that of the new director's assistant, calling from her work number. Wow, that put my heart at ease!

What could I say? I was supposed to talk with my boss last night, so I went straight to the elevator shaft and pressed forty-four.

* * *

"Take a seat, Timothy," the Special Projects Director pointed to the guest chair. "I know you're tired after your game session, but don't worry. I won't be keeping you long. I actually have an important meeting with marketing people about the next big update in ten minutes, so I'll be brief. I want to know about your companion Taisha. Tell me about her."

Yet again... Every one of my bosses had brought up the advanced NPC thief and, for some reason, thought that I was the one who should know the answers to all their questions. So, I had to explain for the umpteenth time that I had a very weak understanding of what was contained in the next generation NPC's algorithms. Also, I said Taisha had been made by the very same team of programmers that had earlier worked on intelligence algorithms for the Gray Pack, and they had worked on the basis of an assignment given by my former boss Alexandro Lavrius. But the thing was that all of them, both my first boss and his programmers had turned out to be mixed up in a scandal selling intellectual property of the *Boundless Realm* corporation and were fired.

"Yes, I was already told that part of the story yesterday at the director's meeting, as well as the fact that no documentation on that project was retained," Max Tohner agreed, but his curiosity was already sated. "I'd just like to find out more, something that goes beyond the bounds of simple words. After all, you've been communicating with Taisha for quite some time. You must have noticed some strange aspects of her behavior."

- A Trap for the Potentate -

"Strange?!" Here I couldn't hold back and laughed uncontrollably. "Yeah, everything about Taisha could never be called anything other than strange! Let's start with the fact that Taisha can now approach player respawn stones, which mobs are not supposed to be able to get near. Without any noticeable exertion, she can get right past magic barriers made to hold NPC's at bay. Taisha can make whole regions of *Boundless Realm* freeze up, requiring insanely huge computing power if she is presented with a complicated or unsolvable mission. Although... that was all fairly long ago. The programmers must have fixed that bug already."

"It isn't totally fixed yet but, as far as I know, they're working on it actively," the director told me. "Some of the most obvious processes leading to memory outflow were discovered and fixed. But the programmers discovered that Taisha's code is very trickily encrypted, and they cannot get through to her logic core. Attempts to copy every file associated with Taisha and move them to an isolated 'sandbox,' in order to figure out her behavior algorithms met with great difficulties. Her program, like a computer virus, artificially hides parts of itself on various cluster servers, doubling important fragments of its body many times, constantly checking the integrity of its files and not launching if it doesn't see *Boundless Realm* around it. And starting recently, this strange program even learned to communicate with the real world. It can activate external libraries and services that are totally outside the virtual game, so tricking it and locking it in a sandbox is practically impossible."

"Yes, Taisha was always interested in the world of the 'undying.' She has a passionate desire to become like a player, constantly asking me to tell her about our world, and yesterday she even called me on the cell phone..."

"That's exactly what I said, just in other words," the director snorted, none too pleased. "It was actually because of that call that all this boiled over yesterday. I think, Timothy, that you must understand perfectly that no computer program, even the most advanced and perfect imitation of human behavior, should act like that. A report about that incident reached the president of the corporation Thomas Heywood, and he took it very seriously. He came back early from vacation and went straight here, immediately calling an emergency meeting. Our experts see just two options. First: we are dealing with a live player or even an organized group, that managed to log into the corporation's servers and is skillfully leading us by the nose. Second: we have come up against something fantastical and previously considered impossible..."

The watch on the director's arm beeped, so Max Tohner broke off and didn't finish his sentence.

"Damn! I'm already late to the meeting. Gotta run!"

The director stood up from the huge leather seat and spun around in front of the mirror. After that, he demanded in an upset tone that the new long-legged secretary tie his tie and fix his haircut.

I'll admit, I had been eying this unknown doll-faced girl since I got here. She had a model's looks and purple hair in a complicated haircut. She must have been the one who called me a few minutes ago. On the director's orders, the girl sat calmly in the assistant's chair, looked at the screen of her computer and pretended she had absolutely no interest in our conversation. And yet, the director's assistant must have been totally inactive for a few minutes, because her monitor screen was now off.

"Is Taisha an artificial intelligence?" I tried to guess the end of my boss's unfinished sentence, but he didn't confirm or deny that theory.

"Timothy, I didn't say that, and it's too early to judge. There are certain facts that prove both possible hypotheses. In any case, don't let your companion Taisha get away from you and observe her carefully. And as for the telephone call..." Here, my boss abruptly turned and stared me stubbornly right in the eyes. "Yesterday, a tester employee asked our In-Game Security Service about that. And so, the direct and extremely unambiguous answer, which the president of the corporation himself ordered sent on to all our departments and official figures is this: no, such a call did not happen and never could! NPC characters are not capable of making phone calls to the real world, period! And I also demand that you stick to that official version of events until the end of the investigation! Consider than an order!!!"

With those words, Max Tohner, taking another look at his watch and spitting another curse, grabbed his tablet from the table and hurried off to a meeting. And although I had a ton of questions for him and, more importantly, objections about keeping Taisha's phone call a secret, I didn't risk stopping my boss. Now was not the time, and it couldn't bring me anything but more problems.

As soon as the doors closed behind him, the purple-haired girl called out, offering to get me a coffee. I was planning to leave the boss's office, but stopped. Coffee was just the thing I needed to perk me up after the sleepless night.

"My name is Tina," the girl introduced herself, even though I didn't ask. "Before this, I worked for the company for three years as a travelling employee. I was a model at all kinds of events. I handed out ads and souvenirs at gaming industry exhibitions, stood at *Boundless Realm* stands and attracted visitors. I went all over the planet in those three years. At first, it's interesting but, soon, you get sick of it. And now, I wanted to switch to a more relaxed position without all that moving around. And although there were thirty-five people who applied to be the director's personal assistant, Max Tohner chose me. Here's your coffee, Timothy. Do you want anything with it? Crackers? Pastries?"

I asked for pastries, and Tina practically ran out of the office to fulfill my request. I'll be honest, I wasn't used to having a peer act so deferential to me. It was even a bit awkward. What was more, I didn't understand why a girl I barely knew would tell me her whole life story, bend over backwards for me, and so obviously attempt to get to know me better.

It could hardly be simple politeness. Tina didn't treat her boss like that. Also, it wasn't part of the job requirements for the assistant to the director of special projects to wait hand and foot on the normal testers. In fact, the director's assistant was supposed to be deeply indifferent to average employees, given that her personal career and salary didn't depend on that whatsoever.

There was the possibility that Tina just thought I was cute, but I didn't consider it seriously. Such a remarkable beauty probably had a steady man already, and maybe even a whole line of admirers. And even if I was wrong about Tina being taken, such stylish model girls knew their own value and would never be seeking relationships with guys they'd just seen for the first time in their life.

"Really?" an internal voice acridly reminded me of Kira, but I immediately found a hundred differences between those circumstances.

At that moment, apologizing for the delay, Tina returned with a tray of pastries. I noticed that, while the girl was gone, she had time to make up her lashes and put on a different, brighter lipstick. Mhm... This was looking less and less like simple politeness.

Probably, a gallant gentleman would express a sense of tact and diplomacy in such a situation, and give the lady a few compliments, take the opportunity for a pleasant chat and get to know her better. But after the sleepless night, I just wanted to finish my business quickly, go home and sleep until my next gaming session. So, I asked Tina a very direct, probably tactless question, asking why she was trying so hard to make me like her?

It came out a bit rude, and I even thought the girl would get offended. Tina froze and looked at me for a few seconds, before she lowered her gaze in shame and answered my question with a question:

"Is it really that obvious?"

I just smiled in silence, which embarrassed her all the more. Tina even went slightly red, then decided to admit it:

~ A Trap for the Potentate ~

"Alright, Timothy, it would be dumb to deny it. I heard about you many times and saw promo-clips about the Goblin Herbalist and his flying wyvern. And yes, I really was trying to catch your gaze. No matter what, it isn't every day you meet a millionaire, who is also a handsome young man, and not married. For me, for example, this is a first in my whole life. So obviously, feminine instinct kicked in."

"What can I say, thank you for the frankness, Tina. But I'm not a millionaire. Not even close," I tried to convince her. "I was not allowed to sell the Royal Forest Wyvern, and my character doesn't have anything else quite that valuable. Yes, I got decent payouts for taking part in the Great Hunt, but that wasn't anywhere near a million, unfortunately..."

The director's assistant shook her head in disbelief and smiled:

"I heard something totally different this morning in this very office. Max Tohner was told by the higher-ups that your character has a strong influence on the NPC Taisha, and that it would be absolutely impossible to unravel her computer algorithms without your help. The Goblin Amra is the only character in *Boundless Realm* Taisha truly trusts, so it is principally important that you be satisfied with your work and remain an employee. The boss was told to treat you as delicately as possible and they said they were afraid that, if you were unhappy, you might simply sell your virtual property for real money and quit, and that the money you could get for that would be enough for the rest of your life. I even heard someone say 'potentially, he's a multi-millionaire, and could easily get by without working here.'"

What could I say? Today, my boss's behavior really was unlike yesterday, and for the better at that. But as for me being a potential multimillionaire, I was totally thrown off and couldn't hide my incomprehension. After all, I had no idea of the total value of my items, but still didn't imagine it came to anywhere near one million. Even considering the percent from the corporation for selling the Great Hunt participation tokens, I still had no more than five hundred thirty thousand. Of course, that was definitely not bad for a person who couldn't make rent just one month ago, but still it was not a million credits, and certainly not several million. I must have been missing something. In any case, the information Tina gave me was valuable and I thanked my new acquaintance for telling me.

But as for the offer to go out for lunch or dinner the girl made immediately thereafter, I refused. Tina was clearly crestfallen and started suggesting other options of how we could spend time together. But I was firm in my decision and didn't want to get to know the director's new assistant any closer than work required. My new acquaintance just didn't understand that her activity might be strongly upsetting to another employee of this corporation, who had the power to not only fire Tina from her new job, but also to make lots of other problems for a romantic rival.

* * *

However, these "other problems" started much earlier, in just fifteen minutes, and with me. The electronic key to call an elevator to floor three hundred thirty-three of the Castle didn't work, and I couldn't get into my place. What the hell?! I tried it a few times on the panel of the high-speed passenger elevator, and also on the panel of the more sluggish freight elevator, but the data reader was stubbornly refusing to accept my card and confirm my ability to access the isolated floor. There was no way except the elevator to get to that floor of the residential skyscraper tower, which Kira owned in its entirety. And only Kira herself decided who got the right to access it and who was not allowed...

Could my girlfriend really have gotten offended and cut off my access? An inner voice was telling me yes. Yesterday evening, when we'd parted ways, we had technically been fighting. She clearly didn't believe me about the phone call from Taisha and asked that very question to the In-Game Security Service of *Boundless Realm*, which had brought it all the way to the leadership of the corporation, including the president. What could I say? From there, it was clear. The corporation had told her no, and now she thought I was a liar and had cut off all contact. It was harsh, but completely in my girlfriend's spirit.

Although... despite all the facts on the ground, I couldn't believe Kira had decided to part with me once and for all. Show her disapproval, sure. And it was even possible that she wanted to show me how much I needed her. But Kira was not the kind of person who would keep quiet and be embarrassed about her decision to end a relationship.

To my eye, the situation resembled our first meeting in some way. Then, Kira felt awkward next to me, avoided me for a few days and was annoyed, expecting that I would be seeking out meetings with her and bothering her with my company. But when I didn't chase after her, she decided to get near me. I think I now needed to act that very same way, not getting on her nerves and letting her cool off. And although I could send a message to Kira through the head of her security team as before, given I still had his number, or at the very least through her influential grandmother, I preferred not to use these options.

What could I do right now? I wanted to sleep horribly. Book a room in a hotel? I had easily enough money to get even the most fashionable apartments in the center of the megalopolis. But doing that without it going up the chain to the police database, and various other organs of state control was impossible, and I didn't want any record of where I could be found. Telling the whole world about my location wouldn't be the smartest move, especially if I considered the fact that the Grave Worms had it out for me.

So, what remained? I remembered that I had the experience of napping during the day in my work cabin right in the uncovered virtual reality capsule, and had even gotten decent sleep. There was nothing else to do. I went back to work. On my way, I went into the supermarket and bought something to eat. I was reminded that, in my game cabin, there was a refrigerator, even though I had never even opened it before. It would seem that the time had come to start using it.

Sometime later, I left the supermarket with full bags in my hands, and called my sister. My sister told me that she had been in the game since the morning and had already led my orcs to the edge of the Great Desert. Now, the orcish army was making camp on a high hill overgrown with thorny brush, and they could already see the bank of the large black river on the horizon. If everything proceeded like that, my brutes would reach the banks of the Styx by this evening.

"Great, Val! As soon as you get there, tell the coordinates of your camp to Max Sochnier, so he can meet us with his galley."

"So, where are you, Tim? I just looked around and Taisha, the Gray Pack and VIXEN are all gone..."

I told Valeria that, last night, I'd managed to reach the subterranean city of Dotur-Khawe and pick up the package. The purchase turned out right and I thanked my brilliant little sister yet again for her wonderful intuition. I also told her that I had to stick around in the dwarven town to make some more purchases and now, the bright light of day would keep me in the caves until evening. But at that, it seemed I had found a good chef for my savages, so the orcs would be fed right, instead of just wolfing down loads of filth.

I didn't mention the strange situation with Taisha, having decided to tell my sister about all that one on one. What was more, I didn't immerse my sister in my problems with Kira, the Grave Worms or our lack of home. Valeria couldn't help me in these matters, but it would spoil her mood for a long time.

I told Valeria I would be sure to visit her in the hospital this evening before work, bring her a bag of fruit and gifts and speak with the doctors. But, I said, if we didn't have enough time to chat, we could keep talking in *Boundless Realm*. Val lit up at my upcoming visit, then changed the topic:

"Tim, I've been studying the map of Styx you gave me last night. And I have a couple very interesting ideas, I'd like to discuss. But that would be a really long conversation, so let's do it not over the phone. So, we can talk in the evening at the clinic or, when we meet at night in the game. I'll tell you the coordinates of the orc camp on the bank of the Styx over the phone, and you can fly on VIXEN after it gets dark."

I got surprisingly good sleep, despite the semi-spartan conditions and constant buzz of many voices coming from the hallway. During the day, there were always dozens if not hundreds of testers talking outside. I was even getting the impression that many noobs spent the majority of their work day, not in their game cabins at all, but in conversations with one another. I had a perfect understanding of how difficult it was for a new tester to pass the trial period, so I was baffled to see them all behaving so carelessly and wasting so much time. If I were their boss, I would install security cameras in the break rooms and fire anyone who was caught on film more than twice in one day. Maybe that was too harsh a measure, but I seriously couldn't understand what all these poor testers were hoping for!

After eating the food I'd bought in the morning, I started creating my daily video report about the adventures of the flap-eared Goblin

Herbalist. There was more than enough interesting material today but, when editing it, I hesitated for a long time deciding which parts to show my viewers. The desert oasis and orc camp, yes. The search for the ifrit den and discovering the heart, yes. After prolonged consideration, I decided to also include my troglodyte gulping down the rare alchemy ingredient and discovering the previously unknown qualities of the Ifrit Heart. Of course, by doing so, I revealed that secret to all players of *Boundless Realm*. But, after the *Legion of Steel* uncovered the mystery and had combed through all markets and auctions in the game, buying up every Ifrit Heart to be found, I had nothing to lose. Plus, it would be sure to increase the popularity of my video clips.

I thought the strongest moment of today's video clip was my big-eared goblin receiving the unique quest Something Different... with the reward One Wish, and summoning the *Legion of Steel* to complete the mission. And here, I had to spend a long time deciding what to do.

On the one hand, I needed to show my viewers that I had successfully completed the mission but, at the same time, I was certainly not planning to reveal precisely what wish I had made to the djinn. I also decided not to show Taisha's wish, or when she received a quest. But then, it was unclear how the djinn had managed to get free, despite all the efforts of the strongest players in the game. Overall, a lot had to be cut out and, in the end, it turned out a bit too condensed. So, I tried to explain the unclear moment to my viewers, telling them that the wish made to the djinn was very personal and secret, so I didn't show it. And I said the djinn was freed right after granting all wishes (which was technically true), sending many players to respawn including Amra and Valerianna Quickfoot.

After finishing the edit and uploading the video, I went to the clinic and talked with my sister. Val was clearly recovering from all her internal worries and was inspired and full of energy. She now had lots of friends, who she spent practically all day talking and playing with. That was good. I finally saw my little sister truly happy and was sincerely glad for her. The attending doctor had a positive opinion of Valeria's psychological progress after her recent suicide attempt, and he also had an optimistic outlook on the upcoming complicated procedures to implant electrodes into the girl's limb stumps. He even pointed for me at the bionic legs made specially for my sister stored in a sterile transparent container. They were practically indistinguishable from real legs. The doctor assured me firmly that, in a few weeks, Valeria would even be able to move the toes on both legs, and in a few months, she could even walk in a special walker or with crutches, getting used to her new legs.

Overall, I returned to work from the clinic in a wonderful state of mind. This morning's call of warning about killers from the Grave Worms no longer seemed so ghastly to me, and I even mentally reproached myself for giving in to panic and spending a whole day in a virtual reality capsule that was barely adequate for sleeping instead of a comfortable hotel room. But suddenly, in the revolving doors at the entrance to the *Boundless Realm* building, I passed a person who seemed dimly familiar. I strained my memory and remembered that I had met him a few times in the criminal neighborhood, either in the grocery store or next to the electro-bus stop. This person, it seemed, didn't notice me and walked down the stairs away. At any rate, my fears instantly returned but now many times stronger.

The first thing I did in my work cabin was to firmly lock the door behind me and bash it hard a few times to test its strength. After that, I looked for the contact data of the corporation's Security Service on my computer. It was already almost eight in the evening, time for me to load up *Boundless Realm,* so I wanted to avoid a long phone conversation, and especially a personal visit to security. Fortunately, I could just send this information by email. I tried to give a fairly detailed description of the problem, and sent it off. Considering it a done deal, I laid down in the virtual reality capsule and began the loading procedure.

* * *

The dwarven lady's son looked very much like his mother in body proportions. On the doorstep of the alchemy shop, there was a practically spherical dwarf, whose head, hands and squat legs seemed like strange nubs protruding from an ideally spherical body. Adding to that picture was a mail suit, which was clearly too short and narrow for such a body. It didn't cover his protruding stomach even to the navel. Add to that a haughtily luxurious golden helmet with lowered visor, red and green stretchy pants tucked into boots and a set of pots, ladles, and pans hanging from a wide leather belt, and you understand what a sight was drawn before me.

Tondik Exuberant
Level-43 Dwarf Chef

I walked a slow circle around the chef, who was frozen in indecision, looking with curiosity at the extremely outlandish spectacle.

"And where is your weapon, dwarf? Or were you planning to fight off the swamp beasts with your ladle, using a pan as a shield?"

The chef remained silent and just lowered his gaze, but Pirona Zealous hurried out of the alchemy shop to defend her youngest son:

"Mr. Amra, don't you worry about weaponry. Tondik is great with knives and can hold his own in a fight."

For some reason, I had great doubt in the accuracy of these words, but I still didn't insist on a test. What was more, I had a more serious reason to worry. For some reason, I didn't see a single trader of weaponry, armor or ammunition, even though I'd given extremely clear instructions to Pirona Zealous on what precise objects I was planning to buy, where and for how much. After seeing how confused I looked and how I was looking around, the owner of the alchemy shop explained:

"They aren't coming, Mr. Amra. I'm afraid I'm to blame here. I got into a big fight with my neighbors today, because they didn't believe in my son at all, trying to outdo each other in mocking Tondik and saying that he'll never find a wife. And one of my neighbors is an armorer and the other is a weapon-smith... All in all, it turned out bad. However, I did pack three big bags of supplies for the road," said the mother, pointing at several huge piles of massive bales stacked in the corner. "There are some victuals, various items, a tent, and everything one needs for a long journey."

It wasn't good, but I didn't get particularly upset, because I saw something of a balancing of game algorithms in the NPC conflict. And that unobtrusively reminded me that this was not the real world, and that certain fixed rules did exist here. Instead of walking alone through a huge subterranean city and buying each type of item from a different person in a different place, I wanted to save time and gather all the necessary traders in one spot. But there was no such thing as a free lunch. The game algorithms of *Boundless Realm* had created a conflict of NPC's to make me seek out the traders I would need.

I took another critical glance at the bales packed by the doting mother. I was positive VIXEN wouldn't be able to take off with so much stuff. And she probably couldn't deal with Tondik's weight, either. But it was no big deal. The wolves of the Gray Pack had plenty of inventory space, and I could let the fat chef ride on the strong Fimbulthul. After ordering Tondik to drag the bags to the nearest exit from Dotur-Khawe, I promised to come by a bit later. I still had an hour before sunset, so I set off to find the right shops.

The Banks of the Styx

I NOTICED THE ORC CAMP when I was just a few kilometers from the Styx. Between a pitch-black swamp, strange gloomy starless sky and anthracite black river, they had lit bright bonfires and dozens of torches, like the landing lights of a large airport. Steering my Royal Forest Wyvern right into the middle of the camp, I brought VIXEN down next to the very largest central tent, justly assuming it was mine.

The second I jumped off my mount, the entire Gray Pack appeared next to me: Akella, Lobo, Blanca and White Fang, the level-45 Hardened Wolves, Darius and Darina, the level 13 Wargs, and also the huge shaggy level-59 Mythical Hound Fimbulthul. On the icy-white hound, feverishly latched onto his thick fur, the Dwarf

~ A Trap for the Potentate ~

Chef was half lying, half sitting, his face white as chalk. His skin color even matched the fur of the unique animal.

"Climb off Fimbulthul before his back breaks under your weight, and unload your bags from the other wolves!" I ordered Tondik, myself turning to the whole delegation of NPC's and living players who came out to meet me.

"Amra! How glad I am to see you!" I was so happy to see the beefy Ogre Fortifier, that I even allowed Shrekson to lift my goblin with his huge arms and squeeze me tight in a burst of emotion. "Max Sochnier and I got here just a half hour ago on his galley. The Naiad Trader is overseeing the unloading of goods from his *Tipsy Gannet* right now... Actually no, there he is!"

The fish man in a dashing captain's tricorn with differently colored feathers and unusual scaled armor was hurrying to greet me. I was very glad to see my friend, but there was also a high-level player behind him I was seeing for the first time. I froze, reading his information.

Antonius Just
Human
Level-138 Healer [LIGHT]

"You yourself asked me to get a map of the Styx or find people who had already been here during the previous twenty-six unsuccessful expeditions," the Naiad Trader began explaining in an energized tone, pointing at his companion. "Just imagine, I managed to find such a person! And you won't believe who he is! Timothy, this is my nephew Martin! He's been playing for two years and has leveled up well in that time. Anyway, it was Martin who suggested I look into a job as a *Boundless Realm* tester, when I was looking for work a month ago. You could even say my nephew led me to the game. Timothy, don't pay any mind to the fact that he has a marker from the clan of wandering healers *Lifegiving Light*. Martin is a loner by nature and might leave the clan, if need be."

"Yeah, I can leave whenever," the healer Antonius Just confirmed, entering our conversation. "I've been playing in this clan for three months, but they're real boring and passive. There has only been one mass-scale event since I joined. The leaders of the clan tried to organize an expedition up the Styx on three ships to the undiscovered lands, because one of our clan members got a rare or even unique quest up there. We fought our way through the rougarou territory. We also managed to get through the lands of the giants, although they kicked our asses. I died three times myself. But we eventually got stuck on a sandbar and couldn't keep going by water. The river rapids were too strong. But going on the shore is just not an option. There are cyclopes there, who will instantly kill anyone they see. We tried all kinds of ways for three days, and each player died at least five times, but it was all pointless. In the end, we just gave up and never went back..."

The forest nymph, standing in silence not far away and surrounded by my orc cutthroats, unexpectedly lit up and asked the healer:

"So then, the unique quest remains uncompleted? You wouldn't happen to know what the mission was called, would you?"

"I once overheard the clan leader say we were three hundred twenty kilometers from the map marker, so we didn't complete it, of course. I'm not sure about the name of the quest. Something about the twelve guards of Elgar, or something like that."

Until that moment, I had been just partially listening to the conversation as I looked in thought at the mini-map, showing Max Sochnier's nephew as a black skull (meaning he was more than fifty levels higher than me). I was alarmed by some red text saying this character was on my black list.

It was a great shame, but Antonius Just was one of the four undying who I promised Taisha to kill for burning down the village of Tysh. A very unexpected coincidence... What was the chance, after all, that a player I was searching for would come to me all on his own? It was easier to win a million credits in the lottery than to have a chance meeting with a specific player in *Boundless Realm*, which was larger than the surface area of planet Earth. Perhaps this was no simple coincidence, and there was something I was missing.

All the same, when he spoke of the "twelve guards of Elgar," I left my considerations and jumped into the conversation, carefully asking my new acquaintance:

"Maybe it isn't the 'Twelve Guards of Elgar,' but the 'Twelve Élivágar Guardians?'"

I had a ring with such a name on my finger, and also, the full name of the Mythical Hound Fimbulthul contained the phrase Élivágar Guardian, so I had that word in the back of my mind.

"Yes, it seems that is exactly what that quest was called," the Human Healer confirmed carelessly. "But, in any case, it was impossible to get there, so it doesn't matter. We only reached the rapids of the river Styx. But, I have maps of the locations, so I can share them with you and tell you how we got past the tricky spots."

Valerianna Quickfoot looked me right in the eyes and nodded in silence. My smarty-pants sister had clearly understood everything about the still unfinished quest, which would most likely give yet another unique Mythical Hound. And I myself understood perfectly how intriguing it would be to finish that mission and thus reinforce the Gray Pack with such a rare creature. But getting to the place on the map the healer had so vaguely described as "three hundred twenty kilometers above the rapids on the Styx," where no player had ever gone before, would be really hard. To say nothing about completing the unique mission itself, which would probably also be quite difficult.

Our conversation was interrupted by a ghastly blood-curdling wail coming from somewhere near the river bank. The whole Gray Pack instantly shuddered and turned their snouts to the sound. VIXEN even took off into the sky.

"That howl has already been going on periodically for forty minutes, sometimes further down the river, sometimes up," my sister commented. "He's walking around us, but won't come near the camp. I don't know what it is, but your orcs have never fortified this vigorously. I ordered them to make a defensive rampart out of thorny bushes in a semicircle around the tents, and another two rows of sharpened stakes at an angle with the points out."

"Only pointing at the dry land? But what if something dangerous crawls out of the river?" I asked, on guard, but Max Sochnier started laughing and hurried to reassure me.

"Amra, don't you worry about the river. My girlfriend the nereid Olilissa is on guard there, and she's seven meters of pure muscle, shark teeth and a sharp trident in a pair of strong hands. I'll have to introduce you to my sweetheart today. I'll be honest, I didn't want to take her on the dangerous journey, but she insisted and has been swimming behind my galley the whole way. Sea creatures don't find it very comfortable in rivers, and Olilissa is complaining that the water tastes nasty, but the nereid is the strongest and biggest thing in there, so she scares away all the river creatures with her mere presence. What's more, Olilissa has help from my pet Claymore. The three-meter-long blazing-fast swordfish, but my little fish is also feeling like hell in the fresh water."

Just then, First Mate Ziabash hardy ran up to me wheezing. The huge orc's hands and clothes were caked in black dirt and swamp muck. His eyes were sagging in exhaustion.

"Captain Amra! You came at just the right time! The orcs building the camp fortification are saying they can see fast shadows moving about in the distance. Lots of shadows. And also, big red eyes are gathering on the nearest hill, watching us. And there's also that howl, which rattles the bones..."

I could sense that my first mate, who'd taken part in many ghastly sea battles, was now feeling close to crapping his pants in fear. I suspect that many of the other orcs were not in the best psychological condition now either, affected by the gloomy atmosphere of the swampy banks of the river of death, the darkness of the moonless night and the monsters gathered around the camp. I supposed now was the very time to show some leadership and invigorate my soldiers.

I got up on Fimbulthul to get a better view of my squadron and what was going on around me, then loudly commanded:

"Shrekson, as an experienced Fortifier, I need you to get to building right away! Ziabash, tell your orcs my order: they must not stop working on the fortifications for a single second! And at that, break off all the soldiers into groups of ten and send one group at a time to the galley. Our soldiers there will be given good weapons and armor."

Foreman skill increased to level 32!

Foreman skill increased to level 33!

Here my gaze caught on Gnum Spiteful, the level-50 Dwarf Mechanic, who crawled out of one of the tents, looked around with her eyes tearing up in the bright light of the fire and started limping in my direction in a bouncy gait. Everyone in my army knew Gnum as a reckless dwarf adventure-seeker with fierce mannerisms and a complete lack of self-preservation instinct. Even the savage orcs were wary of contact with her. But I knew that the bearded lady hadn't yet fully recovered from a very severe, nearly deadly wound. But I really needed her help right now.

"Gnum, may your beard be burnt! Take your crutches and go help with the construction! Look after the wild cutthroats, most of whom are not able to tell a saw from a hammer. But first..." here I noticed that the Dwarf Chef was still standing helplessly next to a pile of his things, "help this walking misunderstanding. He's one of your kind, after all," I said, pointing at Tondik Exuberant. "He needs to pitch his tent and set up a field kitchen. After the long march today, the soldiers want to eat, so help him get to work!"

Foreman skill increased to level 34!

After giving the most necessary commands, I went off to the edge of camp, in order to watch the fortification work and, at the same time, catch a glimpse of the monsters my first mate said were gathering nearby.

Mhm... The situation was a bit worse than I was expecting. There was obviously not enough construction material for anything resembling a serious defensive bulwark, although my orcs had already cut down all bushes and trees near the camp. The wall of stinging plants reached waist height at its highest point, and was generally even lower. The orcs were sharpening stakes and driving them into the ground, but it was obvious that they wouldn't be enough for decent defense.

~ A Trap for the Potentate ~

And the worst part was that, as for the great many monsters, Ziabash Hardy hadn't been exaggerating one bit. Hundreds of pairs of red eyes were observing our camp carefully from the nearest hill and, with every second, the enemy was getting reinforcements, pouring in from all the nearby swamps.

Successful Perception check
Experience received: 160 Exp.

Swamp Spirits, Ghosts, Banshees, skeletons of all kinds of creatures that had drowned in the local swamps... Among the enemies there were a good deal of undead from levels eighty to one hundred. And at that, the undead were peacefully coexisting with living creatures, also from levels eighty to one hundred: Plague Rats, Jerboas, Swamp Wolves, Leshies, all kinds of poisonous snakes and unbelievably huge insects. Despite the variety of species, this army of all stripes had no internal conflicts and was simply standing on the hill, growing in number with each passing minute.

I was extremely displeased to see the enemies had significantly higher average level than my orcs and already equaled us in number. In the case of direct wall-to-wall conflict, we already had quite low chances and, in an hour or two, the situation threatened to become utterly hopeless.

"Apparently, there's no avoiding a battle," the thoughtful voice of the Human Healer rang out behind my ear, also having come to evaluate the situation. "And much to my dismay, there's no respawn stone nearby..."

"We didn't see a single respawn point in our whole day traversing the desert, either," the mavka added, also looking in fear at the enemy forces gathered in the distance. "So, the closest place is that oasis we left a day ago. It's a pretty good slog, for what it's worth... Maybe we should retreat to the galley?"

But I really didn't like my sister's suggestion of retreat. If I did manage to get the three hundred wild orcs on the *Tipsy Gannet*, then together with its crew of one hundred and fifty, we'd be packed like sardines in a can.

And also, if I thought about it, we couldn't just hide on the ship forever, right?

As far as I knew, the *Tipsy Gannet* was preparing to go back down the delta of the Styx into the sea right after unloading, returning to its usual cyclical trade route. In any case, the trade galley couldn't make it very far up the river. So sooner or later, we'd have to come ashore, where the situation would only be worsening with every hour. What was more, if we couldn't handle the dangers here, how could we ever hope to get higher up the Styx, where both the concentration of monsters would be higher, and their level significantly more respectable?! No, we needed to deal with this problem right here and now.

Battle was inevitable, everyone understood that perfectly. As they also understood that, with their numbers and high levels, the swamp beasts would simply wipe the floor with us if we didn't change our defense strategy. I got up on the icy-white hound to a slightly elevated area and called my orc cutthroats to attention, pointing to the pitiful attempt at a defensive bulwark:

"This border is pointless! Only a creature with no legs couldn't jump over it! Dismantle three sections of the fence at once, purposely leaving seven-to-ten-step-wide gaps. Remove the stakes from these passages, using them to reinforce the other parts!"

The savage orcs were bewildered by the order, not understanding the reason for my decision. I had to chew the idea over for them, explaining my plan in detail:

"There aren't enough of us to reliably hold the whole perimeter. So, we should concentrate in smaller sections. Keep in mind that there are only stupid, brainless undead and wild creatures against us, which will certainly run down the most obvious path precisely to the gaps I left. That is exactly where we'll meet them!"

I jumped down and walked along the barrier, choosing a place:

"Make the central passage here. I'll be posted here with the Gray Pack and I swear by my ears that no one will get past me! The main passage will be defended by the Ogre and Naiad, and I'll place thirty orc warriors with wide shields and long spears with them. The spearmen's mission is to hold the enemy back while our bolts mow them down. I'm sure that fifty crossbowmen will be more than enough. To the left then will be the very strongest orcs from my guard, led by Ziabash Hardy. Fifty soldiers with yataghans will stand at reserve behind the defensive bulwark and help with defense wherever needed. That division will be headed by our mountain troll... Where is he, by the way?"

"Right here, Captain Amra!"

Said the muscular, level-65 Troll, overgrown with reddish fur, his hands dragging on the ground as he pushed his way through the dense crowd of orcish soldiers. I could now read his name: "Vaash." Before, his opinion of me was too low, and I could only see him as Troll Enforcer.

"Vaash, you have earned my confidence with your bravery and strength. You are the one I'll entrust to command the reserve division. You and your fifty fearsome orcs will have to stop the enemy, if they get through our defense at any point. If you do well enough tonight, you'll get a whole hundred to command!"

Vaash thumped on his chest with a huge fist

and roared out so loud that my Goblin Herbalist even got the deafened effect for a few seconds. Overall, my confident speech had a very positive effect on my subjects, and I heard shouts glorifying the captain's name from all directions. The orcs were clearly inspired.

Foreman skill increased to level 34!

Foreman skill increased to level 35!

I called them all to silence and continued:

"While we still have the time, everyone keep building and, at the same time, reinforce our defenses by digging out a ditch in front of our fortification. This is a swamp and the ditch will quickly fill with water, so the monsters will have no way to get to us except through the three passageways we leave open!"

Foreman skill increased to level 36!

My skill grew again, and just in time. It was getting easier and easier for me to command the wild horde, giving orders to my subjects and setting them to work, which then leveled my Foreman skill even more and increased my influence on the orcs. I waited for their enthusiastic cries to die down and continued:

"Proud warriors! Now, all of you will receive

good armor and weapons so you can really make a name for yourself in the upcoming battle! Once you get your weapons, Ziabash Hardy will assign you to a division. Whoever doesn't end up defending the three passageways will line up along the defensive bulwark and defend their section. But if there aren't any enemies near you, don't just stand around and pick your noses, take up crossbows and shoot enemies over the barricade! Valerianna Quickfoot, you're in charge of the ranged soldiers. You are all to obey the mavka same as me!"

Now in a normal voice, not shouting at full throat, I turned to my sister:

"Valerianna, you're our main damager, and strike force. You're experienced in battle, so you decide where best to position yourself to do as much damage with your magic as possible. Don't be stingy with the mana. The enemies are high-level, so you'll get good experience for killing them, and with every new level, your mana will be totally restored. But at any rate, I have more than enough mana potions. I bought plenty in Dotur-Khawe, so take as many as you need."

"And what should I do?" the Human Healer asked, overhearing our conversation.

"What a strange question!" I exclaimed in surprise. "You stand behind the soldiers and heal the wounded. Only spend your mana on healing, paying no mind to the enemies. Basically, the upcoming battle is a test of your professional abilities. If you prove yourself to be a skilled healer, you can come with us right to the upper reaches of the Styx. But if you act dumb and don't manage to heal the wounded, I'll personally send you to respawn, I promise! By the way, healer... I don't see any pets with you. I'd never in my life believe that such a high-level mage doesn't have any. Where are they?"

Antonius Just paused for some reason, as if deciding whether he should obey a player just one third his level. But then, he chuckled awkwardly, and three bright flying pixies showed up next to him. The miniature girls had variously-colored sectile butterfly wings behind their backs. Every pixie was the size of my pointer finger, and all three of the winged beings were totally naked without the slightest hint of clothing.

The Naiad Trader shook his head in reproach and brought his nephew down a peg with the words: "You're a damn shame! You need to meet a normal girl, not spend day after day doing nonsense in this game." And my sister walked up closer and commented on the healer's unusual winged pets:

"I saw pixies like that in the corporation's online store. Pixies restore mana for their master, which is very useful to any mage, and they also cast strong spells on enemies. But they cost fifty credits each. And I seem to remember them being dressed in different colored skirts made of flower petals..."

"Yes, the pixies really are from the store, and were initially clothed," our new acquaintance agreed easily. "But I had a good reason to change their appearance. They're much cooler this way! And the pixies don't only charge mana, they make my magic reserves a whole sixty percent higher! They've very useful companions for a mage, and they are nice to look at!"

Knowing my sister well, I could see that Valerianna was distinctly disapproving of such a vulgar choice, and also didn't have a friendly opinion of our healer overall, although the mavka didn't confirm that aloud. However, Valerianna voiced a different thought completely, which needed to be considered before the upcoming battle:

"Amra, I'm surprised so many totally different monsters aren't fighting amongst themselves. That is very strange, because it really shouldn't be. Wolves are made to hunt rats, and undead to attack the living, but for some reason that isn't happening. It seems to me that, if we can understand the reason for our enemies working together, we'll immediately realize how to fight them!"

* * *

~ A Trap for the Potentate ~

Taking advantage of the fact that the other players were busy, the mavka took me aside and asked, barely audibly:

"I can see that you don't want to say anything in front of the others, but you can be open with me. What's wrong with our healer? You were looking at him like you wanted to strangle him with your bare hands."

Hmm, I didn't think my private thoughts were so obvious. I hoped very much that the other players hadn't noticed. My sister understood me much better than the others, though. I had no secrets from Valeria, so I explained the reason for my doubts:

"Antonius Just is on my blacklist. He was one of the players who attacked the goblin village of Tysh, and even took direct part in the murder of Taisha's sisters. I gave Taisha a promise before the gods of *Boundless Realm* to kill this man. But he found us. And now, I have quite a dilemma: ignore an oath I swore before the gods of *Boundless Realm* with all the resulting negative consequences like severe debuffs and streaks of bad luck or lose an experienced, high-level healer, which would be very undesirable before the upcoming heavy battle."

"Is that it?! I thought it was something serious," my sister chuckled, showing her sharp predatory teeth. "To appease the gods of *Boundless Realm*, you just need to make sure Antonius Just doesn't survive this battle. Just make it all look like a coincidence, so the healer and his relative Max Sochnier don't suspect us."

"Us?" I asked, and the forest nymph bared her teeth yet again.

"Of course! You're my brother, after all, and you can always count on me for help. As for Antonius Just, don't lose your head, I'll deal with this problem myself and promise that the gods will be left satisfied. And I'll do it with great satisfaction. I don't feel any sympathy for that healer, much less trust. That dude appeared at just too convenient a time, given you were searching for him in this huge world. Such things simply do not happen. Maybe you called him by name in one of your video clips?"

"No, of course not. But from what I did upload, my audience does know that I promised Taisha to find and punish those at fault in her sisters' murders. Although I, naturally, didn't say their names."

The forest nymph made an anguished grimace, showing a strong doubt in my mental capacity and, at the same time, marveling at how I could possibly not understand such elementary things.

"Tim, your big-eared Goblin always had Intelligence as the weakest stat, but you could understand yourself that all the TOP clans have already put two and two together and figured out exactly which players you promised Taisha to track down for the torching of Tysh..." the mavka turned around and looked carefully from side to side to make sure that we were still talking alone. "By the way, as the topic has turned to your beautiful green-skinned thief, would you mind telling me where she is? I was embarrassed to ask with everyone else around."

With no reservations, I told Valeria the situation with Taisha, about the unique quest, our duel and my secret mission for the NPC thief. My sister stayed silent for a long time, then spoke out barely audibly, looking me right in the eyes:

"Well, Tim, I hope you understand you will be spoiling your relationship with the strongest clan in *Boundless Realm* once and for all. After all, if Taisha does manage to steal the unique item from the *Legion of Steel*'s treasure room, they'll never forgive you. Also, even if the theft is unsuccessful, the leaders of the *Legion of Steel* will be frightfully angry at such impudence."

I already understood perfectly, but didn't see any other way to get the item and, at the same time, express to the *Legion of Steel* how upset I was with their attempt to steal my unique NPC companion. Valeria gave a heavy sigh, shook her head, then changed the topic once again:

"Doesn't it occur to you, Tim, that we might be going about this all wrong? We're trying to reach the upper Styx by force, repeating the error of the previous twenty-six expeditions. But all their pitiful experience shows that, no matter how strong the initial expedition members, sooner or later, they came across an equal force and had to stop. Some players made it further than others, sure, but eventually they ran into monsters they just couldn't handle."

"And what do you suggest?" I asked, my interest piqued.

The forest nymph shrugged her shoulders unconfidently:

"I'm not sure, I have only one suggestion for now. In essence, after all, our army is made of NPC orcs and is moving through territory controlled by other NPC's. As a rule, different groups of NPC's are rarely hostile to one another, especially if there are no living players nearby. It's logical, otherwise all the computing resources of the *Boundless Realm* servers would be wasted calculating which NPC predator saw which NPC prey, managed to sneak up to it, or take it down. The world comes to life only when there is a living player nearby to witness it. It is, after all, for our benefit that all this beauty is made. Approximately the same thing happens with intelligent NPC races, clans and armies..."

I caught my sister's idea and, after some thought, agreed with her:

"That's true. That goblin village of Tysh, for example, stood for years unnoticed, until me and you showed up. As soon as there were players nearby, everything turned on right away. The goblins scurried into action, and started generating missions for us, trading, and discussing. But if we weren't nearby, everything would stay frozen, or work in background mode with minimal use of computing resources."

"That's exactly right! And now, imagine this: a squadron of NPC orcs is walking into desolate unpopulated lands where not a single living player can be found. Those unpeopled regions are probably in a 'half-asleep' state using as little computing power as possible. Let's not consider you and I and say that it's just our orcs on the march. You can't seriously think that, just because of such a modestly sized group of NPC's, whole regions of *Boundless Realm* would be activated, and the expensive computing resources of corporation servers would be wasted on their upkeep? I'd never believe it on my life! Most likely, it would just calculate the speed of our squadron and, as a result, the game system would spit out where it would be at a given time. After all, recall after we got that message from Taisha, your orcs walked in peace to the copper mine near Dotur-Khawe, and probably didn't meet anyone along the way. It was as if they were simply walking, not interacting with the game world and, at the calculated time, simply appeared at their destination."

I hadn't considered that before. But she was right. Why simulate the movement of every NPC in the huge *Boundless Realm*? Also, there wouldn't be enough computing power for that truly titanic effort, even in the most powerful game cluster! Players only care about what is happening next to them, and the system devotes its main resources to showing its users a vibrant and interesting *Boundless Realm*. In fact, a simple squadron of NPC's without living players had much higher chances of reaching a certain map point without coming across any difficulties. That had to be thought through.

Our conversation was interrupted by the flapping of huge wings over my head. VIXEN had returned from her nightly hunt. My winged snake brought a half-suffocated Desert Jerboa and I thanked the fortunate hunter for taking care of her hungry master. I extended a hand to stroke my emerald beauty as usual, but the Royal Forest Wyvern unexpectedly pulled back from my affections and stuck her toothy maw and long neck toward me. I got confused and didn't realize at first what my flying mount might want but, after that, I realized my winged scout wanted to share some information.

I took a step closer and leaned the forehead of my big-eared goblin against VIXEN's head. Just then, a kaleidoscope of pictures ran before my eyes like screenshots of the game taken from up high.

~ A Trap for the Potentate ~

A hill next to the orc camp, densely crowded with so many different monsters there wasn't even room for a falling apple to hit the ground. Most of all, it was large toothy rodents: rats, jerboas, hamsters... very, very many rodents. Although there were also plenty of wolves. There were also a decent amount of reanimated animal skeletons, partially decayed zombies and a few tall leshies, armed with blowguns. That was unpleasant information. I was working under the impression that the enemy wouldn't have any ranged weaponry. And above this motley crew, there was a whole swarm of large winged insects and a few ghosts. Our defensive bulwark could certainly not hold back these creatures. The flying beasts could attack my army from any direction. And further over the hill... it got much more interesting.

Saddled on a very large reddish-brown swamp wolf, there was a huge two-headed monster that looked like two overgrown rat bodies fused together. But one head of the strange Siamese twins was dead and without eyes, having long ago turned into bones stretched over with dried-out skin. It wasn't clear how it was still moving and flapping its lipless gums. But at that, the second rat head was totally alive and darting its evil red eyes at VIXEN flying in the sky. The monster was equipped with a heavy black cuirass with two head holes. One paw was holding the reins and the other had a glimmering staff, clearly filled to the brim *with strong magic.*

> *Hyenarius*
> *Rat King*
> *Lord of the Swamps of the Styx*

I had apparently discovered the black-magic being that united this ghastly army of the living and the dead.

Blood-Soaked Swamp

I TOLD VALERIANNA about the rat king and described him in detail. The forest mavka considered it for a minute, then suggested a few options of how to try and reach the enemy leader. But she tore apart all her own ideas in short order, because we wouldn't manage to reach the hostile military leader either in stealth, on the Gray Pack or on VIXEN. And we certainly couldn't kill him in any kind of reasonable timeframe. The king was guarded by a whole army of dangerous high-level creatures, including flying ones which made the mission of taking him down extremely complicated.

The forest nymph adjusted her hair, messed up by the cold bursts of wind coming from the river and our camp, and took a heavy sigh:

"Let's hope that, right before the attack or during the battle, the Rat King will come to within striking distance of our arrows or spells. Then we can try to get rid of him. I can just feel that, with the death of the leader, this whole army will fall apart all on its own!"

I also thought so. In all of *Boundless Realm*, the undead could not coexist with the living, and the only possible reason for this exception was the half-dead half-alive Rat King.

From the direction of the orc camp, the wind carried an intoxicating scent I wasn't expecting — donuts frying in hot oil. It seemed that Tondik Exuberant had finally gotten to his chef duties. The mavka also picked up the smell and asked to explain about the fat chef. I told her about Tondik and his doting mother, and also about what I'd bought in her alchemy shop. At the same time, I complained that I hadn't found anything interesting from the weapon-smiths or armorers in Dotur-Khawe. I mean, of course I managed to get a new blowgun, cloak, mail, boots and leather pants that were much better than my old stuff, which was for a level-fifteen or -twenty character, but everything I'd bought, if it had any magical bonuses at all, was just average and boring. The Forest Mavka heard out my groaning and laughed happily in reply:

"Big-ears, did you think you'd find sets or unique or legendary items in a normal trade shop?

~ A Trap for the Potentate ~

The whole reason such items are valued is that they are found very rarely... What's that?"

The mavka asked, seeing me do something unexpected. My flap-eared goblin squatted down and was digging in the thick grass, gathering some large yellow berries.

Herbalism skill increased to level 16!

Miraculous Cloudberry (alchemy ingredient)

Herbalism skill increased to level 17!

Fame increased
Present value: 8

You are the first to discover this plant in Boundless Realm

Two skill increases in a row?! I could understand the first. I had not received any increases in Herbalism for a long time, even though I was stubbornly gathering plants all the time, if I happened to come across them. But what was the second for? For discovering a new type of plant? Apparently.

I told my sister about my discovery and the double growth in skill, at the same time showing her the unusually large berries. The mavka then immediately asked that I give her one, so she could determine the properties of the new plant, because Amra didn't have enough Intelligence to do so.

"It gives a decent boost to Regeneration, but for quite a short time," the forest nymph shared her conclusions. "Tim, I've got a feeling that, if you made a concentrated elixir of these berries, it might give complete regeneration like trolls have, and even restore lost limbs. But that's just a feeling. You should check it. By the way, here's a good way to quickly level Herbalism. After all, we're going to wild and unknown lands, where very few Herbalists have been before, if any. I suspect that you will come across a good number of new plants. I think, if you manage to raise the skill fast enough, your director will be satisfied..."

Our conversation was interrupted by the piercing wail of a signal horn. One of the sentries watching the enemy army had seen them go into action.

"It seems to have started," the forest nymph made a few passes with her hands to renew her defensive spells. "Best of luck to us all! And don't forget to eat that Jerboa before battle," my sister said, pointing at the barely living creature that was still in VIXEN's mouth, after which she headed out to her defensive sector.

"I won't!" I promised the mavka, looking around for prying eyes.

The Swamp Jerboa died from just one Vampire Bite. I shared its body with the ever-

- A Trap for the Potentate -

hungry VIXEN.

Experience received: 1105 Exp.

Achievement unlocked: Taste Tester (88/1000)

Racial ability improved: Taste for Blood (Gives +1% to all damage dealt for each unique creature killed with Vampire Bite. Current bonus: +26%)

Not bad, not bad. The hunger passed, and my Thirst for Blood was also totally sated, so I didn't need to worry about that for the next thirty hours. After wiping the traces of blood off my face, as not to betray my secret, I hurried to the most dangerous and important defensive sector and immediately jumped onto Fimbulthul's back while running, so my short flap-eared Goblin could see at least something in the distance.

It seemed the alarm had been raised by Johnny, the eagle-eyed sentry boy who had come from the *Tipsy Gannet* to my pirate crew on the *White Shark*, then followed the orcs into the desert.

"Captain Amra, the enemies have come down from the hill into that ravine!" Johnny pointed into the darkness. "You can't see them from here because of those thick bushes but, when it was light out, we walked through there, the ravine leads along the river right to our camp!"

Holy Moses! The Rat King had shown a bit of tactical trickery, trying to get his army into our camp unnoticed. What could I say? The defensive trench had been dug, sharpened stakes were placed, the barricade was reinforced, and my orcs were already equipped with new weapons and armor. The enemies would be forced to approach our fortification through the sections we'd left open, only three or four monsters per passage at a time and, meanwhile, my crossbowmen would be constantly zinging enemies with bolts. The rest of the monsters would simply not fit and just trip each other up, pressing into their allies' backs. We were ready!

I thanked Johnny for his good vision and attentiveness, then sent the young chap to the rear. The front lines were no place for a child, even if he was a level-35 Sentry. I also didn't want to lose the only human in my orcish and goblin army. The boy tried to object, but I was insistent and even thought up an explanation:

"Chef Tondik is cooking donuts back there, take Irek and Yunna and start handing out food to the hungry soldiers. And you can eat too. But if I see any of you at the barricades, I'll tear your ears off!"

Foreman skill increased to level 37!

~ A Trap for the Potentate ~

But then I was quickly left speechless. Behind the nearest bush-covered hill, I could see enemies just two hundred meters away. What surprised me was that the enemy army was moving in silence, trying not to reveal their approach too early. My crossbowmen fired a volley on Valerianna's command, and I saw a few monsters fall and roll on the ground, immediately trampled by the innumerable paws of their attackers.

Only in our direct zone of sight after being entirely convinced that they were revealed did the enemies break their strange and utterly unnatural silence and start giving off a ghastly howl with hundreds of different voices. An enemy arrow passed just one centimeter from my head. I noticed it at the very last moment and dodged by some miracle.

Dodge skill increased to level 23!

"All bowmen first fire on the leshies, they can hit us from afar!" I shouted out, not wasting any time and activating the Gray-Pack-control interface.

I made sure that, above all else, the wolves, wargs and Mythical Hound had the Pack Hunter perk, increasing attack numbers, resistance and armor by ten percent for each member of the Gray Pack with the same perk active. After that, I changed Fimbulthul's second perk (available for all pets level-50 and higher) to Bloodthirsty, which made his health go up for every bite he landed. And finally, I looked at the list of beasts I could include in the Gray Pack.

There were lots of options. The Rat King's army had no less than forty Swamp Wolves of all different levels. I could take any three of them into the Gray Pack just by dragging them into the slot. I chose the three highest-level wolves, and immediately gave them the Pack Hunter and Bloodthirsty perks, then set them against a group of leshy archers.

Animal Control skill increased to level 27!

My three new Swamp Wolves didn't survive for more than six seconds, swept away by a wave of enemies piling on them. The wolves didn't get close to any of the enemy archers, or even get out of their tightly-packed groups. The resulting scuffle did delay the wave of attackers by a few seconds though, allowing my crossbowmen to get off another volley.

After tossing the gray inactive wolves out of the Gray Pack, I chose new Swamp Wolves. This time, I didn't even choose perks, immediately ordering the predators to run away from the enemy armies, setting a far-away point on the map. The result was similar. A great many teeth and claws tore the three wolves to pieces in a matter of seconds. Without the Pack Hunter perk, they had no chance. Their armor and health were just too low. Damn!

And although I could seriously weaken the enemy army this way, taking all wolves from them one by one, I was still hoping to find a better application for these predators than simply offering them up to the horde of rodents and undead.

My third attempt was also not too successful. I tried to give the wolves the Pack Hunter perk and also increase their defense with the Dense Fur perk, after which I set them on the nearest Jerboas. There was a scuffle, and a bit of chaos. The attacking monsters were distracted by the sudden appearance of enemies in their midst. I managed to stop the approaching wave of monsters very briefly although, this time, they were just one hundred steps from our positions. The horde of monsters were stuck through with orcish crossbow bolts, taking a bloody harvest. Valerianna Quickfoot once again applied her focus, creating one double, then again and four identical forest nymphs opened fire on the enemy with the speed of a machine gun, sending an unending stream of icicles, lightning bolts and fireballs at the beasts.

Level forty-six!

From time to time, an orc would light up with various colors. The warriors were leveling up quickly. For now, my calculation was fully justified. The enemies were high level, and the reward for killing them was quite generous.

The fourth attempt to take Swamp Wolves under my control was more successful. With the Swift Feet perk, two of the three predators managed to escape the dense crowd and threw themselves at the leshy blowgunners. I immediately added the Pack Hunter perk to these two wolves, in order to increase their combat stats and that calculation fully justified itself. These two creatures' lives came at a high cost, eliminating three of the leshies and pulling a significant cohort of the enemy army away to chase them.

Animal Control skill increased to level 28!

The next three Swamp Wolves joined the Gray Pack, immediately throwing themselves at their neighbors and causing a general brouhaha. In theory, the decision to simultaneously change out my level-45 Forest Wolves for stronger Swamp Wolves at 80-100 seemed tempting. It would have been a totally logical move to strengthen my ranks, but I refused to do it. Akella, Lobo, White Fang and

~ A Trap for the Potentate ~

Blanca had been with me practically from the very first day in the game and tossing them aside felt like treason against my loyal pets. Yes, these four Forest Wolves were just NPC creatures, banal pieces of program code, but they had earned their own names and, although it was just that, they were now different from other wolves.

The enemies were now close enough that I could shoot them from my Blowgun but I didn't, because it wasn't the most effective use of my time. Instead, I launched a Frost Breath ice bomb at the approaching wave of enemies. The effect was beyond expectation! Two dozen enemies turned to ice statues frozen in monstrous poses, which allowed my crossbowmen and Valerianna to shoot the motionless vulnerable targets with ease, once and for all crossing half of them off the list of dangerous enemies.

Level forty-seven!

Yikes, just a flood of experience! Too bad I only had one Ice Bomb Valerianna Quickfoot quickly drew the necessary conclusions, though, and all four copies of the forest nymph started emphasizing ice and freezing spells. However, my sister soon lost interest in the enemies on the ground. Ghosts and huge winged insects had begun to target the caster determinedly from the air.

Her pack of fierce hornets met the enemy, and the quick-winged VIXEN raced back and forth, spraying the beasts with acid and poison. Quite a serious air battle was taking shape in the night sky. Half of the crossbow orcs turned to air defense, and orcs with shields were covering my sister, but the enemy was fast and deadly.

I noticed one of the mirror copies of the forest nymph get dashed to pieces with a ringing echo, struck down by a ghastly shadow nosediving from the night sky. Bad news! My sister had once said that she needed a whole hour between casting the doubling spell, so the magess would not be able to replace that copy any time soon... The firepower of our very strongest damager had dropped, although it was still hard to say by how much exactly. From what I could see, the majority of my sister's hornets were still alive and doing most of the Beast Master's damage.

Soon, I lost interest in observing the mavka. The first enemies had reached the central passage: a level-82 Flaming Skeleton with an old serrated cutlass, a level-80 Fetid Zombie and a level-89 Royal Cobra.

Right from Fimbulthul's back, I tossed my throwing net on the zombie, trying to hold down the dangerous undead, which was giving off a nasty-smelling poisonous gas. I wasn't worried I'd be poisoned. No matter how you sliced it, Amra's resistance to poison was very high. But my wolves could be poisoned, paralyzed or even killed by these stinking wisps of green air. Not doubting that the Throwing Net would hit its target, because it was hard to miss the slow-moving zombie, I jumped off the back of my hound toward the Flaming Skeleton, waving my Blow Gun in the air and using it as a simple club.

Acrobatics skill increased to level 19!

Critical hit: 2880 (1440 crushing damage from Blowgun*2 — armor ignored)

Exotic Weapons skill increased to level 15!

Exotic Weapons skill increased to level 16!

The extremely nonstandard application of the Blowgun probably used Strength rather than Agility, but the game system considered it valid. My strike broke the Flaming Skeleton's head clean off, flying somewhere far into the swamp, fractured its right shoulder and lowered its health bar by seventy percent in one go. My enemy stumbled and missed the chance for a counter attack. My second strike left the Flaming Skeleton nothing but a pair of legs on the ground, the rest of its bones flying in all directions.

Experience received: 62480 Exp.

Level forty-eight!

I saw that the Fetid Zombie was caught in the net and wouldn't be a threat for some time. However, the Royal Cobra had sunk its poisonous fangs right into the chest of my Mythical Hound and was starting to coil its huge body around my pet! The icy-white hound would have met it's end right then and there, but Fimbulthul bit the snake back, partially restoring his health. All the other wolves and wargs were hanging off the huge many-meter body of the cobra and tearing into its flesh, quickly lowering its health. But I still understood that they wouldn't manage to kill the venomous beast before it bit the Mythical Hound again, which was a guaranteed respawn for my pet.

The enemy had to be killed quickly and for certain. I knew only one such method:

"Have at ye, beast! I'll show you how to bite!" screaming that, my big-eared Goblin threw himself at the dangerous snake and bit right into the Royal Cobra's yielding throat.

Experience received: 11050 Exp.

Achievement unlocked: Taste Tester (89/1000)

- A Trap for the Potentate -

Racial ability improved: Taste for Blood (Gives +1% to all damage dealt for each unique creature killed with Vampire Bite. Current bonus: +27%)

By doing this, I had revealed my vampiric nature and was expecting a negative reaction from the orcs, wolves and wargs who'd seen me, but... several seconds passed, and nothing bad happened. Either no one had noticed in the heat of battle, or they all considered a goblin biting an enemy totally explicable and natural. Well then? All the better.

Experience received: 3015 Exp.

I didn't have to deal with the zombie. Poked full of crossbow bolts like a pincushion, the undead creature finally died and collapsed to the earth. But another group was already coming to replace the first bunch of enemies in the narrow passage: a level-90 Swamp Jerboa, a level-99 Plague Rat, a level-88 Swamp Wolf and a level-81 Mutated Centipede. Behind them was a dense pack of dozens of other high-level monsters.

I tossed a Flame Rage fire bomb deep into the enemy horde to immediately reduce their health and break the nearest group off from the others, then I pointed the orc crossbowmen at the

Plague Rat:

"Everyone shoot at that beast! Then the Jerboa!"

The rat, preparing for a jump and crouching down on its back paws, reeled back but its place in the narrow passage was immediately occupied by a Swamp Wolf, growling and baring its sharp teeth. I wasn't prepared to kill him, in fact I was smiling:

"Now you will serve me, and not the Rat King!"

After choosing that precise Swamp Wolf from the still long list of other canines, I included it in the Gray Pack, immediately activating the Pack Hunter and Bloodthirsty perks, and changing its fur from dirty brown to hot pink. Yes, now the wolf looked very stupid but, at the same time, my crossbowmen were sure not to confuse it with an enemy. I chose another two wolves at random and included them in the Gray Pack, but they died almost instantly.

Animal Control skill increased to level 29!

Foreman skill increased to level 38!

A whole bedsheet of messages about experience gain followed. Apparently, some of the wounded victims of my fire bomb had been killed by Valerianna or a bowman. Then came a new system message:

Level forty-nine!

The Gray Pack, reinforced by their new member, tore up a Swamp Jerboa double time and latched into a centipede. The predatory insect incautiously turned its mandibles toward Fimbulthul, presenting its side to Lobo and Blanca. But I made the final bite. When else would I manage to find such a rare insect for my vampiric collection.

Experience received: 9050 Exp.

Achievement unlocked: Taste Tester (90/1000)

Racial ability improved: Taste for Blood (Gives +1% to all damage dealt for each unique creature killed with Vampire Bite. Current bonus: +28%)

Ha! Hot diggedy! Another Jerboa appeared nearby, which the Gray Pack tore up on their own, along with a level-80 Night Shadow that came down to earth. The vigor of battle overflowing from me, I howled out just like a wolf, and the Gray Pack was inspired by my canticle of strength and confidence. The enemies around, both undead and living, all recoiled at once, not wanting to meet forces with such fearless enemies.

But the situation didn't come together quite so pleasantly on all defensive sectors. I noticed that the forest nymph had only four insects left from her whole swarm of hornets, and that the magess herself only had two mirror copies now. But worst of all was the right flank. I couldn't see Max Sochnier at all. The Ogre Fortifier had lost his huge mount the Moose Lil_Timbo and was struggling desperately with his bloodied club against the many enemies all around him.

"Reserves to the right flank!" I shouted out at full volume, but my sister immediately answered with a private message:

"The right flank will make it, but the left one is a total mess. And our healer is all the way out of mana. I already gave him half my Elixirs of Magic."

My Goblin's short height prevented me from seeing what was happening on the left flank, so I climbed back up on Fimbulthul. Yikes, shit... Our defenses there were broken through. The flow of creatures was practically unobstructed through the passage, now abandoned by its defenders. Overcoming the noise of the battle, I heard a frightened wail from the chef, then an echoing blow, as if someone had struck a gong. I turned the Mythical Hound to the left, preparing to attack the enemy army, but got another message from

~ A Trap for the Potentate ~

Valerianna:

"No! Don't go left! The troll has already opened a breach with the reserve division. Ziabash and the rest of his division has also regrouped, and me and the other ranged fighters are helping out over there. Better look at the hill to the north west. Here is our chance to win the battle!"

I turned to where my sister had indicated. On a small hill overgrown with thick brush three hundred meters from my camp, the two-headed King was saddled on the huge brown Swamp Wolf Alpha! The living head of Hyenarius shrieked and sprayed saliva, the eye sockets of the dead rat's head lit up a shade of blood-red, and the magic wand in the hands of the strange Siamese twins lit up with purple sparks.

The path to the King was practically free, disregarding a few wounded survivors writhing on the ground. The enemy army was divided into two streams, attacking the right and left flanks of my defenses, while totally ignoring the center. Even the totally brainless zombies had already stopped trying to force their way into my central passage. But in that I had no faith in the high intellect of the undead, I thought the Rat King must have been commanding the army, sending the attackers to weaker sections in the defense.

Anyhow, without skipping a beat, I activated the whole Gray Pack at once and ordered them to run toward the enemy leader at full speed, and avoid any random squabbles along the way. I selected the first Swamp Wolf in the list for one of the two free slots in the pack, but I decided to leave the tenth and last one open for now. I'd taken quite a liking to the Rat King's shaggy mount! If his master were a living player, I'd doubt that it would be possible to attach him to my pack. The time with Fimbulthul was an exception, made possible by many uniquely convenient circumstances. But an NPC character, even a two-headed half dead one could not have pets by definition, so the huge swamp wolf was an independent gaming unit and could potentially be drawn to my side. And although I hadn't yet seen it in the list of canines I could add to the Gray Pack, that may have only been because of the large distance between us.

"Giddy-up!" I spurred the hound on with my feet. Fimbulthul burst from place and shot forward like an arrow, not lagging even a step behind the fleet-footed wargs.

Athletics skill increased to level 17!

Riding skill increased to level 20!
You may now choose your first specialization in this skill

Quite a positive message, but also very bad timing! I swiped the text off the screen, so it wouldn't hamper my vision, and concentrated on the dangerous enemy. He had already seen me coming. Hyenarius turned toward me with both of his heads and raised his magic wand.

Shit... A purple lightning bolt stretched toward my chest from almost half the distance between us, bursting on my mail with brightly colored, unpleasant sticky droplets.

Damage taken: 2285 HP (2285 from Death Magic spell Touch of Death)

Damage taken: 0 HP (0 damage from spell Cold of Space, immunity to cold)

A hard hitter! I felt like I'd been slammed in the stomach with a sledge-hammer. My goblin nearly flew off his mount! From just one lone strike, Amra was left with just thirty percent of his health, so I had to immediately take some healing elixirs. The very idea of attacking such a dangerous enemy started to look foolhardy and unsound, so I even started thinking I should retreat before the Rat King could get off another shot. It seemed the enemy leader didn't even believe that one magic lightning bolt hadn't struck down such a weak low-level enemy. The living head of the rat reflected surprise. But the ghastly mutant didn't shoot a second time, perhaps due to the spell recovery time or needing to recharge the wand. Instead, the Rat King sicced his shaggy mount on me.

That was the wrong move. The predatory beast started running in my direction, letting out that very same icy howl that had scared my orc army, then the Amulet of Fenrir kicked in and listed the Swamp Wolf Alpha. I saw him appear on the list of potential Gray Pack members and didn't miss my chance. Got him! My new pet immediately got a running-speed bonus and a direct order from his master to go full speed toward the black river and throw himself from the hill into the cold water, sending his ghastly rider into a whirlpool below. The Styx was close at hand, less than fifty meters away, so the Rat King simply didn't have time to react to his mount's change in behavior.

Animal Control skill increased to level 30!

Foreman skill increased to level 39!

I saw a beautiful and long jump from the powerful creature and, a second later, the Swamp Wolf Alpha and his rider were swallowed up by the black waves. The situation in the battle changed immediately. From the top of the hill, I could see perfectly as the once united army broke ranks and started a disorderly retreat, fighting amongst themselves. The surviving camp defenders, not yet believing in their victory, didn't follow the enemy and just reinforced their positions, linking their shields tighter and holding their spears out in front.

I spent a long time standing at the very banks of the Styx staring into the dark surface of the river. The Swamp Wolf Alpha' life bar had long gone gray. The creature had drowned and been sent for respawn. Neither Night Vision, nor Search for Life could help me find Hyenarius, but his heavy metal cuirass didn't allow him to swim to the surface.

Nevertheless, three lingeringly long minutes passed before a sharp rise in experience confirmed the death of the Rat King.

Level fifty!
Attention! You have reached level 50
You may now improve your character's survival by choosing a modification

I sent my sister the approximate coordinates of the Rat King's death. That beast could easily have had interesting loot, so it would be a good idea to dive in the river in search of trophies. Almost instantly, Valerianna Quickfoot answered that she'd understood the mission and would send Max Sochnier down to have a look. So, the Naiad Trader had survived after all?! This was very good news.

As was the message that came from my sister after that saying that the "healer is no longer an issue." I didn't know what exactly had happened to Antonius Just, but I intended to find out after returning to the camp. For now, I needed to distribute my built-up stat points, improvements and perks. Strength and Constitution were increased automatically with each level, and I placed the other free points according to my habitual scheme: one third in Agility, two thirds in Charisma.

It was also totally simple to handle the modifications: as I had initially decided to make my Goblin Vampire less conspicuous, I needed to keep going on this path. Especially given that, every time, the bonus from the modification was more and more significant: the first time, at level twenty, it gave just minus 1% to discovery radius then, at level thirty, minus two percent. At forty, it gave minus three, and now it was down to minus four. To be honest, I didn't fully understand from the description exactly how the effect of a few levels of modifications stacked with a -20% perk to discovery radius from Stealth but, in any case, Amra would now be harder to see, which meant he had a better chance of surviving when meeting with dangerous enemies.

It was just as simple to choose the Riding skill specialization. Given how my Royal Forest Wyvern was potentially the second fastest flying creature in *Boundless Realm* after the mythical Phoenix, I needed to purposely choose specializations to emphasize this advantage. Plus fifteen percent to movement speed was more than decent! Also, the Gray Pack acquired the very same ability and became stronger.

Much more interesting was that, at level fifty, my big-eared Goblin got another primary and secondary skill slot. But the next such expansion was only possible at the ephemerally far-off level one hundred, so I needed to think very carefully about what skills Amra should gain now in order to reach that coveted level as quickly as possible. Also to just get to it at all.

After the Battle

I STARTED UNHURRIEDLY back to the orc camp, finishing off wounded and crippled enemies who hadn't managed to retreat with the scattered army.

Legless skeletons crawling who-knows-where, headless zombies chaotically wandering about the swamps, a Gigantic Praying Mantis and Royal Cobra locked in a battle to the death... I killed the Praying Mantis myself with a Vampire Bite, because I didn't have anything like it in my "collection" yet, while I let the Gray Pack rip the wounded cobra to shreds.

Achievement unlocked: Taste Tester (91/1000)

~ A Trap for the Potentate ~

Racial ability improved: Taste for Blood (Gives +1% to all damage dealt for each unique creature killed with Vampire Bite. Current bonus: +29%)

Akella, the first and most leveled of my Hardened Forest Wolves, had already reached level-49. Lobo, Blanca and White Fang were still languishing at around 48. In any case, either today or tomorrow, they would all most likely get a second perk, which would give me significant leeway to vary their abilities depending on the situation. Darius and Darina, level 49 Wargs, were dawdling in the squelching thick muck behind me, and Darius was panting noticeably. He had been seriously wounded in tonight's battle. The phlegmatic level-62 Mythical Hound Fimbulthul was interested only in grub as usual, and he was vacuuming up any traces of food he found on the ground, not having an aversion even to the bones and flesh of the undead.

But my two new Swamp Wolves felt timid in the unfamiliar pack and were anxiously pressed up against my legs, seeking protection from their master. It looked quite funny and even awkward with their levels at 88 and 89. The pink wolf was especially shivering and putting his tail between his legs, as if he was also embarrassed at his stupid appearance.

I had yet to decide what to do with these two,

because I was hoping to find more interesting and stronger pets higher up the river of death, and I would need empty slots in the Gray Pack for them to occupy. But for now, I kept the Swamp Wolves in, because it would be stupid to part with the strongest and most dangerous of my pets (except, of course, the Swamp Wolf Alpha, which hadn't respawned yet. I wasn't sure of its level, but it was certainly higher than that of my other pets).

Oh! Plant! My big-eared Goblin Herbalist nearly stepped on a black, practically invisible flower in the dark swamp. Only the stench of death exuding from it warned me, and I stopped literally one step away.

Nocturnal Corpse Flower

Herbalism skill increased to level 18!

Fame increased
Present value: 9

You are the first to discover this plant in Boundless Realm

Great! Another increase in Fame for discovering a new plant. Most likely, these swampy shores were covered with a good deal of flowers, which opened their petals only at night, and could only be seen then. Few players had come through these parts even in the daytime, and there probably were even less Herbalists. So, at night... I was probably the first Herbalist to ever walk these ghastly swamps in the dark... I had to test that theory, because every new plant gave me a generous +1 to Herbalism and +1 to Fame.

After gathering the black, unpleasant-smelling blossoms for future study of their alchemical properties in a calmer setting, I told the mavka about my discovery and Herbalism growth in a private message, and also warned my sister that I would be walking around the camp for a bit, telling her not to worry about my absence. My sister immediately answered that she understood, and would send the orcs to loot corpses and gather pelts and meat before the bodies of the dead animals disappeared.

I walked an unhurried circle around the nearest hills, gathering rare herbs, berries and mushrooms. I still didn't risk getting too far from the defended camp, because there were plenty of dangerous beasts wandering around, but I could allow myself a half hour or two to level Herbalism. And although, in the end, my skill managed to raise up to level-19, I didn't find anything more, just plants already known to other players. That didn't upset me one bit, though. After all, this was just the start of my journey and, higher up the Styx, I could expect to find even wilder undiscovered places.

There was one more reason I was in no rush back to the orc camp. I... was afraid. Yes, yes, precisely! After clearly demonstrating my vampiric abilities during the battle, I was worried about the upcoming conversation with my warriors. A decent amount of orc defenders had seen me bite the cobra during the battle — both the crossbowmen and spearmen with large shields blocking off the path behind the Gray Pack. It would have been naive to hope that none of the dozens of orcs had seen the Vampire Bite. So, my secret was most likely already revealed, and the orcs would probably fear and hate me. But I couldn't put the difficult conversation off forever. Sooner or later, I'd have to talk about it with my crew...

I was fifty steps from the fortifications when a huge muddy brown beast appeared next to me. The Swamp Wolf Alpha had respawned. Only now could I appreciate his truly fearsome dimensions and familiarize myself with his impressive combat statistics.

Level-110 Swamp Wolf Alpha

High attack strength, armor, hitpoints, and wonderful endurance. My new pet had practically triple the stats of Akella and the other forest wolves. The beast held himself proudly and confidently, looking at the‘ various predators surrounding him with superiority and even obvious contempt. The Alpha didn't dispute my power and treated his master with great respect, but emphasized with all his behavior that Amra was the only one he would obey. I immediately decided to keep this brown wolf and tried thinking of a nickname that was appropriate to his character. For some reason, the name Baron came to mind. I felt it represented strength, independence and power. I immediately renamed my new pet.

It was as if Baron could see the name changing over him, and gave me a dog-like lick on the face with his scratchy tongue, then he gave the same ghastly howl that had scared my orcs. I turned an old leather belt into a collar for the huge beast, because I wasn't sure I could keep the wild and dangerous creature in the camp otherwise.

Animal Control skill increased to level 31!

Foreman skill increased to level 40!

And so, holding the huge wolf by the collar, as he bared his teeth spitefully and lunged at everyone he saw, I walked into the camp. The orcs bowed their heads in respect and made way for me. I then saw my first mate Ziabash Hardy at the fire, and went over to him. The orc had always listened to the opinion of the rest of the crew, knew the mood of the group and could speak for all his compatriots, so he was just the person to discuss my vampirism with.

When he saw me approach, Ziabash Hardy lowered his head dejectedly:

"Captain, I wasn't able to do my part and hold my flank... There were so many beasts pushing on our shield wall. Something inside the defenders broke... Everyone just forgot about resistance, and wanted only to survive... Flinging up our heels, we scampered to the very center of the camp... And I ran as well, damn near first of the bunch. And if the monsters hadn't gotten distracted by the smell of food from the kitchen..."

My heart stopped at these words. A wave of monsters had reached the center of the camp and attacked the kitchen?! But that was where Tondik Exuberant, and Gnum Spiteful were with Irek and Yunna! What had happened to them? Fortunately, his very next words reassured me a great deal:

"If it weren't for the bravery of the fat chef, who held off the boldest attacking rats with his two-handed pan, the consequences could have been most dire... But Gnum Spiteful got them with his terrifying hammer, and a few orcs from the barricades came to help, as well as your goblin niece and nephew. Then the troll Vaash led his fifty berserkers into battle and the crossbowmen and mavka shot them all down. My soldiers and I were ashamed and joined the main formation. All in all, we managed somehow. Eventually, the enemies suddenly stopped coming forward, then just ran for the hills. We didn't understand what happened at first. But then the mavka explained that it was you, our captain, killing the Rat King... Overall, that's what happened. Captain, it's for you to decide what to do with me and my cowardly soldiers. I will accept any sentence..."

"What were our losses?" I asked the most important question, and Ziabash Hardy said with sorrow in his voice:

"Eighteen orcs were lost, of which eleven were under my command. The Goblin boy Irek was also killed, but he's already been reborn, I just saw him alive and well. And the Human Healer died somehow. To be honest, I didn't see. But he's one of the undying, so he will probably be reborn as well. There are forty wounded and crippled. I ordered them brought into the big tent. Shaman Ghuu, Yunna and the mavka are attending to them now. And also, Tondik Exuberant and Gnum Spiteful suffered badly, but they're lying in a separate tent. And I also heard that seven people from the *Tipsy Gannet* were laid out on the right flank."

"What?" I couldn't believe my ears. "What were they even doing there?"

"Well, there was the Naiad Max Sochnier, captain of the galley. He first sent Jonny to the ship for aid, then ran off because his people didn't believe the young scout. Help arrived just in time, and the monsters weren't able to break the right flank. Not like my left..."

It hadn't all turned out as bad as I might have expected, given the initial balance of forces. If not for one "but..."

Lowering my voice to a whisper, I asked my first mate:

"Who in our crew knows about my vampirism? And how did the orcish soldiers react to the news?"

Successful check for Ziabash Hardy's opinion

Successful check for Vaash's opinion

Successful check for Gnum Spiteful's opinion

Successful check for Ghuu Gel All-Knowing's opinion

Successful check for Johnny's opinion
Successful check for Orc race opinion

All conditions met (6 of 6)

Hidden mission completed: Our Captain's Eccentricities (racial, rare)
Reward: 24000 Exp., +30 to any check of your crew's opinion

~ A Trap for the Potentate ~

Veil skill increased to level 15!

Veil skill increased to level 16!

Stealth skill increased to level 24!

Foreman skill increased to level 41!

Foreman skill increased to level 42!

Ziabash Hardy's eyebrows shot up in surprise:

"Hmm, Captain Amra, when even was that...? Talk started of a vampire on board the *White Shark* when you first traded wine for blood... Or was it even earlier? I can't remember anymore. First of all, everyone was on guard, of course. There was a lot of chatter, how can you not gossip about something like that...? But they eventually got used to it. The crew never thought too badly of you for it. In fact, it was the opposite. They saw that our captain is courageous and favored by fortune so, if he has some weird habits, that's his business. And when Taisha asked us to build a tent in the sunny desert for Captain Amra, everyone understood why. Also, the winged snake is constantly bringing still living beasts for the captain, and he doesn't eat them, just kills them. All in all, our crew has long known about our captain's vampirism, but none of our soldiers will give up your secret, you can be sure!"

Woah! The whole pirate crew had long known about their captain's predilection for blood but, all that time, they had reacted fairly calmly. My goblin stroked his huge ears in contemplation. Ugh, if I'd have known earlier that I didn't have to shiver over my secret, think how many nerves I could have saved! My mood was plainly improved, and I patted the nervous orc reassuringly on the shoulder:

"Ziabash, it isn't some deficit of thought that caused the gap in your flank, because cowards would never be able to look such strong and ghastly beasts in the eyes. As far as I can tell, the reason was insufficient preparation and the soldiers' lack of ability to fight in formation. But your group wasn't the only one to have this characteristic, all our orcs did. It would be stupid to punish you for that. But it is clear that intensive training is not only important, but vitally necessary! The forest nymph will lead this initiative starting tomorrow morning. Valerianna Quickfoot has a lot of experience in such matters."

Leaving the orc to keep resting by the fire, I headed into a tent for the wounded. At the entrance to the tent, I ran into Shaman Ghuu Gel All-Knowing, who happened to be on his way out. The normally sprightly and strong shaman was now barely able to stand due to overexertion.

~ A Trap for the Potentate ~

Looking at me with his eyes sagging wearily, Ghuu pointed at the rows of orcs lying on bed-mats:

"Captain, I've done all I could. Some of the wounded will be back in shape tomorrow, others a bit later. But there are five badly wounded. They have very bad tear wounds from the claws and teeth of the undead, and all five have begun to be infected. As bad as it may be, I'm clean out of healing elixirs..."

Mission received: Orc Infirmary
Mission class: Normal
Description: Get thirty Minor Elixirs of Healing and five Elixirs of Cure Disease for the shaman
Reward: 4000 Exp., Alchemy +1, your squadron will be ready to keep moving

Everything in the mission was totally usual and predictable, but I was slightly put on guard by the line "your squadron will be ready to keep moving." What the heck did that mean? If I couldn't find the proper number of elixir bottles would we be stranded here forever?! And what about the option of leaving the wounded behind? Of course, I did have a large reserve of empty flagons, and a whole stack of healing herbs towering in my inventory. I was not planning to leave my orcs behind, but it still seemed a bit illogical.

I promised the shaman to handle the alchemy a bit later and prepare everything needed for healing, then headed off to find my sister. Valerianna Quickfoot was in the dwarven tent and let me inside, pointing at both of the wounded soldiers:

"Here they are: the true heroes of tonight's battle! They held out alone against an attacking wave of monsters. They did get pretty seriously hurt though, especially the fatso..."

The chef was obviously not doing well. There were so many cuts and bites on his body that there wasn't a single fresh patch of skin. All the bandages on his chest and head were soaked in blood. It also looked like Tondik's right eye had been poked out. There was an uneven bloody scar running across his empty eye socket, cheek and upper lip, stitched up tight with thread. But the worst wounds were to his arms and hands. His right was missing two fingers, and all that remained of his left was a stump at the elbow wrapped in rags...

At that, Tondik was still conscious, recognized his captain and even tried to stand up from the cot:

"Captain," I could hear despair in the dwarf's voice, "those rats came at my kitchen and ate all the food! What kind of a chef am I without flour, grains, sugar and spices?! I tried to stop them, stunned them with the very biggest pan...

when I still had two hands... Then jabbed with the knife until I was dragged off..."

It was unbelievable, but the chef was much more worried about the loss of foodstuffs than his severe injuries!

"Tondik was raging like a real berserker," Gnum Spiteful spoke up with a weak voice from the neighboring cot, "beset by enemies on all sides, the chef didn't notice his wounds and kept fighting, even after a huge swamp wolf bit off his hand..."

The dwarven lady was also seriously wounded. Her right hand was hanging limp in a bandage, both legs were splinted, and her beard was matted with blood. Some beast had tried to bite the Dwarf Mechanic's throat. But still, Gnum Spiteful's state didn't worry me seriously. She would be good as new in no time. Unlike Tondik, who was seriously crippled.

I took a step forward and went down on one knee next to the chef's bed:

"It is a great honor to have such a valiant warrior in my squadron! I'd long known about Gnum Spiteful's fearlessness, but you really surprised me with your determination and valor. I want both of you to know that the orcs are impressed with the bravery of the dwarves and say that it was your example of fearlessness that stopped the panic in our ranks!"

Foreman skill increased to level 43!

Would you like to take the primary skill Warchief (Ch P)?

Would you like to take the primary skill Diplomat (Ch I)?

I dismissed both suggestions. I needed to take an intelligent approach to choosing my new level-50 skills, and think it over carefully, not act spontaneously. Here, the forest nymph cut into the conversation:

"As for more victuals, don't you worry Tondik. Sure, there may be no more flour, but we've got so much meat that our squadron will eat for a week! It just needs to be dried or salted so it won't spoil in this hot and humid climate. We also have plenty of herbs and spices, so there's plenty of work for a chef."

The fat dwarf sat up on his bed once again and said, giving a chuckle with his stitched upper lip:

"Thank you for the trust, undying forest nymph. Of course, I will try to cook with one hand, but I'll need time to get used to it."

"Tondik, I'll help you in the kitchen as soon as I can stand!" Gnum Spiteful said unexpectedly. "And I'll be sure to make you a prosthesis for your hand with all kinds of adaptations, so you can work more comfortably in the kitchen."

The chef overflowed with words of gratitude for his compatriot. Valerianna and I left the dwarves and went behind the tent door flap. As soon as we were out, the Nymph whispered in my ear, pointing behind her back at the tent:

"Big-ears, here's your chance to try out the new regeneration potion!"

I in complete agreement with my sister, as I had come to the same conclusion already. All in all, I needed to practice Alchemy seriously in order to prepare all the necessary elixirs both to finish the quest, and to heal the chef. I started heading to my tent, planning to set out vials and herbs, but Valerianna stopped me:

"Wait, Amra, don't rush. Alchemy is important, but it isn't going anywhere. I just got a curious idea for how to quickly level Herbalism. If you can find new types of plants no one has ever seen before on the banks of the Styx, just imagine how many you'll find under the black water, especially at night! When Max Sochnier and I dove down to search for the body of the drowned Rat King, we could barely move due to the overabundance of seaweed, floating and underwater plants, flowers and roots. All the flora wasn't marked for us at all, because we don't have Herbalism, but you should definitely take a look at the underwater vegetation! I suspect that, in these dangerous waters, no one has ever searched for plants before, especially at night. This is basically Klondike for an Herbalist! And don't worry about safety. The nereid Olilissa is reliable protection. I almost fainted when I saw her for the first time. Now that's power and grace!"

"By the way, did you find the body of the Rat King?" I asked, and the forest nymph took a glowing purple scepter from her bag with pride.

"Anything useful?" I asked, because I couldn't see the object properties myself due to low Intelligence.

The forest nymph laughed in satisfaction and loosed a purple lightning bolt into the dark cloudy sky.

"Decent bonuses to Intelligence and mana regeneration. But the most interesting part is that it allows access to the same death magic spells available to an equivalent-level necromancer, and the ability to cast Kiss of Death once a minute without wasting any mana. In fact, I was planning to take death magic at level one hundred as a primary skill, but now I don't even see a particular reason for it. This scepter isn't legendary, nor unique, but it has interesting properties. It can serve me well until level one hundred twenty easy. The Rat King also dropped heavy armor. I gave it to our Ogre Fortifier. Of course, it looks a bit strange to see him with the extra head hole, but the armor has simply excellent defensive characteristics!"

~ A Trap for the Potentate ~

Over our conversation, we reached the very edge of the water. The bank was boggy. My goblin was almost up to his knees in the black oozy muck. The mavka was equally deep in the slow-flowing black water and dragging her feet. She stopped short and started looking attentively, as if expecting something. I was standing a step from my sister not understanding why she hadn't yet placed the underwater breathing spell on me.

Suddenly the water just one step from me stirred up. Huge jaws gnashed with terrifying teeth only one centimeter from my nose, and the long scaly body went back under the water, giving a lash with its tail one last time on the surface, soaking the mavka and I from head to toe. I froze for a few seconds in surprise, then reached for my knife, but the forest nymph stopped me:

"Amra, put your weapon away! It's just Olilissa having some fun!"

"If that's what you call fun!" I objected justly, although I still took my hand from the weapon. "I'm still worried. My heart is beating a mile a minute and cannot calm down! What if there was an elderly person in my place? I wonder if many players of *Boundless Realm* have died of heart attacks?"

The water stirred again but, this time, I was morally prepared. Her shark-like nose popped out of the river and she stared at me with huge unblinking eyes. After that, the nereid's lips stretched into a smile, making her toothy maw all the more terrifying.

"Hey there, little goblin! You must be Amra. Maxy told me about you. He warned me that you'll need some of my blood. I'm ready to share."

I turned in incomprehension to the mavka, but she just shrugged her shoulders in surprise. Meanwhile, the huge nereid flicked her tail a few times and came even further into the shallow water, allowing me to see her in all her glory. The huge predatory fish's seven-meter-long body was covered with scales, but the front third was still somehow reminiscent of a human. It was far from the complete resemblance of mermaids, but she did have hands (or more likely strong muscular flippers with webbed fingers to hold her trident, which was sharper than a razor), and something like shoulders. At any rate, that was where her similarity with humans ended. Over her neck, there was a toothy fish head. Before me was a creature that inspired respect with just its appearance and was ideally adapted to kill everything that moved in water. And that which didn't move, she could also kill with a flick of her wrist or trident.

"Here, I'm ready. Stick me with your knife and collect some blood," Olilissa turned her stomach up, presenting her less-armored belly. " Maxy said that you'd need one flagon of my blood for alchemy experiments, no matter how much I don't like it."

I walked up to the gigantic creature and carefully pierced the thin fine scales on the nereid's belly with a dagger. I took one flagon of blood and put it in my inventory, not wanting to risk demonstrating my vampiric inclinations in the presence of Max Sochnier's girlfriend.

"Is that all? Or do you need something more from me?"

I thanked the nereid for her help and politely asked Olilissa to protect me while I gathered plants and seaweed underwater.

"Of course! I'll do anything for a friend of my sweet Maxy!"

It was a long, but very fruitful night. First of all, I really did manage to significantly improve the Herbalism situation, going up by eight whole levels! My sister, as usual, was right. The banks and bottom of the Styx had abundant plant life, and I found new species there that had never been picked or described before. Six new kinds of lily-pad, lotus and riverbed seaweed gave me +6 to Herbalism and +6 to Fame, while the other two skill points were earned the usual way simply by gathering plants. In the end, I brought my Herbalism skill to 27, and for the first time felt a glimmer of hope that I might complete my mission and level the skill to 45 in the five days I had remaining.

At Herbalism level 20, I could choose a new perk. There were plenty of options. I could improve my plant-detection radius, or luck in finding rare species, take the mushroom or epiphyte specialization, increase the number of useful ingredients I could gather from a single plant and lots of other stuff. But I chose Replanting, the ability to not only pick flowers, leaves and berries, but dig them up carefully with the root and transfer them to another place. Sure, roaming actively around *Boundless Realm* as I was now, that skill seemed quite useless, but I was hoping to eventually find a secure place to call home, where my Goblin Herbalist could set up a rare-plant farm.

I also got my first perk in a secondary skill, Athletics. As it turned out, this skill was excellently levelled by swimming and diving. I didn't spend a lot of time trying to be clever, and chose to have my Endurance restore quicker. Beyond that, while gathering underwater plants, Amra reached level-51. My Strength and Constitution grew by one point automatically, leaving the other three free, which I distributed according to my habitual scheme: two into Charisma, one into Agility.

During my night swim, my sister and I had also had a good think about my Amra's further

~ A Trap for the Potentate ~

development. It was clear that we needed to make some adjustments to our former plans because, due to the bonuses from Fenrir's Cursed Regalia, Strength and Constitution had become my goblin's main stats, no longer Agility. Along with that, Amra also needed to pick a weapon for high Strength, some kind of axe or hammer, or even hand-to-hand combat. But, we decided, I should make that skill a secondary not a primary, so I wouldn't be punished by the goblin race's 50% penalty to Strength growth.

Valeria asked me not to rush that decision. My sister wanted to first study the *Boundless Realm* forum and see what high-Strength weapons were recommended by more experienced players. But at that, the mavka now suggested I move Riding from secondary to main. Amra regularly rode VIXEN or Fimbulthul, so I was using it a lot, and it also leveled Agility which, with my 30% racial bonus to Agility, was very nice.

My sister also suggested I make a choice: would Amra become a powerful lone wolf with a team of predatory pets at his beck and call, or remain in command of a large squadron of NPC warriors? These two different paths demanded different skills, and a slant toward different stats. The issue really was leading to the following: was the orcish crew a temporary whim for me, a single-use tool for completing the concrete mission of reaching the upper Styx, or was I truly planning to develop that skill, level and strengthen my soldiers, and increase the numbers and power of my NPC army?

I had already long determined my answer to that question, so I told my sister that I would not abandon my orc pirates and would lead them further. And that was exactly what Valerianna was expecting:

"What can I say then, Tim? You need to think about leveling the army. The average level of the orcs is about fifty now, but the enemies here are eighty to one hundred and, higher up the river, it'll only get worse. You have to level your warriors quickly, that's obvious. To do that, you also need to add strong new soldiers to the squadron, and increase the level of those you have. But level isn't everything. Discipline, coordination, and the ability to work in combat formation are also important. Beyond that, you need to provide useful bonuses to the army — defense, morale, and number of hitpoints... What can I say? I'll think about how to help."

Taking advantage of the fact that there was no one around except the big coils of Olilissa twisting around us, I asked my sister about the death of the Human Healer Antonius Just. For some reason, I had no doubt that my sister had somehow been involved in the very timely end of the high-level player from my blacklist. Valerianna Quickfoot confirmed my guess:

~ A Trap for the Potentate ~

"Tim, I didn't lay a finger on the healer, just... how can I put it... I didn't point out a crude error he was making and let that kill him. Antonius Just was squandering his mana for no good reason. He was supposed to be healing the NPC orcs. And although he was standing at the back, he placed a bunch of protective spells on himself that ate up his magical energy. He was constantly demanding more and more elixirs of magic from me to prop him up. What did he think I was, a walking storehouse or something?! You have to agree, it looks strange to see a level-one-hundred-thirty character in battle totally wasting his own mana, then taking advantage of a level-sixty-three player! When the orcs wavered, I simply 'didn't make it in time' to give him another portion of vials and didn't warn him about the breach in the line, hurrying away together with the rest so I wouldn't get caught on the front lines. But the healer must have slept through our retreat. He was too busy writing angry messages to me in a private chat, demanding mana elixirs. In the end, he was left without mana and surrounded by enemies. Antonius Just died almost instantly..."

I had some doubts about whether the healer dying by the teeth and claws of NPC monsters counted as me fulfilling my oath before the gods of *Boundless Realm*. All the same, Valerianna Quickfoot was fairly convincing, arguing that all the conditions of the oath had been fulfilled, and the Human Healer's death was not so different from the time I'd let VIXEN chop down the she-elf bowwoman, another player in my blacklist.

Finally, my inventory was filled with water plants, and I crawled up onto the shore. Valerianna, who was accompanying me during the underwater work, also came out of the water and removed the underwater breathing spell from both of us. My sister yawned in exhaustion and was preparing to quickly leave the game.

There was around an hour and a half until the sun came back up, and I was preparing to devote that time to Alchemy. When Valerianna heard me say that, she unexpectedly laughed:

"Big-ears, your Intelligence is obviously limping with both legs. It's been like that for a while. But your Perception isn't supposed to be so bad. Have you really not noticed?"

What was I supposed to notice? I looked all around for something unusual. Darkness, swamp, the loud croaking of gigantic toads in the distance, the well-lit orc camp in the other direction... What was the matter? The sky in the east was turning slightly pink, but it looked like today would be a cloudy day. So, I said as much to the mavka.

"Tim, are you so lazy you didn't even read the reports of the last twenty-six expeditions? There are a lot of threads about the river Styx and its weather on the *Boundless Realm* forums. It's always cloudy here, Amra! And higher up the river, there will be such thick cloud cover, that you can't even see past your own hand. There's no reason for you to play only at night, Tim. This is the ideal place for a vampire!"

Emissary of Darkness

MY CAMP HAD an unexpected visitor at dawn. By that time, I had already finished my alchemical experiments and was preparing to go wake up Shaman Ghuu Gel All-Knowing and tell him I'd finished the quest. Everything it needed was already prepared: there were thirty Minor Elixirs of Healing and five Elixirs of Cure Disease lined up in neat little rows on my alchemy table. Other than that, I had made a whole bunch of Middling Elixirs of Healing and Middling Elixirs of Magic, one vial of the rare Elixir of Regeneration made of Miraculous Cloudberry, three portions of Elixir of Underwater Breathing made of seaweed and a few poisons with all kind of different effects. All that raised my Alchemy skill by four points to level twenty-eight.

~ A Trap for the Potentate ~

Other than Alchemy, I had been intensively levelling Stealth. To that end, I did all my alchemy in a hidden state. Being inside a tent in the middle of my military camp, I was technically in the sight radius of hundreds of NPC's, but unseen. In theory, in such conditions, Stealth should have been levelling quickly but, at first, I didn't notice any effect. For some reason, the skill didn't want to activate, as if someone could still see me. The fabric of my big tent was not transparent, Irek and Yunna were sleeping inside on bedrolls. Other than them, there was just the Mythical Hound lying at the entrance. I checked. Both of the goblin teens were really asleep, and even had their faces turned to the wall, so they clearly wouldn't be able to see me. That meant they couldn't be the problem. I had to put the dozing Fimbulthul outside the tent with the rest of the Gray Pack, despite his protests. He must have grown used to his privileged position next to the master and clearly did not understand why his status was being lowered.

After that, my Stealth bar started to quickly fill. I was potentially in the detection zone of three hundred different NPC creatures, but none of them had been able to detect me in the last two hours, which raised my Stealth by six points to level thirty. What a great way of rapidly levelling Stealth! I was very satisfied with the result and was not preparing to rest on my laurels, but my preparations were interrupted by a piercing buzz from the signal horn of an orcish sentry, having spotted a potential danger.

I already knew that the sounding of the orcish horn could mean different things depending on the type of threat, so I perked up my huge ears, listening to the melody. A one note staccato, meaning this was not a mass attack, nor a natural disaster, just a lone enemy. I immediately calmed down. Clearly, this was just a high-level creature near our fortification, which would quickly get spooked by the loud sound and leave. But the sounding of the horn didn't stop. What was more, the sound of that one alarm horn was soon joined by several others, which clearly overturned my theory about a random wandering creature.

Around the walls of my tent, I could see the shadows of soldiers tossing about. The orc camp was hurriedly waking up, getting ready to meet the rude stranger. So, I quickly threw all my new elixirs into my inventory and hurried to the exit.

Successful Perception check
Experience received: 100 Exp.

I was struck and put on guard by the fact that the whole Gray Pack had their tails between their legs and were whining mournfully. The Hardened Forest Wolves, normally striving to show their fearsomeness at every turn, were now cowering behind me and clearly not burning with desire to meet our morning guest. Darius and Darina, with the arrival of morning, usually took on human form, but were still in their warg shapes for some reason, baring their teeth. Fimbulthul, taking advantage of the open tent flap, immediately hid inside. Even the huge Baron lost his proud appearance and was now more reminiscent of a terrified beaten puppy. To put it lightly, my pack was acting strange...

Before I could come to any conclusions on their unusual behavior, though, I heard a wave of moans and frightened cries from all around the orc camp.

Darkness Magic resistance check failed

Damage taken: 0 HP (spell Wave of Horror, immunity to fear)

What a way to start the day! Before, I was yawning wide, insanely tired by the long difficult night. But, after the attempted magical attack, I instantly shuddered. Not a trace remained now of my former sleepiness. Based on what I could see, I was now being protected by the Fenrir's Paws gloves, which gave complete immunity to fear. But what was this creature that could bring a whole military camp to a state of terror?! I ordered the Gray Pack to follow me, then hurried to the fortifications.

At the barricade, seemingly all soldiers who could hold weapons were already gathered. In the ranks of the orcs lined up to meet the enemy, I even saw a few who still should have been in the infirmary. The mood of the defenders was determined. I didn't see any signs of fear, much less panic. Ziabash Hardy and the Troll Vaash were loudly commanding and generously slapping their yawning or confused warriors awake, setting the spearmen in two rows with large shields, and placing crossbowmen behind them. Shaman Ghuu was doing a strange wild dance behind the formation, waving his crooked staff and putting some blessings on the orcs as they prepared for battle.

All in all, these were positive signs. The lesson of our recent battle hadn't been in vain. The division commanders were working carefully. The soldiers mostly knew their places in formation, and even the threat of a ghastly creature didn't stop the orcs from quickly taking up defense. But where was the enemy? Amra was too short to see anything over the much taller warriors.

I called the nearest sentry and demanded an explanation. But I could understand very little in his disjointed and faltering speech: something about darkness, dread and burning red eyes. I could only make out that the enemy had been seen on the nearest hill two hundred steps from the camp, but then went down in a hollow and disappeared from sight. Perhaps he had retreated, although the sentry couldn't say for certain. Fortunately, the shaman finished his dance right on time and ran up to me:

"Captain Amra, I sense an evil presence! I do not know who it is this time, but the spirits are telling me this is a very strong enemy, who is nourished by our fears. So, I called the sprits to help and give our warriors the gift of bravery."

"Great, Ghuu! Excellent thinking!" I tried to speak confidently and loudly, so as many orcs as possible would hear me. "Our enemy has never before come up against truly fearsome orcs, so he was counting on scaring us and making us run away in fear! What a naive fool! If our enemy really is nourished by fears, he will have to go hungry! Isn't that right, my brave warriors? I want you all to shout out together what body part orcs show their enemies to suggest they either surrender or retreat!"

In reply I heard a coordinated and confident roar from a hundred throats, then a loud chuckling, which rolled over the surrounding area for many kilometers. I smiled in satisfaction from ear to ear. If I were a creature nourished by fear, I truly would not want to come up against these inspired orcs.

Foreman skill increased to level 44!

Would you like to take the secondary skill Warchief (Ch P)?

The game system was suggesting I take that skill for the second time now. This time, I didn't dismiss it right away, and called up the in-game guide:

Warchief. Allows a commander to inspire his warriors, giving them random positive bonuses. As this skill grows, the chance of bonus increases, and the effects grow stronger. At higher levels, this specialization allows multiple bonuses (including multiple identical bonuses), increased bonus duration up to permanent, and the use of spirit- or mind-magic spells on one's army. ATTENTION!!! The Warchief skill will not work and does not level if the subjects have a low or negative opinion of their commander.

I couldn't understand from the skill description if the effect would work on the whole army or just individual warriors in it. I also couldn't tell if there were limits on the size of the army a commander could control, or if the bonuses would stack (for example, increased morale and loyalty) with the effects given by the Foreman skill. Nevertheless, it seemed very, very useful to me, as I'd decided to continue leading the army of orcs.

> **You have taken Warchief as a secondary skill**
> **Skill level: 1**

Secondary skills chosen (6 of 7)

"Captain Amra, I can sense that the enemy hasn't left and is still circling our camp!" Shaman Ghuu pointed with his staff, vaguely indicating the enemy's location.

What could I say? This was a perfect time to try out the new skill. I ordered the shaman to roll out some barrels of rum and give one cup to every warrior as we had previously done on the pirate bireme before a dangerous encounter.

> **Foreman skill increased to level 45!**

> **Warchief skill increased to level 2!**

> **Warchief skill increased to level 3!**

In reply, the crew roared out in elation. The orcs were waving their yataghans in the air and banging their weapons on their shields, expressing their complete approval of the captain's decision. Over the heads of some of the warriors, I saw bright shining symbols and read the effects with curiosity. Increased Morale, Increased Strength, Increased Speed, Immunity to Fear, Hunger Sated, Night Vision, Increased Luck. The effects were random and of all different kinds. What could I say? I now knew how the Warchief skill worked.

And then, it was as if a gust of evil cold wind came over the camp, wiping the happy smiles off their tusked faces and causing a distressed gnashing of teeth.

Darkness Magic resistance check failed

Damage taken: 0 HP (spell Wave of Horror, immunity to fear)

The beast had tested its fell magic on us once again! I looked at the rows of orcs with alarm. They had stopped baring their teeth in pride and were now feverishly clutching their weapons. The orcs looked around unconfidently, as if searching for help from their neighbors. Many looked to me as their commander. However, I didn't see any acting cowardly or abandoning their positions. Just then, Johnny shouted out:

"There it is! It's riding straight for the camp!"

I demanded the shield-bearers make way and let their captain come out in front. The rows of huge orcs obediently made way, and I finally saw the cause of all this fear with my own eyes.

Well, well! Our morning guest really did

make an impression. His appearance was mortifying. It was a huge dark rider astride a giant black stallion. The face of the rider was not visible because he had a hood thrown over it. All I could see under the black ovular gap was two bright-red eyes. The body, clothes and even horse were seemingly formed of tufts of thick black cloud, so I was not even sure they were material. What was more, the horse was not a separate creature, more like an inseparable addition to the rider, a part of his terrifying look.

Dark Rider
Emissary of the Dark Sovereign

There wasn't very much to be gleaned from the description. The fact that before me was a rider, and a dark one at that, I had already noticed. But now, I could also see a black-skull marker on the mini-map, signifying that he was more than 50 levels higher than me. But that was hardly surprising in such a wild, remote place. Although an emissary, if you think about it, is something like a messenger, a representative. But then who was this Dark Sovereign? I had never heard of this melodramatically named character before. Our morning visitor stopped one hundred meters from the barricade and froze motionless, as if awaiting a representative from our side.

What could I say? I'd be getting answers to

all my questions right now. I ordered my warriors
to remain in place, called Fimbulthul over and,
gracefully jumping on the Mythical Hound's back,
steered him forward. When I was just ten steps
away, the emissary raised his hand in warning,
commanding me to stop. Not looking for trouble, I
came to a halt.

"Hey! Are you from the Global Modeling
Department? Or a tester from the Special Projects
Department?" I tried addressing the stranger like
a living player, because he really reminded me of
the glowing angel Keeper, just his complete
antipode. Clearly, both of these creatures had
been made by the very same *Boundless Realm*
artists and programmers.

The Dark Rider ignored my question, just as
any NPC should when discussing things beyond
the bounds of their virtual world. It was clear that
this was just a program, not a living player. Then
I called him by name and asked why he was near
my camp. The Dark Rider's voice was hoarse and
howling, like that of a ghost:

"You have crossed into my master's
holdings. You have also killed the lord of these
swamps, a loyal vassal of my sovereign. It may
have been out of ignorance, so I have come to warn
you that it is forbidden for anything alive or dead
to travel up the river of death. You and your army
must leave this place at once!"

Woah! This was the first time I had heard of

such a rule. Antonius Just hadn't mentioned any Dark Sovereign or the borders of his lands. Also, my sister Valerianna had scrupulously studied all available materials on the previous missions up the Styx, and not encountered anything like this. In any case, I had an unexpected problem before me.

"How much time do we have to think? And what will happen if we do not obey?" I asked the ghastly rider.

"There's nothing to think about. Go back to where you came from or be destroyed! You have until sundown to tear down your camp but, by nightfall, neither your camp nor your ship shall remain! And just so you understand the serious nature of my words and pack up your tents quickly, here's a clear example of punishment for impudence and disobedience!" With these words, the Dark Rider threw up the sides of his cloak of black clouds and pulled a bow from under his clothing, which was also seemingly made of black cloud.

That made me seriously afraid, because my respawn point was devil-knows-where, and coming back to the river camp would take me a few hours at least. I even feverishly activated my vampiric ability Undead Apathy, although I strongly doubted that the emissary of the Dark Sovereign counted as a restless dead. I do not know if my ability helped in this situation or not, but the Dark Rider shot not at me, but my mount.

Fimbulthul gave a short howl of pain and collapsed on his side, no longer breathing. I barely managed to jump off my shaggy hound before his hefty body came down on top of me.

Riding skill increased to level 21!

Acrobatics skill increased to level 20!
You may now choose your first specialization in this skill

Then, after somersaulting off and jumping to my feet, I grabbed my Throwing Net. But the Dark Rider had already turned his huge mount around and was spurring him on. Completely silent, without the clopping of hooves, champing of mud or any other sounds, the black stallion dashed a few steps and dissolved in thin air together with his ghastly rider, like a wisp of cloud.

"What a beast!" I was planning to keep swearing with even more rage, and really let it out, but I froze.

The flesh of the dead hound was decaying right before my eyes, leaving behind white bones and revealing an evil predatory whirlwind swirling inside his chest cavity. What the hell was this?! It very much resembled the most dangerous creature I had ever seen... Already realizing the answer, I raised my hands in warning and shouted out to the orcs and Gray Pack, who were rushing out to help me, not to come near. The wolves and my soldiers obediently froze fifty steps from me, and just in the nick of time. I finally managed to read the information on the flesh-eating whirlwind, and my very worst guesses were confirmed:

Midnight Wraith
Level unknown

The very last thing I needed! I finally had identified the mortifying creature that had devoured the flesh of my mount and the arrow, immediately remembering how I knew the name Dark Rider. Once upon a time, I had a fragment of a Dark Rider arrow, which the Keeper had paid me generously for, respawning my NPC Goblins and making Yunna and Irek immortal. But as there was such a creature before me again, I already knew the way to fight it. I would have to try to minimize the level of its opponent, because the insidious dark monster was always twice as strong as its highest-level enemy.

"No one come near! There's guaranteed death here! This battle is for me alone!" I reminded my subjects. I also gave a separate command to the level-110 Baron to go to the opposite end of the camp and stay there. After that, I started thinking hard.

Now, the Midnight Wraith would

theoretically be level one hundred and two because the only character nearby was my level-51 Goblin Herbalist. At level one hundred, the beast was immaterial and probably extremely hard to damage with melee weapons, perhaps even having complete immunity to physical attacks. My character didn't have any magic at all, but I needed to handle it myself, and very soon, before the terrible monster ate up the rest of Fimbulthul and left to cause mischief in the surrounding area. If the Midnight Wraith moved toward the barricades with the orcs, it would cause some tragedies there. The orcs would be incapable of doing any harm to the immaterial ghost, and he would take a bloody harvest from the inhabitants of my camp.

Last time, I had just passively stayed aside, making use of my defensive ability Undead Apathy, then set my Royal Forest Wyvern against the Midnight Wraith, having used a special poison to lower VIXEN's level to one. I had such a poison with me now. In fact, it was even stronger due to my improved Alchemy abilities, and could lower a victim's level by a whole 28 for forty seconds. But there was just one hitch. VIXEN had reached level-43 since then, and, even with the poison, would be level 15, giving her no chance to fight against an enemy twice her level. Using this poison directly on me was practically useless. After all, my Goblin Herbalist had an 80% resistance to poison. There was a very high probability the negative effect wouldn't work, if I drank the vial of poison, or that the poison's effect would be greatly reduced. Damn! Now here was a stupid situation, suffering from my own high resistances...

I saw the orc Shaman Ghuu Gel All-Knowing in the crowd gathering in the distance and shouted out to ask if he could curse me to temporarily reduce my resistance to poisons. I had to repeat the question two times, because Ghuu didn't believe he had heard his captain properly. I assured the shaman that he had understood everything right, and I needed it for the fight with the ghastly undead.

Successful check for Ghuu Gel All-Knowing's reaction!

Check for Ghuu Gel All-Knowing's reaction failed!

LOGICAL ERROR! Mutually exclusive actions
NPC $FF0270-CC0083 is attempting to commit an act of aggression against an ally based on high opinion of that ally
Error code #LOC/ER-007941
This message has been sent to Boundless Realm *tech support*
We apologize for the possible inconvenience

~ Dark herbalist Book Three ~

SYSTEM ERROR!

Opinion variable of NPC $FF0270-CC0083 undefined

Error code #LOC/ER-040056

This message has been sent to Boundless Realm *tech support*

We apologize for the possible inconvenience

CRITICAL ERROR!

The Boundless Realm game client will now be restarted

We apologize for the possible inconvenience

The world around me started to fade. A black screen appeared, with lines of technical commands running past. I mean, god damn! All I had done is made a friendly request for the shaman to curse me... Around a minute passed before the image lit up again.

So, what was the result? The Midnight Wraith had already eaten the last remnants of the huge hound. The orc shaman then confirmed that he could curse me and was ready to do it. Then, without delay, he started doing a strange jerky dance with howling and epileptic convulsions. In any case, I sent the Gray Pack further from the shaman, so the wolves wouldn't throw themselves on the man for attacking their master.

~ A Trap for the Potentate ~

Animal Control skill increased to level 32!

Finally, the shaman finished chanting and dancing and shouted out something strange that sounded like swearing, pointing his crooked staff in my direction.

Death Magic resistance check failed

Critical fail in Intelligence check!

ATTENTION!!! A fearsome curse has been placed on you. For the next two days, you will not be able to use any weaponry in your left hand, your character's movement speed will be reduced by 42%, your resistance to poison is reduced by 53%, damage taken from all kinds of attacks is increased by 200%, and experience gain is reduced by 77%.

Aw, fu...! Just damn it. Now this is what it looked like to be whole-heartedly cursed by someone giving their all for their beloved captain. It can't seriously be impossible to limit this to only reducing my defense against poison, right?! But I'd deal with that later. The most important thing now was taking down this dead creature. I took a vial of poison from my bag. The chance of successful poisoning was 73%, which was still no guarantee.

It worked! My Goblin Herbalist fell to level... one??? But why not to twenty-three as I was assuming? What was more, my leather pants, cuirass, helm and other equipment instantly fell off me due to their level requirements. In fact, I was left in nothing but my initial "diaper," a couple of rings and the cursed amulet and gloves from Fenrir's Regalia. My big-eared Goblin probably looked funny, and my audience would like it, but I'd have to think about that later. The main thing was that the Midnight Wraith had transformed from a dark immaterial whirlwind into a ghastly half-meter-long worm . I just stomped it with my foot.

Experience received: 1 Exp.

Hrmph, I'll be direct: not much for killing a beast that could have easily destroyed my whole military camp. Pulling the black arrow, covered in inky goo, from Fimbulthul's body and trying not to touch it with any uncovered body part, I rolled the dangerous trophy up in a rag and put it into my inventory.

I waited for the effects of the poison to roll back, got dressed and spent a little while just standing in worry that the Keeper might appear and demand I give him the dangerous item, but nothing happened. Based on that, the big update was no longer so far beyond the horizon, as the Global Modeling Department decided to let me keep the trophy.

I returned to my orcs and, first of all, walked up to the very nervous shaman. Ghuu was clearly not yet sure that he had done the right thing by putting the curse on me, but I gave the young shaman a comforting slap on the shoulder and assured him that I wasn't offended. At the same time, I gave him the items from the Orc Infirmary quest.

Mission completed: Orc Infirmary
Reward: 920 Exp.

Alchemy skill increased to level 29!

Warchief skill increased to level 4!
Foreman skill increased to level 46!

The shaman assured me that he would immediately give the medicine to the wounded and, right after that, our group would be able to pack up our tents and head off wherever their captain desired. I answered the shaman and my first mate standing next to him that I would tell them where to go, then went to the dwarf tent and gave an elixir of regeneration to the crippled chef. I waved off the words of gratitude that followed, saying the chef had earned this potion with his bravery in battle.

Then the camp was packed up. The orcs

dismantled their tents and put out the fires. My tent was one of the first to go. I was standing and watching them work when I got a sharp tug on my sleeve and turned around.

Darius and Darina, now in human form, were standing before me. They were wearing dirty torn villager clothing, a far cry from the expensive aristocratic costumes the werewarg teens normally wore in the daytime.

"Our master and alpha," came Darius, beginning the conversation with a strange flair for the dramatic," my sister and I humbly request the right to leave the pack!"

My eyebrows shot up in surprise. I was intending to immediately give a negative answer, but then Darina hurriedly jumped into the conversation, pushing her brother aside:

"Mr. Amra, our strength and agility have grown a lot with your pack and we are grateful for that. But at the same time, we're growing up, which causes certain problems. In animal form, we cannot think like humans..."

"Yes, that is true," her brother cut into the conversation again. "At night, I see only a young female in heat, not my sister, and it is very hard for me to overcome my animal instincts. Alpha, nothing irreversible has happened yet, so we ask you for permission to let us return to our lands, where we can find others of our own kind. Or at least let one of us go, and the other can remain with you in the day as a servant and helper, and at night as a fanged warrior..."

"I'd die of sorrow without my brother! Master, I beg you to let us both go," the girl interrupted her brother, "the *Tipsy Gannet* will soon go out to sea, and the sailors don't know anything about our beast forms. I spoke with them. They're willing to take us to the nearest port, but only if our master agrees. In such simple villager's clothing, we won't attract any attention and can disappear into the mass of people."

Mission received: Children of Wargs
Mission class: Rare, racial
Description: Come to a decision on Darius and Darina's fate
You may:
- *Keep both wargs in the Gray Pack: +2 to Gray Pack member limit, +3 Animal Control, -15 to warg opinion*
- *Keep one warg in the Gray Pack: +10000 Exp., +1 Animal Control, -5 to warg opinion*
- *Let both wargs go: -2 to Gray Pack member limit, +25 to warg opinion, variable reward*

I read the conditions over and over, but couldn't come to a decision.

On the one hand, if I gave in to the teens'

request, the Gray Pack wouldn't only lose two very strong members, but every remaining member would get weaker by twenty percent due to the reduced Pack Hunter effect. And that was to say nothing of the fact that both Darius and Darina had practically reached level fifty and would get their second perk fairly soon. After that, the wargs would only grow more useful and versatile. Some vague, variable reward was hardly enough to recoup all the negative effects of such a choice, while I was lukewarm on a +25 to warg opinion, given there would be no more such predators in the Gray Pack.

Leave one in the pack? That would give me a pitiful +1 Animal Control, which I'd get fairly soon anyway. Ten thousand experience was almost unnoticeable for my character, especially given this curse of -77% experience received. I'd be getting nothing but crumbs. Also, having all wargs think less of me was unpleasant.

Leave them both? At first glance, it was the best choice, purely based on game considerations. I'd get a sharp spike in Animal Control skill, but most important was two new slots in the Gray Pack and a strengthening of my predators by 20% from the Pack Hunter perk. My relationship with the wargs would be spoiled, of course, but that was absolutely nothing in comparison with the pluses. It seemed to be an obvious choice. However, it looked totally different in light of what Darius and

~ A Trap for the Potentate ~

Darina had told me. I had no idea how I could look Darina in the eyes when she inevitably got pregnant from incest. Also, the promised +2 to Gray Pack members would be occupied by practically useless newborn pups at level zero, the product of an immoral liaison between brother and sister. But if there weren't any free slots for the children in the Gray Pack... I immediately remembered Blanca eating her young. Would Darina eat her children or drown them? I didn't know, and I definitely didn't want to find out.

Ugh... I took a heavy sigh. My little sister, who was calculating and sometimes even cynical, would kill me when she found out about my decision, driven purely by emotion, but I had made my choice:

"Darius, Darina, I release you from the Gray Pack! Take this coin purse. You'll need the money for your journey. I'll speak with the captain of the *Tipsy Gannet* and tell him to bring you to the port of your choosing, as long as it's on their route. I wish you luck in the search for your compatriots!"

New Patch

"**Y**OU'VE LOST your mind, Timothy!" my boss was clearly not overjoyed by my newest video clip.

And my director had plenty of reason to get worked up. In today's video report, I told the viewers that, on a mission from the corporation, I was playing a vampire, and checking to see if one could now live while infected with porphyria in *Boundless Realm*. I even showed scenes of me using Vampire Bite, when my flap-eared goblin had struck down the gigantic praying mantis and royal cobra. I said the truth in my video clip and nothing but, but I didn't put any special emphasis on when my character had become a vampire. That little hidden fact was meant to make my viewers think Amra had been infected with vampirism quite recently, when he successfully passed the Great Hunt and the corporation offered to make him a tester employee.

The night's harsh battle in the swamps, the Rat King, Olilissa and the Dark Rider were also quality and interesting material for the viewers, but they were still dim in comparison with player reaction to the news there was another vampire in the game. Based on the more than eighteen thousand views in the first two hours, the fact that someone was openly announcing their vampirism had aroused great interest in the players. But my boss clearly did not like Amra having such ill-gotten glory. However, I couldn't help but notice that Max Tohner was trying to hold back and treat me with as much respect as possible. And now, with a cup of coffee in hand, he was leaning back in his seat and carrying on in a calm tone, trying his best to curse as little as possible.

"Timothy, you're a valuable employee, and you create unique and interesting content, but that is not your main job as a tester. You're a Goblin Herbalist, and you're supposed to be emphasizing the advantages of that very combination of race and class. And let me note that, up until now, you've been doing a decent job. There are now three and a half thousand Goblin Herbalists in *Boundless Realm*. Not all of them are having such brilliant success as your Amra but, overall, your gameplay has shown the viability of such a combination of race and class. The forum even has a separate thread called Goblin Herbalist where players discuss the best choice of skills and weaponry, and share advice and useful experience. You're a great authority there and an example to be imitated, as the first to discover this approach, so it would be nice to see you going on the forum to answer questions, and give commentary and advice to your followers from time to time."

I promised my boss to support the Goblin Herbalists as much as my free time and energy allowed, and the director bubbled with enthusiasm. He even promised to get me moderator rights for that section of the official forum, so I could make sure it stayed orderly.

After that, the topic of discussion returned to vampirism. I explained my thinking to my boss, saying it seemed relatively safe to reveal my secret here in the wild remote parts of *Boundless Realm*, because vampire hunters would not drag their asses so far afield, and would most likely wait for me to return to the more densely populated world. And in fact, I might never return, or I could use clandestine methods in populated places, so no one would recognize me. So, I didn't see a particular problem for my goblin vampire, but the plusses from increased player interest in Amra and his video reports was obvious.

"That's all true, Timothy, if not for one

~ A Trap for the Potentate ~

'but...'" Max Tohner said, setting his empty mug down and looking at me with a sour face. "It was a bone-headed move on my part to send you up the river Styx! Of all the hard-to-access parts of *Boundless Realm*, I chose the worst. I could have sent you to Dragon Ridge, or the Shifting Sands of Etta, the Ancient Swamps or Rainforest of the Amazons. Those places don't see a single living player for months at a time and they all have thousands and thousands of square kilometers of territory. But the upper Styx is exactly where we're preparing a big new event with creatures of darkness invading the game world and soon, it will be an arena for high-stakes battles! I myself only found that out last night in a meeting about the new patch with the marketing team. Soon, a new game update will come out, and its most distinctive element will be a mass scale event that will touch all *Boundless Realm*! We expect tens and even hundreds of thousands of players to come, including some of the strongest clans, to make war against the army of the Dark Sovereign for fun and glory, unique missions and legendary items. And on the way, they're bound to chance across your Amra who, as of today, will be known to all *Boundless Realm* as a vampire!"

Mhm... I guess that turned out less than ideal. I was in complete agreement with the director here. However, it was too late to change my plans now. I had told my viewers for the past three days about my desire to do the impossible and reach the upper Styx. They were already buzzing with the idea. I'd wasted a huge amount of money and power to organize this expedition, dragging my friends and sister along with me so, on my end, it felt wrong to turn tail.

What was more, the director had just shared a company secret, and I wasn't supposed to know about the contents of the new game update in advance, so I could not be suspecting that loads of players would soon be flooding into the lands around the Styx. And now, If I were to cancel my expedition before the patch, or try to leave the potentially crowded areas, the players would have lots of very unpleasant questions for the corporation, which would just put more fuel on the fire of rumors that tester employees were privileged over normal players.

And that was exactly what I said to my boss. Max Tohner considered it, then frowned and was forced to agree. We could easily expect the players to react negatively.

"Your expedition up the Styx must go on! And given that you already represent our corporation in the mind of most players, let's think of a way to help you within the rules and without breaking the game mechanics. The battle last night came at a great effort, and the monsters will only get stronger from there. It won't look great, if an official tester has to stop so early and can't even get as far as dozens of previous expeditions."

I considered it, then asked the director for some advice on how to find information in the game about a unique object, if it hadn't been detected at any auctions, described in the forum, or found in the game knowledge base.

"That's pretty weird," my boss said, frowning. "Information about new unique and legendary objects is added to the knowledge base automatically when a player discovers an item. The name of the owner, item properties and acquisition conditions won't be visible, but it should be in the database. Are you sure you looked thoroughly?"

I gave a short nod, not wanting to go into detail on my sister and I's efforts to find the components of Fenrir's Cursed Regalia.

"If the item is dropped by an NPC monster or rewarded after a quest, the Traders' Guild should be able to track it down," Max Tohner suggested another option. "If sufficient money is offered for the service, the traders will dig through all regional markets and auctions of *Boundless Realm*, look up the logs of big battles, check through freight lists from customs agents in all ports, and search in a few other places as well. In the end, you won't always get accurate information, but at least a broad estimate of where the item may be located. That takes time, though... What are you even looking for?"

"I need information about the sixth object from Fenrir's Cursed Regalia. Most likely, it's a helmet, because I already know about the other items, which form a set of armor. The name should probably mention Fenrir or wolves, but that's not certain. At the very least, I didn't find anything relevant from a knowledge-base search."

Max Tohner quickly typed a command on his keyboard, pressed enter and spent a long time staring at the monitor. After that, he shook his head shortly, drummed his fingers in thought on the tabletop and led an absent gaze around the office.

His gaze stopped on his assistant Tina, who was bent over in an overly short skirt as she dug through a filing cabinet.

"Ah, what about my assistant? Let's give her the mission! This is a good chance for Tina to get some experience using service tools. She shouldn't just be pouring coffee all the time! I promise, Timothy, that by this evening you will have all relevant information about Fenrir's helmet or, tomorrow, I'll have a new secretary!"

I repeated what I knew about the item to Tina, and she promised to have the info by this evening.

Max Tohner gave a satisfied nod, again typing a service command on his keyboard, and turned his monitor so I could see the screen.

"Now let's look at your character together."

- A Trap for the Potentate -

Name	Amra
Race	Goblin Vampire
Class	Herbalist
Experience	1062111 of 1112000
Character level	51
Hit points	2586/2586
Endurance ιts	1869/2172
Statistics	
Strength (S)	103 (403)
Agility (A)	105 (308.4)
Intelligence (I)	5 (25.8)
Constitution (C)	105 (430.5)
Perception (P)	3 (63.5)
Charisma (Ch)	100 (125)
Unused points	**0**
Primary skills (7 of 7 chosen)	
Herbalis m (P A)	27

	Trading (Ch I)	25
	Alchemy (I A)	29
	Dodging (A P)	23
	Stealth (A C)	30
	Exotic Weapons (A P)	16
	Riding (A C)	21
Secondary skills (6 of 7 chosen)		
	Veil	16
	Acrobatics	20
	Athletics	20
	Foreman	46
	Animal Control	32
	Warchief	4

First of all, my boss wanted to know why I still hadn't taken one secondary skill. I answered that the next slot was reserved for a weapon that used Strength, and that I was still thinking about it. That answer didn't satisfy my director at all:

"Well, that's stupid! There are lots of weapons that use Strength in the Exotic Weapon category: all kinds of sickles and bolases not only for throwing, but also for melee. There are even kukri and karambits that are governed by Exotic Weapon, not Dagger. Sure, such weapons aren't especially commonplace, but they can easily be found at auctions and, as a rule, the price is acceptable due to low demand. Why should you waste a valuable slot for a weapon skill, when you already have one that gets little use?!"

I promised my boss to think over his suggestion and search for something appropriate to my Amra at auction. Max Tohner then grumbled a bit about my weak skill leveling for a level fifty-one character, expressed satisfaction at the increase in my Herbalism, and then ended the meeting.

The director was purposely avoiding bringing up Taisha and, every time I mentioned my goblin companion, he immediately steered the conversation in another direction. What could I do? I didn't insist, especially because I didn't know what was going on with Taisha now and was seriously worried for her. But still, I asked the director to give me another few minutes.

"Today, along with a few others, I finished the Children of Wargs quest. It gave me a serious debuff, reducing the number of pets I can control, a minor improvement of my relationship with wargs and nothing more. In the mission conditions, there was a variable reward listed, but it seems I didn't get it."

"Let's check..." the director turned the monitor away from me again and started using the service console to enter commands, spent a long time looking at something on the screen, then his lips stretched into a smile. "No, everything is correct, Timothy. There's already a reward coming your way, you just haven't gotten it. I won't tell you what it is exactly. Let that be a pleasant surprise for you. Very pleasant."

* * *

Valeria was in a great mood when I came in and was combing her stylish long hair, sitting on the bed next to a cracked opened window. I saw a dish on the bedside table with peeled mandarins, sliced apples and kiwis.

"Kira came by," my sister commented, having seen my interest in the fruits. "We spent a whole hour walking around the hospital garden together and talking about all sorts of stuff. She said goodbye just a half hour ago and went off to do something."

Woah! Very positive news. That meant that, despite the fight with me, Kira was still talking with my sister. And had Kira perhaps asked about the goblin thief girl Taisha? It was hardly plausible of course because, technically, my sister thought her new friend was the owner of a designer fashion store, not a highly experienced tester for the *Boundless Realm* Corporation and the most powerful Queen of the Harpies. But how great would it be if they had! After all, Val was one of the few who could say how extremely unusual the NPC girl was, and that would be the beginning of Kira and I making up. As if out of nowhere, I asked Valeria what they'd talked about.

"Fashion, dresses, modern art and literature, all kinds of ladies' secrets... it would have bored you to death. We also spent a long time talking about my new biotic legs. The operation is scheduled for the day after tomorrow, then I'll have to spend two days laying on a special hospital table, stuck full of wires and all kinds of readers while the doctors make sure my body doesn't reject the devices. So, for three or four days I'll be out of the game and you'll have to get by in *Boundless Realm* without my help."

The news was a double-edged sword. At first, I didn't know how to react. Of course, I was strangely glad that my beloved sister would finally get legs, but... it was such bad timing! I suppressed my annoyance. I couldn't be so egotistic! No virtual game or quests were worth Valeria's tears! So, I put on a happy expression for Val and reassured her. She was a bit nervous before the upcoming operation.

We took a walk in the hospital garden. Valeria simply clicked "repeat previous route" on the console of her wheelchair and it followed the paths on its own. Its rubber wheels gave a slight whirr on the white sand. We spoke exclusively about *Boundless Realm*, especially what had happened this morning and our plans for the evening.

This morning, when Valerianna Quickfoot had entered the game, she had convinced me, Max Sochnier and Shrekson Bastard to try and have the NPC orcs move automatically on the map. The naiad and the ogre were not too happy to exit the game when they'd basically just entered, but they still agreed to give it a shot. The ogre quickly hacked together four sedan chairs, where we undying sat down and I chose the very strongest orcs to carry them on their shoulders.

I placed a target on the map for Ziabash Hardy where it read Lower Fort, a fortification on the very edge of the lands of the savage rougarou. What kind of fort it was, who built it, and if someone lived in it now I did not know. All the same, the forest nymph confirmed that it would be a decent place for us to spend the night, because many expeditions had used it before. The fort was seventy-two kilometers away and, by my calculations, the squadron of NPC orcs should reach it before it got dark outside.

- A Trap for the Potentate -

Everything was ready for the expedition, but Max Sochnier asked us to wait a bit before we left, because he was waiting for his nephew to come back. I didn't understand how the Human Healer would be getting back to us after dying in last night's battle and respawning who-knows-where, but the Naiad Trader said it was possible:

"Antonius Just can create magical scrolls, and he told me he made a teleportation scroll to this orc camp, just in case he happened to die. I figured that, in the morning, my nephew would already be back but, for some reason, he just isn't coming..."

Max Sochnier even left the game to figure out the reason for the delay. He came back a few minutes later, angry as a devil:

"Antonius Just won't be coming, he changed his mind. He said there's some interesting stuff going on in his clan and he'd rather do that."

Unlike my friend, I was more glad than upset. Antonius Just gave me a kneejerk feeling of anxiety and mistrust, so I wouldn't be missing his company one bit. The orcs lifted the sedan chairs and started on their way. I left *Boundless Realm* not long after, as did all the other undying.

And now, walking around the park, my sister and I were actively discussing the game and worrying about our army's progress. Had they gone anywhere, or were they just staying in place? There was no way to go in during the day and check. It would immediately violate the whole concept of moving safely through the desolate, unpopulated lands of *Boundless Realm* because, in the presence of a live observer, it would load the whole dangerous location with all the obstacles, thick swamps, dense thickets and deadly monsters.

My sister assured me that there was nothing unusual in moving this way. Once before, we had traveled on the dwarf train and, on reentering the game, we'd found ourselves in a moving vehicle, not where we'd exited *Boundless Realm*. Also, when traveling by ship, we hadn't just shown up in the middle of the open ocean where we'd left the game, but in our cabin. In theory, our situation was no different from those previous examples. All in all, my sister managed to convince me there was nothing to worry about, and she was right. But Valeria started beating herself up over a different issue: she didn't know about the rare sickles, kukri and other Exotic Weapons that used Strength.

"I was planning to waste your last skill slot for such a stupid thing... I nearly hobbled your character, Timothy! I'm a worthless advisor..."

I reassured my sister saying everything was fine, it wasn't too late, and we had acquired valuable knowledge about the game. Nevertheless, Valeria's mood was ruined. My sister took her mistake very hard and suggested we go back to her hospital room, where she could search auctions on her tablet, and immediately order something for delivery to the Lower Fort.

* * *

I didn't even manage to enter the corporation skyscraper before an armed guard standing at the entrance hurried to leave his post and blocked my path.

"Not so fast! I have an order from the Security Service to bring you to their office. It's right here on the first floor. Follow me."

A thousand worrisome thoughts were spinning in my head. I tried to imagine why I'd caught their interest. I really hoped I hadn't unknowingly broken a corporate rule, or accidentally spent another player's money on a real-world purchase. Come on, I basically only made purchases with prize money from the sale of Great Hunt tokens. Or was it somehow connected with Kira? I was reminded that her guard team was composed of Security Service employees.

As it turned out, it wasn't the first, second or third option. Once in the office, an elderly man with a mustache in a Security Service uniform immediately cheered me up by saying that they'd followed up on my inquiry, done some checking and, as a result, two members of the Grave Worms had been exposed and detained. Both of them had been hired by the *Boundless Realm* Corporation for a trial period in different departments within the last few days. Next to me, a projector was displaying the faces of the two young men on the wall.

They were clearly immigrants from the Middle East and, in a certain degree, even resembled one another. It was the first time I'd seen one of them, but I recognized the second immediately. He was the guy I'd bumped into in the revolving door to the corporation building, who I had crossed paths with a few times in the criminal neighborhood. That was exactly what I told the man.

The gray-haired security guard gave a nod of satisfaction, then told me that both of them had already been interrogated, and everything I said was confirmed:

"The ringleaders of the Grave Worms have promised seven thousand credits to whoever can kill you, and this information is known in the whole neighborhood. It's a very, very significant sum, from what I understand. What's more, they'll let anyone do the killing, it doesn't have to be someone in their gang..."

Seven thousand was a huge amount of money for the vast majority of people in this city, not just those who lived in poor neighborhoods. I immediately felt extremely uncomfortable, seeing a gun in the man's belt holster. It seemed the guard also sensed that, because he gave a kind-hearted chuckle and continued:

"Timothy, your personal file is secret, and I would need a special permission to access it. But from what I could get my hands on, you've had some unpleasant run-ins with this gang before. Their desire to get revenge and punish is basically easy to understand. But both people we arrested told us independently that whoever wants you dead had an extremely unusual condition: you were only to be killed while inside a virtual reality capsule. Only in that case would the seven thousand be paid out. In all others, the assassin would be tortured to death. This is the first time I've come up against anything like it in my practice. I'll admit, I'm at a loss. Maybe you have some of your own ideas about who might have put out such an unusual hit?"

No, I had no idea. Maybe the Grave Worms wanted to demonstrate that even the most powerful protectors couldn't keep runaways from payback? All in all, I didn't understand at all, either. The mustached guard took a disappointed sigh and slumped his shoulders. It seemed he was hoping I could help him solve the riddle. After promising me that, from now on, all new hires would be checked for ties to the Grave Worms, the man wished me a good shift and let me go.

* * *

"Come in, Timothy," the assistant to the head of the Special Projects Division joyfully threw open the doors before me. "Mr. Tohner just left, but I found all the necessary information for you! Would you like some coffee?"

I didn't refuse, and told Tina she was amazing, along with some other words of admonition for her spending work time on my problems.

"And what is the name of the sixth item from Fenrir's Cursed Regalia?" I inquired while the girl was making coffee, not hiding my impatience.

"The Mask of Fenrir!" Tina answered readily but, seeing me reach for my smartphone, she rebuffed me. "Don't search for it, Timothy. It's no use. The object isn't in the knowledge-base, because it was never added to the game."

"How's that?" I asked, simultaneously surprised and horrified.

What did that mean? My grand dream of gathering all six items from Fenrir's Cursed Regalia was impossible even in theory??? But Tina clearly did not consider the conversation over, nor her discovery pointless. More likely, it was the opposite. The girl was overflowing with enthusiasm. She handed me a cup of coffee and sat in a chair opposite mine, crossed her legs and said with a satisfied smile:

~ A Trap for the Potentate ~

"So then, Timothy. You won't be able to squirm out of a serious conversation. One hundred thousand credits, and the item can be in your inventory today."

I nearly spit out my coffee. One hundred thousand?! She'd lost her mind! But Tina didn't think so:

"The price is totally justified, considering how much getting the whole set is worth to you. Just so you know, without my help, the item will never exist in the game. So, think carefully."

I was sitting in the chair, drinking the strong coffee in small sips, not rushing to answer. One hundred thousand! That was a huge amount of money by any standards. I didn't want to waste the money, but that wasn't even the problem I was fearfully displeased by the whole situation. It just looked too much like the old scandal with the wyvern egg, where Alexandro Lavrius had tried to put an item into the game by unsporting means and give it to a certain player as a payoff. I knew perfectly that that story had ended quite badly for all the employees with unclean hands.

What was more, I couldn't write off the possibility that there was no sixth object, and I was now just being tested to make sure I followed the rules. My agreement to this unclean deal could lead to instant loss of employment and an accusation of theft of the corporation's virtual property. But maybe my fears were overstated and, by refusing, I was missing my last chance to get the whole set.

Seeing that I was in no rush to answer, Tina continued:

"The Mask of Fenrir was not put into the game, because they haven't finished calculating what might happen if one player got all six objects. At the very least, that was how it was explained to me by tech support. Basically, from what they said, the idea of Fenrir's Regalia came spontaneously and wasn't thought through all the way. But our programmers have created the mask. It has a unique number, so it would be a small matter to put the object into the game with service commands."

While Tina was speaking, I finally made my choice:

"No, Tina. I refuse to acquire the object by dishonest means. It isn't worth the helmet itself, nor even the whole set to be booted out of work, and also be accused of stealing the corporation's virtual property!"

"Great decision, Timothy!" I then leapt up in surprise when a raspy woman's voice rang out from a seemingly inactive computer. I quickly realized that someone else was carefully listening to our conversation via webcam. "Tina, you should have asked for a smaller amount! I told you like thirty or forty thousand, where'd you come up with one hundred thousand all of a sudden?!"

~ A Trap for the Potentate ~

The girl shuddered in fear and lowered her head in shame. I then finally recognized the voice coming from the speakers. It was Inessa Tyle, Vice President of the *Boundless Realm* Corporation, one of the richest women on the planet and Kira's very own grandmother. So, this really was a test?! I didn't even know if I should get mad at my highly-placed superior for such a guileful examination or be happy that, with some sixth sense, I managed to root out the trick and had not taken the bait. And meanwhile, Inessa Tyle said in a raspy old-lady's voice:

"Timothy, forgive this old bat for the little show. I want to see you in my office. You do remember how to get here, I hope?"

I confirmed that I did, and headed straight for the exit so I wouldn't keep such an important person waiting. And when I said goodbye to Tina, I saw a strange and complicated mixture of admiration, curiosity and sadness. It seemed that my boss's assistant didn't know I was already familiar with the second person in the *Boundless Realm* Corporation. As a perspective suitor, I had just grown significantly in her eyes but, Tina now must have thought her chances of getting with me were much lower.

* * *

This time, there was more than enough vigilant

security on the seventy-seventh floor of the skyscraper. I had to go through several guard posts, where I was X-rayed and searched before being allowed to pass into a room with glass walls where I was already awaited by the gray-haired lady lounging in a deep armchair. The elderly woman was wrapped up tight in a warm shawl. For some reason, I didn't notice right away how severely the old lady's fingers were shaking.

"Normally, I greet guests on my feet but, for some reason, I'm tired today..." the lady said in response to my polite greeting.

In fact, Inessa Tyle did not look too healthy. She was in no way reminiscent of the nimble vivacious woman who had been feeding fish with her own hands on my last visit. Now, she really seemed like a ninety-year-old woman, not trying to hide her age or artificially rejuvenate herself.

"Let me beg your apology again for that little test of honesty. In my defense, I can say that I studied your detailed dossier fairly well, which included a psychological portrait, and I had no doubt in your honesty. Overall, if I had been wrong about you..." Inessa Tyle gave a predatory smile, showing her perfectly maintained teeth, "let's just say I really don't like when people disappoint me..."

I didn't answer although, mentally, I was surprised that the vice president of a huge corporation wanted to acquaint herself with the personal dossier of one of her many thousands of employees. I'll admit, I still didn't understand why I aroused such stubborn attention of the upper leadership, and that frightened me. Meanwhile, Inessa Tyle continued her speech:

"You see, Timothy, Fenrir's Cursed Regalia was created on my direct orders. And I was also the exact person who reversed that decision and prevented one of the items from being added to the game, because I wasn't sure of the consequences. I didn't want to take all the responsibility for the fact that the huge pack of predators was back, and could threaten all *Boundless Realm*. Last time, it took the coordinated efforts of twenty-eight thousand players to get the better of the threat. But this time, it won't be a program controlling the Gray Pack, but a living player, who's tricky, smart and unpredictable! Who knows where that might lead?!"

It seemed she was trying to convince me that I was in too great a rush to collect Fenrir's Cursed Regalia and had failed, because the full set would never appear in game. I needed to immediately intervene and convince Inessa Tyle, otherwise my dream threatened to remain unfulfilled. Choosing my words carefully, I tried to express myself to the important Vice President:

"But from what I've heard, the global event with Fenrir was praised very highly by corporate leadership. The predatory, uncatchable pack forced players to leave the cities, which they were sick to death of, gave birth to a number of clans and forced them to act together, keeping several regions in a state of agitation, adding precisely what the users craved: intrigue, excitement, and an element of danger. As far as I know, all corporate employees who took part in the mass event got significant bonuses, and some even got promoted. Meanwhile, the experience of creating intelligence algorithms for the Gray Pack is what allowed the programmers to make Taisha, a next-generation NPC!"

The gray-haired lady smiled a somewhat tortured smile and pressed a button on the armrest of her chair. A young woman immediately entered the room with a deep bow and placed a glass of shimmering bubbly lemon-colored liquid on the table before Inessa. The Vice President waited for her to leave, took a small sip and continued:

"My heart is acting up... Anyway, back to the conversation. Timothy, your view of the Fenrir event is too positive. It wasn't all so smooth, even though there were lots of worthwhile moments. The programmers created a force so strong the players couldn't ignore it. Reining it in was quite difficult. The main feature of the pack is that it quickly restored its losses by adding more NPC predators, while the program controlling it was self-teaching and took its errors into account.

~ A Trap for the Potentate ~

There were times when it seemed the power they created was out of control and growing without limit, so the only way of solving it was to artificially shut it down. But the players eventually handled it on their own. It was all they could talk about on the news for many days. It was quite the uproar..."

Inessa Tyle went silent, thinking in agitation. I was just trying not to bother the Vice President.

"Maybe you're right, Timothy," the old lady said in the end. "The idea of a living player as the new Fenrir really is not so bad. What's more, you'll clearly need the forces where you're heading. Higher up the Styx there are more territories of the Dark Sovereign, the new uber-boss of *Boundless Realm*. That said, our designers and programmers are still working on him, so he isn't in the game yet, but his armies are already large in number, and his underlings are not very welcoming. You've met one of them already, so you have experience!"

I raised my head in surprise, and Inessa Tyle laughed with an old lady's voice:

"Yes, yes, Timothy, don't be surprised. I have been attentively watching all your video clips. Vampire, owner of a flying snake, alpha of the Gray Pack, commander of an army of Orc Pirates and the legal husband of an NPC thief... It's created a very unusual cocktail! But you still aren't living up to your potential. All in all, Timothy, I'm not against you becoming the reincarnation of Fenrir, but I'll only allow it under the condition that the Gray Pack will not attack cities or come to the most populated regions of *Boundless Realm*. All the same, no matter how you spin it, the vast majority of our players prefer peaceful gameplay, crafting, trade, and easy questing... Such players bring the company most of its money, and there's no reason to saw off the branch we're all sitting on."

I confirmed to the vice president that I understood everything perfectly and was not planning to break the game world, which most players liked just the way it was. And after that, I cautiously inquired why Inessa Tyle thought the new Fenrir had to be me. Say what you will, but I had only three out of the six Fenrir items, and some other player could easily start trying to collect them all as well.

The old lady in the chair drank down her medicine and placed the glass on the table. After that, she leaned in my direction and said:

"I would never allow someone I didn't know to collect the whole set. But I like you. You're proper and honest. You help your friends and sister, and you aren't even remotely selfish. So, I feel like an old tortoise trying to give a golden key to a mischievous lad that's caught my fancy. Have you ever heard of Tortila?"

I shook my head "no," as this was the first time I'd heard such a name. It seemed Inessa Tyle was somewhat upset:

~ A Trap for the Potentate ~

"Mhm... I sometimes forget that I'm a prehistoric dinosaur who's outlived my epoch. Modern youth don't know about Buratino... Anyway, it doesn't matter. As far as I know, only you could have gotten several of the Fenrir items, and found out about the bonuses by doing so. The rest of the players see only cursed items, which are very hard to take off, so they don't seem particularly valuable. Anyhow, I don't see the sense in wasting time throwing the Mask of Fenrir up for auction, or giving it to anyone else. You'll get your hands on it eventually no matter what. It'll just cost you time and money. So, I'll have that girl you were talking to in the office add the Mask of Fenrir to your inventory."

Would you look at that! I'll be honest, I could barely hold back from hugging and kissing the sweet old lady. I was overflowing with the wildest elation! Inessa Tyle, who had easily guessed my emotions, smiled good-heartedly.

"You heard about one of the other objects from the Djinn Sultan. It's a bit far away, of course, but your flying snake will be able to get you there. The last object in the set is now located in Taisha's inventory. A few days ago, I'd have said that meant it was already yours, but I'm not so sure anymore..."

"Why not?" I asked in surprise. The Vice President's assertion both made me glad and confused.

"You see, Timothy, Taisha feels quite happy in the *Legion of Steel* and seems to be satisfied with life. Yes, I know you and her having certain understandings, but it's been two days since then, and lots has changed. Your girl has grown a lot in level and skill, made a bunch of new friends and acquaintances and may not want to return after so much time with the 'stars' of the game. And there is one more reason for my doubts, of a totally different nature. The In-Game Security Service has traced a few phone calls from *Boundless Realm* and believes it may have been your green girlfriend that hired the killers!"

Now that was a twist... The news was clearly shocking, although I believed the Vice President at once, because it explained the strange fact that I was supposed to be murdered while in my virtual reality capsule. It seemed my NPC wife had made the wrong conclusions from Valeria's recent suicide attempt and wanted to make my Amra stay in *Boundless Realm* forever!

Lower Fort

I DON'T REMEMBER leaving the Vice President's office, it was like I was in a cloud. I hope I at least said goodbye to Inessa Tyle, although I was not totally sure of that. All my thoughts were occupied with what she'd said about Taisha. How could my virtual girlfriend have dared to treat me that way?!

On the tester floor, Leon and Max Sochnier were already waiting for me. The clock was showing seven thirty PM and, theoretically, our orcs already should have been nearing the Lower Fort.

"You're late, Timothy," Leon reproached me. "You said we'd meet at seven twenty, and then all log in together at seven thirty."

I didn't try to defend myself or tell them I'd

been on an urgent call to the VP. Instead, I suggested we not waste time and load up the game. In my work cabin, I didn't even have dinner, even though I hadn't eaten anything today except a light breakfast, and my stomach was slightly groaning in hunger. But there was no time for food now. I had to go into the game.

A message jumped in about a few incoming letters and a package, but I didn't waste time reading them, having decided to handle the correspondence later. The letters had probably, after all, come from players who wanted to kill the rare vampire in the game, and were making me offers. And the package probably contained the spiky ball on a strong metal chain my sister and I had chosen today as my goblin's exotic melee weapon.

So then, loading. The world lit up. I saw myself sitting on a sedan-chair on the ground. All around were some hurriedly nailed-together wooden buildings. Over my head was the evening sky, thick with clouds. Next to me was a whole horde of orcs and wolves with a friendly opinion of me. Meanwhile, on the mini-map, there were fifteen unknown players in my immediate vicinity!!!

I shuddered in surprise, seeing so many undying next to my Amra. Who were they? Were they just here by coincidence... I saw a clan tag reading [LIGHT] next to a few names. It couldn't be pure chance then. These people were from the same clan as Antonius Just, the Human Healer I had a firm mistrust of. These players had clearly come for my head. So, I acted more intuitively than consciously:

"Orcs, on the attack!!! Take them all down!!!"

Warchief skill increased to level 5!

Foreman skill increased to level 47!

It probably would have been good to at least take a closer look at the enemy for a start, see their levels and classes, but I was hoping to catch them by surprise. And it turned out to be the right decision. It was all over in just twenty seconds. I didn't even manage to take part in the battle and try out the fearsome-looking spiky metal ball on a chain, which I found a step from me. The dozen confused players didn't have time to get any serious resistance together and were literally torn to shreds by the horde of bloodthirsty orcs and the Gray Pack, rushing in from all sides. I barely managed to stop my warriors before they took down two inactive players, who were standing slightly aside, clearly away from their computers.

"Tie them up!" I ordered my cutthroats, pointing to the undying prisoners. "I'll interrogate them later. Where's our Ogre Fortifier?"

Shrekson Bastard ran up to me, looking

somewhat strange and even funny in the dark armor suit with two head-holes. I saw a bloodied hammer in the titan's hands and the bright red Criminal marker over his head. Our ogre had managed to "caress" one of the enemies with his frightening sledgehammer. And it should be said that the Naiad, the forest nymph and I also had such markers over our heads.

"Leon, I see a respawn stone right here in our fort on the mini-map and, probably, all of the people we just killed managed to change their respawn point there. You've got just an hour to surround the whole area with sharpened stakes! Don't let any of the undying respawn! If need be, let Max Sochnier and Valerianna Quickfoot help you. I might join up a bit later. And don't count on the other members of the squadron helping you out. NPC's cannot come near."

"Great idea, big-ears!" the forest nymph supported me. "But there are two things I'd like to know. First: how are you able to hand out quests left and right? Just now, me the ogre and the naiad got a group, time-limited quest. And at that, the reward is so generous that we now have no choice but to try. And second, how were these enemy players able to track us down?!"

"Nothing to fear," the Naiad Trader jumped into our conversation, wiping blood from his trident. "As I already said, my nephew has the ability to create magical scrolls, and he could have made portals here for his clan. Or maybe they still had some left from their previous unsuccessful expedition."

Most likely, that was exactly what had happened. But as far as I knew, all teleportation-scroll copies made from one original could open a portal only to one specific point. That meant we needed to find that point and go there to meet the guests with traps and spears at the ready. First, I tried to use my wolves' sense of smell, and my Perception to determine where exactly the players had shown up. But I met with failure. Everything inside the small fort was densely trodden, so I couldn't follow the footprints. But then I got a better idea.

I walked up to the two bound players, a level-88 Bowman, and a level-95 Paladin. Both were inactive as before, but that wasn't what I needed now. I twirled the spiked ball in my hands with doubt, and decided to put my new weapon in my inventory. I might accidentally kill the prisoners that way... Instead, I took out my dagger and made a small wound on the bowman's neck, lowering his health-bar by a quarter. It wasn't deadly, but it was immediately noticeable. I activated my Veil icon immediately, changing the logs. Here was the log the player would have seen:

Damage taken: 331 (418 Dagger strike — 87 armor)

But I changed it to something else entirely, much more worrisome:

Damage taken: 331 (418 Vampire Bite — 87 armor)

ATTENTION!!! Your character has been infected with vampirism
You have just 48 hours to cure the disease, otherwise the effect will become permanent, and you will become a bloodthirsty vampire!!!

Veil skill increased to level 17!

I did the same with the bound paladin, then ordered the four orcs to guard the prisoners and immediately tell me if they woke up or moved. I then met with Ziabash Hardy and ordered my first mate to guard the fort, placing sentries on the walls and assigning posts and shifts. I told him to also make sure the rest of the soldiers were well fed and would be sent to the different buildings to get some sleep.

After Ziabash Hardy left, I found myself in calm circumstances, so I set about studying the Mask of Fenrir, which had already been added to my inventory. But I froze stock still when I saw the fat chef walking around the camp with heavy bags. Tondik Exuberant still had just a rag-wrapped stump instead of a left hand, and his right was still missing two fingers! How?! Had the Elixir of Regeneration not worked?! I thought the chef would now be making dinner for my orcs, but he was still wounded and could barely handle his duties.

"Captain Amra..." the fat dwarf's only remaining eye was cast down at the ground. The chef clearly didn't know where to begin. "I immediately realized... Here's the thing... Captain, did you know... my neighbor in the tent Gnum Spiteful isn't some gloomy and fearsome mechanic man, but a dwarven lady from an influential family?"

"Of course. I've known that for a long time," I said, not trying to clarify that I had only found that out by coincidence in the subterranean city of Dotur-Khawe. "Wait, Tondik, can't you tell by looking?"

"That's the problem, I couldn't tell..." the fat dwarf grew even more embarrassed. "I thought my neighbor was just a bearded redheaded dwarf, quarrelsome and squat. And that's why I was acting that way. I was rude, swearing, vulgar. We talked about the kind of things one is ashamed to discuss with a girl... What an idiot I must have looked like! But this morning, we started talking about our relatives, and..." Tondik Exuberant took a heavy sigh, "well, I know her family, and quickly realized who it was before me. So, I gave the Elixir of Regeneration to her. A dwarven man can survive with just one eye and one arm, but a pretty girl shouldn't feel mutilated..."

During his speech, Tondik was looking at the floor and couldn't see that Gnum Spiteful had come up to us now on both legs without any crutches, and was carefully listening to the words of her compatriot. Vanessa didn't say anything, just gave Tondik, who'd just noticed her and fallen sharply silent, an approving slap on the shoulder. All the same, from the words that appeared before my eyes, I realized everything would be ok.

Mission renewed: Marrying off a Son
Additional condition completed: Make Tondik Exuberant a well-known dwarf traveler and find him a wife

I asked both dwarves to start making dinner for the whole army, promising to send my "niece and nephew" Irek and Yunna to help them, along with the cleverest orcs in my squadron. We still had plenty of meat, and the orcs had discovered some provisions left behind in a store room by a previous expedition. There were all kinds of vegetables, rings of dried fish, corned beef and a barrel of beer, so there was no chance my warriors would go hungry.

Finally, after dealing with the camp's defense and feeding the soldiers, I took advantage of a free minute and removed the Mask of Fenrir from my inventory. It looked fearsome, like a snarling wolf's snout.

Fenrir's Mask helmet (unique item)
+250 Constitution, +250 Strength, 50% resistance to elemental magic, +50 to reaction of the following: *Demonic creatures, Mythical creatures, Unique creatures*

Attention!
Your character's level is too low to use this object
Requisite level: 125

Just what I was afraid of. I needed a very high level to use the mask. And although I still had two Ifrit Hearts sitting around, which could remove level requirement, there were three more objects in the set...

There was nothing to be done, I'd have to use one of the hearts. I popped the black stone into my mouth, and it gave a beat in my goblin's toothy maw.

You have activated a magical item
You have the choice of what effect you would like to receive:

I removed level requirement from the Mask of Fenrir and strapped the helmet onto my head.

Immediately, my goblin's shoulders grew broader. His muscles even visually grew larger. No matter how I tried to keep my flap-eared Amra small, funny and inoffensive, I was looking less and less that way all the time. My goblin was now bigger and more muscular. Before my eyes then there ran a whole bedsheet of text:

You have equipped four items from Fenrir's Cursed Regalia

Set bonus unlocked: all members of the Gray Pack will receive a bonus of +100 Strength, +100 Agility, +100 Constitution, +75% movement speed, +75% experience gain

Mission completed: Fenrir's Legacy (2/4)

Reward: 25000 Exp., +10 Animal Control, +50 Strength, +50 Agility, +50 Constitution, Gray Pack member limit raised to twelve

The helmet looked very impressive, I could tell that as soon as I opened my character equipment window and looking at my goblin from all angles. The viewers would also like the snarling wolf snout with its scary fangs. But, the bonuses given by the unique object were much more important than appearances. It restored the Gray

- A Trap for the Potentate -

Pack's member limit to twelve, so I now had two free slots for the Gray Pack! And also, I was just a handful of experience points shy of level fifty-two, less than three thousand. If it weren't for the curse, which gave a serious penalty to Amra's experience, I'd have already grown in level.

All the same, I wasn't allowed to spend too long admiring my new item and noticeably increased combat characteristics — the tied-up paladin had come to his senses and I hurried to talk with the captive.

Lancelot Knight_of_the_Round_Table
Human
Level-95 Paladin [LIGHT]

The bound captive didn't look scared at all, more like surprised and slightly pensive. I walked up to the paladin and spoke first, immediately trying to take initiative in the conversation:

"Lancelot... or more likely Sir Lancelot, given that you're a knight... you've most likely already noticed that you've been infected with vampirism. Yes, don't be surprised, I did it on purpose. Your friends were trying to catch a vampire, and now I'll give them that chance. You have been tied up, and cannot escape the vampire hunters. If they did manage to move their respawn point here to the Lower Fort, your clan-mates can have as much fun as their hearts desire, killing a vampire over and over again..."

Lancelot was clearly imagining everything I was telling him in great detail, and he didn't like the perspective. His face reflected not mere fear, but full-blown panic. And while he was in that state, I continued my speech, just working the man over:

"By the way, in the early stages, vampirism is not all that serious and, for the first few hours, the disease is easy to cure. All you'd have to do is drink a Major Elixir of Health or an Elixir of Cure Disease. But if you take too long, the situation will get more complicated. Then, you'll need rare elixirs and purification in temples... Why am I telling you this? Well, I want to propose a deal. You tell me honestly why the members of your clan came to the Lower Fort, and I'll give you a healing elixir. By the way, if you do not agree to negotiate with a vampire for some reason, I have another option," I pointed at the inactive tied up bowman.

Trading skill increased to level 26!

There was no cause for worry. The captive agreed to work with me practically at once. And the more he said, the gloomier Max Sochnier, who was standing next to me, became. My mistrust and suspicion when it came to his nephew was now one hundred percent justified. Yes, all of this activity of the clan *Lifegiving Light* had been organized by none other than Antonius Just, and with just one goal, to capture a vampire player by the name of Amra and give him up to anyone who might want to kill a bloodsucking monster.

From what the paladin said, it remained unclear whether Antonius Just had decided to betray us from the start, or if he'd come to that decision after watching my last video clip where I'd announced my vampirism, but it didn't really matter. What was important was that I had gotten too relaxed and careless, and acted too predictable.

Before, during the Great Hunt, I had always stayed a step ahead of the majority of players, who were easy to predict, making unexpected moves and muddling my tracks. But now, Antonius Just had predicted the route of my army and the place I was most likely to spend the night, the well-defended Lower Fort on the banks of the river Styx. The only thing the traitor had been mistaken about was that he had seriously underestimated the movement speed of my army and supposed the orcs would arrive to the fort at night, along with their vampire chieftain, who should most likely be afraid of sunlight and thus could not appear in *Boundless Realm* until sundown.

The *Lifegiving Light*'s calculation was based on letting me get to the fort and change my respawn point here. After that, they would suddenly open a portal and the whole clan would burst into the fortress to destroy everything alive.

At the same time as that landing party, another fifteen players from the first group were going to log in, having jumped to the fort earlier using just such a portal scroll in order to evaluate the situation on the ground.

"As far as I know, there were other players preparing to jump through the portal together with our clan. The greedy Antonius Just even sold 'tickets' to the vampire hunt. But they were only expecting activity closer to eleven this evening, or maybe even midnight. Who could have thought that you'd get to the fort so early...?"

I asked the paladin, as if in passing, where the portal came out in the fort and was told it was right on top of the respawn stone. Great! That simplified things greatly! The captive couldn't have known about our preparations but, meanwhile, my friends should have been nearly finished booby-trapping the stone. In just a little bit, the unfortunate guests and any players trying to respawn could expect a big surprise!!!

Considering the conversation with the bound prisoner finished, I fed him a whole vial of Elixir of Cure Disease with my own hands in order to imitate healing and not have to explain why he'd never truly be infected with vampirism. Then, I gave a wave to Akella, who was standing nearby, and the Hardened Forest Wolf quickly tore open the throat of the helpless prisoner, sending the paladin to respawn.

~ A Trap for the Potentate ~

Animal Control skill increased to level 43!

Experience received: 4720 Exp.

Level fifty-two!

I noted with satisfaction that my loyal Akella had gone up seven levels from just one lone enemy and was now even higher level than his master. I barely got a few drips of experience for that...I supposed, considering the curse, I needed to do whatever I could so Amra wouldn't share their experience, otherwise it would just disappear into thin air. And as for the "particularly sweet" enemies, I should purposely feed them to the Gray Pack, because my predators were getting a respectable 75% bonus to experience.

Based on those calculations, I didn't help my friends place sharpened stakes around the respawn stone. Let the forest nymph, ogre and naiad share the likely large prize among themselves for the attackers landing in the trap. I told my friends my decision, and found complete understanding. And while my companions were busy with construction, I decided to deal with my new messages and... froze in surprise.

The spiked ball on a chain had long been in Amra's main weapon slot but, meanwhile, there was still a message flickering that I had a package waiting for me. What the hell?! I opened the message and, just then, a couple of ghastly looking winged demons appeared a step away. They threw a wooden box bound with metal bands carelessly at my feet, then disappeared without a trace.

On the outside of the heavy and apparently voluminous box there was a sheet of paper affixed with red wax, and I read the measured calligraphic handwriting:

"Our new confrere! You're just the eighteenth of us in all Boundless Realm, and the youngest of our cohort. Take this gift from more experienced and cautious players, and may it help you survive in this harsh and unjust world."

The latches of the box were easy to throw back. As soon as I had the lid open, I saw a bunch of flasks carefully placed atop fresh hay. Each of them had a barely visible tag describing the contents. A plaque on the inside of the lid read: "Complete Collection of Blood Samples of the Inhabitants of the Lilac Mountains of the Eastern Continent, Fifty Vials."

I didn't find the name of the mystery sender, and the strange letter disappeared from my mailbox as soon as I opened the package. But such clandestine secrecy was perfectly understandable. Apparently, a vampire player with carefully guarded anonymity had decided to help me level my vampiric abilities as fast as possible.

~ A Trap for the Potentate ~

Although... If I thought about it, the box of blood samples could have been sent with just as much success by someone trying to pretend to be a vampire to earn my trust. In any case, the blood was real, which I immediately became convinced of after tasting a few samples:

> *Achievement unlocked: Taste Tester (93/1000)*

> *Achievement unlocked: Taste Tester (94/1000)*
> *...*
> *Achievement unlocked: Taste Tester (100/1000)*

> *New racial ability unlocked: Incorporeity*
> *Your character may become incorporeal for thirty seconds, making him invulnerable to physical damage*
> *Using this ability will cost 50 Endurance Points, recharge time is 24 hours*

A new cloud-shaped pictogram popped up on my screen next to the icons for Night Vision, Search for Life and Undead Apathy. What could I say? This was great news. Now, Amra could escape a battle if everything turned out wrong. But after that, I decided to stop the blood sampling, so I wouldn't repeat the error I'd made drinking too much blood in Dotur-Khawe. Last time, my Goblin Vampire had become intoxicated for a prolonged period. What was more, the boy Johnny, the best sentry in my army, came up to me just then:

"Captain Amra, there's a thick white fog coming up the river. I can't see through it at all, but I heard a few splashes and screeches from the river, as if someone was rowing with oars. The other sentries are laughing at me. They say I've been bitten by the fear bug. But I decided to warn you just in case..."

I always took Johnny's warnings very seriously, because the smart and ambitious boy had proven several times that he was the best sentry in my squadron. So, I ordered the orcs to carry the heavy chest of vials into my tent, which the orcs had already pitched in the very center of the fort, despite the fact that there were little houses perfectly suited for their commander to live in. I then went up to the northern sentry tower after Johnny. The area beyond the fort walls was so thick with fog it looked like the river and earth were covered in a layer of milk.

"Hey, I heard a sound from over there!" said the boy, pointing in one direction, but immediately slightly shifting his hand. "No, the sound is coming from over there! Can you hear it? It sounds like oars splashing!"

Perception check failed

- A Trap for the Potentate -

No, I couldn't hear any suspicious sounds, no matter how I strained my huge green ears. There was no oar splashing, nor any screeching of oarlocks. Just the croaking of some far-off frogs, the barely audible lapping of river waves on sand and the abrupt guttural cries of a swamp bird. Nevertheless, I had no reason not to trust the observant sentry boy, so I activated Night Vision and Search for Life, making the gloomy world more contrasting, and warm-blooded creatures easier to see. I nearly shouted in fear!

On the river, just fifty meters from the walls of our fort, there were at least ten long narrow boats filled with huge creatures! The unexpected visitors were stealing right up to our fort under cover of fog. There were more than a hundred, maybe even nearly two. I could see that many of them were armed. It seemed these mysterious strangers had aggressive intentions, but I couldn't tell why they were going so slow and not attacking the fort.

By the way, as soon as I noticed the attackers sneaking up to the fort, their markers appeared on the mini-map, and they were round and red. NPC's, not living players! Also, the mobs were aggressively inclined and, what was more, I saw black skulls over the figures on the river, which meant they were more than fifty levels higher than me. My heart still slightly slowed its pace.

Then, suddenly, there was a break in the fog, and I saw the unexpected guests clearly. Strong muscular figures, some of them were wearing leather vests or chainmail, but most of the warriors were stripped to the belt and marked with screamingly loud war paint on their torsos. But most importantly, they had the heads of canines on totally human bodies. Rougarous! I immediately remembered that the Lower Fort was located on the border of their lands.

I sent my sister a private message about the arrival of our aggressive rougarou neighbors, and asked her to organize our defenders on the walls without too much noise. I then ordered Johnny to remain here on the sentry tower and blow the alarm horn only if something happened to me and decisively jumped off the sentry tower down to the wall of the fort. Yes, the height was extreme, seven meters, but I did a somersault down a slope when I landed, significantly easing the fall, so I didn't get seriously wounded.

Successful Agility check
Experience received: 17 Exp.

Acrobatics skill increased to level 21!

At first glance, my actions may have seemed spontaneous, senseless or poorly thought out, but they were nothing of the sort. My big-eared Goblin Herbalist had a very significant bonus to the reaction of rougarous, so I wasn't expecting them to be aggressive toward me. And if that didn't work, I could always include the two most dangerous enemies in the Gray Pack, thus removing them from the enemy army. But I had to figure out why the high-level rougarous had shown up near the fort before the dog-headed creatures collided with my orcs in battle.

I didn't even manage to get to the water's edge before a whole bedsheet of messages ran before my eyes about successful Charisma checks and rougarou reactions. The NPC markers on the mini-map changed color from red to yellow. The hostility had dissipated. The bowmen I had not noticed earlier, who'd already managed to land on the bank and hide in the rocks, dropped their weapons on my approach. So far, my calculation was fully justified.

"What a splendid little goblin boy! His ears are so cute! I want to take him as my pet!" came the dainty voice of a capricious girl from one of the boats. I turned to the sound.

Chai-nee Shu
Princess of the Clan of the White Lily
Level-84 Rougarou Huntress

At the very bow of the boat in a long dark-green cloak, there was a pretty girl, whose anthropoid body transitioned surprisingly harmoniously into the snout of a shaggy little dog. Huge "anime" eyes, gold earrings on fluffy protruding ears and sharp teeth completed the image of the Rougarou Princess. Overall, the huntress looked funny and unusual. By the way, she was the only one marked with a red skull, not black, meaning she was "just" 20+ levels above my Amra. Also, Chai-nee Shu's marker on the mini-map was the only green one, meaning friendly.

"Bring him to me, I'll take this little goblin as a living toy!"

What?! That was already an excessive and perverse expression of friendship. I was not at all at peace with the living as the house pet of an NPC princess. But meanwhile, the two soldiers nearest me had already jumped from their boats into the shallows and were lunging in my direction to carry out their Princess's order. I had to demonstrate my power to the rougarou. I grabbed one of the clawed paws stretching out toward me and squeezed it in my hand.

Successful Strength check
Experience received: 180 Exp.

The distinct crunch of breaking bones rang out, drowned out by shouts of pain. I didn't torture the Rougarous, who hadn't done anything wrong, and quickly let the crippled warriors go. After that, annoyedly dismissing the popup system messages suggesting Amra take Hand-to-Hand Combat or Butcher as secondary skills, I spoke loudly:

"Great and wonderful Princess Chai-nee Shu! It seems there's been a misunderstanding and you've taken me for someone else! I assure you, I am not some inoffensive little critter, and certainly not a house pet. Allow me to introduce myself. I am Amra, the leader of an orcish army. And if you were leading your brave warriors to this fort, I'm afraid I have to upset you. My savages have already cut down the group of undying inside. Orcs and Goblins are not enemies of the Rougarou, so I am enthusiastic to see your war party at the walls of the riverine fortress, because we have something to offer you, something to warn you about, and something to ask of you."

The rougarous didn't reach for their weapons, although that was thanks to the fact that they were still watching their Princess, awaiting her decision. Chai-nee Shu, meanwhile, was in pensive silence, and I couldn't predict her response based on the bored expression frozen on her fluffy snout. I mean, even professional poker players showed more emotion than this frozen hairy mask!

Finally, one of the large rougarous in the boat walked up to the Princess and whispered something to her barely audibly. Amra failed another Perception check, so I couldn't hear a single one of her advisor's words. At the same time, I was attentively watching the quite remarkable rougarou:

Uvari-Dor Shu
Regent of the Clan of the White Lily
Level-124 Rougarou Druid

Regent?! So here was the true leader of the clan, as Princess Chai-nee Shu was still considered underage! And she clearly heeded the words of her advisor because, right after his hint, she finally came to a decision and pronounced in a celebratory voice:

"An enemy of an enemy is practically a friend! The Clan of the White Lily is happy to discuss any issue with you and invites Captain Amra, as well as all of his warriors to our camp. How many of you are there?"

"I have around three hundred under my command," I answered honestly. A strangely long pause followed.

The Regent whispered something else to the Princess, but this time the girl objected:

"But I already promised I'd invite all of Amra's warriors! I cannot go back on my word!"

"Very well, My Princess," Uvari-Dor Shu answered with a deep bow of respect, "we'll bring enough boats to the fort to carry all our guests."

Land of the Giants

T HE LAST THING I saw on the shore of the River of Death was a blaze so bright it turned night into day, with huge tongues of flame lapping above the walls of the Lower Fort. No, we didn't torch it. It was as reliable a shelter for those travelling along the Styx as could be imagined. The huge hot fire was burning right on top of the respawn stone. My sister thought it would be a better trap than sharpened wooden stakes. Valerianna Quickfoot had reinforced the raging flames with ghastly spells from her death magic arsenal. Shaman Ghuu got in on the act as well, adding his magical contribution and guaranteed me that the fire would kill anything alive and carry on burning until at least the middle of the next day.

I was next to the Princess in the boat, and Chai-nee Shu was enthusiastically telling me the story of her tribe. Constant border wars with neighboring clans, temporary alliances and breakdowns over issues that seemed minor, but were moments of principle to the rougarou. For example, who got to sit to the right of the chieftain of a united army during a banquet, or the use of notched arrows in a hunting competition during the Autumn Rut.

But with all their many-year if not many-century history of constant border conflicts between tribes, the rougarou had certain rules for their warfare. For example, the conflict immediately ended if any member of a ruling family was taken prisoner, at which point the parties negotiated only about payout size. Also, an injured enemy was never killed, and none of their neighbors even thought of raising a hand against a child or pregnant female. These eternal conflicts kept the warriors in good shape, but didn't threaten the existence of the clans themselves.

But everything changed when the undying came...

"It's like they simply have no understanding of honor!" the Princess lamented, raising her paws to the sky in a vain attempt to call vengeance on the lowdown newcomers. "For the undying, there's no difference between a warrior and a helpless newborn. They kill everyone! They even killed our truce envoy, even though he came to their camp unarmed and with peace symbols on his body, in accordance with every rule! Why do they act this way?!"

In her naivety and faith in justice, Chai-nee Shu reminded me greatly of Taisha in the very first days of our acquaintance. The Goblin Girl had also sincerely not understood why players had attacked the NPC village of Tysh, saying the peaceable goblins living there hadn't done anything wrong to them, so the undying had no reason to attack. Now, I guessed that before me was another next-generation NPC and, to test that theory, I started talking about the world of the undying, but Chai-nee Shu immediately dropped out of the conversation and let all my words go in one ear and out the other. All the same, as soon as I returned to in-game events, the Princess latched back in with vigor.

In the last year and a half, the Clan of the White Lily had seen several harsh undying attacks and, three times, had even been forced to move their main camp. The last attack had happened just two months earlier, when undying traveling on boats up the black river had discovered the rougarou camp and cut down practically half of its inhabitants. Among those killed in the cruel carve-up were Chai-nee Shu's parents, after which power in the tribe had gone to the young princess. According to the huntress, the rougarou of the

Clan of the White Lily had learned a painful lesson
and hidden their new camp location well so, now,
it would only be possible to reach it by water, and
only by those who knew the lie of the confusing
waterways and swampy banks of the black river.

"This evening, our scouts saw some people
at the fortress. What was more, my subjects
recognized some of them. These people were
among those who killed my parents and many
other clanmates. So, I ordered all warriors of the
White Lily to prepare for battle and, together, we
swore to get revenge on the newcomers for that vile
attack!!! But you got them first..."

I couldn't tell if the Princess was speaking
with reproach or not but, in any case, I hurried to
answer the furry girl:

"Yes, we cut down the first small group, but
that was just scouts before the main invasion. So
said our prisoner. The main forces of the undying
are supposed to come to the fortress tonight,
which was why we started that huge fire where
they should be showing up. For some time, the
devastating flame really will hold back the
enemies, but it won't stop their inevitable
invasion. The undying will come no matter what,
and there will be lots of them!"

The Rougarou huntress clearly wasn't
taking me seriously enough, because she
answered carelessly that the Clan of the White Lily
was not afraid of low-down undying. The warriors

- A Trap for the Potentate -

of her clan were many and brave. They were prepared to die for their Princess, and would never retreat. I didn't try to convince her otherwise, seeing how we'd arrived at our destination. The boat touched the mucky bottom and gradually came to a stop. At that very moment, the Princess gracefully hopped ashore and disappeared into wisps of white fog. Following the princess, all of her bodyguards also left the boat, even the oarsmen, taking the oars and leaving me all alone.

I took a look around as much as I could in the dense fog. The gentle slope of the shore reeked of ooze and rotting river plants. The smell was so strong that it seemed palpable and stuck to my clothing. There was no wind and there was such thick fog all around that I didn't even have a close appreciation of how the Rougarou could navigate here. Both my Goblin Vampire's Night Vision and Search For Life were worthless in the thick fog. By the way, it was quite strange that I couldn't detect any living creatures near me. After all, in theory, we were supposed to be arriving at a large village...

At that very moment my sister, as if sensing my alarmed state, sent me a private message:

"Big-ears, these dog-headed helmsmen left me and the others on some uninhabitable riverbank, then took off with most of the boats and all the oars. It's dark here, there's dead swamp forest all around, and the place is totally wild and impassable. It doesn't seem like anyone lived here

at all ever. Where are you now?"

I told Valerianna Quickfoot my coordinates and almost immediately was answered that I was more than four kilometers away from the others. How could that be?! The rougarou must have purposely separated me and my warband, setting the orcs down in some desolate place and leaving them without means of transportation, leaving me here on this boggy shore. I wrote Valerianna to get the orcs into combat order and stay on her toes, start building a fortification with the help of our Ogre Fortifier if possible, and then be sure and try to start carving new oars for the boats.

"Oh, I just got new quests from you! Don't worry, Amra. We'll do everything."

I was less and less happy with what was happening. The Gray Pack didn't show up next to me, either. The wolves appeared by me only when they were very far away and had lost their master but, if the distance was not so great, they simply tried to reach me on foot. So now, it might take them quite some time to reach me along the mucky swamps and many streams. It had turned out badly with the wolves, but what could I do? Rules are rules...

But I was especially worried by the fact that, in the river next to me, I saw some bizarre movement. I heard strange gurgling and splashing sounds, as if a large lizard or crocodile was swimming in this foggy branch of the Styx.

~ A Trap for the Potentate ~

I tried to call VIXEN so that, in case of danger, I could fly away on the winged snake, but my mount didn't answer for some reason. Something must have happened to the Royal Forest Wyvern. Meanwhile, the strange splashing was getting closer and closer. The unknown monster was approaching...

And then, when I was just about to dash away from the water at full speed, the dark tall figure of an oarsman came through the dank fog.

It was unexpected, I'll be direct. An intelligent creature?!

I froze in place and prepared to either speak with this approaching stranger if he was peaceably inclined, or run or defend myself if not. All my attention was now concentrated on the mini-map. It was very important to see the marker color of the oarsman as fast as possible and figure out what I could do from there. A red marker meant aggressive, yellow indifferent, and green friendly.

I mentally spun my options over in my mind for every possible scenario... but the color of the marker I finally did see was gold! A unique creature?!

Charon

Ferryman of the River of Death (unique creature)

Charon?! I'll admit, I was totally confused, and didn't quite know what to do. Running away

~ 333 ~

from a deity was obviously stupid. And hoping to match forces with such a powerful and most importantly immortal creature all the more so. And the problem wasn't even that there was a black skull over the ghastly figure of the ferryman of dead souls...

Back in school, when we went through the myths of Antiquity, I had to make a report about, coincidentally, Charon. So, I had some idea of who this being was. Grandson of the primordial deities Chaos and Caligo, son of the black night goddess Nyx, and the god of deep darkness, Erebus. Charon's brothers and sisters were just as fearsome as him, too: Thanatos god of death, Hypnos god of sleep, Nemesis goddess of retribution, Lyssa goddess of madness, Apate goddess of deceit... And even the goddess of strife Eris, who'd started the legendary Trojan war. The Three Fates were sisters of Charon, as well. The only person who'd managed to overcome Charon in his many millennia (and still hadn't destroyed the ferryman of souls, just managed to take the haggard old man's pole), was the legendary Hercules, but I was far from the greatest hero of all times and peoples...

His small boat stopped just two steps from me, and I managed to see the time-blackened boards of the boat, the long strong pole and the ancient man's bony fingers in perfect detail. Charon himself was tall and gaunt, his thin gray hair didn't even come close to covering his dark, liver-spotted scalp. He had chalk-white unmoving eyes, more reminiscent of a blind man's, a wrinkled face, and blackened uneven teeth. Charon's clothing was nothing but a foul sack cloth, decayed by time and with many gaping holes. And nevertheless, I didn't forget for a single second how powerful a creature had turned his attention to me, and made a low, waist-bow of respect to the ancient being. Nevertheless, I was certainly not expecting what happened next.

Successful Charisma check
Experience received: 210 Exp.

Successful check for unique creature reaction
Experience received: 1700 Exp.

Successful check for Charon's reaction
Experience received: 28000 Exp.

"Are you lost, boy? Need a ride?"

The deity's voice was croaking and sickly and, at the end of his short introduction, the old man erupted into a coughing fit. Nevertheless, the fact that Charon had begun speaking with me was surprising all on its own. However, I was in no rush to agree to his offer, keeping in mind that, based on all the legends, Charon transported the souls of dead people to the kingdom of the dead, from whence they could never return. And that was like, not on my way.

"Everything is so simple with the dead," the ferryman said, as if reading my thoughts. "You take your payment, bring them to the same old place, and your work is done. With the living, it's also clear. I can bring them to the kingdom of the dead, if they ask nicely but, once there, they quickly become indistinguishable from the other inhabitants. But as for you, the undying, it's all much harder... What sense is there to bring you or your souls to the kingdom of the dead, if you are just reborn in one hour anyway?!"

An unusual point of view. I'd somehow never thought before about how Charon might look on the players of a virtual game. Technically, I could try and ride his craft... Or was it better to wait for VIXEN?

"Your flying snake got too distracted hunting for local game, and became someone's lunch..." the immortal ferryman said, easily demonstrating his omniscience, a distinguishing feature of the gods. "She's still got forty minutes until she's reborn so, if you don't want to wait that long, hop into my boat. I'll take you wherever you need to go."

Mission received: Crossing the Styx
Mission class: Rare, personal
Description: name a location and come

~ A Trap for the Potentate ~

*to an agreement with Charon about payment
for passage*

*Reward: 10000 Exp., Fame +3, +50 to
Charon's opinion of you, +10 to the opinion of
Charon's family*

I was somewhat worried by the issue of
payment. As far as I knew, in Ancient Greece and
Rome, a small coin was stuck under the tongue of
the dead especially for Charon. But how much
could the old man want to transport a living
person? Something was telling me that, in this
case, payment wouldn't be measured in money.
Hercules had paid for passage in pelts, while the
greatest musician of antiquity, Orpheus, had
played for him on the cithara. But what did I have
to offer the deity?

My gaze again hooked onto the time-
blackened boat, which looked quite rickety, like it
could sink at any moment. Maybe I could offer
Charon a newer boat? As a matter of fact, I did
have the one the Rougarou had brought me here
in, while the ferryman already had his own pole to
steer. However, as soon as I hinted about an
exchange, the old man laughed uncontrollably:

"That new thing will be history in ten years!
But my boat has served for millennia, and will
continue to serve millennia from now."

Trading skill increased to level 27!

My offer made Charon laugh, but his laughter gave way to yet another heavy hoarse cough. I took a risk nevertheless and jumped into the black boat. Where did I need to go? At first, I was planning to just join up with my friends, but now, I had sharply changed my decision. The pitiful four kilometers separating me and my warriors was a distance I could overcome by simply waiting for VIXEN to respawn, or at the very least by walking and swimming. It was totally irrational to squander divine intervention on such a modest goal. But what if...

"Three hundred twenty kilometers above the rapids of the Styx, there's a place where a Mythical Hound can be found... Or perhaps a not fully-grown hound, but simply a puppy..." I said, remembering that Mariam Standing_Right_Behind_You, when completing a similar quest with Fimbulthul, had spoken of a small puppy, which she then raised. "Could you bring me there? And how long will it take?"

"Yes, I know of such a place..." Charon finally stopped coughing and was now stroking his disheveled gray beard in thought. "I'm not received too cordially up there. That place has its own gods. But I can take you. As for time... what does it matter how long the trip takes, if all around is only fog and cold black water? There's nothing for the eye to even catch on..."

- A Trap for the Potentate -

The ancient old man started into another heavy coughing fit, and I extended him an Elixir of Cure Disease. To my surprise, my gift was accepted with favor and immediately used as prescribed. Growing a bit braver, I offered the ferryman another vial of medicine, but Charon refused:

"It isn't a problem for me to heal myself. I still have a bit of Olympian ambrosia and, beyond its intoxicating effect, it heals all illness," with these words Charon pulled out an opaque amphora caked in dried mud and gave it a slight shake. I heard a few droplets splash around the very bottom. "But there isn't much ambrosia left, I have to save it. When Zeus organizes another feast, and I can refill my stores..."

If that wasn't a hint, I'd never played a computer game before! Instantly, I removed a barrel of beer from my inventory, which I had taken today in the Lower Fort. I wanted to also take out some appetizers. I also had corned beef and dried strips of meat, but my sensitive nose caught the smell of dried fish. Not yet believing it myself, I looked under the mat on the bow of Charon's boat. Underneath were fishing lines braided from horse hair, primitive goose feather bobbers, and hand-made wooden hooks...

"Sometimes, I go fishing, when no one is around to see," the old man seemingly grew slightly embarrassed, and even started trying to justify himself. "What else is there to do on the river of death when there's no work? Only fish. Yesterday, I almost caught a catfish this big!" Charon spread his arms wide, demonstrating the size of his escaped prey. "Without a net, it was hard to get such a beaut' into the boat, but I lost my net six centuries ago near the sandbanks of the Styx. Three hundred years later, I tried to find it. I even dived in the black water, but I quickly got grossed out and gave up..."

In reply, I told Charon about the underwater city of Ookaa and the professional fishermen from the ranks of the undying who spent days on end on the banks competing amongst themselves in the art of fishing. I also told him that I could order good tackle with delivery, and I'd just need to tell the magical courier where to bring it.

The ferryman noticeably lit up, having seen a careful listener in me, and began telling me his fish stories with clear satisfaction, recalling the most curious cases and best fish of the past thousand years. I listened to his fish stories, cleaned a dried fish I found under the mat for the both of us and poured some fine beer from the barrel into some wooden mugs I found on the boat.

Mission completed: Crossing the Styx
Experience received: 2300 Exp.

Fame increased

- A Trap for the Potentate -

Present value: 18

"So, do you keep up with your family at all?" I asked Charon, and the old man choked on his beer in surprise. Coughing and wiping the foam from his beard, he asked what I knew about his relatives. It seemed to me that Charon wasn't too happy to discuss this. He was either embarrassed as his origins, or thought discussing his relatives would totally kill the trusting and careless atmosphere of our spontaneous feast.

I readily told the immortal ferryman of souls everything I knew about his parents, brothers and sisters. It seemed I managed to surprise the deity with my deep knowledge of his genealogy, and also with the fact that I didn't show any fear discussing the god of death, goddess of madness and the others. Slightly slowing down, Charon admitted that he did keep up with them and even regularly met all his many family members, except the goddess of strife:

"Little Eris isn't gonna poke her nose into such a desolate wasteland just for me. My sister loves big noisy groups and mass gatherings. Those things give her huge satisfaction. But every time she shows up, there are scandals, swearing, and immortal gods getting punched in the face. For mere mortals, that's thousands and thousands of lost lives. I haven't seen Eris since the Trojan War. Although..." Charon dug into the bosom of his shirt, which looked like just a hole-ridden rag, "I used to have a gong to summon her... Ah, here it is! If you want, take the gong. It's just been laying around in my stuff for thousands of years."

With these words, Charon handed me a time-darkened bronze plate with worn, unreadable words and barely distinguishable drawings of athletes or warriors, along with a small bronze hammer attached by small chain.

Gong of summoning the goddess of strife Eris (indestructible item)
Recharge time after use: two hundred years

What a dangerous thing! With extreme caution, I took the plate and hammer from the slightly tipsy deity, trying to prevent any chance of their touching one another. I suspect that, if an unforeseen summoning had happened, Eris would have been unhappy with being forgotten for millennia, and would have found such sharp words for her brother that the deities would inevitably start fighting, which would lead to my just as inevitable respawn as an undesirable witness to their argument.

As soon as I'd placed the bronze gong in my inventory, Charon told me we'd already arrived. To be honest, I hadn't even noticed any difference in the surrounding landscape: it was the very same night, black water and impenetrable fog, also we didn't seem to have gone up any rapids. All the same, I didn't doubt the deity's words. Charon had been traversing the river of death on his boat for thousands of years and, though unhurried and even-paced on first glance, he had overcome a huge distance in remarkable time by lazily operating his pole.

"Right there, a high-powered river flows into the Styx called the Gjöll," the ferryman said with an indistinct wave of his hand into the fog. "There, you'll find the Gjallarbrú, the legendary golden bridge between the world of the living and the dead, the land of the giants and the queen of the dead lands, Hel, with her very unpleasant daddy Loki... Those are other gods, and they don't receive me and my kind cordially, so I won't go near the bank. But you can walk through the shallows here. I don't know, Amra, why you wanted to visit these unwelcoming lands, but we have come to them from the world of the dead, and the local inhabitants don't expect guests from over here."

I thanked Charon for the help and gave him a bow at the waist. After that, I jumped off the boat to a sandy spit extending far into the river. My boots gave a strange hissing sound, as if they were in acid, but I quickly got up on the sand. As soon as I'd come out of the water, the ancient ferryman dissolved in the fog like a ghost together with his black boat. And another second later, the Gray

Pack appeared next to me in full and I heard VIXEN's wide wings flapping overhead. The game algorithms thought my animals were too far away, so they had sent them to their master.

The wolves put their tails between their legs and started whining plaintively, feeling very uncertain in these borderlands of the world of the dead. Even the huge Baron had his ears pressed against his head and was crawling on half-bent paws, nuzzling up to his master, as if I could protect him from danger.

I opened the map and tried to get my bearings but, other than a small bright circle of river and a piece of shore around us, there were only undiscovered lands. I had to spend a long time zooming out before I could see the area of the Styx Antonius Just had shared with me: Upper Fort, rapids, the land of the cyclopes, a bunch of markers warning of danger... And that was where the *Lifegiving Light*'s expedition had ground to a halt. Oh, how far I was from those places! Going by the map scale, it was three hundred kilometers and maybe even further... I suspected that no players before me had ever before managed to come this far up the Styx.

I closed the map and gave a heavy sigh. I couldn't afford to make any mistakes. One wrong move could lead to death in this ghastly dangerous place, and I would not get another chance to be up here. After ordering my wolves and wyvern to simply wait and not do anything, I threw an old cloak with Stealth bonuses over my shoulders and activated all kinds of protective effects: Undead Apathy, Night Vision, Search for Life. I then went into stealth mode and carefully walked onto dry land.

* * *

It was a wooden house. A normal house made of time darkened beams, but it was of truly colossal dimensions. In comparison with this, even the blockhouse my sister and I had stayed in near the village of Tysh, which was built by giant ogres, seemed like a mere dog kennel. This side of the huge building was apparently the back yard with storehouses, sheds and other utility buildings. Other than a dozen ghastly-looking hounds, dozing in the interior courtyard braided into a ring, I couldn't see anyone.

Guard dog
Level ???

I couldn't see the level of these terrifying mutts. Their markers were simply accompanied by black skulls although, based on their titanic dimensions, I could suppose at least level two hundred, if not three. But I wasn't particularly afraid of the dogs, supposing that I would be protected from their frightening teeth by my huge positive bonuses to the reaction of any canid. What was more, in case of alarm, I could try and lure up to four of the fanged guardians to my side, after which the other hounds would quickly stop caring about me.

No, I didn't misspeak. It really was four and not two, because I'd decided to get rid of the two Swamp Wolves. I had no attachment to them and there were now somewhat stronger candidates. I kicked the two brown wolves out of the Gray Pack, supposing they would simply walk away. But no such luck! A blistering fight sprung up and the Gray Pack on the shore of the river immediately sated their hunger with their former compatriots... Hrmph. That was a bit uncomfortable...

Stealth skill increased to level 36!

Seeing that system message run before my eyes, my big-eared Amra smiled in satisfaction from ear to ear. Yes, my Stealth skill was rising quickly, which was one of the reasons I was in no hurry to crawl out in front. My Goblin Herbalist was hiding behind a bunch of stinking trash in the immediate vicinity of a dozen very dangerous high-level opponents but, due to my cover overpowering any smell I might have given off, the camouflage cloak and my bonuses to stealth, I remained unnoticed by the big-toothed guard dogs. The game algorithms considered this a spectacular success, and my Stealth skill bar was filling up right before my eyes, giving me a new level almost every minute.

But that wasn't the only reason I was taking my time. I had already reached the inner courtyard just twenty steps from the titanic cabin of the giants, but I still had yet to see my target! What was more, the game algorithms of *Boundless Realm* had yet to give me the Twelve Élivágar Guardians quest, which is why I had come to these lands in the first place. I thought, and Charon had confirmed that somewhere in the land of the giants and gods of Scandinavian legend, there must be a unique mythical hound, a brother to my Fimbulthul. But where was he?!

Stealth skill increased to level 37!

Somewhere very far away on the boggy shore further down the Styx, my friends were probably worried about me and didn't understand why I wasn't answering their messages. My brothers in arms could see that Amra was alive, but they couldn't tell where he was located. The squadron of NPC orcs was probably calling and searching for their missing commander. They might even rebel and refuse to obey the mavka without me. Meanwhile, I was just lying on my stomach next to a pile of trash, and couldn't do anything about it...

It wasn't clear how long I could keep this up but, just then, a very subtle squeak rang out from the direction of the huge house. My huge green ears immediately perked up and tried to determine the source of the sound. It seemed the squeak was coming from under the porch. Yeah, that was right! One of the huge black dogs had woken up and gone to hide under the porch. It was a feeding female, based on her milk-filled pendant nipples.

The mother's arrival was met with elated yelping. There must have been a couple of puppies under the porch. Based on the squeaking, it seemed there were three, no, actually four puppies! Very slowly, I left the very comfortable and safe shelter and started peeking out to the side, trying to take a wide curve around the yard to catch a glimpse of what was happening under the stairs.

Stealth skill increased to level 38!

Finally, I managed to see the puppies and could barely contain a howl of joy. There it was! Among the puppies drinking their mother's milk, one was marked with a gold marker on the mini-map. A unique creature! But... the puppies were still just level zero and not yet independent creatures. I couldn't simply pick them from afar and include the blind little black pup into the Gray Pack.

~ A Trap for the Potentate ~

What should I do then? Naturally, I didn't have a few days to wait for the puppies to grow up. Also, it was easily possible that the puppy might remain in such a small inactivated state for many weeks and even months, only turning on when one of the players who'd received the Twelve Élivágar Guardians quest showed up. After all, it was supposed to be for someone who had honestly overcome all the obstacles and traps, crossed the bridge between the worlds of the dead and the living, fought with the pack of malicious dogs and earned a reward in the form of a unique pet... But this player wouldn't be me, because the game system hadn't given me this unique quest.

I wasn't sure how much longer I could have watched the puppies and mentally self-castigated, but my goblin accidentally met eyes with the feeding female.

Check for Guard Dog reaction failed!

After such a message, there was no more guessing if she'd noticed me or not. What was more, the marker of the feeding mother momentarily changed shade from neutral yellow to red. Aggression!!! I ran forward at full speed, tacking between the huge awakening beasts as I ran. Meanwhile, I just rudely jumped over or on top of several of their furry backs.

Dodge skill increased to level 24!

Dodge skill increased to level 25!

Acrobatics skill increased to level 21!

Animal Control skill increased to level 44!

Of the four enemies I tried to take under my command, I only managed to include one into the Gray Pack. But even that was a great success, because the animal increased in size instantly from the bonuses and distracted the other defenders. I then, barely managing to dodge the jaws gnashing at my very throat, crawled under the belly of my hound, which hopped to its feet, and found myself facing the female. She bared her teeth, protecting her young and gave a deafening roar right in my face.

Damage taken: 0 HP (spell Psionic Strike, immunity to fear)

The female lunged her toothy maw in my direction, then tried to lie down and cover her pups with her huge body, but I was already jumping toward the valuable loot.

Got it! I managed to grab the puppy with my hands. Mine!!!

~ A Trap for the Potentate ~

Ow... Even at my high Strength and Constitution the huge guard dog pressing down with all her weight was too heavy. My bones and joints creaked. How painful!!!

Damage taken: 310 (crushing, armor ignored)

Damage taken: 278 (crushing, armor ignored)
Damage taken: 390 (crushing, armor ignored)

I tried not to think about the fact that there were puppies in the very same situation. My life was flowing away quickly. In ten more seconds, I'd be dead. I didn't have enough Strength to lift the furry creature...

Despite the pain and stress, I still had enough intelligence to change tactics and not try to escape from under the huge press. Carefully placing the black puppy in my Inventory and making sure he was alive, I activated my vampire ability Incorporeity for the first time.

How wonderful it felt to be free from that pressing weight! It was as if I had freed myself from the strangling embrace of a python!!! The huge enraged mother gnashed her jaws impotently, but her terrifying teeth passed right through me, not doing any damage.

Dodge skill increased to level 26!

Dodge skill increased to level 27!

Acrobatics skill increased to level 22!

But, unfortunately, this invulnerability was very short in duration. I had just thirty seconds, or to be more accurate, twenty-seven, so I ran toward the river as fast as my feet would take me. The battle in the courtyard was still going on, although my hound had already collapsed to the ground and was being torn to shreds. Nevertheless, the main contingent of guard hounds was occupied, and just three were chasing me, including the female herself. I tried to get those three onto my side one more time, but again without result. The chasm dividing our levels was too wide, and the chance for success with hostile beings was quite small to begin with.

In such a fleshless state, I could move very fast, and the guard hounds couldn't keep up. As I ran, I ordered VIXEN to wake up, spread her wings and be ready to fly. I was planning to use her to take off into the sky to evade pursuit. And as for the Gray Pack, I ordered them to run away as fast as possible because, if my wolves met with such deadly enemies as those bounding after me now, they didn't have a single chance to escape.

My last few seconds of being immaterial were ticking away as I ran up to the banks of the

~ A Trap for the Potentate ~

Styx. My pursuers were forty meters behind me, but barking desperately with every second, trying to hit the impudent fleeing goblin with waves of fear. That didn't worry me much, due to my complete immunity to fear. But as for VIXEN... As shameful as it was, the Royal Forest Wyvern couldn't hold out and, sharply flapping her wide emerald wings, took off into the cloudy sky, leaving her master to be torn to shreds...

"Amra, over here!" the familiar rasping voice of Charon drew my attention when my incorporeal state had passed, and I already thought I had no more chances for rescue.

I didn't think it over and, without slowing down, made a running jump into the cold black waters of the river of death. When I landed, I was up to my belt in the water, which was freezing, simply icy, but also burned like fire.

Successful check for Poison Resistance
Experience received: 370 Exp.

Successful check for Poison Resistance
Experience received: 370 Exp.

Charon extended me his long pole and brought my big-eared goblin on his boat, even helping me climb over the side. The three guard dogs stopped at the water's edge as if riveted in place, not wanting to crawl into the dangerous river.

"Let's go before their masters notice what you've taken!" the old man commented aloud, and sharply pushed his pole off the riverbed.

A moment later, the land of the giants was gone, lost in the fog. But at that, something was telling me Charon's boat and that dangerous riverbank were now separated by a huge distance, and I no longer had to worry about pursuit.

"Thanks, Charon! You showed up just in the nick of time. Another couple seconds and those dogs would have torn me to shreds..."

"Oh, it's nothing!" the ancient man waved off my gratefulness. "You're undying, so you'd just be reborn in a different place no matter what. I just wanted to tease those foreign gods. Also, you're an interesting guy to talk to. Well, and we didn't finish the beer," Charon chuckled, taking the small barrel in his hands and giving it a shake, making a noticeable sloshing sound. "Just enough for the road! Amra, at least show me what you took from the giant Modgud."

Modgud? So that was who lived in that huge house! I'd heard the name Modgud before. The giant lady was a guardian of the golden bridge between the worlds of the living and the dead, one of the servants of Hel, the goddess of the afterlife. I got it out of my inventory and showed Charon the tiny black puppy, blindly nuzzling my finger.

~ A Trap for the Potentate ~

Gjöll
Élivágar Guardian
Level-0 Mythical Hound (unique creature)

"Just that..." Charon said, drawing out his words in disappointment, immediately losing interest in my trophy. "You could have found some more interesting stuff in the home of the giantess Modgud. If you'd have just told me you were interested in unusual dogs, I'd have shown you the three headed Cerberus from afar, now that's a ghastly creature! Even the gods try not to tangle with Cerberus, but as for people..."

Charon went sharply silent and spit into the water. It seemed to me that the ferryman of souls wanted to tell me the story of Hercules and one of his twelve feats, the capture of Cerberus, but remembered that, on his way to the kingdom of the dead, the legendary hero had walloped Charon himself to get across the Styx.

Anyway, his mood was spoiled. He drained the rest of the beer in the barrel in one swig and asked in a none-too-friendly voice where to let me out.

"Next to my orc squadron, if possible," I answered.

To that, the ferryman pushed off with his pole a few times on the bottom and pointed his hand at the dark shore that appeared from the fog with far-off gloomy fires:

"We're here! Oh... You need to intervene right away. Jump off quick before the rougarous smash your orcs' faces in!"

The Clan of the White Lily

THE SCENE I ARRIVED to was not pleasing. The black river was crowded from an abundance of boats full of dog-headed warriors, many of which were bombarding the shore with slings and short-bows. On the shore, there was a battle underway. Orcs, covering themselves with wide shields in something like a turtle formation, were reflecting a forward group of rougarou trying to land their boats. Charon let me out right in the midst of all the chaos near a barricade erected by the defenders. The ferryman himself had already dissolved in the thick fog.

"Who can explain what's going on here?!" I

shouted, attracting attention from both sides of the conflict.

"Amra is back!!!" An elated roar from hundreds of orcish throats rolled over the swampy land for many kilometers.

Foreman skill increased to level 48!

Warchief skill increased to level 6!

Warchief skill increased to level 7!

Warchief skill increased to level 8!

Dodge skill increased to level 28!

I just had to say one sentence, but look what it did! Different markers lit up over many of my warriors, showing bonuses from inspiration. The orcs made their traditional war cry (consisting exclusively of curse words) and, walked forward in formation, cut the few rougarou warriors who had made it onto the swampy banks into shredded cabbage. The other dog-headed warriors quickly decided not to make land and immediately led their boats away from shore. Some of the enemy archers trained their fire on me, but I quickly sought shelter behind the shields of my orcs.

"Where'd you disappear to? Why weren't you answering my messages?" the forest nymph threw herself at me, appearing from invisibility.

"I'll tell you later. It's a whole story," I waved off the untimely questions and gave an involuntary whistle of surprise when I saw Valerianna Quickfoot's level, ninety-three. I was also surprised to see the red skull symbol over her head. "Better you tell me where that flea-ridden princess went to after leaving me alone in the middle of the swamp!"

"If you're talking about Chai-nee Shu," the mavka said, immediately guessing who I had in mind, "the rougarou Princess landed on that side of the island with her tribe's main army," my sister said, waving her hand somewhere opposite the river. "The rougarous were nearing our camp with war cries, but were impressed by the strong fortifications made under the leadership of the Ogre Fortifier and refused to attack head on, instead trying to land at our backs from the river."

I had formed a mental picture of the opposing army's position, but I still didn't understand the reason why the rougarous, who had met us in such a friendly manner, had suddenly changed their minds and decided to sabotage us. It wasn't that I was worried about the outcome of the battle. Our position was strong, and my orcs were brimming with vim and vigor, but I still wanted to avoid unnecessary losses.

"I need to speak with that furry deceiver! I don't like being tricked!" I started off determinedly toward the fortification, but stopped short when I saw Max Sochnier.

The Naiad Trader still had the criminal symbol shining over his head like a beacon, and along with that marker, I saw the red skull symbol as well. My French friend's character was now more than twenty levels higher than mine!

Max Sochnier
Naiad
Level-87 Trader

Just twenty? He was a whole thirty-five levels higher than me!!! How?! Next, I saw the Ogre Fortifier running toward me, and he was at level-ninety. That really perplexed me. What had happened here?!

"Amra, the undying managed to get through our barrier at the Lower Fort!" the giant said with agitation in his voice. "At first, it all happened just as you predicted. The players opened the portal to the Lower Fort and flooded through in one group. Their first wave was entirely laid out by the metal spikes in the magical fire! It was awesome!!! I now have the achievement 'Killed Three Hundred Forty Players!' I leveled up forty-two times in just over a minute!!!"

"Oh yes, it was unforgettable!" the fish man laughed uncontrollably, rubbing his webbed hands together in satisfaction. "I leveled up forty times in just a minute and a half and, for a long time after that, I couldn't get on my feet, because I was overcome with ecstasy. It was much better than sex!!!"

I looked attentively at my underaged sister, who had also leveled up at this advanced rate, gaining thirty-five levels, but Val didn't comment on how it felt, just blushed and looked away. The ogre, meanwhile, continued his story:

"But our opponents quickly accounted for their error and, a half hour later, another, better prepared group came through. We could see the huge flame go dark from here, and they got through. The dead also respawned and got through on their second attempt. We saw a few messages in the local chat, and realized they would certainly be after us. But we, as bad luck would have it, are stranded on this swampy island and can't run for our lives!!! And now, the rougarou have us under siege, so we can't go anywhere!"

What could I say? The situation really had come together unfavorably, so I needed to figure out the reason for the conflict with the rougarou fast. But first, I needed to safeguard myself, hiding my location from the pursuers. I wanted to ask my friends, if they'd all turned off message receipt from unknown players in their settings, so no one could find us by that very simple method, when I suddenly slapped my own forehead in vexation.

Why should our pursuers be clever and triangulate our position, or use other search methods when we still had their captive in our camp? He should have come to his senses long ago and now, despite the black blindfold over his eyes, he could simply tell them his coordinates in real time. We needed to kill the captive right away! Although... I got a better idea, and called VIXEN over.

The huge Royal Forest Wyvern tried to snuggle up to me and ingratiate herself, but I pushed her toothy maw away in distress:

"You haven't earned it! How could you have abandoned me to be torn apart by the guard dogs?! Well, you want to make peace? Then look for the rougarou village from the air. Yes, I know it's night and thick fog, but still try. If you can find it, consider yourself forgiven!"

Animal Control skill increased to level 45!

The huge winged snake flapped her wide wings noisily and disappeared in the wisps of dark cloud. I then turned to Max Sochnier:

"Is your Olilissa here? Great! Ask her to overturn all these rougarou boats! She might even eat a couple of the dogheads as a warning, so the others will think thrice before either swimming or taking their boats across the river. If she can, have her push the boats to us on shore. We'll need them later. Then send her to the Lower Fort to swamp the players' boats, if they decide to come after us. Those boats not only can, but must be broken and sunk so they cannot be repaired afterward. By the way, also send your swordfish to smash the players' boats."

Foreman skill increased to level 49!

How could that be? That message made me think. I had just given a mission to a living player, not an NPC. How could my Foreman skill have increased?! Or were the *Boundless Realm* logical algorithms taking into account that I was sending messages through him to his nereid girl? In any case, I wasn't going to bust my brains over it for long, because I had another very small but urgent matter. I called the she-wolf Blanca over and, at the same time, asked Valerianna Quickfoot to come over as an experienced Beast Master.

"Val, you need to make sure this fluffy little miracle gets fed!" with these words, I extended the tiny Mythical Hound Gjöll to my sister.

"Aww, so cute!" the forest nymph exclaimed, immediately picking up the blind helpless and turning it belly up. "It's a girl! Leave her to me! You'll only get in the way! By the way, now I understand why all the *Lifegiving Light* guys were getting so mad in the local chat. They kept saying they'd failed a unique quest. They started to fight amongst themselves and they still haven't figured out whose fault it is."

I walked away. The mavka then called the goblin girl Yunna, now a level-forty Wolf Rider, over to help. Together, they made a little bed for the wolf pup out of rags and straw.

I remembered how harshly Blanca had treated her unneeded puppies, and was slightly worried for the unique pet, which had been so hard for me to acquire. What was more, I was not sure the NPC she-wolf still had milk.

But all my worrying was for nothing. Blanca understood her role instantly. The she-wolf still had milk, and the puppy started suckling on her new mother's teat without hesitation. It was an idyllic scene, but I needed to deal with other urgent matters. Valerianna Quickfoot was also needed elsewhere.

"Yunna, you'll answer for Gjöll with your head!" I said strictly, and my NPC "niece" confirmed that she understood perfectly, and wouldn't be going even a step away from her.

The mavka and I then hurried to the barricade surrounding the camp. This time, the orcs had enough logs and branches from the dead swampy forest to build an adequately tall and sturdy fortification, not like that pitiful parody we'd constructed for the army of the Rat King. From atop its three-meter height, I could see many bright figures through the constant fog with my Night Vision. There were more than a hundred of them. The rougarou on this side of the island were not particularly active, but had begun sieging our fort. My interest was immediately piqued by a marker in the distance. It was many times larger than the others. Some kind of mount?

"The rougarou brought one cyclops with them," my sister explained when I asked the question aloud. "It still hasn't been brought anywhere near our fortification, but I can see its marker and label on the map. Level-one-hundred-thirty-eight Cyclops."

"Just what I needed... Alright, we'll handle the cyclops later. Now, enhance my voice with magic. I want to talk with Chai-nee Shu."

Valerianna Quickfoot said a sentence in an unfamiliar language and made a few passes of her hands, after which she told me that my wish was granted, and the volume of Amra's voice would be like the horn of an ocean liner for the next few minutes.

"Check, check..." my voice now really was loud enough to drown out thunder. "This is Amra, commander of the orcish warriors. I'd like to speak with Princess Chai-nee Shu!"

No answer followed, even though I kept it up for a few minutes.

Finally, my patience gave out,

"Rougarous, where is your Chai-nee Shu.

That flea-ridden bitch doesn't know the meaning of the word 'honor' or understand the laws of hospitality! I don't know what misunderstanding led to this mindless female becoming Princess of the proud Clan of the White Lily, but I do know one thing: in the whole rest of the world, attacking guests is considered a horrible shame! And now, I just want to talk with Chai-nee Shu and find out why she did such a despicable thing. I want to speak on good terms, one-on-one without weapons, meeting in the no-man's-land between our armies. Rougarou of the Clan of the White Lily, I promise that, after this conversation, your Princess will be returned to you alive and unharmed! But if Chai-nee Shu doesn't have the bravery to come out, look me in the eyes and explain herself, I swear that I will find her and treat her the way out-of-control bitches deserve. I'll give her a collar, put it on a chain and make her guard my house!!!"

My hateful and intentionally offensive speech was then interrupted by an outraged and insulted voice from the rougarou warband:

"Enough shaming me! I'm not flea-ridden!"

Trading skill increased to level 28!

Warchief skill increased to level 9!

Would you like to take the secondary skill Minstrel (Ch P)?

~ A Trap for the Potentate ~

Would you like to take the secondary skill Diplomat (Ch P)?

Would you like to take the secondary skill Lothario (Ch P)?

Despite the serious nature of the moment, I couldn't help but laugh. I mean, come on? What the hell did I need Minstrel for?! After hearing a serenade like that, any girl would pour the contents of a chamber pot on the head of such a hacky troubadour! Lothario also was hardly appropriate to the situation, and my whole style of gaming. But as for Diplomat... I unexpectedly found myself thinking it over.

The game system had suggested such a choice to me before. And I had conducted some complicated negotiations: with the dwarves, the Emissary of the Dark Sovereign, and these very orc pirates on our first meeting. With time, I suspected, negotiations would become a totally normal affair. Sure, the diplomat skill was not so great for me as a primary, because the goblin race didn't have a bonus to Charisma, and had a 50% penalty to Intelligence but, after all, I was planning to put the skill in my secondaries, so it didn't make a difference. So, it was decided! I put that skill in my last free slot.

Meanwhile, two figures emerged from the

enemy army and started off unhurriedly in our direction. Strange that there were two negotiators. After all, I had clearly said we should talk one-on-one. But I didn't make a fuss over such small matters. The rougarou princess had agreed to negotiate, and that was what mattered! Alright, seeing as there were two of them, I'd also make slight adjustments to my plans and jump on Baron. The level-111 Swamp Wolf Alpha should emphasize my power and significance. Yes, it would have been better to take the extremely high-level Guard Dog instead, but it still hadn't respawned.

As soon as I made a move forward, the *Boundless Realm* algorithms established a mission for the negotiations:

Mission received: Negotiations with the Rougarou (1/2)

Mission class: Unusual, racial, time-limited

Description: Figure out what made the rougarou hostile and convince them to cease aggression within a half hour

Reward: 16000 Exp., +15 to the opinion of the Clan of the White Lily, +5 to the opinion of all other clans

Penalty for failure: Hostility with the Rougarou

~ A Trap for the Potentate ~

Just a half an hour? That time limit was incomprehensible to me. In all other ways, the mission looked totally logical and was perfectly in line with my plan: to find out the reason the dog-headed men were angry with me and force them to retreat by any means necessary.

We met half way between our armies. The second negotiator from the rougarou side was the Regent Uvari-Dor Shu, a level-124 druid. What could I say, as the princess was too young to make her own decisions, the presence of an advisor was totally explicable and even necessary. I didn't object to that one bit.

"For a start, I demand an apology for your insulting words!" the princess declared proudly, looking to her advisor for approval at the end of her sentence, and the druid gave a nod.

"You demand?!" I replied in an intentionally offended voice. "Well, big-eared girl, you aren't in a position to demand anything. The losing side can only request mercy and ask for the terms of their capitulation."

"I must have missed something. Did we lose?" the regent cut into the conversation with an acrid smile of his fanged snout.

"Yes, advisor, you have lost, although you may not know it yet! Your fleet attacking from the river has been eradicated. All their means of aquatic transportation have been destroyed, and it would be no trouble at all for me to do the very same with all the rest of your boats. So, I'd say you don't have such a great choice. You could stay here on this swampy muck island forever and build a new camp for your Clan of the White Lily, seeing how going into the water means instant death for your warriors. Or you could try to attack my camp. But I have to warn you: trying to assault my fortifications will mean all your rougarou warriors will die, and even the cyclops will not help."

Diplomat skill increased to level 2!

Diplomat skill increased to level 3!

I saw my words make an impact of some kind and the rougarou began to think but, for now, both the negotiators had clearly underestimated the difficulty of their position. Perhaps, if Amra had been higher in level, they'd have paid my words more mind, but the rougarous saw a weak and inoffensive Goblin Herbalist before them, so they didn't take me seriously.

"Amra, even if you aren't lying about the boats being sunk, my warriors are still many in number and each of them is stronger than any of your orcs. I will give the order to attack and, soon, you won't have a single living warrior left!"

I smiled, showing my sharp predatory teeth:

"Princess, you're still too small and naive, so you can see only raw force and underestimate the power of magic! Your warriors will fight amongst themselves and tear each other's throats out, while me and my warriors simply watch the whole performance from afar!"

As a demonstration, I opened the Gray Pack control interface.

I clicked on the list of available creatures and selected a Level-84 Rougarou Huntress named Chai-nee Shu.

Successful check for rougarou reaction
Experience received: 800 Exp.

Successful Charisma check
Experience received: 1600 Exp.

Successful check for Animal Control skill
Experience received: 3200 Exp.

Animal Control skill increased to level 46!

I succeeded at including the rougarou princess in the Gray Pack!!! I didn't risk carrying out the same experiment with the regent. He was of a noticeably higher level than the Princess, and his druid profession meant high Intelligence, so he would be good at resisting magic. If I attempted to control him and failed, the whole effect would come to naught. Anyhow, as a demonstration of my abilities, the Princess was enough all on her own.

Jumping off Baron, I unhurriedly walked over to the girl, who was frozen and clearly afraid, not knowing what was going on. I started giving Chai-nee Shu commands liked a trained dog:

"Sit! Wag your tail! What a good girl! And now hold your arms against your body and stick out your tongue! Good girl, here's a piece of meat for being so good! And now scratch your ear with your left leg. See, you've clearly got lots of experience. And you said you didn't have fleas!"

The regent, watched the messy spectacle for some time in horror, but then decisively reached for his weapon. I calmed the druid with a gesture and immediately set the princess free. Chai-nee Shu sprung instantly to her feet and disgustedly spat out a chewed piece of dried meat, which I'd just given her as a reward for good behavior.

"Amra, never do that again!" I could read superstitious horror in the Princess's eyes. The girl even hurried to run away and take shelter behind her advisor.

"Beg your pardon Princess but, without a clear demonstration, you would have never believed me. You should know, though, that I am far from the strongest mage in my squadron. The forest nymph is much stronger and can take several dozen creatures under her control at once. So, back to the topic of a possible rougarou attack. Your warriors would start to fight with each other before even reaching the fortress, first taking down the cyclops, then one another!"

A tense silence arose. My opponents had yet to recover from the demonstration and were now digesting what they'd heard.

"Alright, Amra. Let's say you're right. The fleet in the river was destroyed, and our attack along the bank will drown in blood. What do you offer us?" the druid inquired, squeezing the girl tight to reassure her, as she whimpered in indignant fear.

"Before I make an offer, I need to know why we're even having this conflict. My orcs have never been hostile with the rougarou and, what is more, our squadron even contained a member of your race at one point... Just a second, my girl wants to tell me something. Please don't be afraid of my wyvern. She's well-trained and obedient."

Just then, we heard the flapping of wide wings coming down from the dark sky, first barely detectable, but more distinct with every passing second. VIXEN made a big circle over the island, searching for me in the thick fog, and finally noticed her master, plunking down right in the dirt just five meters away. Not paying any mind to the rougarou, grumbling unhappily after being splashed with swamp muck, the Royal Forest Wyvern crawled over to me and extended her long neck, offering to send me the information I'd requested. I walked over to my precious pet and touched my forehead to hers.

Black river. Lots of islands. A whole labyrinth of silted-up passageways. Everything in such thick fog that she had to fly right over the water, nearly touching the surface of the black river. Fires in the fog! A sharp turn toward them, gaining height. A big island. Straw huts. Many. A central square in the middle of a large village. A tall pillar with a totem in the shape of a white flower over a fanged canine mouth. Just what I needed. My master will be happy.

"Yes, exactly what I was looking for!" I confirmed, embracing my winged sweetie by the neck, and stroking the wyvern's emerald scales. "You're completely forgiven! What a smart cookie!"

The huge winged snake wagged her long scaly tail from side to side in the swamp mud just like a dog then, overcome with emotion, she tried to lick my face with her split tongue and lightly nibbled my hand.

Successful check for Poison Resistance
Experience received: 1300 Exp.

"He-ey, you don't need to be that sweet! Don't forget, you're poisonous after all!" I pulled my hand from the frightening jaws and pushed her snake-like head away good-naturedly. "And now, VIXEN, I've got a new mission for you. You're gonna like this one. Go to the orc camp, pick up our prisoner and bring him to the place you just showed me. When you get there, take off his blindfold and wait for him to take a look around, then gulp him down!!!"

Animal Control skill increased to level 47!

VIXEN flapped her wings excitedly and, taking off noisily and splashing mud, headed toward the orc camp to complete her mission. I then sent my sister a private message:

"Val, I just had an idea for how to get the players off our trail. VIXEN is gonna come now. Give her the captive. She will take him to the rougarou camp, let him take a look around and get the coordinates of our 'secret refuge,' then eat him on an altar. However... we shouldn't let all the experience for killing a level-88 Bowman go to just one creature. Let Yunna first give the prisoner a little stab with her dagger to share the experience. My 'niece' needs to level up quickly to get back to where she was."

"So then, respected Princess and advisor, I beg your forgiveness for the brief delay and suggest we return to our negotiations."

"What prisoner were you talking about planning to execute?" the princess's advisor wondered, on his guard, clearly having listened carefully to me.

"Don't you worry, he isn't a rougarou. He's a scout we caught from the first squadron of the undying. It's just that, not far from this island, the countryside is lousy with enraged undying. We tried to hold them in the Lower Fort and even sent many of them to respawn but, in the end, they made it through. And so, now we have to take measures to track the movement of our enemies and not let them take down my squadron."

"But... why?" asked Chai-nee Shu, still hiding behind her companion. "Amra, you're undying, after all. And my warriors saw another few undying in your squadron. Why don't you come to an agreement amongst yourselves?"

The cute big-eared dog-faced girl reminded me distinctly of Taisha in her earlier days with her child-like naivete. She had once thought that, if I could just speak with other undying, and they would immediately be ashamed at their unlawful behavior and stop destroying the goblin village of Tysh. How could I explain this in simple words, so the Princess would understand?

"Sweet Princess, the undying are very different, and it has nothing to do with origin. The ability to never perish once and for all gives many undying the idea that everything is allowed, and nothing is punished. They kill simply for fun, especially when they see creatures of other species and races. Among the undying, the majority are people, elves and half-elves, and they don't even think about legality or morals. When they see my orcs or your rougarou before them, they simply kill. But I don't consider the rougarou my enemies, so I was not planning to attack your villages and exterminate your people. I was simply planning to lead my orcs through your territories quickly without getting into any conflicts. We're on our way past the rapids of the black river, to a place where the undying cannot get us."

Diplomat skill increased to level 4!

Diplomat skill increased to level 5!

Trading skill increased to level 28!

"I did not know that," the princess admitted honestly. "I thought all the undying were identically evil. That is why I agreed to the advice of my regent to lure the dangerous newcomers from the fortress and leave them on a desolate island in the forest far away from the rougarou village. If the orcs had returned our ships, and hadn't started making new oars to replace the ones my oarsmen took away, we wouldn't have attacked."

"You leave guests in a desolate place they aren't familiar with, which just so happens to be an island, then expect them to simply sit with their hands crossed and not even try to leave?! Ah,

Princess, your naivete impresses me!"

Chai-nee Shu got embarrassed and fell silent, but instead of her, the druid joined the conversation:

"We treated you the way we treat all enemies. Yes, it was I who suggested my Princess use some military cleverness and lure your squadron away from the fortress," the regent admitted. "But we became enemies before that. The rougarou are subjects of the Dark Sovereign, and we swore to defend the borders of his territories. We received news of the battle in the swamps and the death of our neighbor the Rat King. He was also a subject of the Dark Sovereign, and our ally. We saw a giant in your squadron wearing the late King's armor. His magic wand is with the forest nymph, and you yourself are riding the Swamp Wolf Alpha, his former mount."

Woah! I didn't answer immediately, but first walked up to Baron, who he'd mentioned and thoughtfully stroked the huge dark brown wolf on his powerful furry chest. I never would have thought all this hubbub was due to our victory over the mixed army of the living and undead. It wasn't exactly possible to come to a peaceful agreement with them. The army of the Rat King attacked us as soon as they saw us! But now, when the true reason for the rougarou's hostility was revealed, we could try to resolve the root of the conflict and solve things peacefully. What about declaring to the rougarou that we were not enemies of the Dark Sovereign and were going to meet him and join his army?

Beyond that, as a video game plotline tester, I was interested in being on the same side as all those inhabiting higher up the Styx. What if I managed to join forces with the Dark Sovereign?! I wondered if that was even possible. At the very least, it was worth a try, because it wasn't just an unexplored scenario, but also an interesting way of behaving and, if I could pull it off, it would allow my squadron to walk unimpeded up the Styx through all territories of the Dark Sovereign!

I walked away from Baron, shifted my tone from confident and decisive to tired and pensive, then said:

"I'll admit, I really don't understand why the Rat King attacked my squadron... Orcs have never really been considered one of the 'forces of light,' in fact it's more the other way around, and we could easily have become loyal allies or even subjects of the Dark Sovereign. And also, the Emissary of Darkness, who showed up after the battle, just kept telling us to turn back like a parrot instead of offering different options. We're just looking for a calm place to settle higher up the black river, where all the people and elves of the undying will not follow us. And if the Dark Sovereign could give us some territories to settle, we would develop them and defend them valiantly."

Now came my opponents' turn to think seriously. The princess and her advisor walked farther away and started whispering. I didn't listen in. Despite my huge sensitive ears, I just wasn't feeling like it. Valerianna Quickfoot wrote that Max Sochnier's girlfriend Olilissa had been seriously wounded and the Naiad Trader's pet swordfish Claymore had been killed. More than three hundred players had left the Lower Fort and were making their way up the Styx, apparently heading in our direction.

"Ready the boats, and be prepared to leave at any time."

We needed to move on immediately before this wave of players caught up to my squadron. But here, the rougarou negotiators came to some kind of decision and returned to me. Princess Chai-nee Shu bowed with a proud look and told me:

"Amra, the Clan of the White Lily is prepared to allow you and your squadron passage through our territories. What is more, we will get in touch with neighboring clans and ask them to do the same. Our influence on other subjects of the Dark Sovereign is too small to influence their decision, but we will still tell the cyclopes and mountain giants of your arrival, so they won't attack you out of ignorance."

~ A Trap for the Potentate ~

Mission completed: Negotiations with the Rougarou (1/2)
Experience received: 4320 Exp.
Opinion of the Clan of the White Lily increased by +15
+5 to Rougarou opinion

Diplomat skill increased to level 6!

Trading skill increased to level 29!

The markers on the mini-map for the Princess and her advisor changed to a neutral yellow color. However, I was no longer hot or cold to their agreement or disagreement, because the Clan of the White Lily couldn't stop my orcs from leaving by boat but, as for what they said about the other clans, cyclopes and giants, that was just what I wanted to hear. I bowed and thanked the Princess and her advisor for the wise decision then, in a burst of good nature, decided to tell the rougarou about the three hundred undying on the way to their camp.

"They don't know about our camp, so we'll be safe," the druid said, waving off the threat as inconsequential.

"A village with straw huts on a large island where, in the middle of the square, there is a tall totem with a white flower over a fanged wolf mouth? The undying have already discovered it and will soon flatten it."

The tranquility instantly flew off Uvari-Dor's face, and the more emotional princess started whimpering in fear. Uvari-Dor Shu reproached me:

"Amra, my tribe could be wiped out. You knew about it but kept silent?!"

"One minute ago, we were enemies, so I had no reason to help you," I said, giving a just objection to his reproach. "In fact, I was even planning to use your village as a lure to draw the undying and allow me and my squadron to leave. But circumstances have changed. You stopped being hostile, so I honestly told your clan about the approaching danger. And if we were friends I'd even help warn the residents of the island, who don't suspect a thing, to get them out of their doomed village."

Diplomat skill increased to level 7!

Diplomat skill increased to level 8!

"Can we warn them?" the young Princess asked, looking to her regent and awaiting his answer. But the druid just fatefully lowered his fanged snout after some thoughtful silence and said:

"My princess, we don't have any more boats to send a messenger and tell the peaceful residents of the camp about the approaching danger. I'm afraid the residents of the village are doomed... No matter how intensely pitiful it may be, we are in no condition to help them, and our priority now is to save our very strongest warriors by making sure the undying cannot find them. The skeleton of a warband will survive. We'll still have our territory and can make a new village. Also, new residents will show up sooner or later."

"NOOOOO!!!" the young Princess shouted out in despair. "That is a very bad solution, advisor! If we cannot deal with it ourselves, then let's ask Amra and his orcs for help!"

Mission received: Negotiations with the Rougarou (2/2)

Mission class: Rare, racial, time-limited

Description: the village of the Clan of the White Lily will be attacked by players very soon, while the warriors of the clan will not be able to get there fast enough to help. Come to an agreement with the rougarou to work together and reach the village fast enough to warn and evacuate as many villagers as possible

Reward: 32000 Exp., +15 to the opinion of the Clan of the White Lily, +5 to the opinion of all other clans

Penalty for failure: Hostility with the Rougarou

Bonus condition: Rescue all the peaceful

villagers
        Reward: Loyalty of the Princess of the Clan of the White Lily
        Bonus condition: Rescue all the village's warriors
        Reward: Loyalty of the Regent of the Clan of the White Lily
        Reward if all conditions are met: Alliance offer from the Clan of the White Lily
        Time limit: 17 minutes 32 seconds

The Princess begged, promised and even tried to kneel, but her advisor and I didn't allow Chai-nee Shu to lower herself so much, picking her up before she hit the ground. All the same, I wasn't fully listening, so I didn't give a concrete answer. I was more interested in the mission description. First of all, I opened the map and looked at the distance between my camp and the island village. Four and a half kilometers?! Come on, are you kidding?! Just getting there would take at least half an hour, and maybe even twice that! Why was it giving me so little time?

All my showy pretense and confidence instantly flew away. I needed to act very quickly, because every second counted. And it seemed that, without using magic, there was nothing to be done. I told Valerianna Quickfoot about the situation and ordered her to get in a boat, but not go anywhere yet and wait for the rougarou warriors. I also called VIXEN and told my flying beauty to come to me as fast as she could.

Finally, I got up to the totally despairing and lost rougarou huntress, who was crouching right in the mud and wiping bitter tears from her snout. The regent didn't even try to comfort her, because he understood that any words now would be pointless and empty.

"Princess, I'll help you save your subjects. But you need to trust me. We're going to fly together to the island village of the Clan of the White Lily on my wyvern. It's the fastest way. The rougarou won't believe me on my own, so I need you to come with. Meanwhile, your advisor Uvari-Dor Shu can talk with the rougarou warriors here on the island, and they can enter the orc camp. My warriors will let them in unimpeded and show them free places in the boats. Rowing to your island will take all our strength, and I'm very much hoping for magical support from the mavka and my shaman. Also... there is a seriously wounded nereid by the name Olilissa in the water next to the island. Uvari-Dor Shu, as far as I know, druids have healing magic. I ask you to help the nereid, because Olilissa is very dear to my friend."

The regent gave a dignified, barely noticeable nod. The princess then hopped up and threw herself around my neck, embracing me and not so much kissing as licking my face like a dog.

Diplomat skill increased to level 9!

Foreman skill increased to level 50!
You may now choose your second specialization in this skill

* * *

We just barely made it.

I mean, VIXEN proved herself above all praise, bringing me and Chai-nee Shu to the village of the Clan of the White Lily in the blink of an eye. The girl was terrified the whole ride and held onto me tightly. The residents immediately ran out of their huts to see what the alarming sound of warning was. And it didn't take them long to pack up. The rougarou just grabbed their most valuable possessions, above all their children and hurried to the dock. But there weren't many boats left in the village, and only a third of the villagers could fit. The others had to wait for the warriors to arrive and quickly take their places at the very last moment. We could already hear the ghastly wail of a great many approaching monsters through the fog. In front of the army of undying, there was a cohort of the most unbelievable pets.

"Let's go! Down that channel! I'll create an illusion of shore and pebbles!" Valerianna Quickfoot commanded, and the magic wand in her hand lit up with a dark blue flame.

~ A Trap for the Potentate ~

The chain of boats with the last runaways hid in the channel. The Princess and I, though, stayed back a bit. The girl was getting some of the clan's valuables and relics from the chieftain's hut, and I was pulling up some large, unusual, white, orange, and light-blue lilies growing next to the totem pole, taking some with the root so I could replant them later.

Mystical Royal Lily (alchemy ingredient)

Dappled Royal Lily (alchemy ingredient)
River Royal Lily (alchemy ingredient)

You are the first to discover these plants in Boundless Realm.

Herbalism skill increased to level 28!

Herbalism skill increased to level 29!

Herbalism skill increased to level 30!

Herbalism skill increased to level 31!
...
Fame increased
Present value: 21

What a successful feat! My boss would be quite satisfied at such speedy leveling of my

Herbalism skill! I was reminded that, quite recently, Chai-nee Shu had told me that their village had twice been devastated by undying. But that meant there wasn't a single Herbalist among those players, because no one had discovered these rare yet prominent plants before. My theory that the higher up the Styx I got, the more unknown herbs and flowers I would find was now proven.

Only when attacker markers showed up on the mini-map did I take off into the air with VIXEN. Holding the furry Princess in front of me with one hand as she shivered in fear, I banked a steep turn and, at a blistering speed, carried us right over the forward group of approaching players. In that squadron, there were forty or fifty players, and there were some there of every kind! Elemental Mages, Necromancers, Bowmen, Druids, Paladins... They were going to the doomed village through the water or, to be more accurate, on ice created by their mages. They clearly weren't expecting to see me overhead. After us, there whistled a couple belated arrows. Also, a fireball loosed by a mage flew up into the sky.

Animal Control skill increased to level 48!

Dodge skill increased to level 29!

~ A Trap for the Potentate ~

Riding skill increased to level 23!

"Too bad you aren't a dragon," I said, patting my emerald darling on the back. "Maybe we could try and melt the ice under their feet. Not too many of them have heavy armor on though, so most of them would be able to swim... Alright, let's make another circle and distract the undying so our boats can get a bit further away."

VIXEN made a second turn back, but sharply recoiled and even started spinning, letting a huge ballista bolt go past us, followed by a swarm of crossbow bolts and arrows of a more reasonable size.

Successful Agility check
Experience received: 23 Exp.

Dodge skill increased to level 30!

I barely managed to keep hold of the wyvern during her high-octane maneuvers and ordered my mount to fly higher, out of range. I didn't know that our enemies had brought war machinery with them. Also, the players weren't even remotely surprised by my wyvern... Our midair pirouettes started looking a bit foolhardy. We might not get so lucky next time. What was more, the rougarou Princess sitting in front of me was all green and whimpering through clenched teeth that she had motion sickness. I had to get away, taking a very wide curve and changing flight direction a few times so none of the pursuers could guess where we were going.

As soon as VIXEN got a bit further from the players and disappeared from view, I saw a message from Antonius Just in the local chat:

"It's no use to run, Amra. We're gonna catch your squadron either in the Upper Fort or at the river rapids, where you'll be forced to come ashore. So, let's not waste time and agree right now. You understand perfectly we're interested in you as a vampire. I want to know your terms."

Mission completed: Negotiations with the Rougarou (2/2)
Experience received: 8640 Exp.
Opinion of the Clan of the White Lily increased by +15
+5 to Rougarou opinion of you
Reward for bonus condition: Princess of the Clan of the White Lily's opinion increased to +100
Diplomat skill increased to level 10!

Chai-nee Shu's marker on the map changed color not just to green, but straight to blue for ally! I spent some time staring at that change with a satisfied grin, then it hit me — hey, where was the reward for the second bonus condition? And where was the alliance offer from the Clan of the White Lily? They hadn't lost a warrior, right?! My sister answered my question in a private message:

"The cyclops couldn't fit in the boat, or even two boats tied together. We had to leave him next to the camp and tell him what direction to go in so the undying wouldn't find him. But he was very slow and, it seemed to me, not overly intelligent."

The cyclops? But he wasn't a rougarou, why had his death affected my mission?! But when I told my companion about the death of the cyclops, Chai-nee Shu got very upset and even afraid.

"That was Yuwuu, the youngest son of the cyclops chieftain. We have a treaty with our neighbors: two of my cousins live with them, and Yuwuu with us. They're all guests and, at the same time, hostages. It's an age-old tradition and something of a guarantee of peace... Yuwuu has been living with the Clan of the White Lily for a long time and was even considered an honorary rougarou... What will happen now? The cyclopes are sure to start a war when they find out what happened! My cousins might as well be dead already..."

The girl started wailing and, turning to face me, tucked her little snout into my shoulder. I embraced her and was preparing to give the unfortunate Princess words of reassurance when suddenly, in a gap in the clouds, I saw a sight that both impressed and shocked me: up to her knees in black water, holding the hem of a long dress with her hands, a huge woman was walking through the Styx. She was roughly as tall as a nine-story building! Her long dark hair was unkempt, and her eyes were flickering with a hateful orange and red fire.

The first thought to bubble up in my head was that this was the Cyclops's mother, coming to take revenge for her fallen son, but this woman had two eyes, and not one. Soon, though, VIXEN flew up closer, and the woman made another step forward in the river of death, so I could now read the giant's name:

Hel
Ruler of the World of the Dead (unique creature)

The fog around hid me from the fearsome goddess but, just in case, I turned the Royal Forest Wyvern sharply, so I wouldn't accidentally run into the frightening lady in bad visibility. All the same, two hands popped up from the sheet of cloud and very skillfully plucked VIXEN out of the air like a dragonfly. My emerald beauty batted her wings, nearly breaking them, and tried to poke her long neck out between the giantess's fingers, but Hel was holding my Wyvern tight in the trap of her two folded hands. Chai-nee Shu gave a howling wail, and started whimpering in fear. I completely understood and shared her feelings, although I would not die once and for all.

"So, here you are, the thief who dared to intrude into my lands and steal from my guard Modgud!" the fearsome goddess was looking at me through the gaps between her fingers. "Did you think that because you'd escaped, you'd gotten away scot free and I wouldn't find you?!"

Island Duel

IN THAT TENSE moment, I wasn't thinking about myself at all, and not even my beautify emerald wyvern. With all her colossal dimensions and deadly power, Hel could easily send us to respawn. Yes, it would be unpleasant, but we only risked losing a bit of experience and time. For the young rougarou Princess, though, this would be her only and final death.

I liked Chai-nee Shu. She was fun, cute and fluffy. She also had her own point of view on *Boundless Realm*, a distinct character and convictions, creating a mixture of pride, high-handedness and naivete. I had already started making certain plans for the rougarou Princess and her clan, and I was thinking about ways to bring them with me on the journey up the Styx.

~ A Trap for the Potentate ~

The viewers of my video clips were sure to like such a companion for my Goblin Herbalist, while two hundred rougarou warriors with average level around one hundred would be a great reinforcement for my army. Also, I was sure I could find an application for the three hundred rougarou with peaceful professions. I had seen smiths, weavers, bakers and carpenters, and they would all have work.

But all these plans threatened to collapse because of this immortal lady, who was now looking at us through the gaps between her fingers like some silly little animals through the bars of a cage. The giantess could have easily crushed us with her huge hands, smashing us like pestilent insects, but she was in no rush.

"Don't leave my side!" I whispered to Chai-nee Shu, who was shaking in terror. "I'll try to protect you as best I can."

The girl nodded in silence and pressed herself closer to me as her only hope and protection. Of course, it was very arrogant and even naive on my part to hope even I could escape this situation, and all the more so to promise to help the Princess. Although Amra's Strength and Constitution were much higher than other level-52 beings, the immortal Goddess Hel wouldn't even notice my resistance, if she wanted to close her hand. As if reading my thoughts, she strengthened her grasp. VIXEN started shrieking in pain as the bones in her luxuriant wings crunched.

What could I do?! Could anything really stand up against such a powerful and high-level creature? Maybe... a creature twice her level? I then opened my inventory, searching for the Dark Rider's Arrow but, at the last minute, snapped my hand back, not wanting to use such a dangerous and unpleasant object. A Midnight Wraith twice the level of one of the highest goddesses of the Scandinavian pantheon is not the kind of creature you'd want in your vicinity. That would have meant certain death to everything around.

At that moment, a desperate idea came to my head to bite Hel's finger before the Goddess crushed us all. I sunk my teeth into the nearest finger, as big around as a hundred-year-old oak and with skin as tough as tree bark.

Achievement unlocked: Taste Tester (150/1000)
Regeneration improved to 50 HP/Minute
Resistance to death magic increased to 10%

Fame increased
Present value: 22

My Taste Tester had grown by fifty points in one go! The blood of the gods was much more potent than that of mere mortals.

"Ow!" I suspect the giantess shouted not so much in pain as in surprise. "A vampire?! You insolent bloodsucker! Now you'll see why I'm called the sovereign of the world of the dead. Even the undying find it extremely difficult to escape my gloomy lifeless lands and get back to the world of the living!" And here, Hel suddenly froze and slightly opened her fingers. The eyes of the goddess grew wide in surprise. "Now this is really interesting... The soul of my brother lives in your puny little body!!! Fenrir, is that you?!"

Woah! The surprise of the goddess was simply nothing in comparison with my own. Was Hel Fenrir's sister?! I'll admit, I had a poor understanding of Scandinavian mythology, so I didn't know. Now that would be an unexpected twist! But to me, it was a great chance to escape and also save VIXEN and Chai-nee Shu.

"I'm not Fenrir yet, but I am trying to become his reincarnation!" I shouted to the goddess, and she completely unclenched her fingers.

"Fool, why didn't you tell my servant Modgud right away?! You dragged away a puppy, but you could have chosen any of the grim immortal hounds of the Wild Hunt! And what use are ghostly hounds? In Modgud's kennel, a litter was just born that included the four-eyed Garm, the 'greatest of dogs!' Now that's a pretty little animal! After he grows up a bit, he'll become the pride of our whole land. Then you'll see! Even the much-vaunted Cerberus of the ancient gods won't come close! You could have walked up to my servant like a master and just taken Garm, but you didn't. You crawled into the garden like a thief... Eh, what am I talking about dogs for, your own children are the heavenly wargs Sköll and Hati. They'd have followed you with just one word!"

The more Hel spoke, the lower my head drooped. As it turned out, on the border between the worlds of the dead and the living, in the land of the giants, there were so many possibilities I could have just extended a hand and taken, but I didn't even notice! Now though, it was too late to change anything. According to the goddess, if fate had wanted to give me something other than the pup Gjöll, I would have gotten it. But as I hadn't taken anything else, that meant I wasn't meant to have it. Somewhat strange logic, to my eye, but I didn't want to risk arguing with the fearsome goddess.

"By the way... who dared put a curse on you?!" lightning bolts of rage flickered in Hel's eyes again.

I explained to the giantess best I could that it was done on my own request to help me take down a Dark Rider and a cunning Midnight Wraith. But the curse was no longer important and, if my sister were to remove it, I would only be glad.

~ A Trap for the Potentate ~

Hel led her hand over my head, and Amra had a wave of sparking golden air flow over him. I got a message saying the curse had been removed, and that I had received quite a weighty divine blessing:

Divine Blessing!
For the next 72 hours, your character will receive 200% experience
For the next 72 hours, you will be immune to the rays of the sun and holy magic

Next to me, the Princess was laughing in joy, having received complete immunity to fear and death magic for the next three days. VIXEN then spread her beautiful emerald wings once again. All her broken bones and wounds had healed instantly.

"It's time for me to go," Hel said, bowing and carefully placing her hand on the ground, offering to let us out on the banks of the river. "If there's any way I can help you, brother, now is the time to say. If you want, I could take all the pursuers after you and bring them to the world of the dead, for example."

It was very tempting to send three hundred hostile players to respawn, but I still refused. It wouldn't really be of any use: I wouldn't get any experience from their death, and the players would just respawn to threaten me and my squadron again. But if it was possible to stop them from getting in front of my squadron and not let them organize a siege of the Upper Fort or at the rapids of the Styx... Wait! Why was I thinking so one-dimensionally?

"Hel, if you really want to help, I need a portal for my whole squadron to the upper reaches of the Styx!"

Diplomat skill increased to level 11!

Trading skill increased to level 30!

"Could you be more specific?" the goddess clarified. "The river of death is unbelievably long and doesn't have a source. Many different small rivers and streams, which begin both in the world of the dead and even in Chaos, the first thing to exist, join up with the Styx. Where do you need to go, brother?"

Woah... I didn't know these details about the geography of the Styx, so I didn't have any idea of how to put my question more specifically. If it wasn't possible to find the source of the black river, then where did I even need to go? And how could I even fulfill my promise to the viewers, if the black river had no beginning?

"I can open gates to the very farthest borders of the land of the giants, where my territory and power ends. From there, you will find the lands of the Dark Sovereign, although I don't know much about those areas, and even less about their ruler."

"Yes, that's exactly where I need to go!" I assured the goddess, and Hel extended me a long bright-red thread, which she plucked from her dress.

Single-use magic portal circle

"Connect the two ends, throw the circle on the ground, and gates will appear! Although I don't understand, Amra, what you want in those gloomy lands. The water of the Styx there is so cold and toxic that everything alive will die just by touching it. Eternal twilight, vast hordes of starving wights and creatures warped by magic, which no longer belong either to the living or the undead... Even I, the ruler of the world of the dead, find them terrifying!"

Chai-nee Shu gave a somewhat stupid smile when she heard these words, like a student high on pot. The rougarou girl clearly found it funny that the goddess of the world of the dead was afraid of dead things. I shook my head reproachfully. Immunity to fear wasn't always a boon to the health, and I was afraid that Hel would get offended she was being laughed at. The goddess really did look unhappily at the Princess, who had shown joy at the wrong time, but didn't say anything out loud. Instead of that, the giantess tore a dark hair from her head and gave it to me with the words:

"At least take a normal weapon to use against the inhabitants of those places. I mean, your spiky ball isn't going to do any damage to ghosts!"

Hair Whip of the Goddess Hel (unique weapon)

Indestructible

+35% chance of ignoring armor, +47% chance of ignoring incorporeity, +18 Exotic Weapon skill, +112% damage dealt to undead and dark creatures

A serious weapon! I wanted to thank the giantess for such a luxurious gift, but the huge woman just smiled, took a step back and dissolved into the dense fog. And something was telling me that there was no longer any sense in searching for her nearby. The goddess may have been hundreds or even thousands of kilometers away.

* * *

The next stage of the negotiations with the rougarou took place on a small rocky island in the middle of the black river.

~ A Trap for the Potentate ~

The Clan of the White Lily was represented by the Princess and her Regent and, from our side, I took Valerianna Quickfoot for support and advice.

"The Clan of the White Lily isn't going anywhere! This is our land, and we've lived here for centuries!" Uvari-Dor was annoyed and categorical. He simply ignored all my reasoning about the coming of the undying.

"I'm afraid, Uvari-Dor Shu, that you simply underestimate the scale of the threat." During my speech I was stroking the red fur of the huge and ghastly level-two-hundred-twelve Guard Dog, who was lying at my feet and groaning in satisfaction. "Just an hour and a half ago, three hundred undying nearly cut down your whole clan, including nursing babies. And well, those three hundred undying haven't gone anywhere! They're roving about somewhere nearby in the fog and, sooner or later, they will find us. The twelve kilometers we put between us and the island village is basically nothing to their scouts! We need to get further away, where the undying will not find your rougarou, and using a portal is one way to do that!"

Diplomat skill increased to level 12!

It was obvious that the Princess was prepared to approve my plan and take her whole Clan of the White Lily far away from the impertinent undying, who were becoming the scourge of these regions. But the girl either was not accustomed to making such serious decisions without the approval of her experienced advisor, or simply didn't have the right. And the conservative druid was categorically against resettlement, so the negotiations had come to a standstill. Just then, a private message came in from my sister, and I took a break to read through it.

"What are you dawdling for, Tim? The two hostage cousins of the Princess you told me about have already been executed by the cyclopes, so the overall opinion of the Clan of the White Lily is now equal to the arithmetical mean of the opinion of the Princess and this stubborn Druid. They're the last two key NPC's, so their whole clan's opinion depends on them. The Princess is completely loyal and, if she were to become the only key character, the whole clan would follow you to the ends of the earth."

Technically, my sister was suggesting I simply kill the stubborn hard-headed druid and thus gain control of the rougarou clan through the Princess. It was harsh but, clearly, the forest nymph no longer saw any other options. I'll admit, I had already lost my patience with the unsuccessful attempts to convince the regent. All the same, I tried one more time to solve the issue diplomatically:

~ A Trap for the Potentate ~

"Advisor Uvari-Dor Shu, as you can plainly see, I am one of the undying. Let's not argue whether that's good or bad for the rougarou now, because there is no conclusive answer. But I am aware of a few plans, and can assure you that those three hundred undying we saw in the Lower Fort are just a pitiful advance party before a truly huge army! Soon, tens of thousands of undying will be passing through these lands, and the Clan of the White Lily won't have a single chance of survival. I sincerely want to help your clan! I like Chai-nee Shu, and don't want the sweet young girl to die!"

Successful check for Chai-nee Shu's reaction

Check for Uvari-Dor Shu's reaction failed

"How can I know whether your words about an undying invasion and desire to help are true and not a lie??? For now, I see an obvious trap. You're suggesting that my clan leave its homelands, and pass through a portal to such wild and dangerous places that only undead and mutants live there, where the water is poisoned, and there isn't enough light to grow grain! After the portal is closed, we will not be able to return, and will die in those ghastly lands!"

The regent had now built up to a hysterical scream, which clearly didn't make him more convincing in the eyes of the Princess, more likely the opposite.

Unlike the advisor, I spoke in a calm and confident voice, and could feel with my very skin that my reasoning was being accepted by Chai-nee Shu:

"The lands under control of the Dark Sovereign are expansive. There are plenty of dead places, but also places that are just fine to live in. Our shared mission is to achieve an audience with the Dark Sovereign and, after assuring him of our fidelity, obtain fruitful lands for both for orcs and rougarou where the undying cannot come."

Diplomat skill increased to level 13!

Check for Uvari-Dor Shu's reaction failed

"Never in my life would I believe it was possible to meet the Dark Sovereign himself!" Uvari-Dor Shu went back into a hysterical shout. "This whole fairytale looks too fantastical and adventuresome! No, no and no again! My clan will not follow outsiders and, what is more, will never follow a bloodthirsty and cunning vampire!"

The yellow marker of the druid on the mini-map changed color to a fully hostile red. I don't know if Chai-nee Shu had told her advisor what the goddess said about "bloodsucker," or if the druid found out my secret by some other means, but the racial penalty of vampires giving minus fifty to the reaction of any living creature was coming at a very bad time! Convincing the already obstinate druid had become practically impossible...

"My clan?" Chai-nee Shu suddenly perked up her ears. "Since when, advisor Uvari-Dor, does the Clan of the White Lily belong to you?"

"I meant to say the clan temporarily entrusted to my control, until your highness comes of age," the rougarou druid prattled out, afraid and embarrassed, but the forest nymph cut him off with a gesture:

"Princess, if you'd please answer, I'm just curious... Who would be in charge of the Clan of the White Lily if something were to happen to your Highness?"

The young huntress thought about it briefly, then pointed with a clawed paw at the regent. The forest nymph started laughing acridly and shook her head in reproach. I caught my smarty pants sister's idea right away and tried to build on it:

"Then I see why your advisor is so impatient to place the Clan of the White Lily and its Princess in harm's way. All of your relatives are dead, and all your advisor has to do is get rid of one last representative of the old dynasty, then power over the clan will be fully transferred to him. Technically, Uvari-Dor Shu is already the leader. The Princess trusts him and, from here, it's just a technical matter of making sure the naive girl dies in the upcoming encounter with the undying."

Diplomat skill increased to level 14!

"Yikes..." the Princess's already big eyes had grown huge in surprise, like those of an anime character. She clearly hadn't ever even considered the line of succession in the clan before.

"How dare you accuse me of betrayal?!" the druid objected, walking up to me and starting to growl, showing his fangs. "I have served Chai-nee Shu's relatives faithfully my whole life and, after their death, I have served their daughter!!! But you, vampire, are foreign to our rougarou clan! Get out of here with your orcs and leave us in peace!!! Princess, order Amra to leave!!!"

Successful check for Chai-nee Shu's reaction

Check for Uvari-Dor Shu's reaction failed

The girl went silent and just lowered her snout to the floor, starting to whine just like a dog. We had reached a dead end. The young rougarou Princess didn't want to leave without me, but she also couldn't find the resolve to contradict her advisor.

"It seems this interminable situation can only be resolved by a ritual duel!" the regent roared, frightfully upset by the Princess's silence.

- A Trap for the Potentate -

"We will have a battle to the death! One-on-one! One rougarou from the Clan of the White Lily against any of your warriors! If my duelist wins, you and your orcs get out of here and leave our clan in peace forever!"

The Princess started trying to break up the fight, but it was too late. No one was even listening to her anymore. My sister then gave an approving hand clap and wrote me a private message:

"Alright, finally! I was starting to get worried. My operation is in two hours, and you were just tongue-tied, unable to solve the rougarou problem. Agree to the duel now, before this mutt changes his mind."

"Sounds good!" I agreed, barely able to hold back a smile after reading my sister's message. "But if my duelist wins, you must obey me and lead the rougarou of the Clan of the White Lily wherever I say!"

The huge shaggy dog-headed man stretched out his lips into a ghastly fanged smile:

"Agreed! Fortunately, I'll never have to see such a shameful act, because I will be the rougarou duelist! And now, name your fighter!"

Valerianna Quickfoot took a step forward and, skillfully tossing her shining scepter from hand to hand, asked:

"Amra, let me fight! You've seen me in action many times, and know perfectly well that this hard-headed fur ball doesn't stand the slightest chance against me! My hornets will devour his frozen corpse in a matter of seconds, even through his thick fur!!!"

"Hornets?" the high-level opponent faked amazement. "We were talking about a fair one-on-one fight, without the whole pack of other beings that accompany every undying!"

If the mavka, a Beast Master by trade, got embarrassed, her behavior didn't show it. I had no doubt in my sister and understood perfectly that, if the forest nymph had spoken so openly about hornets and ice spells, then she was probably preparing a totally different plan for this battle. Valerianna was strong not only from her pets. She could also use Water Magic, Illusion Magic and Death Magic and, with my sister's rich imagination, the variations for combining spells and tactics could be truly limitless.

But appointing Valerianna or anyone else instead of myself... it was hard to find the words... was it not right or something? After all, in this ritual duel, we were technically deciding whether Amra was strong and capable enough to replace Chai-nee Shu's advisor, and lead the five-hundred-strong rougarou clan after him. So, it would be more correct and honest for me to take part myself, despite the huge chasm in level between my level-52 Goblin Herbalist and the level-124 Rougarou Druid.

"I'll fight you myself!"

- A Trap for the Potentate -

Mission received: Negotiations with the Rougarou (additional stage)

Mission class: Required, personal

Description: Defeat the Regent Uvari-Dor Shu in a ritual duel to the death without using your pets

Reward: 48000 Exp., +15 to the opinion of the Clan of the White Lily, +5 to the opinion of all other clans, -30 to the opinion of Chai-nee Shu

Penalty for failure: Hostility with the Rougarou, -70 to the opinion of Chai-nee Shu

The Princess was already crouching and whining in sadness. What was that? The girl must have been categorically opposed to her two closest friends fighting. Clearly, this was the very reason. No matter what the outcome of the duel, the Princess's opinion would noticeably fall. My little sister was also obviously upset, but not over the duel, because I had refused her help.

"It's your choice, Tim. I hope you know what you're doing."

I sent the Gray Pack to the furthest end of the island to avoid any excesses, ordering the wolves to lie down and not intervene under any circumstances. At the same time, the orcs and rougarou from a few boats landed on the island and formed a small circle thirty steps across, thus blocking off the area for the ritual duel. In that perimeter, I saw the familiar faces of Ziabash Hardy, Irek, Shaman Ghuu and Gnum Spiteful. But the main part of the audience preferred to remain in their boats and observe the duel from afar. At the same time, many of the rougarou were loudly cheering their fighter on, also shouting out curses and insults at me. My orcs were silent at first, not accustomed to such spectacles, so they slightly lost courage but, after that, they totally lit up:

"Show this flea-ridden mutt who is the terror of the seas! Captain, bite his nuts off!!! Amra, break his neck!!! The staff, pull the staff from the rougarou's paws and stick that curvy branch where the sun doesn't shine!!!"

Valerianna Quickfoot, who should have been maintaining order, spent a long time comforting the weeping Chai-nee Shu, and finally convinced the Princess to leave the circle.

"You may begin!" the forest nymph exclaimed before also leaving the perimeter, in order not to interfere in the duel.

One after the next, I drank down an Elixir of Agility, Strength, and Speed, after which I took my whip in my hands and prepared to meet the huge shaggy rougarou, who had thrown off practically all his clothing, leaving just a chest sling, and was stretching just twenty steps from me. The huge rippling muscles of the druid were distinctly visible even under the layer of thick brown fur, which inspired enthusiastic shouts from his tribe members, especially the females. By the way, the druid did not leave his staff and was spinning figure-eights in the air with it, stretching the hands of his clawed paws.

And then... without coming near me, the druid grabbed the staff with both of his paws and raised it over his head, shouting out a curse as he did! A crack formed in the dense gray clouds, and a bright ray of morning sunshine lit up the ground. Sun!!!

Damage taken: 0 HP (Immunity to sunlight)

I tensed up in fear for a few seconds, morally prepared for a rapid death but, other than a few messages popping up about immunity to sunlight, nothing too scary happened. It was funny, but my Dodge bar was quickly filling up. The game algorithms thought my character was dodging the deadly dangerous rays by some kind of miracle. I snorted happily. I mean, it sounded pretty funny, dodging the sun! I wondered if I would have to move faster than the speed of light to really dodge the sun. Didn't that go against the laws of physics? In any case, I would have to thank Hel if I got the chance. It was her divine blessing that had allowed me to survive.

Clearly, the druid was counting on a

different effect when he had called the bright sunlight down on my vampire, because the huge rougarou was batting his eyelids in surprise, and even lowered his staff. And while my opponent was still in a confused state, and the high-level druid hadn't readied something deadlier from his rich arsenal of spells, I dashed out in front, closing the gap. From seven meters away, I gave a flick and lashed my opponent deeply with the unique hair whip. Got him! Hit! The whip strike connected with the rougarou's shoulder, deeply splitting his flesh and spraying drops of blood. However... my opponent's life bar went down by, at best, three percent, but probably less!!!

Damage dealt: 314 (2467 whip strike — 709 armor, 70% resistance to physical damage)

Exotic Weapons skill increased to level 17!

Now it was my turn to stand in confusion with my jaw hanging down, and for the druid to touch his wound and be surprised at the lack of serious damage. What was more, Uvari-Dor Shu's excellent regeneration quickly healed the wound over, and the druid's life bar filled back up right before my eyes. I made another couple whip lashes but, other than raising my Exotic Weapons skill to 20, no effect was achieved.

~ A Trap for the Potentate ~

Uvari-Dor Shu recovered from all the damage quite quickly and easily and, on my next blow, he made a clever move and grabbed the whip as it curled around his hand, pulling the weapon away from me. However, his long and heavy druid staff was nowhere near the greatest weapon against my nimble goblin, and Amra easily dodged the bulky inert bludgeon:

Dodge skill increased to level 32!

Dodge skill increased to level 33!

Dodge skill increased to level 34!

Acrobatics skill increased to level 23!

For now, I was getting lucky. The druid hadn't hit me once. Nevertheless, my brain was fitfully searching for a way out, or better tactic. Should I just keep fighting and hope that, with my rapid leveling of skills in this duel, in five or six hours, my stats would be strong enough to do more serious damage to the enemy? Funny! I would get tired much faster than that. My endurance points would go down to zero and I would begin to take heavy damage.

But the druid decided to change tactics first. After throwing his useless staff aside, Uvari-Dor Shu got down on his haunches... and his body began to quickly change! All druids had the ability to take animal form in battle! I took advantage of his temporary vulnerability and gave him a Vampire Bite, a few strikes with my clawed gloves, and even threw my Throwing Net over him.

Exotic Weapons skill increased to level 21!

Athletics skill increased to level 22!

But from there, it got dire... A huge brown bear straightened up to his full four-meter height and tore the Throwing Net to bits with ease, as if it were a spider web, then pinned me under him and started tearing with his fearsome claws!!! I answered with blows and occasionally restored my quickly falling health with Vampire Bites, making bleeding tear-wounds, but I couldn't keep this going for long, because my endurance was falling.

"Don't hold me back, let your rage out. Otherwise, we'll lose!"

A voice rang out right in my head. It was definitely not a message from my sister or any other player.

What the hell?! Had I started hallucinating due to lack of air? The bear really was pressing on me with his paws and starting to strangle me. My ribs were creaking and threatening to break at any moment. I couldn't breathe. At that, I could barely hold back his fearsome jaws and stop his bear teeth from sinking into my neck. It seemed that, no matter how I resisted using the arrow of darkness, I had no other way out. The druid had gained the upper hand in the ritual duel.

"Don't think about the pain and possible loss! Only rage and battle lust, only the intoxicating taste of blood! Let me out!!!"

There was that voice again! I understood it clearly and... believed it! Just then, I wailed in unbearable pain, when my own body began to transform. My bones stretched out, my jaw grew longer, my green skin grew black fur and gruesome claws grew out of my furry fingers!

Level fifty-three!

A huge black wolf, no smaller than the brown bear, had taken the place of the small and scrawny goblin in this fight. Two huge predators intertwined into a tangled ball with a roar and, rolling along the wet ground, were tearing into each other with teeth and claws. I couldn't see my audience and their reaction to what was happening, because I was too busy tearing into the flesh of the enraged bear and getting soaked with blood, both his and my own, which was abundantly lashing from many wounds. It was the most natural mindlessness, pure intoxication of battle, like that experienced by the ancient berserkers. I didn't care about my own wounds, all the more so given that the blows and bites I was making were slightly restoring my character's health and healing my wounds.

The scales on the altar of victory went back and forth for some time, but then started tipping distinctly in my favor. Finally, three minutes later, the exhausted bloodied bear unclenched his gruesome embrace and collapsed onto his back. All that remained was for me to bite open his throat, and I sunk my fangs into the neck of the brown-furred predator. I wondered how many levels I would get for a solo victory over a creature that was seventy-one levels higher than me, especially considering the triple experience bonus I had! Twenty-five or more like twenty-eight levels...

"NOOOOO!!!!!" breaking through the perimeter, Chai-nee Shu ran onto the little square.

The Princess threw herself on the bloodied and wheezing bear. Bubbles of blood were already coming out of his mangled throat. The girl covered my prey with her body.

"You must eat her as well!!! Before anyone else does!!!"

But I was already in complete control of my character and suppressed that spark of rage. Grudgingly unclenching my fangs, my huge black wolf stepped back, angrily whipping his tail at his feet. The pain returned. My body started squeezing back down to size. A few seconds later, next to the barely living regent, who had already returned to his dog-headed appearance, there was a Goblin Herbalist covered head to toe in blood.

"Was that... Fenrir?" the druid rasped out, finding me with his half-mad gaze. "I... can't believe... I held out so long..."

"That was only the shadow of Fenrir," I said wearily, "but you did fight honorably."

The Princess, leaning over the wounded figure, muttered words of encouragement and, one after the other, poured healing elixirs into the regent's mouth. I then picked up the whip I'd lost in battle and walked around them both, thinking over what to do next. Clearly, finishing off the wounded rougarou after the Princess's intervention wouldn't have been merely bad form, but fundamentally improper. I wasn't even feeling so sorry for the lost experience and levels (although I was sorry for that, what's to hide?) — what could I do now? — worse was that the still-active mission said battle to the death, but none of the conditions it listed had come to pass.

The druid then, with the help of his young ward, stood heavily on his shaking legs, but immediately went down on one knee and bowed his head in respect. And together with him, hundreds of other rougarou also bowed down, both on the island and in the many boats. Chai-nee Shu then, the only member of her race still on her feet, walked over to me:

"Amra, open your portal. The whole Clan of the White Lily will follow you. And..." here, the Princess gave me a totally dog-like lick on the face, "thank you!"

Mission: Negotiations with the rougarou (additional stage) has been canceled

* * *

"Amra, the water in the river is unbelievably cold, and also burns like acid!" The Naiad Trader raised his hand and showed it to me. It was covered with blisters like it had been scalded in boiling water. "I can't believe such caustic water didn't dissolve our boats!"

"It isn't dissolving them yet, but I've been watching the canoes with alarm for a long time now," Valerianna Quickfoot called back from the neighboring boat. "It's more like some kind of poison than an acid. To everything alive, this poison is very dangerous, but it seemingly doesn't work on nonliving material."

"It's so cold!" Yunna, sitting next to me on a bench, was wrapped up tight in a blanket thrown over her jacket. She was also using the blanket to cover the tiny black puppy.

Gjöll had already reached level three and was a member of the Gray Pack, but was still just a tiny frightened pup, afraid of everything around and only at ease in Yunna's arms. The Goblin Wolf Rider had already gotten me to promise that, when Gjöll grew up and got stronger, she would be her rider. Irek obviously envied his sister and even tried to ask me for Fimbulthul instead of Lobo, but the huge shaggy hound didn't give a damn about the goblin boy, and more likely considered him an element of the decor than a master and rider.

"And how am I supposed to find my way around in this darkness?" Chai-nee Shu was also freezing, despite all her fur and warm jacket, but she was trying to look confident and strong, because, in the neighboring boats, her many subjects were watching her, and they weren't too pleased by the weather out here either.

The weather when we came through the portal was a piercing cold wind with snow and a sky as dark as night, even though the clock showed right around nine in the morning. One after the other, we had all poured out of the oval hole that burned with an orange-red fire and found ourselves on an expansive stone plateau, where not a single plant grew. Far below, under the precipice, we could hear the noisy black river. The orcs and rougarou had the foresight to bring our boats through the portal with us, but it was still a whole operation to lower them down to the black water with ropes. Thankfully, the Ogre Fortifier made a block and tackle system that worked very well and allowed us to carefully lower all the boats

~ Dark herbalist Book Three ~

without damaging a single one.

And now, for the last hour, we'd been sailing up river, which was quite swift in these mountainous lands. The Styx here looked nothing like the lazy flow we had seen down below in the swamplands. Here, it was a raging mountain river with lots of whirlpools and dangerous underwater stones. The helmsmen had to constantly be on guard, and the oarsmen couldn't be stingy with their strength. Everyone in the squadron was cold and having a hard time, but the most bothered, I suppose, was VIXEN. She was the only cold-blooded creature, and the cold could give the Wyvern very unpleasant effects. So, I let my pet fly far away from these unwelcoming climes, promising to call her when I needed her, or when our squadron reached somewhere warmer.

"Tim, it's time for me to go. The operation is in a half hour. Wish me luck! And when it's all over, let's take a day and go to the sea. I mean, we live just an hour away from the beach, but we haven't been even once since our parents passed."

"Of course, Val. I promise we'll go on vacation to the sea."

Valerianna Quickfoot started smiling, took a more comfortable seat on the bench and closed her eyes, intending to exit the game. I opened my mouth, preparing to say some words of encouragement before my sister's upcoming surgical operation, when suddenly a familiar voice

~ 422 ~

rang out right next to my ear. It was Taisha:

"Amra! You have to exit *Boundless Realm* right away!!! An assassin has just opened the doors of your cubicle and is coming inside!!!"

Taisha?! I jumped up in surprise and looked around, but couldn't see the NPC thief girl. Although, how would she have gotten to a boat in the middle of the river in such a hard-to-reach place? Also, if I thought about it, how could the NPC have known who I was in real life, or where I worked? All the other players and NPC's on my boat were acting calm and natural. They clearly hadn't heard the voice. It all looked a lot like a stupid trick, but my heart was beating in terror, so I decided to exit the game just in case to check and reassure myself.

I opened the game menu, but I didn't have time to click Exit Game. The world abruptly grew dark before my eyes and, at the same time, my body was pierced by a sharp pain in the chest area... Ow! I shouted in fear. In the panic and pain, I couldn't totally understand if I was in the real world, or still in the virtual one. I tried opening the lid of my virtual reality capsule. It seemed the lid gave slightly, but just a centimeter. Something was stopping it from opening. I felt another sharp pain, as if a red-hot needle had gone into my chest. At the same time, I saw two light spots in the darkness surrounding me. It seemed to be two holes in the virtual reality capsule! I was being killed in the real world while locked inside my virtual reality capsule!

My fear and desperation gave me strength and I pushed on the lid with my arms and legs, managing to break the latch and throw it back. Then, despite the sharp light stinging my eyes, I saw a figure fall on the floor. Someone had been sitting on top of the virtual reality capsule trying to prevent me from leaving with their mass, but I was stronger! The miscreant immediately leapt up and swung something metal at me. I managed to grab the killer's hand, though, and stop it from jabbing the long Phillips-head screwdriver right into my neck!

A grievous fight ensued. I grabbed the killer's hand, but leaned too far and fell out of the virtual reality capsule. I also sent my opponent crashing onto the floor, though. His screwdriver flew somewhere aside, but the killer grabbed me with both hands by the neck and started to strangle me. All tangled in wires and smeared in blood, I fitfully tried to unclench his grasp with my right hand and get a breath of air while, with my left hand, I just kept hitting the killer in the face. And at that moment, I recognized my attacker! It was the very same technician who, one month earlier, had helped me set up the sensor suit and other equipment. What was the boy's name... Arthur maybe? I rasped out that name, trying to bring the killer to reason, but being identified just gave him more verve. I was resisting desperately and hitting his sensitive points purposefully with my free hand, like his eyes and the bridge of his nose, but my enemy just shook his head, not weakening his grasp.

My consciousness had already left me, and my eyes were glazing over when a few other people raced into the room. My opponent was torn off me and I heard a few shots. After that, a dark figure leaned over me and, in a vaguely familiar voice, said:

"Timothy's lost a lot of blood!!! He's dying!!!"

After that, darkness washed over me...

Questions without Answers

WHEN I CAME back to my senses, I was
feeling somewhat the worse for wear. I
had come to a few times, seen some
dark figures, a bright light, an IV, heard muffled
voices sounding as if from underwater, then
darkness came over again. But this time, I was
finally awake, as if surfacing from a clammy
nightmare that just didn't want to let me go.

After my eyes unstuck, I took a look around.
I was in an unfamiliar place, but immediately
guessed that it was not a hospital room. The
furniture was just too luxurious and ornate. The
stucco work on the cciling, paintings and gilded
columns were also totally uncharacteristic of
medical clinics. I was lying on a large unfolded
couch, covered with a light blanket. My clothing
was hanging next to me on a hanger.

~ A Trap for the Potentate ~

Just then, I remembered the attack and my desperate fight with the killer, the blood and the pain. Naturally, that spooked me. But I listened to my feelings, and felt surprisingly alright. My arms and legs could move, my body obeyed me, my brain could think. The only discomfort was this feeling of strange tightness in my chest and above my stomach, as if I had been glued back together, and my skin was stretched. I had read that such a feeling could be caused by stitches after an operation.

I threw back the comforter and carefully lifted the thin fabric of my long underwear, seeing two bandages and traces of dried healing cream. Apparently, the first screwdriver stab had gone right into my chest cavity, and the bone had stopped the sharpened steel from getting deep inside my rib cage. The second wound was in the upper part of my stomach. I was lucky that the sharp steel had not hit my heart or internal organs in either case. The bandages weren't making me too uncomfortable, though, just a dull pain when I pushed on them, but that was nothing.

I finally got up my courage and, readjusting my long johns, got up from the sofa. I was expecting weakness and dizziness due to the serious loss of blood, but there was nothing of the sort. Great, that meant the wounds really hadn't been as severe as they seemed at first. First of all, I walked over to the closed curtains of a huge window and lifted the blinds, wanting to figure out just where I was. And the view from the window was very familiar: a city park, a lake with catamarans, a ribbon of highway, always busy in the daytime and commercial skyscrapers... And although this vantage point wasn't totally what I was used to, I had already seen this scene from the windows of the *Boundless Realm* skyscraper many times. So, I was still somewhere in the building...

After getting on my clothes and not discovering my cell phone in my pockets, I walked through the available rooms, looking at the pictures and sculptures. There were pretty posters of *Boundless Realm* on one wall, and a bar with expensive alcohol on another. The refrigerator was filled with groceries, and the all-in-one PC on the computer desk was off. The virtual reality capsule was of the newest model (though to be fair, not hooked up) in the far room. I pushed on the exit door, found it locked and sat down to wait. Although I hadn't noticed any security cameras, I had no doubt there was one, so I was sure I wouldn't be left to sit around long enough to get bored.

And I was right. Just five minutes later, I heard a beeping and the door opened. A stylishly dressed tall man of middling years walked into the room. I would have to say thank you to Kira when given the chance, as she'd accused me of being thick for not knowing who was in charge of the company. I had taken that to heart and found the time to carefully familiarize myself with my place of employment, and its leadership. So, I immediately recognized the man who'd come to visit: Thomas Heywood, President of the *Boundless Realm* Corporation.

"You can sit, Timothy. Don't stand." he warned me when he saw my attempt to get up from the soft armchair.

After taking a cursory glance from side to side, the corporate president commented:

"I hope you like this room because, from now on, it is your personal office. Today, I promoted you to lead corporate tester, and such valued employees deserve separate offices on the upper floors of the building. If you have any adjustments you'd like to make to the room layout, fill out a form and send it to Office Support Services. But you can do that later... You must have tons of questions about what happened to you. I'm prepared to answer them all in detail."

"As for the past, I actually have no questions," I chuckled, sitting more comfortably in the chair, "but I do have a ton of questions about my present and future."

For some reason, the President found that very funny. Thomas Heywood walked up to the built-in refrigerator, opened it like he owned the place and, running his gaze over the shelves, stopped on a can of beer. He took one can for himself, and threw a second to me, which I deftly caught in midair.

"Are you sure it's ok?" I asked, pointing to my bandaged chest. He answered with a chuckle:

"I wouldn't have offered otherwise. The doctors said you have no more health-related limitations. The sharp point pierced your mesentery artery, which caused serious loss of blood. It could have ended tragically, but help arrived in time, and the wounds were dressed and stitched. By the end of the week, the only thing left will be two small scars. But, as they say, scars are a man's jewelry."

I gave a heavy sigh. Good that everything had ended well. I opened the can and took a sip of the foamy blood of life. The president of the corporation did the same and took a seat in the neighboring chair, crossing his legs:

"So then, Timothy, first about the present. Many people know about the assassination attempt. When the incident occurred, there were dozens of employees on the tester floor. That, by the way, was why the reaction of the Security Service was delayed. After all, no one imagined the murder would happen so flagrantly in the middle of the day. What was more, he was an experienced technician who had long worked for our company and didn't arouse any suspicion right up until he opened the door of your cubicle. But absolutely all witnesses present in the corridor at that moment have already signed nondisclosure agreements. And you, Timothy, I also ask to sign such a document."

Clearly, I twisted my face into a none-too-satisfied grimace, because Thomas Heywood abruptly grew more severe. The smile crawled off his face:

"It was an unpleasant incident, that cast a serious shadow on the reputation of the whole corporation, so it is in our common interest to avoid any leaks. We've basically managed to avoid the information spreading so far. The circle of those in the know won't get any wider, and even your direct boss and coworkers in the game haven't heard. Your sister knows. She started calling you on the phone after the successful operation to implant her new legs, and we had to tell her everything. But I suggest we keep it to just those people. You will also receive appropriate compensation for the psychological and physical trauma."

I understood that now was not the time to negotiate or be fickle. The president of the corporation was in a very determined mood, and arguing with leadership was rarely worth it. So, I confirmed that I understood the full seriousness and would sign a non-disclosure agreement.

"That's great then! And now let's talk about who ordered your assassination. I imagine you know them well."

"Was it Taisha?" I guessed, already having no doubt in the reply. And I wasn't wrong.

"Yes, it was Taisha. But as for who or what she is, it is still hard to give a one-hundred-percent confident answer. One thing is already clear. The NPC is just the tip of the iceberg and, based on the files and fragments artfully hidden on many game cluster servers, it is something truly huge and powerful. Think of it like a mushroom colony. We see just the fruiting body, but most of the organism is hidden safely underground. We have already discarded the possibility that a person may be controlling her. But that means that before us is an independent electronic mind, cautious, tricky and unprincipled. This thing has a very good understanding of the game it lives in, is capable of using admin privileges and tools and, if need be, can even change the world around it to suit its needs."

"Artificial intelligence?" I clarified, but the president just shrugged his shoulders unconfidently.

"That may be, but we still haven't figured it out. The most frightening thing is that *Boundless Realm* isn't enough for it, and it is very actively interested in the real world. But here, it would be on our territory and we can track, control and even direct the activity of the mind wherever we want it to go. So, our corporate specialists immediately figured out that this being... let's call it Taisha,

~ A Trap for the Potentate ~

was searching the global Internet through a special data gateway we provided and have complete control over. It was looking for information about you and your past, the metropolis, humanity in general and its history. It made a whole bunch of phone calls, and even found its way into the video observation system for the building. The vast majority of Taisha's search requests, which we found very curious, were somehow connected with the possibility of writing a consciousness into the brain of a living creature or other media, and obtaining a body. And that means that Taisha could technically be removed from this whole confusing system of encrypted files in a kind of clot, a concentrate that can be separated, and which will contain a self-sufficient fully functioning mind. We want to allow it to do that, but only under our observation, and according to our rules. And to do that, we'll need your cooperation, Timothy."

"Mine? You want to take advantage of Taisha's trust in me?"

"That's exactly right, Timothy. And there's no need to squirm, point to your friendship, conscience or warm feelings. You cannot have sympathy and mercy for this spiteful being. Although it has no physical existence, it ordered your death and could, in fact, have killed you. Yes, we uncovered a money transfer to the account of the unsuccessful murderer, a conversion of fifty thousand in-game coins into a real five thousand credits. The transaction system used was very, very confusing, so the financiers will need time to uncover the schematic and trace it to its source, but just look. Who else would use in-game coins other than a resident of a virtual world!"

Yes, that sounded logical. In the real world, there were tons of ways to securely send anonymous payments, such as cryptocurrency, crypto-offshores and temporary accounts in one-day banks. So, if the hit had been ordered by a real person, they would have used one of these methods to avoid being exposed. In-game coins would be used only by someone who finds such things natural, and doesn't know about the existence of other kinds of payment.

"On the other hand, if she is confirmed to be an Artificial Intelligence, we have a working model already in our hands..." the president's eyes lit up with these words, his voice quavering in anticipation. "Timothy, you have no idea what possibilities this gives to humankind!!! After a bit of adaptation and algorithm decryption, this could be infinite self-teaching scientists in virtual laboratories, and highly intelligent obedient war robots, this is flying cars and electromobiles without pilots or drivers, this is honest judges and politicians who cannot be bribed, this is billions of androids for heavy industry and dangerous factories, this is new and never-before-seen spheres of entertainment and the gaming industry and, beyond that, this is a huge step toward interstellar flight! This is a colossal jump into the future for all humankind, and that very future will depend on us! That is trillions and even quadrillions of credits! That is power over the whole planet!!!"

Thomas Heywood stood sharply from his seat, walked over to the refrigerator and took out another can of beer. He offered me one, but I refused.

"If you say so." The president drained the beer in three big glugs and threw the empty can into the hatch of a trash incinerator. "But now, listen carefully to the introductory information. Not long after Taisha's attempt on your life, she appeared next to Amra. She had died and was brought right to the boat after respawning."

"With Amra?" I asked in surprise.

"Yes, Timothy, you heard right. Amra is still in the game. The sudden disappearance of your player would have caused unnecessary questions, and we also decided to test out some ideas, so we replaced you with an experimental bot that imitates the behavior of a specific player based on previous gaming sessions. Anyhow, we've only had to intervene and correct it two times since you were last in the game. The first time, he decided to kill the rougarou regent for a large amount of experience but, because you had already decided against doing that once, we didn't let the bot do it either. The second time, the bot tried to take advantage of the high relationship of the rougarou Princess and started taking an amorous line of behavior with her, but we put a restriction on such actions because you didn't do anything like that, and the result might not be to your liking, or that of Taisha."

Here I was in complete agreement with the leadership. Chai-nee Shu was more like a ward or even an adopted daughter, not an object of amorous intrigue. Thomas Heywood then continued:

"However, despite all our attempts to imitate Amra as authentically as possible, Taisha behaves very guardedly with the bot and, it seems, can detect some falseness. And that is the very reason we need you in the game. We have to restore the trust of the NPC thief girl, and preferably in a reasonable timeframe, then take Taisha to the citadel of the Dark Sovereign. And that is where your role will end. After that, it will be our concern. Here, the new patch coincided very well with the route of your squadron. No one will be surprised by that or put on guard, and meanwhile, we have created a separate server for the citadel of the Dark Sovereign, which has intentionally not been activated yet and will not be included in the common cluster. As soon as Taisha goes inside, and we make sure her digital consciousness is capable of fully functioning in this isolated area, the server will be instantly shut down and we will catch her! You then will get such a reward that you'll never again want for anything in this life!"

The mission looked quite simple at first glance, but I wondered what hidden obstacles there might be.

"Well, we see there being two. The first complication: Taisha was worked over skillfully and for a very long time in the *Legion of Steel*. They told her who knows what and tried to trick the NPC girl into all kinds of poorly thought out oaths and promises. We know that, in Taisha's inventory, there is a scroll from the *Legion of Steel* that opens a large portal and we're confident she will open it when she sees the Dark Sovereign."

"The *Legion of Steel* knows about the Dark Sovereign?!" I asked in surprise. "Well, the new patch is already out, and information about the new global event should theoretically already be available!"

"Timothy, don't be so naive!" the corporate president laughed. "The *Legion of Steel* is the strongest clan in *Boundless Realm* and certainly not the least well informed. They have several of our employees in their ranks and, as is totally natural, the clan is more or less aware of all upcoming changes to the game. What's more, all global changes in the game are typically agreed upon with the leaders of the most influential clans and even publicly discussed on the official forums. Naturally, just in general terms, nothing concrete. So then, the *Legion of Steel* certainly knows about the Dark Sovereign and most likely wants to be the first to encounter this unique creature. The fact that Amra and his NPC squadron is en route to the Dark Sovereign is also not really a secret. You said as much in your video clips. And now, put two and two together and you have your answer for what will happen as soon as you meet the Dark Sovereign..."

It was obvious. As soon as the Dark Sovereign came into my field of view, a portal would immediately be opened and, a huge cohort of high-level undying would gush out. Just what I needed to make my life complete, a pissed off *Legion of Steel*... What was more the players, after all, would be interested not only in the epic new NPC boss, but also in the vampire player...

"I see. And the second difficulty?" I inquired, and Thomas Heywood made himself extremely put-together and serious again.

"You see, Taisha saw your 'death' through a video camera, and is now all at sea. Before that, she saw a bunch of material online about 'digitization' of consciousness and was clearly interested in the topic. She most likely believes such a thing is possible. We suppose that the reason for her attempt on your life in the real world was in fact Taisha's wish to kill the man named

~ A Trap for the Potentate ~

Timothy, who she saw as stopping her from always being next to her beloved Goblin Amra. As such, Taisha now thinks her plan was a success: the player himself seems to have died but, at that, his character remained in *Boundless Realm* and continues to be active. That has her clearly intrigued, and she is studying the bot from every angle and trying to draw it into a frank conversation. We think that Taisha can sense its true nature, because it is the only inhabitant of *Boundless Realm* that is like her. So then, your mission: support her in this confusion in every way and, although you want to avoid direct answers, do not deny that you died and are now forever trapped in *Boundless Realm*. If you manage to convince Taisha of that, she will fully trust you and follow you to the ends of the earth. And she'll probably even come with you to the castle of the Dark Sovereign. If you do not inspire this level of trust, she may refuse."

And at that, the Corporate President's visit to my new office was over. After promising that the virtual reality capsule and computer would soon be hooked up, Thomas Heywood asked me not to call anyone or go into the corridor until this extremely important mission was over, so I wouldn't accidentally find myself in view of the security cameras and thus upend their whole clever plan. I just gave a sad chuckle. I mean, technically, how could I do either of those things while trapped behind a locked door without a cell phone?

As soon as the door closed behind Thomas Heywood, the careless happy smile ran off my face. I plunked down in an armchair and started thinking seriously. This situation was very much not to my liking. Why was I being held locked up and not allowed to contact my sister? All these conversations about video cameras in the corridor, through which Taisha could potentially see me were empty pretexts! After all, I had somehow been brought here down those very same corridors, and the possibility of her seeing that through the cameras hadn't worried anyone. And anyway, Taisha couldn't track or intercept calls to my phone, so why put such limitations on me?! I could feel in my heart that I was being tricked, especially when he'd spoken of "trillions of credits for us." It was clearly the word "us" that didn't belong there, and Thomas Heywood didn't take me into account. And also, what he'd said about getting a reward, after which I would never want for anything left me plainly afraid, because that phrase could be interpreted two ways...

I walked over to the desk and turned on the computer. First of all, I checked to see if I could install programs or access the Internet. Everything was closed up tight. The only thing I could do from this terminal was go onto the *Boundless Realm* forum and look at various topics, not write messages. It was also possible, after logging in, to look at in-game mail, but I still couldn't answer or create new messages. All of that made me mad and put me even more on guard.

But if that was so... I looked around the forum for information about Amra and my journey to the upper Styx. Yes, there was a topic about it, and they were even having quite the active discussion. Amra had already almost fulfilled the promise to his viewers to reach places where no player before him had ever gone. Oh! And now this was interesting: two new video clips! They weren't very long, just fifteen or twenty minutes, but I was shaken by the very fact they existed. It can't have been that the "bot" made them, right?! I looked at the files. The first showed the short battle at the Lower Fort, Charon's boat and my visit to the Land of the Giants, then my return to the orcish squadron and my duel with the regent. At that, I periodically heard behind-the-scenes commentary in my own voice!

I watched the second video with my mouth open in amazement. Amra and the unified squadron of orcs and rougarou reached some waterfalls, where they were forced to leave the boats behind and continue on foot. An encounter with the undead, a short successful battle and, after that, our path up into the mountains. The dead lands finally came to an end, and a verdant plain emerged, where the Goblin Herbalist regularly found new never-before-seen plants and raised his Herbalism skill to level-52! The viewers in the comments called this clip boring compared to past ones, but I was in shock. I mean, God damn! None of the audience had noticed that a living player had been traded out for a bot. The most surprising part was that I saw Max Sochnier and Shrekson Bastard next to Amra, and they also didn't express any surprise at "my" behavior! I saw Taisha as well. The NPC thief girl really had returned and was accompanying the Goblin Herbalist.

So then, how much time had passed since the attack on me? I was thinking this over for the first time and was horrified after counting the hours. Almost two whole days!!! All that time can't seriously have been necessary to stitch up two wounds?!

As I loaded up the game this time, I was filled with more anticipatory anxiety than the first time I'd gone into *Boundless Realm*. After the emergency exit from my last game session, and a succession of strange happenings and flagrant lies, I was plainly afraid. I wouldn't even have been too surprised, if I wasn't capable of loading up the game world, or if some of the game functions were unavailable. But then the screen lit up, and I breathed a sigh of relief — it worked! And thankfully, I had a fully functional game client. Nothing was blocked, which I checked right away.

My Goblin Herbalist was standing on top of a hill, looking out over a wide plain. Behind my back, the orcs and rougarou were resting, getting a quick trail lunch together. Everything was basically calm. So then, what had happened while I was away? I opened my character window.

Level sixty-two... Well, well! My character had leveled up pretty decently, above all having corrected the Herbalism situation, but also bringing Alchemy up to level-42. In this matter, the program was merely predictable. If I was supposed to be an Herbalist, then this is what the bot would prioritize. It had also used up all the sheaves of plants to make all kinds of elixirs. Just look, almost my whole inventory was filled with vials of all kinds. And also, my Taste Tester parameter had been leveled to 192. The bot had gone through all my blood reserves, and also bit another two on the way...

Now this was cool, the unique Ring of Ice Stream, which had previously allowed me to summon the Mythical Hound Fimbulthul, had changed appearance somewhat, becoming larger and glimmering on my finger. There had also been changes to the item's properties:

Ring of Ice Stream (unique item)

+20 Resistance to Cold, +50 Strength, +50 Agility

Summon Mythical Hounds Fimbulthul and Gjöll (no more than 1 time per day)

The owner of the ring cannot be attacked by Legendary, Mythical or Unique canids

At that moment, as I was looking at the ring's parameters, I heard an unconfident voice behind me that I hadn't heard in quite some time:

"Amra?"

I turned unhurriedly and tossed an evaluating gaze over Taisha, the level-112 thief girl. She had on a full set of emerald dragonskin armor, a pair of daggers overflowing with shimmering magic, an invisibility cloak, and some kind of new belt...

"Of course it's me! Who else were you expecting?" I asked, answering my NPC companion's question with a question, not even knowing how to treat her in light of all the recent events.

"It's just that you haven't seemed like yourself recently," the thief girl answered, staring at me flagrantly. "You're totally alien and somehow... not alive or something. You used to be different... Well and... I'm not sure."

"And what did you expect?!" I went decisively on the offensive. "Should I be happy and cheerful after you put a hit out on me?!"

~ A Trap for the Potentate ~

"What are you talking about, my husband?! What hit on you? Whatever do you mean?"

Her astonishment looked so sincere that I even got confused. Either Taisha was pretending very skillfully, or she really didn't know. That said, fifty thousand coins was hardly a needle in a haystack. It was hard to hide such expenses.

"Show me your financial transaction log for the last two weeks!" I demanded.

Successful check for Taisha's reaction

Before my eyes, a file opened showing all the incoming and outgoing coins of the NPC's account. Holy cow!!! She had a positive balance of two hundred forty-three thousand coins! It should be said that most of Taisha's capital was not on her person, but wisely stored in the Subterranean Bank of Thorin the Ninth. And the majority of these massive funds had been earned by the thief girl in the last four days, above all as her share of the loot from clearing dungeons and treasure troves with a group of players from the *Legion of Steel*. That was all very interesting, but I was now more interested in expenses.

There were also plenty of those: weapon repair, buying healing elixirs and poisons for her daggers, a fee to participate in a tournament of alliances... Woah! I found the payments for her telephone calls from *Boundless Realm*, and there were lots of them... But none of them were what I was looking for. And, even if I added up all the expenses Taisha had incurred during all her time in the game, they totaled a lot less than fifty thousand coins.

"Well Taisha, it's just that I was told so many nasty things about you that... Overall, I was incorrect in my suspicions, I admit that. Please forgive me for my mistrust!"

So, what did this all mean? If Taisha was not involved in hiring a killer, who had paid for my death? Whose toes had I stepped on? And who had an extra five thousand credits sitting around for such a purpose. The Grave Worms gang could only be a middle-man here, not the ultimate source of the order. Also, they couldn't pay with in-game coins. I honestly admitted my suspicions to the beautiful goblin girl.

"How could you think such a thing, Amra?! You're my legal husband and closest friend... I mean, come on, you're the only person I have a good relationship with, both in *Boundless Realm* and the land of the undying! There's also my father, I have a good relationship with him, but he's far away. How could I ever want to lose you, the only thing close to me?! Yes, I admit that, after the situation with Valerianna Quickfoot, I really did get interested in 'digitizing consciousness,' read a bunch of materials on the topic and could now even probably be considered an expert. Which is why I can definitively state that there is no such thing as digitization!!! Amra is here and Timothy is there, two inseparable consciousnesses..." Taisha's voice, before raised practically to a shout, fell almost to a whisper. "So, I don't understand a few things... I'm totally lost. After all, I saw you die with my own eyes, but everyone around is behaving as if nothing happened!!! You wanna explain that to me?"

Remembering the direct order of the corporation president and understanding that there were dozens of watchful eyes on me right now, I didn't want to risk violating my mission for a conversation with Taisha, and went silent. And, to be honest, I didn't fully understand what was happening myself. Taisha waited for a while, then lowered her head:

"Let's leave that difficult topic for now, I need to think seriously..."

"Alright, let's not talk any more about death and killers, because I understand perfectly. But please answer another question for me... Or, to be more accurate, two of them. Your inventory should contain a large portal scroll. Tell me, why do you need it? And let me remind you about the Pelt of Fenrir, you should have that as well."

"It seems you know the contents of my bags better than I do..." amazement was reflected on the goblin girl's face. "I didn't even suspect I had such an object!"

Taisha readily pulled the fur armor from her bag and extended it to me but, as for the portal scroll, something was stopping her.

"I can't touch it. My fingers are going through the parchment!"

I probably could have foreseen something like this. The *Legion of Steel* had made it impossible for Taisha to simply throw the scroll out and deprive them of the chance to be first to reach the Dark Sovereign. But as that was so, I already had no doubt that Taisha contained a script to activate the scroll at the right moment, even if she didn't suspect it. Alright, I'd deal with the scroll later. Now was the very time to handle the Pelt of Fenrir.

Fenrir's Pelt (unique cursed item)
Armor: 1000
+250 Constitution, +250 Strength, +50% resistance to Air Magic and Fire Magic

Attention! Your character's level is too low to use this object
Requisite level: 125

Yep, another cursed item, and another level-125 requirement... There was nothing to be done.

I had to use my last Ifrit Heart to remove the item's level requirement.

~ A Trap for the Potentate ~

You have equipped five items from Fenrir's Cursed Regalia

Set bonus unlocked: all members of the Gray Pack will receive a bonus of +150 Strength, +150 Agility, +150 Constitution, +100% movement speed, +100% experience gain

Mission completed: Fenrir's Legacy (3/4)

Reward: 300000 Exp., +10 Animal Control, +50 Strength, +50 Agility, +50 Constitution, Gray Pack member limit raised to fifteen

Level sixty-three!
Level sixty-four!
Level sixty-five!

"By the way, Taisha," I suddenly remembered somewhat belatedly, "as far as I know, you've had the fur armor in your inventory for some time. What made you wait so long to come back? Why didn't you want to finish the personal quest?"

Taisha lowered her head and answered a good while later. Finally, the NPC thief girl raised her gaze to me and, with sadness in her voice, started explaining:

"In the last few days, so much self-contradictory information was poured out on me that I got confused as to what I could believe and what I couldn't. I had players and other shadowy figures from your world talking to me, offering me various deals and simply wanting to find out some more about me. To me, that was all new, so I needed time to digest it all and form my own point of view. And what was more, why hide it? I liked being in the *Legion of Steel*, and it was definitely interesting, even though I could see all their attempts to manipulate me and place curses from the leaders of the clan. I was protected from all kinds of danger, my caprices were indulged, I was given gifts. It flattered me, I won't hide it. And I wasn't sure it was worth throwing it all away to come back. But when I saw that you risked tragedy, I finally came to my decision and committed suicide."

The squadron, which stretched on for more than a kilometer, was coming down a winding mountain path to a wide plain. I could already see the tall walls, bastions and guard towers of the huge black fortress of the mysterious and ghastly Dark Sovereign in the distance. My sister was walking next to me, but was somehow glum and taciturn, as if she was mad at me. I had already told my sister about my guess that the *Legion of Steel*

might show up, but that just intensified Valerianna Quickfoot's pensive silence. And I didn't bother my sister with interrogations, either. I was too busy sending and receiving all kinds of messages through magical messengers. Sure, it was quite an expensive indulgence, but all of that was still better than being left without allies against the fearsome *Legion of Steel*.

The strongest of all clans in *Boundless Realm* simply had to have some enemies of their own. In the process of their growth, the *Legion of Steel* must have done a bad turn to many clans, put pressure on many players and driven many them from rich lands by force. Today, I was prepared to give everyone who had been slighted and offended the chance for revenge, and many heeded my call. The number of summoning scrolls in my inventory grew frighteningly fast.

But, before Taisha called the *Legion of Steel*, I needed to somehow meet the Dark Sovereign and agree on a new land for the orcs and rougarou to inhabit, but that was not going to be easy...

On the wide field right before the walls of the fortress, our path was blocked by defenders in combat position. There were many thousands of them, and they came from all kinds of species! Squads of skeletons and ghosts, mountain giants and cyclopes, rougarou warbands from unknown clans, trolls and ogres, beasts both from the swamps and forests, and totally incomprehensible magical creatures. The defenders of the fortress were standing in densely packed rows and, apparently, had no intention of letting my squadron through the easy way. And before all these variously-furred, but numerous and dangerous armed forces, there towered four ghastly Dark Riders, frozen stock-still...

I ordered my warriors to stop two hundred meters from my adversaries and called the commanders for a meeting. It was clear that acting by force here would not be possible. But how could I force the enemy to negotiate?

"They look impressive..." said First Mate Ziabash Hardy, stroking the back of his head in thought and clicking his tongue in admiration as he looked over the ranks of the enemy.

"There are rougarou of many clans here, and all of them once swore loyalty to the Dark Sovereign," advisor Uvari-Dor Shu stated the obvious, but didn't have any advice on what to do.

Max Sochnier and Leon just looked at me in expectation of further orders, and even my sister was in thoughtful silence looking over the ranks of the enemy. Taisha paid attention first:

"Look, the fortress gates are opening! Probably, the Dark Sovereign himself will come out for us now!"

And in fact, behind the rows of defenders, the huge metal gates opened without a sound. We were all frozen in anticipation of who would appear from the huge gates. However, a minute passed, then a second, and a third, but nothing happened. What the heck?! Where was the owner of the fortress? Finally, the extended silence was broken by the biting voice of Valerianna Quickfoot:

"Tim, your lack of perception disappoints me yet again. You really haven't figured it out? You're the Dark Sovereign!"

"Me?! I was generally hard to shock, but now was just such a case."

"Obviously! You're a ghastly vampire, a bloodthirsty pirate, the lord of orc cutthroats and fierce rougarou, and practically already Fenrir, the enemy of all *Boundless Realm*! Who other than you meets even half the qualifications of the Dark Sovereign? Go in and occupy the fortress. It's your right as its true owner!!!"

There was a certain logic in my sister's words. Still not fully believing in such a solution, I started forward step by step. I was walking, accompanied by the innumerable watchful eyes of the living creatures and the empty sockets of the undead.

The four Dark Riders started off at the same time in my direction, gaining speed and holding their sharpened pikes out in front. Despite their unambiguously aggressive stances, I just kept walking forward. And I wasn't wrong. A few steps from me, the emissaries of the Dark Sovereign stopped their mounts sharply and threw their pikes upward in a sign of greeting and respect.

That served as a signal. The army of fortress defenders started to part, forming a corridor to the gates of the black fortress. Ancient skeletons, unintelligent beasts, ghosts and cyclopes, trolls and rougarou — they all made way and gave a deep bow. On my approach, it was as if the fortress grew in size, the arrowslits in the walls grew more distinct, the towers shot upward. Most likely, I was now nearing the separate server the President had told me about. These were the very gates I needed to lure Taisha into.

And then, as if sensing that I was thinking about her, the goblin beauty sent me a private message, just like a living player:

"Amra, I sense there's something wrong with this fortress! Be careful!"

"If you want, let's go through together," I suggested, and Taisha unexpectedly agreed.

I waited for the green-skinned beauty to catch up to me and took the girl by the hand. We went up to the huge gates together, but just a few steps from the entrance, I stopped Taisha:

"Wait, I can't do this to you! You have to know!"

And I told her everything! About her uniqueness, about the attempt to capture her AI, about the President of the corporation and this fortress trap made specially for Taisha. The girl listened to me carefully, then answered:

~ A Trap for the Potentate ~

"What can I say, Amra? Truth for truth. I just sent you a message. It contains a video file. Watch it and think it over. You'll find me when you figure out what is happening to you. And now, forgive me. I feel that I need to get out of here as fast as possible! Djinn, save me now!!!"

Taisha touched a ring on her finger and... disappeared. For just a second, the purple cloud of the djinn sultan flickered before my eyes, then Al-Hassan Godsbain dashed away, taking Taisha with him and, together with her, the *Legion of Steel* portal scroll that still had yet to activate.

I then opened my messages and saw that a letter that had just come in with an attachment. There was just one line of text: "Is digitization really impossible?" and a short video file of just twenty seconds, which I immediately played:

Graveyard. Funeral. People wearing black. I immediately saw my sister Valeria, sitting in her wheelchair with her new implanted legs and bawling. Kira was standing over my sister's chair and also weeping. Next to her was a whole crowd of employees of the Boundless Realm *Corporation. I saw my director Max Tohner, I saw Leon and Max Sochnier, I recognized a few other coworkers. What place was this? Who was being buried? Why was my sister there? The camera turned, and I saw a large ornate coffin being lowered into the grave.*

And at that, the short recording, made by god-knows-who cut off, leaving me with more questions than answers. Was the person in the coffin... me? How could that be?! This was probably some kind of edit! But I could perfectly make out a watermark on the video file icon, a digital marker meaning the recording was authentic and unedited.

End of Book Three

About the Author

Michael Atamanov was born in 1975 in Grozny, Chechnia. He excelled at school, winning numerous national science and writing competitions. Having graduated with honors, he entered Moscow University to study material engineering. Soon, however, he had no home to return to: their house was destroyed during the first Chechen campaign. Michael's family fled the war, taking shelter with some relatives in Stavropol Territory in the South of Russia.

Having graduated from the University, Michael was forced to accept whatever work was available. He moonlighted in chemical labs, loaded trucks, translated technical articles, worked as a software installer and scene shifter for local artists and events. At the same time he never stopped writing, even when squatting in some seedy Moscow hostels. Writing became an urgent need for Michael. He submitted articles to science publications, penned news fillers for a variety of web sites and completed a plethora of technical and copywriting gigs.

Then one day unexpectedly for himself he started writing fairy tales and science fiction novels. For several years, his audience consisted of only one person: Michael's elder son. Then, at the end of 2014 he decided to upload one of his manuscripts to a free online writers resource. Readers liked it and demanded a sequel. Michael uploaded another book, and yet another, his audience growing as did his list. It was his readers who helped Michael hone his writing style. He finally had the breakthrough he deserved when the Moscow-based EKSMO - the biggest publishing house in Europe - offered him a contract for his first and consequent books.

Want to be the first to know about our latest LitRPG, sci fi and fantasy titles from your favorite authors?

Subscribe to our NEW RELEASES newsletter:
http://eepurl.com/b7niIL

Thank you for reading A Trap for the Potentate!
If you like what you've read, check out other sci fi, fantasy
and LitRPG novels published by Magic Dome Books:

Reality Benders LitRPG series by Michael Atamanov:
Countdown
External Threat
Game Changer
Web of Worlds
A Jump into the Unknown
Aces High

**The Dark Herbalist LitRPG series
by Michael Atamanov:**
Video Game Plotline Tester
Stay on the Wing
A Trap for the Potentate
Finding a Body

Perimeter Defense LitRPG series by Michael Atamanov:
Sector Eight
Beyond Death
New Contract
A Game with No Rules

**League of Losers LitRPG Series
by Michael Atamanov:**
A Cat and his Human

**The Way of the Shaman LitRPG series
by Vasily Mahanenko:**
Survival Quest
The Kartoss Gambit
The Secret of the Dark Forest
The Phantom Castle
The Karmadont Chess Set
Shaman's Revenge
Clans War

The Alchemist LitRPG series by Vasily Mahanenko:
City of the Dead
Forest of Desire
Tears of Alron

El Diablo by G.Zotov
(a supernatural thriller)

Mirror World LitRPG series by Alexey Osadchuk:
Project Daily Grind
The Citadel
The Way of the Outcast
The Twilight Obelisk

Underdog LitRPG series by Alexey Osadchuk:
Dungeons of the Crooked Mountains
The Wastes
The Dark Continent
The Otherworld

An NPC's Path LitRPG series by Pavel Kornev:
The Dead Rogue
Kingdom of the Dead
Deadman's Retinue

The Sublime Electricity series by Pavel Kornev:
The Illustrious
The Heartless
The Fallen
The Dormant

Citadel World series by Kir Lukovkin:
The URANUS Code
The Secret of Atlantis

You're in Game!
(LitRPG Stories from Bestselling Authors)

You're in Game-2!
(More LitRPG stories set in your favorite worlds)

The Fairy Code by Kaitlyn Weiss:
Captive of the Shadows
Chosen of the Shadows

More books and series are coming out soon!

In order to have new books of the series translated faster, we need your help and support! Please consider leaving a review or spread the word by recommending *A Trap for the Potentate* to your friends and posting the link on social media. The more people buy the book, the sooner we'll be able to make new translations available.

Thank you!

Till next time!

www.ingramcontent.com/pod-product-compliance
Lightning Source LLC
Chambersburg PA
CBHW060758030726
47503CB00002B/304